NO WHITE KNIGHT

NICOLE SNOW

ICE LIPS PRESS

ABOUT THE BOOK

Gorgeous devil. Hate-worthy. Instant enemy.

What's a girl to do when the man she can't stand plays hero?

It's fitting that his name's a four-letter word.

Holt Silverton had me spoiling for a fight the second we met.

He actually thought I'd sell my ranch—to *him*—in what universe?

Oh, I know his reputation. It's mud here in little old Heart's Edge.

He can spare me his pretty words and Hercules good looks.

I'd rather chew nails than get roped up in *anything* with him.

I ain't giving up my home, my inheritance, or my horses.

Not even if I desperately need the cash when trouble comes calling.

But there are two things I didn't count on.

Holt's as stubborn as a bull.

He's also hiding a rough and tumble country boy behind that big city suit.

Everything flips upside down the day he says he'll help save my land.

Lucky me.

I can't let anybody uncover the secret on my property.

Not even gorgeous stallions turning *I-hate-you* into *what-are-we-doing.*

The way Holt kisses proves he's no white knight.

Do I dare let a dark knight in?

I: WILD HORSES (LIBBY)

*G*ive a girl three wishes, and I'll tell you two of them right now.

I should've listened to Dad.

And I should've stayed away.

That's the only thought rattling around in my head as I do a slow blink, staring around at this terrible scene covered in dust.

I can't let anyone find this place.

I wish someone did little old me the same favor.

But there's barely time to breathe, to walk away, to force a painful grin and just pretend I never saw it.

Thank God my arms and legs still know what to do while my brain's turned into a rock.

Close that gate.

Lock it.

Guard it with my life.

Then I turn tail and run, taking off to swing myself back into the saddle and get out of Dodge like a pack of angry hounds are hot on my heels.

I'm alone.

No one saw me here. No one could have.

But I feel like the vacant eyes of death back there are following me anyway.

You know what? Screw wishes.

I've lived enough to know they don't come true.

Holding on for dear life to my horse's reins and leaning hard into his hoof-pounding gait, I make a new wish on the fly.

No one ever finds out what's at the end of Nowhere Lane.

For my father's sake.

For the farm's sake.

And for my own.

* * *

EVERYBODY'S GOT their own intuition.

Some people swear by a spidey sense. Some people's ears burn when they get a close friend in their head, lighting up their thoughts enough to worry. Some people even claim they've got ESP, a sixth sense, whatever you want to call it.

Me?

I've just got a nose for trouble.

When it tells me something smells rotten, I listen.

That dust cloud coming down the highway toward my ranch, catching up the dry summer earth and turning it into a mini reddish-yellow storm churning my way, let me tell you...

My nose does a whole lot more than itch.

It's on fire, 'cause I smell trouble with a capital S for Sierra.

Sure enough.

A minute later, an old Ford Taurus—clean, but its white finish yellowed to a dull shine—sweeps up the drive outside my fence. I'm in for more trouble on top of calamity.

I haven't seen her for years, but I still instantly recognize the woman behind the wheel.

She's my sister, after all.

And wherever Sierra Potter shows up, trouble's soon to follow.

I fold my arms on the fence, leaning against the sun-warmed wood and watching her as she parks the car and gets out.

Sis doesn't see me yet. It's pretty obvious from the self-conscious way she fusses and pats at her clothes like there's no one here to watch her.

She's dressed like all fancy-schmancy. Of course she is.

But if she's fancy, she's *Goodwill fancy.*

I know a secondhand dress like the back of my hand. That bright-pink sheath thing doesn't do much for her complexion or her dirty-blonde hair.

Blue-eyed blondes in eye-melting pink usually do it a bit better, but...well, she's trying.

The thing is, I don't trust *why.*

When my sister's trying this hard, she wants something.

For a second, I bite my lip and blink longer than I should.

Hoping she's grown up.

Hoping there's no ulterior motive.

Hoping I'm dealing with a different woman than the one who ran off and stole my trust with her.

While I'm busy *hoping* my butt off, a warm, velvety nose bumps my shoulder. I turn my head just in time to get a whiff of hay breath.

Frost's snowy dappled head nudges me with a whiny nicker. I'd ridden the Gypsy Vanner out to check the fences and dismounted long enough to leave him restless.

I smile faintly, cupping his cheek and running my fingers along the strong line of his jaw.

"I don't like it either, big guy. Let's go see what she wants, eh?" I murmur. "Then we'll send her packing."

Cruel? *Hardly.*

If you knew Sierra like I do, you'd chase her off your property, too.

Sometimes blood don't mean a thing—it sure as hell never did to her.

3

Frost snorts, tossing his head hard enough to nearly bump my hat off.

Guess he agrees.

"Good boy," I whisper with one last pat to his cheek. I swing myself back up into the gelding's saddle, settling into his comfortable bulk as he plods us forward.

There's a lot to love about Vanners. Not only are they gorgeous with their long, shaggy manes and tufts of flowing hair around their hooves, but they're smaller beasts while still being pretty freaking strong.

A girl with a similar build can relate.

We circle the barn, coming into plain sight of the gate. The instant we emerge, my sister turns quickly, perking up with a smile as bright and plasticky as bubblegum and just as obnoxiously pink as that dress.

Cringe.

She's always tried to dress like she knows what big city looks like. Too bad neither of us ever spent time in the cities growing up, and I'd be surprised if that's changed judging by her wardrobe.

You'd think she'd never seen a horse in her life, either.

The way she eyeballs Frost like he's gonna lunge right out from under me and bite her as I guide the horse up to the fence steams my blood.

We stop right there, waiting.

I ain't getting down until she gives me good reason to.

And I ain't crossing that fence or opening that gate for her.

Maybe this is her ranch, too, technically.

But it's *my* home and Frost's space.

Not hers.

Later, I'll regret that thought like some kinda godawful prophecy.

For now, Sierra idles, clearly expecting me to get down and welcome her with a big hug. Whatever siblings who don't want to tear each other's throats out usually do.

But the longer the silence runs on, the more her smile droops until she's pouting, folding her arms across her chest.

"Really, Libby? You haven't seen me in eight years," she says, "and you're still mad at me?"

"Reckon I'll stay mad," I say, resting my hand on my thigh, right next to the saddle holster for the sawed-off shotgun I keep around to scare off predators. "You got a reason for showing your face here, or are you just doing it to torture me?"

"I *live* here," she huffs out.

"The hell you do."

"Dad's will says I do." Her smile's back then, triumphant, and dread pools in my stomach like thick mud. "My name's on it too, Liberty Jane Potter. And I'm here for my half of our ranch."

This is where I get conflicted.

See, part of me wants to bust out cussing bloody murder.

The rest of me won't give her the satisfaction of seeing me go nuclear.

It's so predictable it's sad.

I should've damn well known.

Sierra couldn't bother coming home for Dad's funeral eight months ago, but when she needs a little scratch?

Why, of course she's hauling her fake-ass plastic smile out here in her crappy little car, blowing in from wherever she marched off to years ago.

All because there's some sweet green vitamin M on the line.

A mosquito heading for a naked rat couldn't move faster than Sierra does with money.

"The ranch ain't yours," I grind out. "You're looking at the lady who's been keeping it afloat for years. Same girl who kept up looking after Dad when he was sick. I don't care what the will says. You're so not breaking up my home."

"Don't be like that, Libby." She sighs, fluttering her lashes. She's got that wilting daisy act down; I'll give her that. "I came here to help you, too. You know the lien on the ranch is public

5

record, right? You haven't been able to pay the property taxes for years, and—"

"And *I'll figure that shit out*," I snap.

She blinks. What else was she expecting?

God. My neck feels hot, and my temper's up, meaner than a cornered rattlesnake. "If I have to, fine, let's make it legal. I'll buy out your half of the ranch. But you're not selling off my land and making my horses homeless."

"*Our* land," she corrects.

Holy hell.

I swear if I was less of a lady—a lady in cutoff jeans and cowboy boots, a lady dirty from wrestling in the hay all day, but still a lady—I'd get right off this horse and slug her in the face.

We've always been like this.

Oil and water.

It's like entire years never passed, and we're teenagers again, bickering over who got the last stinking Pop-Tart. Only, the stakes are a whole lot higher than pastries now.

She gives me that phony smile again, resting her hands on her hips.

"The bank's gonna take it from you once the tax man crawls up their butt. But before they do, they'll try to buy it for pennies on the dollar," she says. "Now for the good news—I've found us a buyer who's willing to pay a hell of a lot more, and he'll even take on full responsibility for the lien."

I fight the urge to check whether or not I have steam shooting out my ears.

Of all the presumptuous, insane, low-down crap—this doesn't just take the cake.

It *chucks* it into the dumpster.

"I don't care. Screw you and screw your buyer, Sierra," I snarl.

"Oh, you'll care when the bank comes calling, Libby."

My hand twitches.

Her gaze strays to my hip, and she sniffs.

"Don't even think about it," she says, holding up a finger too close to my face. "I've got my copy of the will. I'm not trespassing on my own land. You shoot at me, you wind up in jail, and then you can't do anything to stop me from selling."

I hate that she's right.

I'd rather be hog-tied than admit it out loud.

Narrowing my eyes at her, I send up a prayer for a bottomless pit to open up under her feet, but don't say anything.

Something isn't right here, and it's not just her usual greed.

Sierra's not the type to scour whatever they post liens in.

She sure as hell wouldn't be squatting on the papers watching for our property.

This girl ran away from home when she was seventeen.

Stole the last things I had to remember our mama by, her priceless collection of Tiffany glass, and then ran off with some guy who drove one of *those* vans. The kind that smells like old lube and cheap weed and stale cheesy puffs inside.

So it doesn't shock me that she's come back looking for a quick buck.

What's got me suspicious is her showing up *now*.

Right while I'm backed into a corner.

The ranch wasn't doing that great when Dad was still alive and it's only getting worse.

It's been getting harder to keep things afloat with the little scraps I get from teaching horseback riding classes and renting out space in my stables to the good folks of Heart's Edge.

I didn't even know about the years of unpaid property taxes until Dad was already gone, and I got that letter from a bank representing the county Department of Revenue.

Nasty surprise.

Almost as nasty as Sierra showing her face again.

"Listen," she says slyly, leaning against the hood of her car, resting her weight on her hands. "My boyfriend works with the bank—"

"Nope. You can shove it right there, lady," I spit. "Your

7

boyfriends are nothing but trouble and always have been. Why am I not surprised you shacked up with one of those vultures?"

"He's not a vulture!" Her eyes flare. "He wants to help us—"

"What? Help line his boss' pockets?" I blow out a hot breath. "Dammit, Sierra, don't you care that this is *home?*"

Her expression ices over, answering my question before the words even leave her mouth.

"Maybe for you," she says. "It's never been home for me."

I've honestly got nothing to say to that.

She's not wrong.

If our ranch was ever a home to her, then she'd get why I can't ever let it go. Plus, the bigger reason I can't ever let it fall into anyone else's hands.

She'd know the stomach-turning secret at the end of our property.

This isn't just about me and the horses.

Some things are best left to rest, and if I have to stand sentinel here till the day I die...

So be it.

For Dad, if for nobody else.

Frost stamps his foot and snorts, offering his sympathy. He can probably feel the fury bleeding off me.

"I've heard enough crap for one day. Time for you to get!" I say, resting my hand on the hilt of the shotgun lightly. "I may not be psycho enough to shoot my own sister, but I'll blow your stinking tires out and leave you walking back to town."

She wrinkles her nose at me. "You're so uncivilized."

"You're right. I—"

I break off as the distant sound of an engine yanks my attention away from her.

Heck of a time for company.

Looking up, I see another vehicle powering down the road— and this one's a lot nicer-looking than that used-car-lot piece of crap Sierra's driving.

It's black, a glossy Mercedes-Benz so slick it's like the dust can't even stick to it, sliding right off.

I hiss through my teeth. My thighs tighten enough to make Frost snort again underneath me with an agitated little side step.

So help me God, my hand tightens on the shotgun hilt.

"You called the bank out here?"

"Not the bank," Sierra says. "Our buyer. He's just coming to take a look and talk, Libby. C'mon, at least hear him out."

"You had no right!" I shake my head.

Seriously.

I don't know why I even bother feeling betrayed.

This is peak Sierra.

And I'm practically spitting nails while the slick Benz comes cruising up to a halt next to my sister's Taurus, making her car look even rattier next to a beast that screams money, power, bossypants.

Just the kind of bull that attracts Sierra and chases me away.

Disgust wells in the back of my throat like the morning after a bad bender. But I just can't peel my eyes off the shiny black car.

The door opens, and a man who's absolutely everything I expect steps out, adjusting the lapels of his finely pressed double-breasted suit.

Oh, yeah.

I *know* his type.

Swarthy. Strong jawline. Neat, almost razor-sharp trimmed beard.

Hair black as sin, of course, everything smooth, raked back in a classy sweep.

At least he's big and must hit the gym. He looks like the kind of brute who's too big for the kind of suit he wears, but it's been tailored so perfectly that it sits on his body like he was made to wear it. Like he carries his bulk and solid, trim muscle with more grace and elegance than the usual white-collar hooligan.

Perfectly knotted tie.

Pewter freaking cufflinks.

Nice nails, but his hands are square and worn and work-weathered, like maybe, just maybe, he knows what the business end of a hammer actually does, but I doubt it. He probably got those calluses sailing his yacht around or something.

Yeah.

He looks like money.

And those sly, confident, snaky golden-brown eyes look like a big fat *screw you* to any chances of this day having a happy ending.

He comes closer. His face is downright sculpted, graceful angles and sloping, sharp edges, so precise he's almost beautiful.

Fun fact: Fallen angels were pretty, too.

They say Lucifer himself was once the finest creature ever made.

And watching this hulk stuffed in a suit looking over my land like it's already his, his dark, sly brows shadowing a possessive gaze...

I can believe it.

But I won't fall for his lies.

I'm already set to get rough and tumble if I have to, swinging off Frost's back and vaulting over the fence, not even bothering with the gate.

I want Mr. Slick Dick out of here like yesterday.

No, I'm not here to sample whatever pretty sprinkles he puts on my crap sandwich.

That's how men like him get you, but I know a thing or two about making deals with the devil. And the first rule is real easy to remember.

Don't.

II: SERIOUS HORSEPOWER (HOLT)

*W*hen Sierra Potter warned me her little sister might be difficult, I didn't think she'd mean this damn tricky to rip my eyes off of.

Because Liberty Potter is a natural knockout.

That's my first mistake.

Mistake number two: I'm so busy gawking at her that it doesn't register, her coming at me like a charging grizzly, until she's up in my face.

I'm pretty sure I'm in legit fucking danger from this pint-sized terror glaring up at me with her blue eyes like knives.

She hesitates the last couple steps, giving me a second to remember how I jumped at the chance to off myself with this deal.

I won't lie.

I've had a bad feeling about this contract ever since Sierra and her financial rep—which is what I guess we're calling fuck buddies now—showed up in my construction office trailer, settled at my desk, and acted like their cheap knockoff designer clothes made them too good for my mobile base.

Right.

Look, I know style like ducks know ponds.

I know rich.

I know fashion.

I know class.

I've spent years of my life living in a swanky New York City penthouse. The suit I have on right now could make a dent in the back taxes on this ranch.

And Sierra Potter and Declan Eckhard wouldn't know class if it jumped up and chewed their faces off.

I know sob stories, too, and I wasn't really sure how I felt about Sierra sitting in a folding chair across from my desk, dabbing at her completely dry eyes with a tissue and spinning me this tale.

Her poor father died last year—yeah, I remember Mark Potter, a nice, quiet guy always pottering around up in the mountains, pun intended.

I wasn't around when he died. Sorry for their loss.

But I haven't been out of Heart's Edge so long that I don't remember Sierra Potter running off in the back of some sleaze-ball's van. Sheriff Langley had missing person notices tacked up around town for days.

So it's hard to buy that now she's just so concerned about her sister Libby, who's fallen on such *hard* luck with her property taxes, and how if she'd just *sell* the land and split their inheritance, it'd make their lives so much easier.

Sierra said it was all for Libby's own good.

Utterly selfless.

No ulterior motives.

And Declan, well, he was just there from the bank. New place, just opened up in town. *Confederated Bank & Credit Union.*

Never heard of 'em, but supposedly they're a big deal in Chicago.

Declan said he could get the land for pennies, or just wait until enough time passed to seize it in a foreclosure.

But it's in the bank's best interest for Libby to pay off the property taxes when they're acting as collectors for the tax man.

That way, the bank gets the most money out of it, and Libby gets to keep a big stack of cash instead of losing her home and the equity in one blow.

Which means she needs an outside buyer willing to take on the property plus the tax lien.

And apparently, I'm the right man to sweet-talk Liberty out of shooting herself in the foot, if these *wonderful* altruists with *zero* ulterior motives are to be believed.

Believe me. I know better than to stick my head in a tiger's mouth for nothing.

Turns out, Libby Potter's property is actually the key to a major construction contract I've got out on bid with the city council.

If I can go the extra mile to get the land they need for a new road to a planned shopping mall that should bring tons of new businesses into town, then I've got the contract to build that mall in the bag.

Maybe that's why I'm dizzy watching her transform before my eyes.

I can't lie. When I saw Libby sitting on top of that pretty dappled horse with its shaggy mane, I felt like I was looking at something out of a story.

Sun shining off wild blonde hair.

Blue eyes like a frozen lake.

A short, tight body with all the right curves packed in a pair of cutoff jeans.

Tanned thighs. Calf-high cowboy boots. Ass like a peach.

Flannel shirt tied up around her midriff and barely holding in those tits, her chest straining tight against the red-and-black checker squares until I *pity* what those buttons are dealing with.

That goes double for the horse, who just might be the luckiest bastard in the world.

My reaction to seeing a pretty girl with her legs wrapped around a few hundred pounds of solid muscle, her hips bobbing with every stride?

Fucking primal.

I might kill a man in cold blood to trade places with that horse.

And damn, when she swings her legs so wide, the muscles in her inner thighs rippling as she dismounts, her hair trailing behind her like a splash of liquid gold...go ahead and shoot me *now*.

Sure, it's been a while.

I haven't looked at a woman naked since I left New York City.

Sierra even tried to chat me up a little right in front of a sneering Declan, playing on my old reputation as the hotshot panty ripper of Heart's Edge who'll do you dirty in the streets and in the sheets.

I didn't even glance her way.

But I'd sure as hell love to do more than window shopping with the younger Potter girl right now.

And I realize how far I've got my head up my ass when she's standing close enough to hit me.

I can *smell* the sweat beading on her slender, suntanned neck.

Yeah. I think she's been yelling at me for a good sixty seconds without me processing a single word.

Shaking my head, I remind myself where the hell her eyes are, and focus on them.

Nah, at second glance, they're not winter ice.

More like pure blue lasers, and I think she's trying to burn me to a crisp with her hell-stare.

I blink. "Sorry, what did you just say?"

She eyes me up and down, then rolls her eyes.

"You heard me," she snaps, though I honestly didn't. "I *said* I know I don't keep cattle, so I don't get how a piece of crap this big wound up on my property."

The fuck?

I scowl, wondering if I forgot I made a pit stop in her coffee maker.

She's definitely not one of the girls in Heart's Edge with plenty of good reason to hate me.

She's too young. Gotta be mid-twenties at most.

With me pushing forty, by the time she'd have been legal to join my trail of broken hearts, I'd have been long gone out of town.

So.

Either she hates me on my reputation alone.

Or she's just pissed at the guy in the nice suit coming out here to talk to her about the land.

When Sierra said difficult, she'd been sugarcoating *complete and utter hellion*.

"Okay, look," I say, holding my hands up. "I get that you don't trespass on a cougar's territory without getting scratched. But you don't even know m—"

"I know *exactly* who you are," she snaps. "And I know exactly what you think you're doing. I'm not the kinda girl who falls for your bull, playboy. Your shitty tongue won't work on me."

I arch a brow. "No intention of using my tongue on you."

Only, I'm damn well thinking about it now.

About that gap between her thighs, and how that suntanned, velvety skin would taste as I lick my way higher, higher, and higher still.

Rein it in, cowboy, I tell myself.

Especially when it just makes her glare at me harder.

Her little red mouth twists up in a furious rosebud, her cheeks flushed. She's got amazing cheekbones, and that blush—I want it to *be* a real blush, not just a hot rush of anger—highlights how graceful they are.

She's got the face of an angel and the mouth of a trucker.

"That'd make a first fucking time," she says scathingly. "I hear you've used your tongue to get your way in just about everything else, and I don't mean by talking, *Holt Silverton*."

"Glad to hear I need no introduction." I smirk. "You must've been thinking about my reputation pretty hard to remember my name so well." I'm trying to play nice, so I hold my hand out. "It's Libby Potter, right? Haven't seen you since you were knee-high to a rattlesnake. Sorry to hear about your old man."

Her dagger eyes just sharpen with the cold way she looks at me.

And pointedly doesn't take my hand.

Okay, then.

I'm here on business. Not to let this pint-sized firecracker get under my skin, and I plan to keep it that way.

So I let my hand drop but hold my smile. I let my gaze roam over the ranch, taking it in.

It's a tidy little place; a low, sprawling ranch house made out of timber set far back from the main fence. A few well-kept, freshly painted barns loom on the horizon, scattered around.

The land around the buildings looks nice enough. Heart's Edge can get pretty dry and dusty out on the outskirts of the mountain valley, but she's managed to cultivate some impressive grazing grounds—places where horses and even several sheep move under the lazy summer sun, chewing away peacefully.

There's a hint of an old, overgrown road breaking off from a trail circling the fences just outside a long irrigation ditch running the length of the property.

I barely get a glance at it, keeping my eyes trained on her, noticing the gun on her hip.

Let's hope she's not *that* pissed.

Shame to ruin the quiet here by blowing my head to kingdom come.

All in all, it's a pretty nice place. Cozy. Everything a cowgirl could want.

I see why she doesn't want to give it up.

Too bad this is prime real estate. And I can't help but see the business opportunity in every sprawling inch of these gorgeous assets.

Gorgeous assets.

Yeah.

I need to keep thinking about the property, not *her*.

So I focus on the pastures, dredging up every bit of patience.

Then, as pleasantly as I can, I say, "I can tell you've put a lot of love into this place. Never seen horses shine like that."

"Oh, so you remember what horses are?" she throws back. "As old as you are and as long as you've been away, I'd thought maybe you'd forgotten."

I close my eyes. Take a deep breath. Keep calm.

"Think I can tell a horse from anything else that's been between your thighs, woman." I'm just as surprised at how it falls out of my mouth.

She sucks in a breath so loud it's almost a rasp, echoed by Sierra's choked laugh.

Fuck me sideways.

I'm screwing myself over.

I risk glancing back at Libby, but she's got her mouth twisted up in something that's part smirk, part frown, like she wants to laugh at my stupid mouth but she's just too mad.

"What gets between my legs ain't any of your business, Silverton," she whispers. She's got a little of that small-town twang going, just enough to give her voice this alluring, husky lilt. "But I can promise you, mister, it'll never be you in ten lifetimes."

"You think I was offering? Maybe I prefer thoroughbreds to draft horses."

Her nostrils flare.

"See, the problem with you," she says pleasantly—suddenly all sweetness hiding incoming venom, "is I don't know if you meant that literally or not. Considering I've heard you'll take anything on two *or* four legs...I guess that overdone suit's compensating for something." Her gaze drifts over me slowly from head to toe. "Maybe you should stick to two legs. I don't think you've got enough to handle a horse."

Goddamn, this girl hits below the belt.

Literally.

That's one area, though, where I'm never insecure. I'm actually grinning.

There's a fire in her, and frankly, I respect her more for calling me the douchebag I am for coming out here and sizing up her land without even a *how-do-you-do?*

"Don't even try it," I say. "I grew up around here. I know how to handle horses."

"I *hope* you mean riding. Wouldn't know it just looking at you." Another once-over, like my suit's some kind of scarlet letter branding me an outsider. "You look like New York. Tell you what—you ever want your country edge back, I'll break you in until you're raw around the edges and leave you begging."

I arch both brows. "Sweetheart, I don't think you meant that to come out the way it did," I say, biting back a bigger grin.

Libby makes a disgusted huff, rolling her eyes so hard they go white.

"Keep it in your pants, cowboy."

"Again," I point out, "you seem to be putting a whole lot of thought into what's in my trousers. You been missing me, Libby? Had a little crush I never knew about and now we're all grown up and you want to play?"

I step closer to her.

I can't help it.

Women look at me like I'm dinner. Sure, they hear the stories.

I'm bad news, but the kind of bad news you want to hear to learn a few dirty tricks.

Everybody wants a ride.

Nobody ever tries to buck me off.

Not like Libby.

And that just makes me want to get under her skin and live there. I smile slowly, leaning down toward her, close enough to purr in her ear.

"You want to play house," I say, "you gotta call me Daddy."

Her eyes go wider than the moon.

She makes a strangled sound in the back of her throat.

That hot-pink flush in her cheeks turns brilliant red, and there's no mistaking the fury.

Her mouth thins to a tight line.

The only warning I get is Sierra shouting.

"Oh, no, Libby, *don't—*"

Too late. Libby plants her hands square on my chest and *pushes me.*

I mean, hell.

It's a miracle she catches me off kilter, considering she barely comes up to my collar.

But I'm thinking less about being impressed and more about the sky spinning and the world whirling by as I topple backward.

My ass lands *hard* in a puff of yellow dust that flies up and spills back down, coating my freshly dry-cleaned black suit.

I'm dusty all over in an instant. Hurting like hell, too.

Big things fall harder, and I'm a tall man, so damn if my own muscle mass hasn't left me bruised and throbbing in places I'd rather not be.

For a second, I lie there groaning.

Just taking it all in, my arms and legs akimbo while I stare up at the sky.

Then I can't stop laughing.

That gets her attention. I blink, and she's bending over me, filling my field of vision and staring down at me with a scowl like a storm, but her eyes are a little too wide to be pure anger anymore.

"Did you just...hit your fool head or something?" she asks. "What's so damn funny?"

"Nothing," I say. "Except you just did exactly what I thought you'd do. A simple slap across the cheek seems too easy for Libby Potter."

I push up, sitting, not even bothering to dust myself off.

With her bending over me, suddenly we're nose to nose. Eye to eye. Breath to breath.

Lips far too close.

She freezes, her eyes widening more.

I flick my gaze down to her mouth. Her lips are parted like she'd started to bite off an insult and then just stopped.

For a second, I've got her.

And while I've got her, I lean in close, murmuring in that tiny thin skim of air separating our mouths.

"Look at you, gawking at me all scared like you hurt me. Just like I knew you would." I grin real slow. "Regret pushing me yet?"

She stares dead at me.

My inner wickedness has hold. I'm not gonna lie.

"Maybe you want to play nurse instead," I whisper.

Five seconds ago, she'd been about to tear my damn head off.

Now?

She's motionless, caught off guard, staring at me with her lips wet and not a single barb rolling off that glistening pink tongue I can see just past the curve of her mouth.

I could do something wild.

Something hot and hungry and dirty.

I could be exactly the kind of man she thinks I am.

It'd be too easy to thread my fingers into her hair and hold on just enough for her to *feel* it, for her to quiver with the need to give up control.

A few inches forward and I could kiss her until she's melting, her body so soft and hot I could reach down inside her to grab at her heart, making her think she could have me if she just gives in.

But I'm trying to be better.

If I treated her that way, I'd be worse than pond scum.

I'd be disrespecting the first woman I've met in years who actually has the nerve to call me the hell out.

So I don't play games, but I can't let go of the upper hand, either.

Smirking, I just pull away from her and stand, brushing myself off and turning to walk away like I'm not a dusty mess.

Hey—I know it's time to leave the field when the battle's over.

I'll be back after that flare of tension between us cools down and we're both ready to talk again.

But I'm not ready for her voice to follow me, chasing me with something hard to describe.

I think it's the sound of it.

It's not quite anger. Not quite hate. Not even scathing mockery.

It's almost like...disappointment?

Hurt.

"I guess I know who got the good genes in your family," she says quietly. "Blake inherited any sense of honor and didn't leave a bit for you. His biggest crime is that goofy-ass love line conspiracy show."

Damn.

I'd just started to take a step over the plates of dust-caked, corrugated metal forming a bridge over the ditch, linking the lane with the homestead.

When she mentions my brother, her words hit so hard it's like slamming a wrecking ball into my bones.

My foot slips on the plating, and I don't know what feels worse.

The angry bomb going off inside my chest.

Or the way the world upends itself again in a swirl of color.

It's not my lucky day.

I fall on my ass for the second time in about ten minutes.

Only this time I don't land in dry dirt.

I *thunk* down in the muddy water in the bottom of the ditch. Dirt squelches under me loudly as I sink into it, and cold water soaks me from waist to toe.

Part of me doesn't even want to get up.

I'd say I don't know why that last parting shot hurts, but I do. I damn well do.

Doesn't mean I haven't earned it, either.

Fuck, when I first came back to Heart's Edge, my own brother wouldn't believe I wasn't up to no good.

It took me saving his life with a fire truck to make Blake believe I wasn't just here to screw him over.

I don't blame him. Not after the fouled up blood we had growing up together, always undercutting each other for Mama's amusement.

Chasing her attention, fighting to be the favored son, stealing girlfriends.

Well.

The stealing girlfriends part was mostly me.

In my heyday, I've had at least a hot make out session in the back of a pickup truck with ninety percent of the eligible women in Heart's Edge.

Back then, I thought I was sly. A born player.

New York City taught me I don't know what sly even is.

While I *thought* I was cutthroat, it chewed me up and spat me back out to the weird little town I started in.

That's not something I grieve.

I'm ready to come home and continue un-fucking my life.

Ready to make right.

But that doesn't mean people are ready to let me.

So, I think, staring up at the sky, watching a single cloud go skipping along, moved by winds I can't feel down here where I'm stuck in the mud in more ways than one, I can't quit.

I've got to keep trying.

But I've also got to know when it's time to call it a day, and this conversation's done.

Sitting up, I drag myself out of the muck and stand with as much dignity as I can muster.

First I bite my tongue. Then, pretending I'm not dripping

wet and caked in crud, I adjust my lapels, then dip a brief bow to Sierra.

"Miss Potter," I say politely, and then bow to Libby, too.

Sierra's staring at me with her eyes wide and stunned, but Libby...hell, she looks like the cat that got the cream, her eyes glittering with laughter.

Damn little minx.

"Miss Potter," I repeat, adding, "it was a pleasure meeting you. I hope to repeat the pleasure again. A little less dirty talk next time, maybe."

I can't resist.

But it doesn't wipe that smug look off her face in the slightest.

If anything, it grows.

Libby uncurls one of the hands planted on her hip and goes for something almost as deadly as that shotgun.

She merrily flips me her middle finger.

Awesome. There's my cue to go.

I nod one more time, then turn and walk away, my spine stiff.

There's a very *un*dignified *squelch* as I pull the door of my Benz open and settle in behind the wheel, dripping muck all over the leather seats.

Yeah, fuck, it's definitely time to call a time out.

I focus on ignoring how cold and clammy and uncomfortable I am as I start the engine and back the car out of the long winding unpaved driveway.

I'm officially done with the day.

Even if I'm not giving up.

Not on myself.

Not on my chance to rebuild my reputation.

And not on the fascinating hellcat named Liberty Potter.

* * *

BY THE TIME I've cleaned myself up and changed into my work duds, my ego's feeling a little less bruised.

Though my ass is still complaining plenty after taking the brunt of a fall twice in a row.

Still, I'm feeling pretty proud of myself as I do a final walk-through of The Menagerie. It took some convincing with Blake to get Doc to agree on my crew doing the job. But we did it in record time and under budget, leaving his insurance people happy.

My boys did solid work rebuilding Doc and Ember's veterinary clinic. I think they're as happy as their critters to have a proper place again after that botched arson attempt earlier this year left some serious damage.

I just wish it hadn't taken so long to get to it, but there's a lot of work around town, and my crew's not that big. I've been trying to handle it all myself, building up our reputation before the city calls in outside contractors, but considering how shit goes down in Heart's Edge?

Yeah.

Calling this place *unlucky* in the ruins department would be a serious understatement.

First the town museum, after that crazy jackhole blew it up. Then the collateral damage around that blast, working on building a new site where the Paradise Hotel used to be, restoring old buildings, and now this possible supermall project.

I've got my hands full.

It's nothing I can't handle.

Thankfully, there are plenty of college kids home for the summer and looking for work.

Right now, though, my skeleton crew—just a few loyal fuckers who stuck with me and came all the way out to Heart's Edge for a fresh start—did a damn good job with The Menagerie.

I'm as proud of them as I am to know them.

It's nice to be around Doc and Ember, too.

With both of them being old transplants to the town, they aren't quite as familiar with my lifelong—ahem—*reputation*.

They treat me straight up.

Handshakes, gratitude, and compliments on the hard work done to put their practice back together. It leaves me beaming, satisfied I've done something useful with the day besides pissing off Ms. Libby Congeniality.

I don't do *everything* with my tongue.

Sometimes I let my fingers do the talking, too.

After handing me the check, Doc digs around in the pocket of his pressed slacks, pulls out his wallet, and hands me a crisp fifty-dollar bill. I look at him, cocking my head.

"Buy yourself a couple rounds on me," he says, looking over his spectacles. "My patients can't show the same gratitude, but it's the least I can do from all of us."

I thank him, give him a crisp salute, and head out to my car.

Honestly, Doc's orders don't sound half bad after the day I've had.

I'm still riding high on giddy accomplishment when I dust myself off and head over to Brody's an hour later. My fool brother's already staked down a table at the joint.

Imagine a Hooters Lite crossed with an old timey mountain bar and built out of weathered wood. That's our local watering hole. The place where every kid sneaks his first beer and every grizzled old man in Heart's Edge glugs down his last.

I've kept a lot of memories here, playing pool with girls who bent over the tables *just that way* to throw me off my game, or watching from afar while my older brother and his friends hung out and played darts.

It hasn't changed much.

Still the same loud jukebox music, waitresses in denim skirts and short-shorts that wouldn't pass muster, the smell of thick burgers and beer-battered onion rings, noisy college kids and even noisier high schoolers hoping they won't get put out for being too young.

This place is so timeless it feels like I'm the one who's changed.

Not Brody's. Not the town.

But if I've changed, then so has Blake, finally the happily married man he swore he'd never be.

He's quieter now, this big blockhead of a man with russet-brown hair and a silver-flecked beard. Truth be told, we don't look much alike, but after his old man was history, some nameless devil in a moment of reckless passion gave our mama *me*.

Maybe my wandering hands and roving ways are genetic.

I'll never know.

I never had a dad growing up.

Just an older brother who was half my only friend, half my worst enemy, and one hundred percent someone I'd never admit I looked up to.

There's no hint of our old squabbles now.

Blake catches sight of me and lifts his hand, gesturing toward the seat opposite him and the foaming glass mug of beer just waiting.

"Ordered for you," he says, taking a swig from his own mug. "From what I've heard, you seem like you need it."

"Shit, you know?" I groan, sinking down on the wooden seat —and wincing. Goddamn, I really did land hard on my ass. "Word travels that fast?"

"Small town. It's like some kind of invisible telephone tree. Anything that happens, everybody knows in ten minutes around here." He grins at me slyly. "So ya had a little fun with the Potter sisters, huh?"

"You make it sound like a night on the town. Not what actually happened," I mutter.

"Look, I'm not surprised you walked face-first into trouble, man. Libby's lived on that big ol' ranch her whole life. She's not gonna take kindly to strangers trying to buy it out from under her nose, no matter what money troubles she's got."

I shake my head, lifting my beer and taking a swig, letting the mellow taste soothe me.

"I don't know how she keeps that place running if she's so far behind on property taxes. We've got no water out here, and yet she's running irrigation ditches? Where does the cash come from?"

"Mostly, stable rentals and riding lessons, I think. Though I bet she also sells off some wool from those sheep." Blake grimaces. "But I think the Feds will wind up grabbing her land in the end. Real sad. She's got her daddy's energy keeping the place up."

"That's what I don't get about her being so damn stubborn," I say, and I'm not going to lie, it comes out a little heated. Hours later, a successful job behind me, and that girl's *still* got me riled, fire blazing under my collar. "Wouldn't it be better to sell off a little sliver of your land rather than lose the whole wad out of pride?"

"Pride's a powerful SOB," Blake says pointedly, jabbing a finger at me. "Remember, dumb pride was what had us nearly ripping each other's jugulars out just a few months ago. People get stupid over stuff they're attached to. You know how it is."

I take a long pull of my beer, hating how he's right.

No wonder every night owl in Heart's Edge tunes into his goofy love-line show on the radio—all the more reason now with his wife, Peace, playing her pretty music sometimes.

"So if you really want to help Libby, you try to get how *she* feels," Blake says. "Might help her see reason. Then you get your contract and she keeps her farm. Easy peasy."

"It's a thought," I admit grudgingly, though right now I think trying to reason with Libby Potter would be like a snake trying to talk with a mongoose—and I promise you I'm the snake, and she's gonna chomp me right in half. "Part of me gets where she's coming from. Run a major road down the edge of your property, and suddenly you're a scenic attraction. Shoppers and tourists acting like you're part of the mall."

"Yeah, but look at the other side," he says. "More people noticing the Potter place. Maybe hiring out for lessons or rentals, so she gets a bigger steady income and doesn't fall back in the hole."

He's got a point.

Too bad emotions and common sense don't get along too well.

I'll try again, though.

There's got to be some way to work through this.

Because Libby's not the only one who stands to lose everything right now.

"Hey," Blake says, kicking me under the table, just enough to get my attention. "No moping on my watch. C'mon. You finished The Menagerie today, right? This is a celebratory beer."

"Sorry," I say with a dry smile. "Head stuck in the business."

"It's creeping me out, honestly." He smirks. "Where the hell's Mr. Playboy? You're always thinking about supplies and invoices and construction codes...must be a lot of lonely beds in Heart's Edge lately."

I snort. "Not you, too. Does *everyone* think I'm still the biggest man-whore in town?"

"Honest answer or nice answer?" Blake looks at me with his dark-blue eyes twinkling.

"Honest answer."

Blake's smirk widens into a grin. "Yyyep."

"Goddammit!"

"Don't sweat it, bro." He's enjoying this. I can tell. But he's also sincere when he says, "Look, I was surprised as hell when you said you wanted to stay here. But look now—you fit right in. Fixing up the town and all, helping Doc and Ember back up and running. We're getting along like gangbusters. Andrea loves you. You ain't doing half bad, Holt. If people wanna gossip about you and the ladies, well...keeps 'em from getting bored. And as long as you got your reputation, you can always get laid. Bet a whole pack of girls want to know what the fuss is all about."

Shame I'm not interested in just *getting laid* anymore.

New York City took care of that.

My mind tries to push an image of angry blue eyes in front of me, but I shove it away just as hard.

Nope.

Fuck no.

Mixing business with pleasure already screwed me over once.

I'm not messing with that ever again.

So I'm happy to change the subject, talking about how my niece is doing in school, that punk Clark she's still hung up on, Blake's new marriage to his cute little hippie girl, how things have finally quieted down.

Blake says he might even come help out on my crew just to keep busy. In between keeping an eye out for brush fire season to kick into high gear, of course.

Everything else is always a side gig for the town's fire chief.

But as we talk, my gaze roves over the bar.

I don't recognize a lot of the new faces here. I've been away for a good long while.

Some people have grown up and look so different they're like strangers. Others are just people who moved to Heart's Edge for whatever reasons, or folks who stayed here as leftovers once Galentron skipped town.

It's not the same place I grew up in.

But one guy in particular catches my eye.

I don't know him from Adam, but there's something about him that just looks out of place.

He's stiff, wearing a waistcoat and tie in a bar like Brody's, his suit coat draped on a barstool next to him and his slacks so neatly creased they could cut.

Not one strand of black hair is out of place, his face smooth and empty with a brooding touch to it.

The biggest red flag? He's drinking alone.

Everyone else is on their third to fifth beer of the night, but this guy's got *wine*.

Wine—at *Brody's*.

"Blake." I cut off his rant about people being stupid with their propane grills every summer and jerk my chin toward the guy. "Who's that? Never seen him around."

"Huh?" Blake cranes to peer over his shoulder, blinking slowly from his buzz. "Oh, him. Can't remember the name, but he works at the new bank. Y'know, Confederated something or other? They're buying all sorts of shit around town. Saw him talking to somebody on the council outside that old theater that burned a while back."

Interesting. My hand tightens on my mug.

As far as I know, there's only one man from Confederated Bank buying out properties in Heart's Edge. That cold-eyed Declan fuck I'd met with Sierra.

Maybe Confederated Bank is hiring since it's new.

Maybe.

Something about it just weirds me out, though.

I can't really dwell on it too long, and it's only halfway my business because I'm making it my business.

Blake starts blabbing away, I have another beer, and time blurs by while we talk and wait for the buzz to die down so we can drive.

Soon, it's time to hit the hay.

I clap my brother on the shoulder as I stand and head for the exit, only to pause as he calls out to me.

"Holt, wait," he says. "The guest bedroom is still open if you ever want something fancier than the inn."

I smirk. "What, you mean ever since your wife moved into your bed?"

"Hey, we're not talking about my nightlife habits." Blake snickers. He's got that goofy thing going when he's drunk, like a big dog, but it's good to see it. There was a time when it was a mask over trauma, loss, grief, loneliness...but now it's just his genuine happy self coming out, ever since he settled into married bliss. "Look, I'd have something to say if you were parading a different woman around under my daughter's nose every night. But I don't like the idea of you staying in a hotel room all the time when you're family."

Part of me wants to protest.

I'm not like that anymore.

Part of me also almost wants to take him up on the offer.

Just to feel like I'm part of something.

But it's Blake's family, his life, his home. He's newly married with a teenage daughter, and it's not my place to play third wheel.

I'll build my own home when I'm ready.

And when I do, I need to do it with my own two hands.

I'll prove to myself that I can actually *build* things, instead of wrecking hearts and my own prospects for a future. That I'm more than some dude who talks his way into good luck and better graces.

For now, that means going it alone.

Tonight, I'll let my reputation save me.

"I've already got a bed and somebody waiting on me," I lie. "The Fords aren't so picky about my guests. I'll come hang out some other time." I reach over and ruffle his hair. "Tell the kiddo hi for me."

"You bastard devil!" He swings at me playfully, but I'm already gone, spilling out into the bright lights and the dimmer glow of the parking lot.

The Milky Way overhead outshines any street lamps.

Time to get some rest for real.

Got a feeling I'll need it to gird my goddamned loins for another confrontation with Libby Potter and the ranch holding the key to my future.

III: HOOFING IT (LIBBY)

*W*ith my temper, caffeine probably isn't a good idea.

But I've got an addiction to those mocha lattes Felicity whips together at The Nest, and she's one of my closest friends.

I need a friend right now.

I need to be around someone I can trust.

And I shouldn't have to feel that way around my own flipping family.

The only thing I can think, every time I see Sierra, is *what do you want from me now?*

Thankfully, Felicity's easy, friendly company who doesn't expect anything but a smile. Plus, it's pretty sweet having a friend who always gives me free drinks with extra whip.

So that's how, this morning, I find myself perched on a stool in front of the long polished coffee bar at The Nest, listening to her chatter faster than a bright-eyed chipmunk about...

I'm not even sure what she's going on about, honestly.

Something about finding like, a town underneath the town?

It doesn't make sense to me, but Felicity's all excited. It's an archaeological dig or something.

Apparently, towns as old as Heart's Edge kind of build on top of themselves. Foundations of old buildings turn into new ones.

Now underneath all the crap that's gotten blown up and burned down and torn up lately, they're finding pieces of buildings that've been here since the old silver rush settler days. Old antiques, art, tools, clothing, remnants of entire lives. Western stuff.

I don't get why she's so into it, but everybody needs a passion, I guess.

That thought makes my hand drift to my throat, this tic I always do but don't realize until I feel cool reassuring metal and tiny polished stones against my fingers.

It's a necklace—shaped like the constellation Aries, the Ram.

Nine tiny major and minor stars no bigger than grains of sand. All made out of this polished red stone that's rather matte with a pinkish shade. Never found out what it is, but those nine little pieces are strung together with silver rods as fine as thread.

Dad's gift in more ways than one.

Thanks to him and his old NASA career, I can identify every last one of those nine stars, from Sheratan to Mesarthim, whether I'm looking at the fragile necklace in my palm or up at the night sky.

It's the last thing he ever gave me.

The last thing I have to remember him by.

Other than whispered words I try to forget every damn day of my life. I can't stand to think about what they might mean.

Seems to be a theme for me, lately.

Trying to forget the things men say.

Whether it's my father's dying words...

...or Holt Silverton, talking about using his tongue on me, thinking about what's in his pants, all that other ridiculous, low-down, filthy—

God.

He just makes me *mad*.

A swaggering dumb peacock of a man, strutting in and

looking me over like he's already won when he doesn't even know the stakes in the battle we're fighting.

And then to hear him go and say all that dirty stuff...

Damn, did it feel good to watch him fall on his ass.

Twice.

I'm glad he muddied up his fancy outfit.

Looking at him, you couldn't even tell he's *from* here.

But I liked getting to rub his face in the dirt of Heart's Edge.

Just a reminder that he can't wash away who he is that easy.

"—ibby?"

It takes me a minute to realize Felicity's still talking. Whoops.

I'd zoned out, staring at her hands while she cleaned glasses without really seeing her, or much of anything but that devil's bourbon-gold eyes.

"Libby."

"Huh?" I shake myself, blinking, focusing on her face. "Sorry, what's up, Fel?"

"You're what's up," she says, eyeing me. "Your face is red as a tomato. What's on your mind?"

"Have you ever noticed," I say, almost before she can even finish the question, "how some guys think they know every-thing? Like, they can't fathom that maybe they're wrong. Maybe they're just not going to get their way, not with my land and not with *me.*"

Felicity arches a brow, an amused smile teasing at her lips, just a glint of teeth she's trying to hide. "What man's trying to have his way with you? 'Cause if I didn't know better, I'd think Holt Silverton was getting under your skin."

"Like fricking snake venom," I spit back. "And nothing good comes from getting bit."

"Oh, I don't know, I can think of a lot of good things you get from biting," she muses with mock-innocence. "A lot of long, thick, slithering thi—"

"Felicity!" Half wheezing, half laughing, I push myself up on the rungs of the stool, snatch her wet towel right out of her hands, and fling it at her face.

Giggling, she sets the mug she'd been cleaning down and grabs at the towel, pulling it down and blowing her mussed brown hair out of her face.

"And there you are. Welcome back." She grins wickedly. "You're blushing like a schoolgirl in denial, y'know."

"I'm not in denial of *shit*." Grumbling, I flump back down on the stool and take a long cold sip of my mocha latte, then lick a little whipped cream off the top. "Listen, if he goes missing any time in the next week, I'll deny knowing where the body is. And you'll back me up."

"I mean...if you really want to kill him that bad, here's your chance." Felicity smirks at me knowingly, her eyes cutting over my shoulder. "Surprise. He's been watching you for the last five minutes."

Oh, crap. My heart stops.

"What?"

I don't want to turn around.

I just can't freaking help myself.

Wide-eyed, I peer over my shoulder.

Right to where Holt sits at a corner table, sprawled out, looking like pure sin in a tidy package.

Only, he ain't that tidy at all right now.

He sure as blazes doesn't look like the polished city suit I met the other day.

Today, he's actually kinda filthy. I don't think anybody's ever made filth look this good—wearing nothing but a pair of construction coveralls in battered, dirty dark grey.

They're unzipped at the top and rolled down with the sleeves tied around his narrow hips, the white A-shirt underneath so sweaty it might as well just paint the way the fabric clings to his mountain of muscle.

God, I can see *everything*.

From the dark curl of black chest hair crinkling around his pecs right down to the tiniest sculpted detail of his abs.

Mercy.

Those ripples of tight muscle wind on like waves, starting at his ribs and pouring around to his back. He's got arms like cut steel, pure chisel and nothing else, and he's streaked in sweat and grease and grime that just makes you want to rub up against him to get a little of his bad self all over you.

Worst of all, he's looking dead at me.

Practically blinding me with those intense, sultry hazel devil eyes.

A grin plastered on his gorgeously red mouth says he knows exactly what I'm thinking when my eyes dip down over his chest, trailing to the way his wide-spread thighs push against the baggy coverall pants in curves of hard muscle.

"Libby," Felicity says mildly, "put your tongue back in your mouth."

I whip back around to face her with my cheeks lighting up like flaming cherries. "My tongue wasn't—I didn't—don't bring my tongue into this!"

Oh my God.

Oh my God, I'm dead.

I can't be having these thoughts.

Just because he's gorgeous doesn't change the fact that he's bad news.

He still wants my land.

My *home*.

All the things Dad left me to protect.

"Lib-by," Felicity sing-songs softly.

"No," I snap.

"*Liiiibby.*"

I hunker down into my shoulders, folding my arms on the bartop and glowering down into my latte. "What?"

"I think," she says, "our darling Holt would like to speak with you."

"Well, too bad. I don't wanna speak with him. Or anything *else* with him."

"Never said you did."

She's *chortling* now.

Awesome.

Honestly, I've never heard any woman chortle before, never even knew what it sounded like, but now I do—it's that sound when you're trying to talk, but you're trying not to laugh but you can't help yourself, so these silly little *hoo-hoo-hoo* sounds come out around the words while you're shaking yourself silly trying to hold it in.

Just like Felicity is right now.

If she keeps this up, I'm about to be short a friend.

After another snicker, she clears her throat. "Okay. Seriously, it looks like he's waiting. Aren't you at least going to talk to him? Be a little civil?"

I steal another peek over my shoulder, holding my breath, making a wish.

Nope, not granted.

He's still *watching* me.

I can almost feel his gaze, and I want to kill him for it.

As our eyes meet, he arches a brow, then gestures to the chair next to him with a questioning tilt of his head.

I narrow my eyes.

Then pointedly turn back to Felicity and slide off my stool.

"I'm out," I say. "Thanks for the drink, but I've got work to do and a gaggle of kids coming in for lessons this afternoon."

Felicity eyes me. "It's not like you to run away."

"I'm not *running away*," I seethe. "I'm just...prioritizing."

I grab my bag and head out to my battered truck, taking the back door so I don't have to walk by Holt and that insufferable penetrating stare that just won't let go.

But I ain't gonna get off that easy.

I step out into the morning light, bright enough to make me

blink and squint with a little shiver as I slip from air conditioning into brewing summer heat, and it happens.

A tall, imposing frame blocks my path.

I'm so keyed up over Holt I'm ready to start calling him every bad name in the book.

Until it dawns on me it ain't him.

Holt was all dirty and delicious. This other man standing in front of me is crisp and so clean it's like he's an ad for mouthwash or something.

I recognize him in a heartbeat.

Reid flipping Cherish.

The bank financier who was here even before Declan and Sierra, trying to be *reasonable* about talking me into selling my home and giving up everything.

He adjusts his glasses with a low sound, almost apologetic, then clears his throat.

"Ms. Potter," he says formally.

And then he bows.

This dickhead actually *bows* to me right here in the parking lot of The Nest like he's inviting me to dance cotillion. Not like he's trying to help the tax man muscle me out of my ranch.

"Don't you 'Ms. Potter' me," I snap. "And look me in the eye when you try to sell me on your crap."

"My apologies," he clips out a bit stiffly but with no other response.

That's the thing about Cherish. He doesn't get angry, doesn't bark back, just straightens and pushes his glasses up his nose like some kind of robot.

Yeah. I think I'd rather be arguing with Holt.

At least I know I can piss him off.

"Out of my way," I bite off.

"I will be in just a moment. I was simply hoping we could arrange a meeting soon," he says smoothly.

"For what? So you can try to change my mind again?"

An almost pained expression crosses his face. He looks like

some kind of English Lord stuffed into a modern suit, transplanted to the Montana wilds, and left real uncomfy with it.

Good.

I want this particular weasel uncomfy.

"You understand, Ms. Potter, that legally you don't have many options," he says. "Unless you're able to procure the funds to pay your back property taxes and all associated penalties and fees, you have a little less than forty-five days before your property is seized as an asset. You won't get it back. And you'll only lose an extensive court battle trying."

Ever felt two emotions hit so extreme at the exact same time that you feel like a ping-pong ball bouncing between them?

That's me right now.

On one hand, I'm almost sick enough to stagger, to pass out, with how faint I feel at hearing that countdown.

Up until now it'd been a distant *one day,* leaving me hope for some kind of Hail Mary pass.

On the other hand...

I'm white-hot with rage and already gearing up to smack him, my hand clenched into a fist as I stride forward, already drawing back to get the best momentum.

Perfect timing for a second oversized body to throw itself in my path.

I stumble back, barely reining in my fist, as Holt damn Silverton steps between me and Reid Cherish.

"The hell do you think you're doing?" I demand.

Meanwhile, Reid says flatly, "Excuse me, sir, but this is a private discussion and—"

"Nothing private about you harassing a lady in public," Holt growls, and there's a different flavor to his voice.

I blink in surprise.

It's almost like anger dampens his polished New York City crap and brings out the country boy underneath, just a little bit of twang and a little bit of holler.

"You're gonna want to fuck right off and leave Libby alone," he says.

"I didn't give you permission to use my name," I snarl. "And don't you call me a lady. I don't need your help. I can tell *Mr. Cherish* here to fuck off just fine all on my own."

There's a bristling silence.

Then Reid makes a soft, exasperated sound. "I see we'll get nowhere with this discussion now."

I can barely see him around Holt's broad, grungy, tightly muscled back, but I make out him dipping his hand into his suit for something—before he leans around Holt and offers me a business card.

"If you change your mind, Ms. Potter, you know where to find me. There's still time to do something sensible. I'm trying to *help* you," he insists.

I just stare at him flatly.

I'm not taking that stupid card.

He seems to realize it when he pulls his hand back with another barely-there sigh.

"Fine. Good day to you both, then."

Good day?

I don't breathe a word as he turns around and walks back inside The Nest with stiff strides that do nothing to dispel the idea that he's a machine in a human skin.

But the second the door closes and Holt turns to me with that self-satisfied look on his smug-ass face?

Yep, I *lose* it.

"What was that?" I snarl. "Who asked you to do that?"

Holt's face blanks. "Uh? That's the guy from the bank, right? He was bothering you."

"Duh, that's the guy from the bank. Yes, he was bothering me. No, I didn't need you to come swooping in trying to white knight me, Holt. I had it under control."

That actually gets me a skeptical, amused look as Holt cocks his head. "From the way I saw it, your idea of 'under control' involves three to five years in prison for assault. Think you wouldn't even be able to talk old Sheriff Langley out of bringing charges."

"They'd never convict me." I narrow my eyes, clenching my fist. "And I really doubt anyone would take me to court over pelting your sorry ass, either."

Holt just grins, slow and dark, his teeth white against that sinful black beard. "You gonna hit me now, Libby? Your hero?"

Holy hell. No, that did *not* just come out of his mouth.

"Not if you look like you're gonna enjoy it so much!" I sputter.

He laughs, rich and full and deep.

The sun catches those strange whiskey-eyes, turning them into pure, glittering gold. "You're a violent little pixie, aren't you?"

"You really hankering to find out *how* violent?"

I'm so not ready when he steps closer.

When he fills up the space around me, I realize I had no clue what summer heat really was until I felt him. His body too close to me, and now I can smell him, too—the scent of concrete and masculinity and hard work.

Something hot and sharp underneath that should smell bad, but it just gets me dizzy with...

With *him*.

Ugh. I hate the weird, tingly feeling cutting through me.

It's like a million sparks going off, and I want to just scream with the rawness and wildness of it burning up inside me.

It's got to be a trick.

There's no earthly way I actually want Holt Silverton.

Hell to the no.

Especially when I start feeling awfully dirty myself. His eyes dip over me, and he leans down, purring in his rough, velvet voice.

"Go ahead, little lady," he breathes. "Hurt me."

I do the only thing I can.

What feels like a reflex with him.

I slam my hands against his chest and push until my arms burn.

It feels like a desperate act of self-preservation.

Because something about him does something to me when he's this close.

It's like pheromones getting up in my head, drugging me, turning my brain into mush while my whole body just ignites.

It's like I can feel the anger he inspires in me all over my nerve endings, but that heat...

That heat ain't rage.

I gulp a deep breath. He moves a step back. Barely.

This time, on steady ground, there's no knocking him off-kilter.

Guess them big old steel-toed workman's boots are a heck of a lot sturdier than dress shoes. Or maybe I just grossly overestimated my own strength against a titan.

But he's watching me with his eyes narrowed.

It's like we're playing poker, and I just gave away my hand.

Screw him, I'm not out yet.

I fold my arms over my chest like I can contain my racing heart if I just cage it, slitting my eyes right back at him.

Two can play at this.

I can do those skin-stripping stares, too.

And we're like two territorial cats as I ask, "Why'd you chase him off, anyway? Don't you get everything you want if he takes my land?"

"Nah," Holt says. "That delays my timeline and the town's. The thing with government seizures is, I have to buy it at auction later. A lot more competition then. It could be years before they even put the land up. The city council wants to close on this mall deal this month."

I can't help rolling my eyes. "Nice to know you've got such altruistic motives."

"Hear me out." He spreads his hands. "There's a way for us both to get what we want."

I eye him skeptically.

I'll probably regret these words, but...

"I'm listening. Talk," I say.

"No denying you're in trouble. You're not even making enough money to keep the ranch going. Don't—" He holds a hand up as I bristle. "Don't tear my head off yet. That's not your fault, and I'm not criticizing. I know what it's like to fight like hell to keep your livelihood afloat. That's *why* this could work so well for you."

God. I don't want to even think he could know what my life's like.

I don't want sympathy from him.

But I'm still listening, because now that I know what my time limit is, forty-five days...

I'll never admit it to Holt, but that number?

It scares the bejeezus out of me.

"I don't need your whole property," he says. "I've been picking through old town records, survey maps, the works. With the lay of the land and how we'd have to route a road for easy grading to get out to the mall, it'd run along the edge of your property, not cutting through it. We could build the road up on a steep embankment with a guardrail to keep your horses from getting up there, if they get out. And plant trees alongside the road so you've got less noise pollution and don't have to see all the happy shoppers going past."

I give him the side-eye. This sounds too good to be true.

And with men like Holt, that usually means it *is*.

"Okay. You're trying to sell me on what's in it for me," I say. "So what's in it for you? You know you're gonna be responsible for the lien on that acreage, right? In for a penny, in for a pound."

"I know. I'm fine with that. Considering the size of the land, it'd be a small percentage of what's owed overall," he says.

There's something in his eyes, something lit up and almost enthusiastic. "But what we'd pay you for it would be plenty for you to get those property taxes done—or close enough that you can negotiate some kind of payment plan for the rest."

I stare him down, wondering how many seconds it'd take to light his ass on fire.

Oh, but his lips are still moving.

"It's win-win, Libby. You keep your ranch away from the bank, get out of seizure, and I get my contract."

Right. I don't trust it. It's too easy.

And he's being too freaking nice. Talking about making provisions for my horses and my privacy.

Provisions Mr. New York City doesn't have to follow through on once I agree to it.

I can't trust this crap.

And I can't forget the biggest reason why I can't have hordes of people milling around.

People get nosy. They poke around.

Sometimes they find things they damn well shouldn't.

Holt looks at me, his eyes shining and eager.

"No deal, cowboy." I set my jaw, shaking my head.

Holt's face falls.

On anyone else, it might almost be cute.

He looks like a little boy who's just been told he's going to bed without dessert, as if that ain't the damnedest thing when he's as gorgeous as Lucifer. Right down to those shadowy eyebrows that make his eyes smolder.

"Why not?" he asks.

"I said I'd listen, and I did. Don't owe you an explanation," I force through my teeth—and instantly feel like an ass for it.

I don't know why.

We've been trading barbs ever since we laid eyes on each other, and he's still that snake who's after my land—and I *know* his wicked reputation.

So I don't even know why I feel guilty seeing that crestfallen

44

look on his face.

I sigh.

"Whatever, I'll give you three reasons," I mutter grudgingly, then unfold a finger from my clenched fist. "One—an embankment isn't a total guarantee. I don't want to lose my horses to a semi and a tired driver. Two—" I flick out another finger. "That crappy mall is gonna destroy half the businesses in town, and if you think I'm up for helping with that, you've got another thing coming. And three?" I snap out a third finger. "You're twisting my problems to your advantage, mister. Making it sound like you're doing me a big favor. So actually, here's number four —screw you."

He just blinks at me.

I arch my brows, folding my hand against my arm.

Waiting for the insults, the condescension.

Waiting for him to tell me I'm being unreasonable—yeah, I kinda am—but I never claimed to be smart when I'm pissed.

Waiting for him to start arguing.

But he doesn't say anything, and honestly, that's weirder than this entire mess.

"Well?" I growl. "That finally good enough?"

"For me, maybe," he says somberly. "What about Sierra?"

"What *about* Sierra?"

"She won't quit, Libby," he points out—like I don't know it. "And the way she's going, she's probably going to try to take the whole ranch—not just half. The more you stonewall, the better her hand gets in court."

I wrinkle my brows. "What do you mean? Half the ranch is rightfully mine."

"I'm not an estate lawyer, but I know this much. As long as you won't settle on her half to keep her from selling it, she can take you to court for damages and get an award that lands her the whole enchilada," he says.

Crap.

I hate the logic.

I hate that he's right.

I hate that according to the law, I'm the asshat in the wrong here trying to protect what's mine.

But by my heart, by my morals...I know I'm doing what's right.

I turn away from him. I can't look at him right now.

Not with all this panic running through my head.

Not even now, when he's talking to me like a *person*.

"Sierra's my sister and my problem," I say. "Not yours."

"Guess so. I know what it's like," he says ruefully. "Sierra's not the only one coming home after a long time. It's messy as hell."

"That's the thing." I shrug. "People who leave Heart's Edge only come back with ulterior motives. I know hers, but what are yours?"

"Having a life of my own." His eyes narrow, turning a shade darker.

There's a rawness in his voice I'm not expecting—a quiet sincerity.

It transforms that deep voice from husky sin to soft beguilement, heartfelt and wrenching, and my heart skips a beat.

"That's all I ever wanted," he says. "A life I built for myself from the ground up. A place of my own. Friends, family, a place to crash."

I don't know what to say to that.

Especially when I know too well how it feels, fighting to keep my home intact with every last bit of my soul.

The silence between us goes strange, charged.

I keep my back to him because I don't know what I'll do if I turn around.

If I see that earnest look on his face, if I see some weird truth in those gleaming honey-brown eyes.

Or worse, if I see that smirk again.

Then I'll just have to kick myself for feeling anything for his lies.

I shrug. "You do whatever you want, Silverton. Just leave me out of it."

"Sierra's going to make that mighty hard." There's a scuff of his boot, the sound coming closer, and I tense. "You're worried about my motives, but hell. Are you sure you know hers?"

I toss a suspicious glance over my shoulder.

He's looking down at me, his eyes shadowed with the sun at his back, impossible to read.

"What do you mean?" I ask.

"There's got to be a reason why she wants to sell so fast, and she's suddenly putting so much pressure on us both." He shakes his head. "I think it's because that Declan guy's coming down on her. Don't you think it's a little weird that she's dating the bank guy who wants to buy you out?"

"I mean, if I had to pick between Declan Eckhard and Cherish Reid..."

I shudder.

I can't even finish that sentence.

It'd be like picking between an unfeeling android and a stinkin' badger.

"Didn't like the vibe I got when I met them," Holt continues. "Declan seems exactly like the type of dude who'd shack up with a vulnerable, affection-starved young woman with a taste for bad guys and bad decisions. Maybe just to get at her sister and her land."

I can't help barking out a laugh.

It's awful, but damn this boy brings the heat.

It's also the best and worst description of Sierra Potter I've ever heard. There's no way to save her if she doesn't want to save herself.

I turn back to Holt, planting my hands on my hips and eyeballing him hard.

Maybe he's genuine.

Maybe.

Trouble is, I don't know what that changes.

"So what do you want me to do about Declan?" I ask.

"That's up to you." Holt tucks his hands into the pockets of his coveralls again.

Again, I'm struck by the impression of the charming, disarming small-town man instead of the slick city beast when he smiles.

"Is it?" I whisper.

"Sure. And you know, if you let me have a look around, maybe I can figure out if there's something else making them push so hard. Maybe something we don't know about the property that they've figured out. Minerals, a hidden oil reserve that isn't on the survey maps...could even be an old silver vein out there that isn't tapped out. This town staked everything on mining a long time ago."

"If there was oil or silver on my property, I'd know. My dad was a scientist. He studied every nook and cranny," I say dryly. "Again—what's in it for you, helping me sniff this out?"

"For now? Curiosity."

I snort.

At least he's honest.

But I think I see an opening to clean up this part of the mess.

Doesn't mean I don't have to deal with the rest of it or that I'm even throwing Holt a bone. But I'd rather control his so-called curiosity than let it sneak up Nowhere Lane.

"I'll make you a deal," I tell him. "You come out, you have a look around, we walk the property lines together, and then when we don't find anything...how 'bout you buzz right off and stay buzzed off? We got a deal?"

He grins, hazel eyes glittering like fool's gold.

And I guess I'll be the fool to believe him when he agrees.

"I can definitely work with that, honey," he growls.

My cheeks go hellfire red. Damn, he's lucky I'm too tired to give him another lashing when I'd rather be six feet under than be his *honey* any day of the week.

I nod sharply. I don't care if he's lying or not.

I'm gonna hold him to it, one way or another.

This might be the only way to get him off my butt.

It *has* to be.

Because I can't let him see what's on the outskirts of my ranch and discover the secrets Dad took to his grave.

* * *

It's weird to think it's still out here.

The place creeps me out so much I wish I could pretend it didn't exist.

I almost never come out to this distant end of the property unless I'm checking the barbed-wire fences that are more to keep prowlers and predators out than to keep anything in. I don't use barbed wire on anything holding live animals.

But I can't say I really feel bad for anyone who gets themselves tangled up in spikes, trying to sneak onto my land.

There's a rusty-hinged wooden gate almost hidden in the bushes overgrowing the fence out here, though.

This is where the land bumps up against the mountains. They rise up out of the earth pretty suddenly here—just a few tall, tumbled rocks, and then suddenly you're looking up at stone crags dotted with scrub brush and those tiny twisted trees that cling to the face.

And between those high walls of stone, I see it.

A mountain pass.

One that someone, a long time ago, turned into a road.

It's almost gone now, long buried under scrub brush and grass and fallen trees. It's unpaved, just the suggestion of wheel tracks.

It leads deep into the mountains, to places better forgotten.

I can't help but smile faintly.

Dad was a born storyteller. He used to spin all sorts of wild yarns about ghosts and monsters to keep me and Sierra from going down that road.

But while Sierra listened?

I said I was a ghostbuster, and I ain't afraid of no ghost.

So when I got older, I'd try to sneak off down that road every chance I got.

Problem is, when I was a little girl, I had the worst sense of direction.

If pigeons have iron in their beaks that helps them navigate, I must have that kinda weird magnetic metal that makes compasses go haywire.

For the longest time, I'd just get lost. Turned around, wandering in the bushes, prowling through the grass.

I'd go in circles for ages, make a game out of it, act like I was a cougar out there hunting in the grass, pouncing at squirrels and birds with a little growl.

But when Dad would call me in to wash up for dinner, his voice would always help me find home.

It'd usually be dark by then, too, the stars coming out.

Familiar friends.

Show me a constellation, and I'll show you the way home.

It wasn't until last year that I finally got serious about finding out what was down there. I'd forgotten about it for a while, to be honest.

Dad got sick slow at first, then fast, and he stayed real sick for a long time—and ever since I turned eighteen, more and more of the ranch's management was on me anyway.

When you come of age running a ranch full-time and trying to graduate high school, you don't really remember old stories about overgrown, haunted roads. By my twenties, I'd halfway forgotten them all.

You learn real quick not to rely on anyone but yourself, too.

Not on smooth-talking bankers.

And not on dirty-talking bastards with gorgeous hazel eyes.

Dad was kind of a legend before everything went crazy and this little town found new heroes. He was the brilliant NASA scientist who came home to settle down and retire on the land that'd been in our family for generations.

Heart's Edge knew him as a kind man, a gentle man, a wise man with a good heart.

And I want people to keep thinking of him that way.

I want to remember him that way, too.

It's been a struggle ever since I found out about the avalanche of back taxes, went to survey everything myself, and finally found that long lost road again.

I wandered down it and found something I'll never forget.

It wasn't long before the end. In the final days of his life, I hardly got more than two coherent words out of Dad about it.

But the last thing he said to me...

No.

I can't even think about what he confessed, or it's gonna break me, on top of the other stress.

I can't bear to think my father wasn't the man I thought he was.

It won't help anyone.

He always called this road Nowhere Lane, though I doubt that's the official name on any survey maps. He'd laugh and say it's just the path to nowhere, and no one goes down it unless they want to get lost and never come back.

Now they carry an uncomfortable truth.

If people ever find out what's down there, I don't know where I'll be.

I might even lose this land no matter what I do, but this place could take it away a lot faster.

I don't think they let you keep your ranch when it's been seized by the police as a crime scene, all assets forfeited when your father gets posthumously convicted.

Maybe it can't happen.

Maybe it can.

With the way my life is spiraling nose down right now, I'd believe just about anything.

But I'm going to find a way to save this place, one way or another.

I'll make sure of it.

I've always made sure of it.

Everything's going to be okay.

I swear.

* * *

Months Ago

I CAN'T BELIEVE it's gonna end like this.

Dad's the smartest man I know.

He's the kinda smart that finds new planets and can tell you what atmosphere they have from thousands of light years away. All by tiny flickers in light on photographs that aren't much more than grainy spots of black and white taken with a high-powered telescope.

That's what NASA used to pay him to do.

Find new stars and planets.

Reach out across the universe and touch galaxies that might not even be there anymore, full of all those beautiful lights we see up in the sky every night.

But now it's like there's nothing left of that amazing brain that used to be full of so much life.

Just riding with him was like being in school.

He'd tell me about how all the mountains here are full of metal that came from stars, carried by asteroids that crashed into the Earth eons ago.

He'd tell me about navigating by constellations.

He'd tell me what the names of the constellations meant, everything from my own Aries to Ares—the God of War, ruled by Mars—to the much-ignored Ophiuchus that kind of got kicked out as the bastard child of the zodiac.

He'd tell me about moons where it rained titanium and shores of liquid helium oceans made of crushed black diamonds. I'd look up at the shining night sky and wonder how he could learn all that just from the color and brightness of those twinkling lights.

Now? He can't even talk.

He's almost a vegetable, his body wasted away, his tendons ropy and his mouth hanging slack, a bit of drool building in the corner. His eyes are glazed, empty.

He never told me about the cancer, either.

He's always been like that, holding back bad news.

And the thing with cancer is, it can go slow for the longest time, and no one can tell.

But when it decides it means business, it doesn't mess around.

I didn't want to put him in hospice. It wouldn't have made things any easier for him when the doctors already gave us an in-home morphine drip.

I don't want it to be even harder with him surrounded by impersonal caretakers instead of the people who love him.

Not that Sierra's here for this, here to change his feeding tube and wash him down every day, here to sit by his bedside and hold his hand and try not to squeeze it tight enough to hurt him while I struggle not to sob until I'm just a dried-out, mindless husk of who I used to be, too.

Like father, like daughter.

But I know it won't be long.

It started in his pancreas, but now it's in his lungs, his liver, even in his brain.

Eating him alive.

No one wanted to say it when the doctors sent him home.

We all knew they were sending him home to die.

And I'm here wondering who my father really was, after what I saw this morning.

But he's not here to tell me anymore.

His heart may be beating, his hand may twitch feebly in mine as I clutch it softly at his bedside, looking down at him with his white hair spilled across the sweat-soaked pillow.

There's nothing in those eyes.

Until they abruptly snap open.

I suck in a sharp breath, my eyes widening. I almost recoil from him as a stark, wide blue stare locks on me for dear life.

His hand tightens on mine like a vise. The sticks of his fingers are so thin they dig in with surprising strength, and I let out a little hiss of pain, but I don't let go.

"D-Dad?"

He stares at me. Suddenly everything I know as *Dad* flashes in those eyes like he's an empty vessel and was poured back into himself.

He works his dry, gummy lips, his voice a hollow rasp in the back of his throat before he coughs, his thin body shaking, his nostrils flaring around the breathing tubes.

"Libby. Y-you...you have t-to..."

I lean in close. His voice is weak and thready, so hard to hear, but I'm trying, listening with everything, holding fast to his shaking hand.

"L-Libby, you have to f-find it. I can't...I c-can't take back. What I did, I...y-you. The rock! You need..."

"What?" I whisper, frozen, not comprehending.

His gaze darts away from me then, almost afraid, flicking around the room wildly.

"Th-the gun. Where?"

"Which gun, Dad?" We've got tons of guns. Kinda necessary when you run a ranch this size, everything from his favorite rifle to my sawed-off shotgun that almost never leaves my saddle when I'm out for a ride. "My gun?"

"*His* gun!" he flares, starting to sit upright only to collapse again, wheezing. "Have...h-have to hide...his gun..."

That's when I realize.

He's not actually here with me.

He's living in the past.

He's down Nowhere Lane.

And this horrible dread sinks in.

Dad knows exactly what's down there.

Oh, Jesus.

He knows, and he's the one who...

"Oh my God." I cover my mouth with my free hand, my eyes hot with tears—afraid for him, afraid *of* him, afraid of the truth. "Dad? Dad, what did you do?"

But he only sinks down into the bed, that distant gaze never leaving me. His brows knit together.

"The rock, Libby," he whispers. His voice is oddly clear, almost eerie. "It was all for the damn rock."

Then his eyes close, his head sagging to one side.

His hand goes limp in mine.

And those wheezing breaths that were background noise for weeks of my life, constant and steady and loud, just stop.

So does my heart.

He's gone.

I clutch at him, pressing my fingers to his pulse, to his chest, over his mouth.

Useless. Even though his flesh is still warm through that parchment-thin skin, there's no air against my palm, no flutter against my fingertips.

A loud cry bellows up from the bottom of my shattered heart as I fling myself against him and gather him up.

"*Dad!*"

* * *

Present

55

IT HASN'T BEEN SO LONG that remembering that day doesn't still make my eyes burn.

I can tell myself it's the midday sun or the dust in the air all I want.

It'd be a lie.

I still miss him.

Even if I'm afraid to know the truth.

The love he gave me—gave both of us, Sierra included—was real, no matter who else he may have been.

I've just got to hang on to that with all my heart and soul.

Rubbing at my eye, I reach up to touch my necklace with its constellation spelled out in little red stars, and feel a touch of warmth welling up inside me.

Still, I feel heavy as I turn away from the gate and the fence, guiding Frost in a light trot across the even ground.

Out here, it isn't as well-tended as the pastures visitors see. But it's still got that *tended* feel to it that says a long time ago, my family grew crops. Way back when farmstead living was the only way of living if you weren't a miner or a money changer or a straight-up outlaw.

Frost barely makes it a few steps, though, before I realize I've got company.

I'm a little surprised Reid Cherish, Mr. Suit and Tie Robot himself, drives a dusty old decommissioned military Jeep.

But I'm even more surprised to see him this far out on my property, standing on the other side of the fence on the barely-there dirt lane ringing my land, crisp and cool in his suit even under the high yellow sun.

Here comes emotional ping-pong again.

Only this time it's flinging me between pure rage and terror.

He saw me through the gate.

Odds are he'll have questions about that glimpse of road in the scrub just beyond it, vanishing into the mountain pass.

I don't know if I should act casual to throw him off the trail or go all wolverine to chase him off.

So I just settle for not acting like I'm as heart-thumpingly scared as I am and send Frost kicking forward, scowling at Reid.

He doesn't react.

Yeah, that's gonna get annoying.

But what's annoying me now is the way he looks at me from the other side of the fence. On Frost's back I've got height on him, bulk on him, but he still carries himself like he's the one in charge here.

And he looks at me like he knows something's up.

Like he knows *everything*.

"What the hell do you want?" I growl at him. "Who said you could go traipsing around my place?"

He smiles thinly. "Traipsing. Hmm. Never heard a girl your age say that." He cocks his head to one side while I bristle. "Technically, I'm not on your property, Miss Potter. I'm on the other side of the fence."

"Except," I say, narrowing my eyes and letting my hand fall to the shotgun in its saddle holster, "we built the fences a little in so we could run irrigation ditches. Better check your property map before you figure out where it's safe to stand without getting shot for trespassing."

His eyebrow ticks up a tiny bit. "You'd have to properly warn me first in order to legally shoot me for infringing on your property line."

I thumb the hammer on the shotgun, eyes narrowing, but don't pull it out of the holster just yet. "Pretty sure I just gave you fair warning."

Reid's sigh is long-suffering, slow, as if he's just not the slightest bit worried about the angry chick with a gun big enough to roar like a bear.

"I only came to talk, as promised," he says. "I saw your truck pulled up past the fence, and when you didn't answer the door, I thought it might be prudent to seek you out."

I roll my eyes. "Everybody's always showing up on my doorstep. Haven't you or your little buddy ever heard of phone calls?"

"My buddy?" He looks puzzled, then dismisses it with a flick of his fingers along his sleeve, before he adjusts the cuff of his shirt. "If I called, would you actually pick up the phone?"

I snort. "Nope."

"There you have it." He smooths his sleeve against his wrist, then tucks his glasses up his nose with his middle finger—and I don't think it's pointed, but it damn well might be. "May I *please* ask you to come to my office for a meeting next week? We can still negotiate something."

"Like what?"

"If you put a reverse equity mortgage on your—"

"Fuck no."

That's when the shotgun's out of the holster and across my saddle, resting on the horn.

I won't actually shoot him, no.

Sadly, I'm a big old softie under this temper and this mouth.

But he doesn't need to know it.

He just needs to think I might be as psycho as I'm trying to look.

"Mortgaging my house to pay taxes is the same as letting the bank own my place outright. This place is mine, paid off for generations, and it's staying *mine*."

I try not to sigh. Dad wasn't bad with money, but between mounting medical bills and the endless upkeep on a place this size...he fell farther behind. Down a debt hole that still has me plummeting.

"This 'place,' as you put it," Reid says coldly, "is only partially yours, ma'am. Think carefully. If you continue down this path...soon you'll lose this land. A tragic end for a place that's been Potter ground for over a century."

I'll give him one thing—it takes balls to say that to a woman threatening you with a sawed-off shotgun.

I guess it also takes balls to freaking *bow* to her, before turning your back like you aren't just giving her a perfect target.

For a second, I'm sorely tempted.

So tempted I can suddenly understand my father doing something awful in a moment of anger and desperation, adrenaline hot and fear even hotter in the back of his mind.

For a second, my hand tightens on the hilt of the shotgun.

I relax it when Reid Cherish slinks back to his Jeep and calmly backs out, reversing into the little dirt lane.

Leaving me alone with just Frost and the sickly fear pooling in the pit of my stomach.

I don't know if Reid Cherish and Confederated Bank know what my father did or know what's back there.

I just know they're dangerous.

And I've got to figure out how to outwit them.

IV: MUSTANG SALLY (HOLT)

*W*hat can I say? A man can change.

This is the first time in my life I've ever dressed *down* to impress a chick.

Usually it's all suit and tie, or at least a nice expensive designer shirt and a pair of slacks, rarely jeans.

Back in the Big Apple, I did the whole 'dress for the job you want' thing. The job I wanted then was being the most coveted man in New York, both in the construction business and in everyone's bed.

I guess I'm still doing it here.

The job I want now is being somebody Libby trusts so we can find a way to make everything work.

I think I might actually have a soft spot for that little fire-cracker.

Nah, let's be real.

A hard spot, too.

I can't dwell on how much I'd like to let another part of my anatomy talk with her instead.

I'm hardly dressed like a gentleman today as I pull up in my Benz and find her waiting for me with two horses tied up to the fence at her side.

I'm in jeans and an A-shirt with another light flannel shirt unbuttoned over it just to ward off dust and flies. I don't want to sweat half to death. Though it's barely mid-morning, I've already got the sleeves cuffed and rolled up to let me breathe.

She's wearing significantly less.

A tight tank top so close-fit and low-slung that those thin spaghetti straps look like they're about to break free, snapping under the weight of her tits from the sheer *strain* on the dark rose-colored fabric.

Her cutoffs that might as well be panties with how high she's cuffed them.

Fuck.

She's still in those cowboy boots, too, highlighting her shapely, tanned mile-long legs.

Today she's even got on a cowboy hat, too, shading her eyes and the loose tumble of windswept golden curls.

I can't quite make out the expression on her face under it or what she thinks of me as I slam the car door shut and mosey up the little drive. I cross over the plating bridging the ditch nimbly this time, thank you very much.

She tips the brim of her hat with a little curl of her lip. One bright, glowing blue eye rakes over me.

"Did you come to walk the grounds or wrangle cattle?" she mocks as soon as I draw into earshot.

I grin.

"I mean, if you need a little help around the ranch..."

"I don't."

She goes cold on me in an instant.

It's not hard to see she's got an independent streak a yard wide.

Lucky I'm not here to fuss with her today.

I'm trying to play nice.

So I hold my tongue while she turns away, swinging up onto one of the horses—a gorgeous Gypsy Vanner with a solid, graceful build.

61

The other horse is larger. I can't quite tell the breed but the coat's a glossy shade of brownish black that shines almost purple under the sun. The meat in the legs tells me there's some Arab lines in there somewhere, maybe Barbary.

She settles on the Vanner with an easy grace. The horse's broad body stretches her thighs apart and draws my eye instantly.

Straight down to where the denim molds up into the creases where her thighs meet her hips.

Goddamn, I think I'm helpless around this woman.

Everything about her has this hot, feral magnetism that makes me painfully aware of her, of her body, of her raw aggression that could turn into a roaring passion if a man pushed the right buttons.

Maybe I can't keep my eyes off her.

But I'll damn sure keep my hands to myself.

No matter what my reputation says about me, I'm over it.

So I drag my eyes back to her face—and find her watching me with her face set stone-cold, unreadable.

I smile anyway.

"Well," I say, leaning against the fence and holding out my hand to the darker horse to let her have a sniff and get a feel for me. "Since this girl's already saddled up, I'm guessing she's my transportation?"

"Unless you think your Benz can handle the dirt," she says sweetly, even if her expression never changes. "I'd hate to see your poor engine get caked up with all that crud, though."

"You'd be surprised what a Benz is built to handle."

Honestly, I've been pondering selling it soon.

I need something for utility in this town, not show.

But I'm distracted now, and I smile as the dark mare lowers her nose to my palm.

It's warm and velvety, breaths soft against my skin. I stifle a grin. This brings back memories of other summers, back when me and Blake were just kids and we'd borrow Mr. Potter's horses to go galloping along the trails.

I give her a slow look. "What books did he name these two after?"

Libby blinks, actually jerking up in the saddle to make her Vanner prance with a little whinny before settling down. "Books? You know about that?"

"Damn right. Back before Blake and I got into our shit-fight, back when we were barely big as foals ourselves, your old man would let us ride. Sierra was just a little thing back then, and you were practically a toddler, so you wouldn't remember us." I grin, stroking my fingers over the mare's nose. "Two knock-kneed little boys clambering up on these horses that were like mountains to us. My favorite was War. Blake always rode Peace."

Some things never change considering he married a Peace, too. I chuckle quietly to myself.

Then Libby lets out a choked, soft sound I'm not expecting, rough with hurt.

She looks away sharply, covering her mouth.

I lift my head, looking at her intensely, but she's avoiding my eyes. Just staring out over the ranch with her gaze narrowed and that hand hiding most of her expression.

"You okay?" I ask softly. "Shit, I didn't mean to—"

"I'm fine," she says thickly. "It's fine, I just—" She takes a shaky breath. "I forget how much this town loved him and how many people he knew. So for someone else to remember how Dad went through his Tolstoy phase naming horses..."

I smile faintly and reach out to rest my hand against the Vanner's muscular shoulder, near her knee.

"I didn't know Mark that well, Libby, but he was always good to me and Blake. A real kind guy. He'd give us fresh lemonade when we'd come in all hot and sweaty from the trails. And he'd always tell us weird shit, too." I laugh. "Like the molecular composition of silver, and how it's extracted from...from fuck, I can't remember."

"Galena," she fills in. "Yeah. He always knew the weirdest stuff, and he never hesitated to tell anyone. A big nerd to his dying day."

It's almost ridiculous how hard it hits me when she swipes a finger at her eye, trying not to cry.

The urge to pull her down off that horse and hug the fuck out of her.

Until she can enjoy the good memories of Mark Potter without the pain.

"Sorry," I say softly, restraining that impulse to offer some physical comfort when I don't want to upset her, and she might just take my hand off for trying. "I know it hasn't been that long since it happened."

"Yeah. Almost a year." With a fierce, almost irritated sniffle, she rubs at her nose, taking in a shaky breath. "But, well, life happens."

She's suddenly matter-of-fact, shoving her feelings down, and she jerks her chin at the mare.

"That's Plath," she says and then rests her hand to the Vanner's mane. "This is Frost."

I grin. "Authors this time instead of novels? Sylvia Plath and Robert Frost?"

"Nice knowing you can read. He liked to change things up a little."

She smiles back at me then.

Small and distant and careful, but damn, it's *there*.

I'm glad she's slinging barbs again.

The thump that shakes my whole chest tells me my stupid cock isn't the only reason why I can't seem to look away from her.

Plath gives me a good distraction, bumping my hand imperiously. I realize I'd stopped petting her, and I carefully trace my hand up Plath's nose and jaw.

"Not ignoring you, girl," I murmur, glancing at Libby. "So

you think she'll take me all right? I still remember how to ride. It shouldn't be a problem."

"She should," Libby says blandly. "Just in case, she's the horse I usually give to beginners." Her brows arch under the brim of the hat. "Usually when they're in the five to seven-year-old range."

I burst out a snort of laughter.

Shit, at least she keeps me on my toes.

I think I've still got a good feel for a horse, even if it's been a long time and all the horsepower I've been handling has been under the hood.

I vault over the fence, and under Libby's critical eye, give Plath's reins and saddle a once-over.

Never let someone else prepare your tack without checking it yourself.

I make a minor adjustment to Plath's girth strap before putting my foot in the stirrup and swinging myself up in the saddle.

Not gonna lie, I forgot just how high up a horse's back is, and it's a little dizzying.

I remember this.

The feeling of a horse, the solid movement of our bodies, the saddle keeping me balanced while the animal moves in swaying rhythm. Plath sidesteps a little before settling as she adjusts to my weight.

If I'm not wrong, I think there's a little glint in Libby's eyes that says she just might approve.

Though she doesn't say one word, just takes up Frost's reins and steers the Vanner away.

I lean over, unlooping Plath from the fence, and follow.

It takes me a few minutes to get back into the rhythm—to remember how to let myself move with the mare's body instead of tensing up against her gait, and how to guide her with my knees and heels while going gentle on that bit in her soft mouth.

It's like knowing how to ride a bike.

You never forget.

Before long, Libby and I are riding side by side, moving at a light walk that'll let us cover ground pretty easy without lathering the horses in the morning heat, which is only getting worse.

Seasons in Heart's Edge go to extremes. We get buried in snow in winter, tossed in red-gold bursts of leaves in autumn, lashed by storms in spring with gorgeous bursts of flowers.

And in summer?

We sweat half to death, worshiping the gods of air conditioning and oscillating fans.

I can already feel sweat trickling down my spine by the time we pass the barns, heading across the property.

Even with the heat, it's nice out—and nicer with the company, the bright gorgeous sky, the smell of horseflesh and the feeling of settling back into this town like I *belong*.

Hell, maybe I really do.

And if I don't yet, then maybe I *could*.

Even though I've seen the survey files, I never quite realized just how much land out here the Potters owned.

We're not talking a few scrappy acres of farmstead.

It's miles upon miles of space, most of it left to go to scrub brush out here, with only Libby to manage.

From the property lines I've seen, their acreage even extends into the mountains, though the maps made it look like that area was pretty much impassible, dead land—except for a single mountain pass carving a channel through it.

Depending on the final site for the mall, that pass might be our roadway.

Only one problem, I think, as I scan the land with an assessing eye.

We'd likely have to run straight through Libby's ranch to get to that road, instead of skirting the edges of it.

Damn.

I'll table that for later, though, knowing she'll never buy it, and explore other options first.

"What's the plan if you get to keep your ranch?" I ask her, breaking a silence between us that hasn't been easy, but hasn't been hard, either.

Her shoulders stiffen. They're tanned to such a gorgeous shade of gold, gleaming beneath the sun. Her little white tan lines say she puts those tank tops to the test pretty damn often.

I catch myself following the lines of the tank strap down to where the neckline dips.

There, I can see where paler skin arcs up over the edge of the cloth, promising a mouthwatering contrast of tanned skin against white flesh crossing over the swells of her sweet tits.

She's wearing some kind of strapless bra underneath, just a flash of saucy red and tight-stretched cloth keeping her girls from bouncing with the horse's sway.

But hell, that doesn't mean they don't sway just enough to keep me hypnotized and make me forget what I was thinking.

"Don't even say it. There's no 'if,' mister. I'm keeping my ranch. Period and end of story."

"Sorry." Thank hell she doesn't seem to notice my wandering eyes, her gaze fixed between her horse's ears. "Slip of the tongue."

I force my eyes on her face. Not on her chest and definitely not on the way her hips roll with the horse's stride in teasing waves.

Her knowing sidelong glance, part amused and part disgusted, tells me I'm not nearly as subtle as I think I am.

She knows damn well I've been staring at her all this time.

"We're not having any slips of your tongue today," she says, and I smirk.

"My tongue doesn't slip, usually. Slides, glides, twists, thrusts...now all that, yeah, it's practically an expert. Slipping isn't usually in its repertoire."

She flicks me a wide-eyed look before snorting.

Her mouth twitches with repressed laughter. "You trying to convince me to sell—or trying to convince me to dump your body out here and leave you for the coyotes?"

"You keep threatening to hurt me like you think I won't enjoy it," I growl, and she smirks, flashing white teeth in an easy smile.

"You keep pointing that out like you think I won't enjoy hurting you."

I can't help laughing along with her.

I like a girl with a splash of confidence.

I'd probably let her hurt me a little if she wanted to.

Hell, I wouldn't mind her nails scratching up my back. Digging in hard, just like the little tiger she is.

Fuck, I gotta stop thinking like this.

Trouble is, riding with your dick harder than steel and bouncing around the saddle isn't a pleasant experience.

"You still haven't answered the question," I say, conjuring up a sorely needed diversion. "Besides having plenty of places to bury my damn body when you murder me, are you going to do anything with the ranch? Or do you just like having tons of space with no neighbors to chase off your lawn?"

There's something odd about the way she reacts to a flippant comment about her murdering me.

I can't quite put my finger on it.

Her mouth thins, her eyes go strange and wide and fixed, her brow furrowing up.

Then her face smooths again to the stone-faced neutrality you'd expect out of a cowgirl who can talk as much trash as her.

Libby doesn't answer for a bit, just riding along silently with the jingle of tack and the clop of the horses' hooves on dry earth between us.

Finally, she says, "I kinda want to build an observatory."

I raise both brows.

Even knowing who her old man was, that's not the answer I expected.

"Good place for it," I say. "No light pollution. Perfect view of the night sky."

Her lips curve bitterly. "But you're aiming to fix that, right? With a nice, brightly lit shopping mall and all the bells and whistles that go with it. Highway lights, parking lots, cars out the wazoo..."

I wince. "Now, c'mon. It usually takes a whole big city's worth of lights for the kind of light pollution that blocks out the stars."

"Sometimes all it takes is just one light bright enough, and the sky never looks the same." She takes a deep breath, reaching up to adjust her hat. "I don't know. I don't need more than an acre of land for that. The rest, well...the water table's shifted so the land's dried up. I'd like to get it irrigated and growing things again someday. At least enough hay and feed so I don't have to keep buying it."

"That's not a bad plan to boost your income," I agree, and watch her sidelong as we ride. I'd known she was smart from the moment she opened her mouth, but it's impressive to hear her talk about her plans. "What's stopping you?"

"Money." Just one word, hissed harshly. "Always money."

Her hands tighten where they rest against the saddle horn with the reins knotted around her fingers. "Even with machinery, I can't work that many rotating fields of crops by myself. I'd need to hire more than the few part-timers I manage to keep on now, and I can't. Not to mention there're miles of land that need proper irrigation before it can grow anything, and irrigation systems don't pay for themselves."

I hold my fire. Don't point out how she could easily afford all that if she just sold a fraction of her land to me.

"Not that there's any point. Sierra's either gonna cut the whole thing in half so there's not enough left to run a sustainable crop cycle, or she'll make sure I lose the whole thing out of spite." She growls under her breath, teeth clenching, sharp blue eyes flashing in the shadow of her hat. "Why is she even *doing* this? I can't believe she's pulling this crap. It's like...like Dad never meant anything to her at all."

There's rawness in her voice under all the anger.

Yeah, I get it.

She talks like she hates Sierra, but it's not hard to see she feels betrayed by someone she loves, no matter what went sour.

"Hey," I say. "Maybe you can still talk some sense into Sierra's head. It's not impossible that she'll come around. Hell, Blake and I used to not get along, either. We're talking brawls in the streets, pissed off, mortal enemies. He tried to kick me out of town when I came back."

"I heard the rumors," she whispers.

"You heard right, lady. He hated me so much he was willing to believe I was the idiot out there setting fires, burning places down just so I'd get the jobs to rebuild them."

She lets out one of her sharp, quick laughs. "Yeahhh, that sounds like the kinda crackpot theory Blake would come up with. Do you listen to his radio show? I swear he's the dumbest smart guy I've ever met, but plenty brave, too."

"That's Blake for you. He's my brother, though. We worked things out in the end." I shrug, idly running my fingers through Plath's mane. "So maybe there's a chance you and Sierra can, too."

"Maybe." But she doesn't sound like she really believes it. And I can tell she's deflecting, diverting, when she glances at me and asks, "How come I didn't see you around more growing up? You're not that many centuries older than me."

"*Shit*. I'm only forty."

She smirks, lofting both brows. "And I'm twenty-seven. So get those dirty ideas out of your head."

I splutter. "We're not that far apart!"

That just makes her smirk widen.

"So you just confirmed you *have* been having dirty ideas."

"Sweetheart," I growl, "I'm not the one fixated on my crotch."

"No, but you haven't stopped staring at my chest ever since we set out."

I grin, practically baring my teeth. "What can I say? I've got a thing for color contrasts."

She blinks, looking puzzled, then looks down at her own cleavage, the tan lines.

Libby lets out a flustered gasp and glares daggers at me. "Asshole, will you just answer the question?"

That's enough to slap the dirt out of my head.

I grimace. "Ma moved us to Coeur d'Alene after Blake went into the army."

It's hard to keep going. I don't like thinking about Ma much. She wasn't right in the head, made this huge rift between me and Blake just for the hell of it, to feel like she was in control of something.

"And?" Libby spits.

"And then she got sick, and we needed healthcare. I signed up for the Air Force myself to help pay the bills."

That's all I feel like giving.

She just watches me discerningly under her hat, those ice-blue eyes seeming to see far more than I want them to.

"Is your mother okay?" she asks after a few tentative moments, and I wince.

"Nah. It was a couple of years ago, but...you know."

I shrug.

No need to finish.

Let's just say I know too damn well how she feels, even if my ma wasn't as sainted and well respected as her daddy and things were a lot more complicated.

You don't have to be sure how you feel about your ma for it to hurt when she dies.

"So what happened then?" she prompts gently.

I'm grateful for the chance to move on.

Tilting my head back, I squint up at the clear blue summer sky, just letting myself remember, nice and slow.

"I wandered around Spokane after the military for a while, looking for something to do for a big boy career. Tried my hand at construction management, found out I liked it, started up my own gig," I say, letting a touch of pride creep into my voice. "Then I took that gig to New York City."

"But you didn't stay?" That's all she asks, thank fuck.

"My family's been out here for as long as I can remember. Plus, the market's more competitive there, too. After hearing about all the craziness going down in Heart's Edge, I decided to head home and help rebuild, reconnecting with kin along the way."

Libby half-smiles. "Tell the truth. You couldn't handle the city, could you?"

"Sweetheart, the city couldn't handle *me*," I shoot back, smirking. "I turned New York City on its head, drained it dry, and then left for greener pastures."

"Uh-huh. Sounds like the pastures here were already sour on you a long time ago," she says mildly. "What's this I hear about *married* women?"

Oh, fuck.

"*Listen.*" I make a guttural sound in the back of my throat. "That was a long time ago. I was practically a kid. Only two of them were married. And I didn't *know* they were married when we went at it because they sure as shit didn't tell me!"

"How do you come from Heart's Edge and not know who's married to who, who everyone's second cousin is twice removed, and who touched whose hand too long at the checkout counter?" she mocks, and I laugh.

"To be honest, I never paid attention to all that. I was too busy making business for other people to mind."

"Guess you did leave behind a legacy. A couple of effed up marriages, a bad reputation..."

"I'm not back to live up to my fucking reputation," I snap, harsher than I intend. "I'm just here to try to be a good uncle, a good brother. Only girl I'm spending my downtime with lately is my sixteen-year-old niece."

"Andrea? No wonder you get along," she says archly. "You're at about the same maturity level."

I whistle through my teeth, but I can't stop grinning. "*Ouch*, witch. You're not gonna show me any mercy at all, huh?"

"Would you want me to?"

"Point taken. Less fun that way," I mutter, lingering on her. My smile fades as I give myself permission to take her in again, watching how easy she guides that horse like it's an extension of her own petite, beautiful body. "I think I like you this way."

Her gaze locks on mine.

There's this moment where we just *look* at each other.

It makes me wish like hell she wasn't off-limits, that she wasn't a prospective seller I was trying to woo, that my whole damn business didn't hinge on convincing the world's prettiest porcupine to play ball.

I can't cross that line.

I've got a sense of ethics I didn't have when I was younger— even if I had to have it beaten into me by bad experience.

Messing around with her when her ranch is at stake could wind up hurting her real bad in the end.

I won't do it.

That's what I keep telling myself desperately as those pale-blue eyes hold mine and our horses drift closer together until our knees almost touch.

I'm fascinated by the Cupid's bow of her lips. The way summer sweat beads on her jaw in this fine mist, the high dip of her waist, the slender, tautly toned tuck that swells out into a long slope of tempting stomach and curved hips.

This woman's built to ride.

And I'm not talking about horses.

We're so close our thighs brush along the lengths of our horses' flanks. My mouth throbs with a wicked need.

I could do it.

I could lean down right now and—

There's a rustling in the scrubby brush just up ahead of us.

The only warning before this huge brown shape comes rocketing out of the bushes, skittering into our path.

Both of our horses stagger back, but neither of them rear or startle or bolt.

Before I'm really thinking about what I'm doing, I whip out the old Colt pistol hidden underneath my open flannel shirt and holstered on my hip, firing it in the air.

The cougar must feel cornered between these big old horses and that line of bushes.

It holds its ground for a moment, laying its ears back and snarling as it crouches down.

Then it turns sharply and bolts away in a flash, its sandy hide almost blending into the ground as it crashes through the brush and disappears.

We stare at the place where it vanished for a minute before I lower my arm, check the Colt, and then socket it back into its place at my hip.

"That was interesting," I grunt.

"She probably has cubs around here somewhere. Just defending her babies."

There's actually a touch of admiration in Libby's voice—and not a hint of fear.

She's definitely a tough one. Knows her away around and knows what can and can't hurt her.

I like that.

To distract myself from wandering thoughts, I lean down and rub Plath's shoulder. "You've trained these two pretty well. Didn't spook at all."

"I know my horses. And I make sure they're good to their riders as long as their riders are good to them." She tilts her head at me. "Where the hell did you learn to shoot, flyboy?"

"Other than here?" I grin, straightening in the saddle. "Pilots don't just fly. They hand out some heavy artillery."

"A missile ain't the same thing as a handgun."

I laugh. "And neither is a wing-mounted gatling gun, but you can't even get past grunt level if you don't certify in firearms training with a hell of a lot more than my old Colt here."

We both nudge our horses into moving again, heading forward now at a walk. The terrain starts to get a little more rocky, strewn with more scrappy brush that could hide another cougar, a snake, who knows what around these parts.

Libby eyes me, then sniffs. "Please. You're just a flyboy so you don't have to get dirty slumming it with the other soldiers on the ground. You make your messes from far away and rocket out of danger."

"Ouch. So your old man was in the Navy, huh?"

A startled sidelong glance darts my way. "Way before I was born, but yeah. How'd you know?"

"Because sailors can't stand us 'flyboys.' We get to jet off and have all the fun while they're stuck on the water." I smirk. "Hell, I'd tell my kids to hate the Air Force, too, if my only job in the military was to play water taxi for the big boys."

Of course, my wisecrack is as over-the-top as it sounds.

Libby bursts out laughing, throwing her head back, reaching up to tilt the brim of her hat back and press her hand to her brow before tugging it down again. "Hot damn. All those jokes about rivalry between the branches weren't really jokes, were they?"

"Nope. You put us out in the field together, we'll have each other's backs. No question, we'll save each other's lives. We'll fight together like the men we're supposed to be, and we're all equals out there in the battlefield. Off the game, though?" I chuckle. "You can take out an entire bar with the brawl just from fighting over what unit did the *real* work on a sortie, while everyone else just drifted along. We get pretty damn territorial about it."

"Yeah, yeah, I've heard the stories." She gives me that no-fucks-given smirk again. This girl's completely unimpressed by me, and it just makes me grin more. "Doesn't change the fact you're a flyboy who doesn't want to mess up his hair."

"You should see how it looks when I'm just out of the cockpit. Helmet off, sweaty, sticking up everywhere. I'm not always this smooth."

It's gratifying that makes her blush, her smirk briefly fading before she looks away from me pointedly.

That tells me *she* thinks I'm pretty, too.

Or handsome.

Or, shit, whatever.

And here I am, still having evil thoughts I shouldn't.

"It's not all easy coasting up there in the sky," I say. "The G-forces are enough to make you pass out if you don't build up your endurance. It's pretty goddamn terrifying being the only thing in control of thousands of pounds of steel and complex machinery hurtling at speeds that break the sound barrier. Thousands of feet up in the air, you're relying on skill. There's no safety net if you get hit. It's just you in freefall, vulnerable and exposed to enemy fire, hoping if you get nailed by flak or a missile, you won't break apart on impact when you hit the ground."

I'm expecting her to laugh at me again.

I'm definitely not expecting the look she rakes over me, disbelieving. "Like you'd know anything about being vulnerable."

I blink.

If I didn't know better, I'd almost say she sounds mad at me.

For real mad, not the playful teasing we've been throwing back and forth and I've actually been enjoying.

"Pardon?" I growl back.

"Don't you 'pardon' me. Talk like you know where you came from," she hisses, then looks away from me again. "Men like you never know what it means to be vulnerable. I've seen your sort of guy before. You break hearts like pinatas so nobody can ever hurt yours."

What the fuck? I don't know where this is coming from, this sudden bitter, hurt animosity like I left her high and dry personally.

Except, I realize, maybe I *do* know.

Because there've been times when I was pretty skeptical about chicks, after the way my last so-called love treated me. After watching how my brother's first wife treated him, too, and how easy it was for me to almost cheat with her, and she didn't even hesitate.

It's Sierra, I bet. If I'd been watching men fuck over my vulnerable, emotionally needy sister for my entire life, maybe I'd be mistrustful, too.

"Sierra, huh?" I mutter. "You blame the dudes she hooks up with for taking advantage."

Her soft gasp tells me I've hit the mark, but she won't look at me. "Who says that's any of your business?"

"Nobody. Sierra's business isn't mine. I just can't help but notice when you're clearly worried about her." But I can't help but add, almost under my breath, "...and I know more than you'd imagine about heartbreak."

"What was that?" A suspicious look snaps toward me.

"Nothing."

I don't need to bare my demons to her.

She wouldn't want to meet them, anyway.

Some things, I'd rather keep close to home. Especially when I'm trying to forget—and you don't forget bad juju by dumping it on every pretty stranger who'll listen.

Libby looks at me for a long moment, something odd flickering in her eyes, before she just clucks her tongue.

Then she gently kicks her heels against Frost's sides, snapping the reins with a practiced "*Hya!*"

The Vanner lurches forward in a ground-eating run.

I stare after her, wide-eyed, before squeezing Plath's flanks. The horse responds instantly, beautifully, all that surging power under me and the wind whipping me in my face as I race after Libby.

At first there's just the Vanner's lashing tail and Libby's sweeping blonde mane, her shoulders taut, and *goddamn,* her ass looks deadly, spread over the saddle in those tight cutoffs.

But then we're running neck and neck, our horses racing to overtake each other.

My blood burns like the sun blasting down on my face and my heart beats like the thud of their hooves.

The whole thing is a little dumb, a little reckless, a lot spontaneous.

I'm still grinning fit to burst, and so is she.

* * *

BY THE TIME we come up on a fence far out on the edge of the ranch, toward the foot of the mountains, I'm panting and so are the horses—but the air between us is easier.

We pull Frost and Plath to a prancing halt, slowing down to let them breathe.

The moment the world stops blurring by, though, I realize where we are.

We've reached that distant mountain pass.

Only it's more of a road, built into a natural cut-through.

It's real old, never paved.

Looks like it used to be a wagon trail or something from ancient patterns in the grass grown through the ruts. I guess the rest of it used to sprawl across the plains before it fell out of use, and eventually, that road became a forgotten thing of the past.

I can barely make it out past the overgrowth, including the tangled bushes and grass that have almost completely taken over the fence.

Which is odd in of itself.

From what I've seen, Libby's fierce about keeping her place up, every nook and cranny.

All the other fences are clear and well-maintained, everywhere else but here.

I guide Plath up to the fence before pulling to a halt, looking out over the narrow cut through the mountains, steep palisades of stone rising up to either side, jagged and dotted with little trees.

"This is the pass through the range, isn't it?" I ask. "Cuts right through. Saw it on the survey map when we were looking at places to pave a road."

Libby's just a little too slow to turn her head toward the road, a sort of forced bewilderment like she didn't even realize it was there.

"Oh, yeah...that," she whispers.

She swings down off Frost's back, catching his reins—and I realize why she stopped here when she leads him toward an old manual pump tucked against the fence.

She grips the handle and strains to work it, but it's rusted in place. Even though the muscles in her arms tighten sweetly against her tanned skin, it's not budging. She's going to scrape her hands to hell and back if she keeps it up.

"Here," I say, vaulting down from Plath quickly. "Let me."

She makes a sour face at me as I shoulder her gently to one side, then grip the pump handle in both hands, bracing my feet and wrenching it up.

The rusty bastard squeals like an animal—but it moves.

I manage to give it a few good hard pumps, fighting against the rust and grime clogging the workings, before it sputters to life.

First it spits out a clot of mud.

Followed by reddish water spraying out in a spurt that quickly clears, darkening the dry earth around it.

With a cluck of her tongue, she beckons Frost over. The Vanner snorts and thrusts his nose under the spray, splashing us both.

I chuckle, holding up my hands to ward it off. Libby gently grips his head and holds him back so he's forced to drink slower.

"Go easy, guy," she murmurs, and there's a softness in her voice I've never heard, velvety and sweet. "Drink it nice and slow or you'll make yourself sick."

"Here. They can share."

I catch Plath's reins and guide her over, and she thrusts her head under it, too.

Soon they're just making a mess everywhere as they lip at the water and shake their muzzles until their manes are speckled in droplets—and so are we.

It's like the whole universe conspires to make it impossible to peel my eyes off Libby.

Everywhere those droplets land on her shoulders, arms, and thighs, those tiny beads of water catch the light and make her shimmer like she's covered in gold dust.

They speckle her shirt, soaking in, making me painfully aware of just how thin the fabric of her tank top is. Wet spots spread, clinging to her skin in a luscious second layer that makes my tongue ache to taste her.

On her cheeks, they shine like freckles made out of tiny diamonds.

And where they dot her lips, they make them gleam in shimmering red curves so goddamn lush my cock twitches just thinking about how they'd feel against mine; how her mouth would go softer and hotter the deeper and harder I kissed her.

Fun fact: I'm bad at resisting temptation.

The more I try not to think about it, the more I fucking want to.

She'd be gorgeous with her thighs around my hips, riding me like I'm one of her steeds.

Fuck.

Thank God she's not looking at me now because I'm probably staring at her like a starving wolf.

I lick my lips and look away, focusing on that half-hidden stretch of road out past the gate.

"I think," I say, "this puts a hold on at least one plan."

Her head jerks up from watching the horses, her hands steady on both of them while they drink, stroking their noses. "What do you mean?"

"Survey maps made it look like this could be a good path to a build site for the mall," I say. "Take this road through the cut, and then there's a flat sort of hollow between the mountains where that mall could sit all pretty, like the treasure at the end of a trail." I frown, narrowing my eyes as I survey the terrain. "But I don't think it's wide enough for a two-lane road. I doubt I can get zoning rights to cut deeper into the mountains to widen it." I glance at her. "Besides, we've got a bigger problem."

Libby tenses, waiting for the worst.

Makes me think of a woman with a guillotine hanging over her head.

There's something in her eyes that says she's waiting for me to break her, but I don't know what she's expecting to hear.

"What's that?" she asks carefully.

I gesture toward the land around us.

"All of this is your space. Looks like the road used to run through here, but it was tilled over a long time ago. To get here, we'd have to run a two-lane road right across your property. Even if we just do a sharp cut off the main highway on the very corner...it's still going to chew into your space. And we're trying not to do that any more than we have to."

"At all," she corrects sharply, straightening, then stalking to stand between me and that brush-covered gate like a tiny human wall of packaged fury. "You're trying not to do it at all, remember? Because you agreed that once you saw this wasn't gonna work, you'd buzz off." She gestures at the mountain pass. "And that's my property, too. Don't talk about it like it's already yours, and I'm just a speed bump in the way."

"That's not what I—"

"Meant?" she flares, her jaw jut out stubbornly. The tips of her fingers twitch like she's just itching to throw a couple punches. "That's the funny thing. People say what they mean when they don't mean to. I know damn well what you meant."

So much for the cease-fire.

We'd gone from hitting each other with poison arrows to hitting each other with Nerf bats.

Now it's open season on me again.

I don't get why the fuck she's so angry.

Or why she even let me come out here, when it's clear she doesn't want me poking around—doesn't want me to be here at all.

Oh.

God *damn*.

That's what this is about, isn't it?

She never had any intention of even considering my offer.

She just wanted to get me to agree that once I saw the logistical barriers, I'd fuck off and never come back.

Clever.

She's trusting I'll actually keep my word.

That I have some shred of personal honor, and despite my reputation, I'm sincere about aiming for a reset.

Damn Libby Potter for being right.

And double damn me for wanting to live up to the tiny crumb of faith she's put in me in her own angry, messed up way.

"Okay, Libby," I say, meeting her glare head-on with my own eyes narrowed. I'm not getting in a confrontation with her over this and stabbing her buttons even more. "Okay. You win. No more deals."

The look she gives me might as well scream *liar*. Then her face softens a tad.

"You...you mean that?"

I smile faintly, though I'm not really feeling it.

"Yeah. That was the agreement, right?" I hold out my hand. "Let's shake on it."

After a wary moment, she steps closer and slips her hand into mine.

I've never touched a woman whose hands were almost as work-worn as mine, her palm hardened and the fingertips calloused, but the flesh is soft and her fingers still delicate and pretty.

A strong hand, one that's earned its strength by knowing when to be gentle and when to be firm.

There's also equal caring and toughness in her grip.

And something about it makes the respect building inside me for Liberty Potter cement even deeper.

I'm also a good boy—no seductive strokes of my thumb, no little tickle against her palm. I just clasp her hand and give it a firm shake, then let go.

She pulls back, almost like she's surprised I *didn't* try something filthy, pulling her hand against her chest.

Libby gives me another strange look, then turns away and reaches for Frost's reins, gently pulling him away from slurping at the pump before bending to shut it off.

"Come on," she says quietly. "Let's take them back before they get all sun-sick from drinking so much in this heat."

I oblige by stealing Plath's reins and mounting up.

But I can't help but notice as she climbs Frost's back, she looks back.

Libby stares down that old deserted road with a pensive expression on her face.

Finally, she sends Frost trotting past, and I nudge Plath into gear to catch up.

My lips arc down into a slow frown.

There's something else down that old road, I think.

Something she doesn't want me to see.

And I can't help but wonder what'll happen to Libby's secrets when the bank takes this land away from her and hands it over to the county tax man.

I move Plath up closer to her, then settle back down into an easy pace once we're moving neck and neck.

I clear my throat. "I have this thing about not mixing business with pleasure, but since we're not doing business anymore—"

"*No,*" she says flatly, without even looking at me. Her cheeks blossom hellfire-red.

Big mistake.

That just makes me grin.

She might drive my brain crazy, but my dick is a different kind of nuts, knowing my charms don't work on her.

It's nice for a change.

Fun that she sees me as something more than the devil to tame; the bad boy every woman wants to try riding and see if they can break him enough to keep him for themselves.

I never wanted to be broken.

Though maybe I wouldn't mind being tamed a bit by her capable hands.

* * *

LATER, it's hard to keep Libby off my mind, especially when I've got a steaming bowl of *hell no* laid out in front of me.

I don't want to be meeting with Declan and Sierra.

Particularly Declan.

The sleazeball excels at handing out the creeps like Halloween candy.

But since Sierra's the one who contacted me as a potential buyer for the land, and since I'm not following through, I need to close this out and send them packing.

I can't do anything to stop Sierra from raising hell over the ranch, but I can at least honor my agreements. Tell her I'm not working with her anymore.

She sits across from my desk in my mobile trailer office with her legs crossed, wearing a leopard print mini dress that went out of style ages ago.

Declan's more reserved in a suit that could've come right out of my own closet.

He's slick, sharp-eyed, and sharkish.

There's something about him I recognize, from one big city playboy to another.

For me, it was always about charming people into seeing things my way. If I had a few bedmates here and there as a result of it...no harm, no foul.

Declan strikes me as the type who'll double deal someone openly with his cold, flinty way of looking you in the eye. His smile says he'll shiv you in the back the second you turn away.

I know his type too well.

He's looking at me that way right now as I fold my hands on my desk and say, "I'm sorry, but our business relationship can't move forward."

"Um, what?" Sierra makes a flustered noise. "How can it be over if it's barely begun?"

"I can't help you," I say firmly. "Libby won't sell to me. Or to you, if she can help it. There's nothing I can do but complicate matters more, and it'd be unethical for me to mislead you, making you think I can force a sale."

"Unethical?" Sierra flares, her blue eyes snapping. They're not the same shade as Libby's, though. Darker. Less fire, more twilight, and they just don't have the searing burn that gets to me. "What's unethical is you abandoning us, Silverton. You stand to profit quite handsomely, but you—"

"Sierra," Declan snaps. He's got this slow, forceful way of speaking that's like standing in front of a grinding steamroller— he might mow you over, but he'll take his sweet time. "If the man doesn't want to play ball, he doesn't want to. We'll just have to take the more punitive route."

My eyes narrow.

Adrenaline shoots through my blood.

Punitive? I don't like the sound of that one fucking bit.

"What do you mean?" I ask, my hands clenching with instinctive need to *do* something.

To protect Libby, even if she's not here.

Declan turns his slow, cold smile on me. I feel defiled.

He knows I'm on edge, and he's enjoying it.

"Whether Liberty Potter likes it or not," Declan says, "half that land rightfully belongs to Sierra. It's her inheritance by law, same for a fifty percent stake in the house. If we take Liberty to court, Sierra wins—and Liberty will just be shit out of luck."

My teeth pinch together.

Sad to say, the prick isn't done.

"The court will force a division of assets," he drawls in this accent I can't quite place. "Sierra gets her half of the land plus more for damages for her sister dragging this thing out. They'll make Liberty sell off her remaining land simply to cover her legal fees without ending up in the poorhouse. It's a regrettable situation, but since she won't cooperate and you won't work with us...regrettable, it is."

I go cold inside.

Is he really trying to threaten Libby to get me to do his dirty work?

"Look, I can't force Libby to do anything," I grind out slowly, making my words very clear, very precise. "And frankly, it won't look good for you or the bank you work for if you're caught trying to muscle her around." I narrow my eyes. "Isn't this entire deal a conflict of interest for you, anyway? All you have to do is stand back and let the bank foreclose when the time's up."

That actually makes Declan blink. "Time limit?"

I cock my head, looking at him.

Hold the hell up.

I know *damn well* I heard Reid Cherish tell Libby about having less than forty-five days to get her shit sorted when I caught them in the parking lot at The Nest.

Yet this guy's acting like it's the first he's heard of it.

Something isn't right here.

I hold Declan's eyes. He's not talking over me or thinking he can intimidate me in my own damn office.

"Sounds like your coworkers haven't been keeping you in the loop," I say smoothly. "Maybe you should get out and rectify that. Have a little talk with Mr. Cherish. See if he approves of you forcing a court division of assets and sale when your employer's trying to work *with* Libby as an intermediary for the taxing authority." I raise both my brows. "Or maybe I should talk with him myself? See what he has to say?"

Declan goes oddly still.

If looks could kill, I'd be dead in my chair right now.

It's a slow, thoughtful glance, assessing, measuring me up and down like he just realized I'm a possible contender and not an annoying bystander.

With a sniff, he stands, hefting his muscular bulk and reaching down for Sierra's arm.

Not to offer his hand. Not to take her hand. Not to ease her up.

He just *grabs* Sierra's arm and pulls like a dog with a rope.

Though it doesn't quite look like it's hurting her, I don't like the way he uses her arm as a leash to drag her up.

"Come, Sierra," he says. "Negotiations have broken down."

"Negotiations are done," I growl back.

Sierra flashes me a look that's half annoyance as she stands.

But the rest?

The other half of that look feels like desperation, wide-eyed and scared.

This dark, worried sensation churns in my gut as I watch them leave.

The more I see of this shit, the less I like it.

Not at all.

* * *

It's past time to butt out of this.

Too bad I can't when I know Libby could be facing more trouble—and at the very least I can make sure she goes into it with fair warning.

It's a funny thing, sprouting a conscience.

I started realizing it around the time I figured out I had to do the right thing with Blake and his half of the inheritance from our ma. I had to work that man to the bone even after we fixed our shit to get him to take a little money for Andrea's college fund.

Now that I'm looking at this woman who believes I've got enough decency to honor a promise made to her in the heat of the moment, well, hell.

It's taken full root and sprouting leaves.

Something about having a pretty lady believe in you is one hell of a drug.

That's how I end up prying Libby's cell phone number out of a very skeptical Felicity, even if it takes buying four black coffees in a row and getting myself so wired on caffeine I think I could race one of Ms. Wilma Ford's hummingbirds.

I think Felicity's just amused, and not just over my clumsy ass playing superspy.

I wonder if *everyone* can tell how much that little cowgirl gets under my skin.

Back outside, I stab her number into my phone and hit the call button.

"Hello?" When she picks up, she sounds out of breath—and I can just picture her out there, hauling bales of hay or putting the horses through their paces, sweat glistening on her skin.

"Don't hang up," I say quickly. "It's me."

Her voice instantly goes hot with irritation when she realizes who she's talking to.

"*Holt?* Holt Silverton? How'd you get my number?"

"Blame your friend at the coffee shop. For some reason, she

felt like I needed to have it." Out in the parking lot of The Nest, I lean against the hood of my Benz, crossing my ankles and letting my gaze drift over the town. "I'm not calling to be a pain in the ass, promise. Just letting you know how things went with Sierra."

There's a heavy *whump* on the other side, then a wary, "And...?"

"Not well," I admit. "That Declan asshole's advising her to force it in court. And we know that won't be fun."

"No, it really won't be. But if he's spoiling for a fight..." She talks tough but sighs heavily, and it rubs me raw how dispirited she sounds. "Why are you even telling me this? Still trying to help me after I flipped you the bird?"

"Because it's the right thing to do."

She doesn't say anything.

It dawns on me then. She's just as much at a loss as I am.

Doesn't know what to do with me when I'm not trying to charm her.

Just like I'm not quite sure what to do with her when she's not trying to take my head off.

Maybe it's easier when we're only voices on the phone and not sworn enemies in the flesh crossing swords of anger and lust.

"Hey," I tell her. "Listen up. You need more help sorting this out, call me, okay? I'm not sure what I can do, but I'll try."

There's a longer pause on her end.

"Holt?" she murmurs sweetly.

"Yeah?"

"You're weird. I just...I don't get it. What about your contract? If Sierra's pissed at you now, there's no way she'll ever sell to you whether she gets this place or not."

"I'll figure something out." I shrug. "There's got to be an alternate route that doesn't wind up ruining everyone. Might cost a little more money and take more legal hopscotch, but it'll work out in the end. I know it will. Hang in there, honey."

For a second, she makes a strained sound, probably at the pet name.

Then she just gives back, "Same to you."

All words aside, I'm at a loss how this ever ends well.

That thought presses down like a boulder as I end the call.

Yeah, I'm already boned.

The city council won't give me the job if I can't hand them the tidiest, least expensive proposal possible. And without that gig, all these smaller gigs won't be nearly enough to get my business settled on solid footing. We're looking at another six to eight months tops to finish fixing the fire damage around town and throw up a few new buildings.

Then Silverton Construction will be staring down a black hole of nothing.

This is the second time I've possibly fucked over my business for a woman.

But I promised Libby help, and I'd rather wind up penniless than break more promises.

What the hell ever.

If this goes south, I'll just pick myself up a second time, too.

One way or another, I'll get it right.

I'll also make sure I do my damnedest to push Libby Potter's sweet ass in the right direction, too.

V: LEAD A HORSE TO WATER (LIBBY)

I can't believe I'm going through with this, but here we are.

I'm dressed up nice—even if *nice*, for me, is a pair of jeans with no holes in them and a button-up blouse—and waiting for my sister and that weirdo Declan to show up at the house for lunch.

There's a fine line between loyalty and stupidity.

Right now, I feel like I'm tap dancing on it.

But this is honestly my only chance.

I need to talk some sense into Sierra. Remind her we're sisters, we should be on the same team, and we need to leave other people out of this.

People like Holt, people like Declan, people like Reid Cherish.

This needs to be between me and Sierra alone.

If by some miracle we remember we're family, if we act like it, we can pull together and save the ranch.

Because even after the way she left, even after the things she did...

If she really wanted to come home, I'd let her.

If she wanted to be sisters again, instead of enemy combatants, I'd be okay with that, too.

I've had nobody else since Dad died.

No one but Felicity as my friend, plus a few friendly acquaintances in town.

Truth be told, I miss being a family.

That thought hits me with a sudden sharp pang I'm not expecting, making my throat close up and my eyes get all twitchy and burny.

Like hell I've got time for that. Not when I hear Declan's car pulling up in the driveway—a Tesla far nicer than my sister's banged-up Taurus.

For a split second, I can't help but remember Holt talking about his brother and niece when we went out riding.

The way he seemed to ache for something he didn't quite have, too.

I shouldn't be thinking about him now.

Or at all.

Just because he did me a favor doesn't mean I can trust that slick talkin' snake-man in the slightest.

Not even if part of me actually wants to.

I glance up, hearing footsteps on the porch.

I've got company and a lot of slick talking of my own to do.

Hell, maybe I should've brought Holt in anyway.

Fair fight.

Two against two.

His tongue's a lot smoother than mine...and no, thank you very much, there's no hidden meaning there.

When I hear the knock at the door, I'm ready.

Scrubbing my hands on my thighs, I step forward quickly and yank the door open.

Declan and Sierra stand arm in arm on the doorstep. He's in another one of his nice suits. Sierra wears another thrift shop designer knockoff that would be nice if she'd just get things that fit her and take care of them.

That's always been her problem.

She can't stick to things or mind them much.

She's killed goldfish that way, plus an old CD player or two.

Is it any wonder Dad left it to me to run everything when Sierra can't even mend a dress?

My smile turns to gritted teeth when I see the moony way she's looking at Declan.

Ugh. She's downright smitten.

Sometimes you just can't reason with a girl when she's love-struck, and Sierra's always gonna put her flame of the moment over any good sense, good reason, or good family loyalty.

"You're just in time. Lunch is almost out of the oven." I swallow a sigh and step back, opening the door wider.

That makes Sierra notice I'm there.

She instantly glares at me.

Of course.

"What's the point of this, sis?" she asks sulkily. "We already know you're not selling. You're just making things more difficult."

Deeeep breaths, I tell myself.

Don't snap at her yet...

...or murder her.

It takes me a few seconds, and I have to turn away, crossing the big open ranch house to the kitchen and pulling the oven open.

The savory scent of shepherd's pie drifts out. I keep my hands busy—and not on anyone's throat—by tugging on a pair of oven mitts and bending in to retrieve the pan.

"The point," I say—and I can only keep my voice even by not looking at them, "is to try to talk this through. You're right, Sierra. I'm not selling. But we're sisters, and I don't want to wind up in court and bleed us both dry." I turn to set the pan on the counter, eyeing Declan. "I only invited him as a courtesy 'cause he's your man. I don't want him here as a representative of the bank."

Declan sniffs, though he offers me a pretty shit-eating smile. "You do understand I can't *not* take any information I learn here into consideration when handling your case?"

"You can do what you will with whatever, but you're not getting me to sell, buster," I say firmly.

I'm trying to hold my ground without being nasty, without more screaming and hollering and raised fists.

But I have an ugly feeling that's not gonna last.

"So what's your big idea?" There's a spark of hope when Sierra folds her arms over her chest, eyeing me skeptically.

"I'm not sure yet." I shake my head. "I was hoping you'd have some thoughts. My biggest hope, right now, is that if I negotiate some kind of payment plan with the bank, I can buy a little time and do something to pull in enough business to make this work."

Sierra scoffs. "What *business?* Trotting kids around on toy ponies?"

I narrow my eyes. "Look, this could be a full-on cattle ranch and crop farm if we had the money to invest in the right stuff and extra hands on deck. But since the only way to get that money is to sell the ranch, it's a damn conundrum, ain't it?"

She sniffs. "*Conundrum,* ooh. Big word for someone who never went to college."

I rip the oven mitts off, flinging them down on the counter, glowering at her. "And them's fighting words for someone who ran away before she even graduated high school—"

"Libby," Declan cuts in. He's all ingratiating but talking so loud it's like trying to talk over a brick wall. "I'm afraid that's not an option. The bank's not in a position to offer you a payment plan on a lien."

I eye him, crossing my arms over my chest. "Why the hell not? Reid Cherish said—"

"That's just not how it works." There's an odd look on his face, and he clears his throat.

"Oh, yeah? Seems like that's exactly how it works to me." I jab a finger in his direction. "I owe money for back taxes, and since I ain't paid, they put a lien on my ranch. So if I sell, the tax man gets a cut of the property to pay off what I owe, the bank gets their service fee, and everybody's happy. If I don't sell, they get to use your bank to legally pressure me into a damn foreclosure. Now why the hell wouldn't the bank be in a position to take the money I owe? Especially if it means they get the full amount plus interest on a payment plan?"

He draws himself up with his shoulders squared, looking down his nose at me. "I'm afraid it's too intricate. If you'll let me—"

"Don't get snooty with me. Just 'cause I ain't a college girl doesn't mean I didn't learn how this whole ball of wax works the second I got the letter in the mail." I plant my hands on my hips, narrowing my eyes and raking him with an up and down look. "Don't talk down to me 'cause I know your job better than you do."

Declan splutters, and for a second his face scares me.

It's just this mask of pure red-faced hate because I stepped on his dick.

There's violence brewing in his eyes—violence and unrestrained loathing.

I'll be damned if I've ever seen a look like that on any banker's face.

Something about this man stinks to high heaven.

But try telling my sister that when she thrusts herself between us, right in front of Declan like she'll protect him from little old me.

Whatever, maybe she's got a point.

If he makes any rash moves, I'll knee him square in the nuts.

Sierra glares at me, her lower lip thrust out. "Is this why you asked us here, Libby? To insult us?"

"No. I wanted to try and actually figure something out!" I huff. "Look, I'm *trying* to be civil, sis, but this asshole can't even keep his shit straight about the bank—"

"*You* said you weren't having him here for the bank," she says a bit smugly, lifting her chin. "So what does that matter?"

"Don't you try to run that mess on me, Sierra Potter."

"Excuse you, you're not Mom. You don't get to talk to me like I'm a little girl!"

That makes us both stop.

When you lose not one, but two parents to cancer...

Sometimes just mentioning them freezes your heart.

We stare down each other for several seconds.

Then she looks away with a pissy little sound, though her shoulders sag, the wind knocked out of her.

"So what if you can get a payment plan? What then? Where are you even gonna get the money?" Sierra folds her arms over her chest.

"I...I don't know yet," I growl. "There's a lot of idle farm equipment sitting around here. Some of it's real pricey stuff. Dad had four tractors, most of 'em in good condition. I could probably take inventory and sell off excess junk for a decent chunk."

Then an idea hits me on the head.

"You know what? You want money for the land, I'll sell off those big old combines *tomorrow* and buy you out. If we ever get this place going for crops again, I'll find another way. That sound fair?"

Sierra opens her mouth to spit something at me—but stops when Declan lays an almost proprietary hand on her arm.

He pulls her away.

I watch suspiciously as he bends down to murmur in her ear. She listens attentively, nods, and casts me a slit-eyed, almost triumphant look.

God, I don't like the look of that at all.

Especially when she straightens and lifts her chin, eyeing me into the floor.

"I might consider it if the money's good enough," she says.

"But why should I when I can take you to court and get the whole ranch for myself?"

"You don't even *want* the ranch," I say, throwing it out with heat born from pure frustration. "You don't care about this place! You don't care that Dad wanted us to stay here—and he wanted us to keep folks off our land!"

Sierra blinks, her smugness fading to leave blank-eyed confusion, her brows wrinkling, then smoothing as it clicks for her.

"Oh, what? You mean that old road he was always telling weird stories about? The one we weren't allowed to go down?" The look she gives me is almost pitying. "Seriously, Libby. Don't tell me this stubbornness is all over an old man's ghost stories. Did you actually believe all that crap?"

I'm paralyzed.

I can't say anything.

Whatever falls out of my mouth right now might send Sierra hunting down that road just to piss me off. Straight into places she has no business being and secrets I can't trust her to keep.

She doesn't care about protecting this family.

I've known it ever since she sold Mama's things and took away our last memories of her.

Ever since she didn't come home for Dad's funeral.

So why would I think she'd give a single damn about my efforts to protect his name and legacy?

I only shake my head, my lips mute, my mouth dry.

Declan looks at me weirdly, something ugly in his flat granite chips of eyes.

"What road?" he asks.

"It's nothing," I bite off. "Hasn't been a real road for over a century. It's just an old mountain cut, and Sierra, if you think that's the only reason I want to keep our *home*, then you were never part of this family to start with."

I don't mean to be so cruel. But I'm panicking, my palms sweaty, my heart racing, and I...

I'm hurt, too.

Just as hurt as the stricken look on Sierra's face before I turn away sharply, giving them my back.

"We're done here," I say. "Screw lunch and get out. I guess if I see y'all again, it'll be in court."

There's a huff.

A growling mutter from Declan and a rattled whisper from Sierra.

Then nothing but the door slamming shut.

I'm alone with that stupid shepherd's pie, and we're both steaming hot enough to melt through the wall.

Guess I'll be eating alone today.

* * *

I'M TIRED, I need a drink, and I really need advice from someone who understands land deals.

Here comes my next big mistake of the day.

I checked around, and we've got no pro bono lawyers in Heart's Edge right now.

Holt Silverton's the closest thing I've got.

I sit on a barstool at Brody's, nursing a can of beer and wait- ing, listening to the ruckus and the noise. I never really got to be part of the regulars who'd hang out here throwing darts and shooting the breeze.

Growing up, I was too busy already for drunken nights, keeping a ranch operational while minding Dad's declining health.

Sometimes I wonder what it would've been like.

To just get to be a kid, reckless and irresponsible and free.

I guess that's part of why I can't stay mad at Sierra.

She saw her chance to get out, to live without all this respon- sibility crushing her, so she did.

Trouble with her is, she never grew up at all.

I'm lost in my thoughts—and nearly jump out of my skin

when a tall frame slides onto the stool next to mine, body heat rushing against me like a hot gust of summer breeze.

Crap.

It's Holt.

He sits there in a pair of jeans that love his thighs a little too much, his hips slouched forward, an open flannel over one of those clingy undershirts that look damn near obscene on him.

The white ribbed cotton is so thin I can practically make out his pores under it, muscle for days, his swarthy skin changing the color of the material.

"Libby," he says. I don't even have to look to hear the smugness in his growling voice. "My eyes are up here."

Holy Toledo.

I'm sorely tempted to chuck my beer right in his leering face.

"Don't even start, you—" I jerk my gaze up to those hot amber eyes and stop mid-curse.

They're charmingly weird. I've never seen anyone with eyes his shade.

Almost like whiskey, deep and gold and liquid, but when they catch the light they glow like mellow gold.

It's easy to get caught up staring at them, wondering just how the hell any man can have eyes like his.

Easy to get tricked, too.

There's a reason they call it *fool's gold.*

"All right, all right." He props his knuckles against his temples, leaning on the bar—and speaking of fools, he's sure grinning like one. "Did you ask me out to ogle me, or is this just a garden-variety date?"

"This ain't a *date* in any way, shape, or form," I hiss, fingers clenched against my beer hard enough to make the metal can dent. "God, do you have to be a dick about everything?"

"Force of habit. Possibly genetic. I can try to find my off switch, if you want."

"Pretty sure I can find a punch with your name on it if you

don't," I mutter, and he laughs, loud and full and free enough to cut over the noise of the bar.

"You're never satisfied till you get to punch *someone*, are you?"

"So I got a little aggression to work out. So what?" I shrug stiffly.

"Mm-hmm." He subsides into a chuckle, shaking his head. "You know, back in New York there was this fad that was all the rage for a while—smash rooms. Can't remember if that's what they're officially called, but basically you pay up to spend half an hour in a room full of marble busts and a lot of other breakable things. It's just you, a baseball bat, and all the rage you'd want to vent."

I perk up. "Yeah? I could use some of that right now. I'm gonna die of a stress headache, I swear."

"I take it that means your sister's been giving you trouble?"

"Doesn't she always?" I mutter grimly and sigh. "Listen, I was hoping you could give me a little advice. Since you know what it's like to get testy with your family over inheritance crap, I mean..."

He cocks his head, musing. "I can try, but I was practically chasing Blake around trying to throw money at him while he was just trying to shove me away."

I eye him. "I'm sensing a theme of people not wanting you around much."

"Yeah?" he says mildly. "I thought I was the coveted man-whore, master playboy of Heart's Edge, women trailing help-lessly in my wake like the pied piper of pussy. Which one is it?"

I snort—but I'm trying not to grin, my mouth twitching.

"Both. They chase you, then they find out what a prick you are and shove you away. Though you've already dropped them by then, I reckon, so you don't have to care, right?"

Something odd flickers across his face.

His smile fades, and there's just...something like regret?

Whatever it is, it darkens those eyes to brass.

"Fair guess" he says a little too easily. "Can't say I haven't earned every bit of my reputation.."

I frown, folding my arms on the bar and leaning on them.

"Why are you like that, though? I mean, what happened?" I ask. "Did some pretty girl break your heart way back when or something? That kind of old story?"

He's silent, his gaze drifting away from me, skimming over the bottles lined up behind the bar. He's got this distant look that says he's somewhere else, seeing places I probably can't even imagine.

"Not way back when," he finally whispers. "Thing is, once you break a wild stallion, he's busted for good. You can set him free, but he'll never quite go back to being wild again."

I shouldn't be feeling for him.

For that odd melancholy roughness in his voice.

But for all that he acts like this dirty-minded charmer with a silver tongue and flaming filth in every word...there's a real man under there, too.

And somebody hurt that man.

Maybe not too long ago.

He's been nice enough for me to go poking more than I need to.

But before I can think of anything to say, to offer even a word of sympathy, he smiles and shakes his head, raising a hand to signal the bartender.

"So," Holt diverts. "You wanted to ask me about the ranch and the dispute with Sierra?"

I wait while he orders a beer on tap—I'm one of the few heathens who'd order a can at Brody's—before I nod.

"Yeah. We got into it pretty bad earlier. I tried to talk about payment plans and selling off some of the old farming equipment for a little liquid cash to make that work, maybe even see if I could make a dent in buying her out." I shake my head. "But it got crappy real fast. I think at this point she's gonna sue just to spite me."

He whistles softly under his breath. "We need to find a way around that."

"How?" I whisper.

Isn't that the million-dollar question?

"Libby, first I've got to ask. The only solutions I can think of would make sure that land can't ever belong to Sierra, and half of it's rightfully hers. You okay with that?"

I turn my head slowly, dragging a look over him.

"She's part of what I'm trying to protect it from." I grind my teeth. "She'd probably dump it in a short sale for half of what it's worth. Or else sell it to people who won't do anything but use it for a landfill or something. She doesn't *care* about the land, the ranch, our home. She just wants money. So I'll make sure she gets plenty of cash for her trouble, one way or another."

It's always been about money.

The taxes, the bank, my sister.

It's all anyone ever wants from me.

"Home means a lot to you, doesn't it?" Holt watches me discerningly, curiosity glinting in his eyes.

The question catches me off guard, enough that it feels like he's struck me in the chest with it, hard and hurtful.

I hesitate, breathing shallowly, then admit, "Home doesn't leave you."

My throat hurts. I stare down at the open mouth of my beer can.

"People leave. Home stays with you as long as you stay with it," I say.

"Just like your ma left," Holt tells me, his voice gentle with understanding. With warmth. "Then Sierra...then your old man."

Damnation.

How can he see through me like that?

I grit my teeth.

There's a hot anger burning through me—what else is new? —but for once it's not at him.

It's aimed at me.

For letting myself get so hung up on my feelings that I'm not focusing on the problem, and now this man's pitying me for all my regrets over things that never were and never could be.

I clear my throat, forcing a smile.

"Maybe," I say neutrally. "What's your idea for saving the land, though?"

Holt looks at me with those knowing eyes that say he knows I'm deflecting.

Bless his infuriating butt, he lets me.

He takes a slow pull off his beer. "There's always the option of having the entire place declared a protected site."

I roll my eyes. "Oh, sure. I'll just ask the state real nicely to put a rubber stamp on it."

He chuckles. "Hear me out. If we can find some reason your place has any historical significance either in American history or the history of Heart's Edge, we just might be able to get the city council to sign off on protected land status. Then we can use that to petition the higher levels of government. Even if it doesn't work...it ties shit up in the legal pipeline. It buys a lot of time."

Hmm. So maybe it's not as ridiculous as it sounds.

"That kind of petition takes forever to go through. We're talking years," he continues. "Years where the bank can't touch it while you figure out your next step. The only other way to get the land legally declared off-limits is if it's considered a toxic HAZMAT site, but then they'll force you to move. I don't think that's an option."

"You're damn right it's not. Dad never let any of those crazy Galentron bastards on our property, anyway, to mess things up like that," I say. "But tell me more about this protected land thing. What kind of historical significance are we talkin'?"

"I'd have to look into it more. It's not something I've dealt with much in the past, mostly heard stories from other developers. It hit me on the way over here." He turns away from me as the bartender slings a fresh beer down for Holt, dark and foaming and nearly spilling over the mug.

Holt spares a thankful nod, then takes a slow sip, his brows setting in a stormy line.

"Give me ideas," I tell him. "And I'll let you know if it's already hopeless."

"Anything, honey. Finding an old Native village, something that could be an archaeology dig. One of the old silver mines, even. With the silver industry here being big in the olden days, and the stuff tied into the gold rush, you never know. I bet there's a lot of old equipment hanging around that has historical value. It's just got to be important enough to preserve the site for study."

I'm instantly tense.

Because I know a place, yeah.

And it's somewhere Holt Silverton has no business going.

Somewhere *nobody* ever will.

I drum my fingers restlessly.

"Maybe," I mutter. "I can't really think of anything like that off the top of my head."

"I could have another look around. See if anything jumps out at me."

"*No!*" I don't mean to be so harsh, but my heart skips. "I mean, you promised you'd stay off my property after I let you look it over already."

"Right. That was business. This would be more like a courtesy call. Just trying to help, Libby." He leans in closer.

Oh my God.

His voice is low, coaxing, too seductive.

Exactly the kind of husky thunder that says he knows he's going to get his way if he just plays a little longer.

"Look. I don't want to bring this up again, but your best bet really is the unthinkable—sell it to me. That way, you don't have to worry about somebody else barging in and taking over. I only need a portion, Libby. Not sure how much yet, but—"

"But *nothing*," I spit, lifting my head and glaring dead at him.

Forget drooling, I'm right back to wanting to tear his head off.

I can't believe he just said that shit.

My lips tremble.

I shouldn't be this emotional.

Blame it on thinking about my messed-up family life, on stress, on everything building up inside me until I'm ready to go off like a warhead.

But if I'm honest, it's more.

It's *Holt*.

It's me starting to believe him, to trust him, but here he goddamned is, turning on his Casanova act to try to get what he wants now that he thinks my guard's down.

No. Freaking. Deal.

"You can stop right there. You're not getting a thing out of me, Holt," I growl. "And I don't want crap from you. Least of all more *help* you're only offering to line your own pockets."

He gawks at me like a fish out of water, staring like *I* hurt him somehow.

Yeah, right.

Like I'm falling for the wounded puppy act again.

It's my own fault for buying it the first time.

As if he'd just gone soft and changed overnight. I should've known.

A leopard doesn't change its spots.

A rattlesnake doesn't change its bite.

And a liar doesn't suddenly start talking truth.

The only truth here is that Holt Silverton isn't out to help anyone but himself.

I shove back from the bar, tumbling off the stool. We're gonna ignore the fact I'm so mad that I forget there's a long drop between my legs and the ground, and almost fall on my face.

I catch my stumble real quick and turn it into another excuse to push away from him, putting more space between us while I grasp at the bar to stay upright.

"Libby," he growls.

"Nope, we're done," I say as firmly and as coldly as I can.

He reaches a hand out to me. "Libby—"

"Don't you *Libby* nothing!"

God. I don't want to barf up these feelings in front of him.

I don't want to give him the satisfaction of knowing how deep he got under my skin.

So I stand there for a moment, glaring, my lips trembling, while he looks at me all helpless like he still cares.

Hell no.

I can't stand that even now he's trying to make me believe he was ever flipping genuine.

Turning my back before he tries again, before he says another word, I move.

It takes half a second to rummage around in my back pocket and slam down cash on the bar to cover my tab *and* his, because screw him and his money.

Then I turn and march right out with my head held high.

Refusing to look back even once.

That man may have the eyes of the devil, but I ain't got eyes for him.

Not anymore.

Not ever.

VI: BACK IN THE SADDLE (HOLT)

*D*o they hand out awards for epic fuckups?

If so, I ought to be a shoe-in.

After tonight, I don't think Libby ever wants to speak to me again.

Goddammit. I should've checked my tongue.

Everything came out all wrong, and I never got the chance to explain it.

All I wanted was for her to sell me enough of her land to get her taxes paid, and I'd cover the remainder.

I'd fucking hold it for her.

Hold it until she can buy it back, so in the end it effectively stays hers anyway.

Of course, I didn't get a chance to say that, and she didn't give me a chance to finish before that skittish tiger was spooked, taking off with her claws lashing my face.

I've tried calling her a few times over the last few days. Texting her. Anything.

Hasn't done a damn bit of good.

She's just stonewalled me completely.

I think if I tried driving out there, I'd get a load of buckshot up my ass for the trouble.

It's still on my mind days later when I'm looking over the fire damage repairs on a fabric shop that got blown out the back with a makeshift incendiary way back when the whole arson mess in town started last winter.

I'm not thinking about building codes or zoning or fire statutes as I do the inspection with my crew and the owner of the building, a young woman named Carmine Andrews, trailing in my wake.

I'm thinking about Libby, Libby, and oh yeah, Libby.

Damn her.

Girl's worse than an untamed bronco.

She's got her feelings all hot about the mess with her ranch and her pride—and now nothing's going to get through. Push her more, and she'll just dig her heels in.

Stubborn little monster.

I just hate that she's even more gorgeous when she's pissed.

Hate it even more how telling her that would just make her furious.

I can't help a faint smile, though, while I leaf through wiring diagrams where my boys had to put in a whole new wall and salvage what was left of the existing building wiring before patching in new shit up to code.

I'm looking at it, but I'm not really seeing it.

I'm seeing Libby when she basically told me to fuck off a cliff and die, seeing how those witchfire blue eyes just lit up.

If she's a witch, then she's sure as hell cast a spell on m—

"—erton? Mr. Silverton, are you listening?"

"Huh?" I lift my head, blinking.

The owner—it was Carol, right?

No, Carmine. She stands in front of me, looking up with a smile and a little toss of her head. She's clearly expecting an answer.

Aw, shit.

I didn't even realize she'd been talking.

I offer an apologetic smile. "Sorry, ma'am, a lot on the mind. What was that?"

She falters but then starts over. "I just said I wanted to thank you for the *personal* attention and detail you put into this job. You live up to your reputation for a man who likes working with his hands."

I flash her another quick smile and look back down at the wiring diagrams, checking one last thing. "Is that my reputation around these parts now? I'll take it. Just glad you're happy with the job, ma'am."

She doesn't answer, which gets my attention more than anything.

I look up again, and she's staring at me with her brows knit together and a bit of a pout.

Then, with a sniff, she turns and walks away, pretending to be too interested in arranging one of the display dummies just fresh out of its box of packing peanuts.

I glance over at my crew foreman, Alaska Charter.

"What'd I do now?" I mutter from the corner of my mouth.

"It's what you didn't do." He snorts, a chuckle that makes his burly chest shake. He's a big man, the kind of cement slab of a human you want to have on your crew. Leaning toward me, he mock-whispers in my ear. "Girl was trying to hook up with your clueless ass, boss."

"Oh."

Oh, shit.

I take a second look—really *looking* at her this time.

She's tall, a little over average height, shapely with thick, lush hips. Today she's dressed to accent all her best assets. I can't help but wonder if she's always got her blouse unbuttoned enough to see the scalloped lace edges of her bra.

Or if that's my invitation, and I missed it.

I hadn't even noticed.

Think I've missed a lot of things, honestly, like the glossy shine of her lips or the deliberate toss of her hair. I replay the highlights reel of the walk-through and only then do I realize the number of times this woman must've looked up at me through her lashes, waiting for me to notice and live up to my *other* reputation.

It just hadn't sunk in.

Now, there she is, ripe for the plucking.

Here I am, cataloging details instead of salivating to take her home.

"*Oh*," I repeat, and Alaska snickers.

I smack his arm and give him a dirty look.

"Stop that. She'll realize we're talking about her, and you're going to hurt her feelings."

"Oh, so you're caring about their feelings now and not their cup size?" He smirks, giving me a once-over like he's never seen me before. "I thought you'd be after her number in a heartbeat. Or maybe these small-town pickings aren't good enough after you left your supermodel harem behind in the city?"

I roll my eyes and thwack his arm again.

"You know I didn't have any sort of harem," I mutter. "And you know damn well my name's like mud here."

"Only because you broke a few too many hearts a long time ago, from what I hear." He grins wickedly. "No woman hates you quite the same as a woman who used to love you."

"Then you haven't seen the way Miss Liberty Potter hates me," I snap—then shut my mouth firmly when Alaska raises a thick, bushy eyebrow.

"Liberty Potter, you say?" His grin peeks past his dense mountain man beard.

Ah, fuck.

I think I just gave myself away.

Grunting, I turn away from the rather annoyed-looking Carmine and bump Alaska's thick arm again. "C'mon. We've still got four more rooms to inspect."

But he's not about to drop it.

He's the type that seems big, dumb, and loyal, but underneath it he's sharp as a tack and far too shrewd.

"So that's what happened," he says, stroking his beard with a thoughtful rumble as he falls into step with me. "You went and got yourself collared by a girl who can't stand you, and now *you* can't stand to look at anyone else."

"Cut the shit," I growl. "There's no point."

Not when Libby won't trust me in this lifetime and maybe several more.

Not when my name's clearly so vile she has every reason to believe I'm just trying to swindle her, jumping to conclusions without giving me any hint of a chance.

It's almost like she knew me back in New York.

Back when I was *that* guy.

A man I'm not proud of.

A man who had to lose everything he had to learn that, deep down, he had nothing worth keeping to start with.

* * *

Two Years Ago

WHEN CALYPSO TOLD me to meet her at Le Bernardin, I thought we were just having a celebratory dinner.

I'm about to close on a big development deal that'll value close to eight figures for the contract, with seven figures in profits.

A whole fuck-wad of zeroes that'll look mighty pretty in my bank account.

Just as pretty as the ring I bought will look on her finger.

It's the perfect setup.

Meeting my girl at one of the most exclusive, upscale restaurants in NYC, and it was her idea, so she has no clue I'm about to propose.

I'm finally ready.

Ready to settle down and let go of my hundred-woman ways.

Ready to stop playing games and find something stable.

Ready to make a life.

A real life with permanence.

It's all going according to plan, too.

Until I check in for our reservation and I'm escorted to the table.

Calypso's already waiting.

Settled into a booth and snuggled in close...

...next to another man.

And not just any other man.

Barry Hensworth.

If there was a Who's Who of New York Construction, Barry would be on the first page, and every other page. His family's been a bastion of New York real estate for nearly a century—and just like mob families, they're all about power, control, and who sets the rules.

They like the cushy contracts going to their guys.

You've got to play smart, play fast, to get around them and find your own niche. Make your own way.

I thought I'd played smart and fast.

Thought I'd found investors who'd take a chance on a hungry small-town boy gunning to upset the Hensworth iron fist in this city.

But the fact that my girl—my fucking girl—is hanging on Barry's arm?

It tells me without even saying a word that I didn't play fast or smart enough.

There are three place settings. Two in front of them, one in front of the empty side of the booth.

They want to play this nice. Congenial. Mafia-style.

Fine.

I'll play along.

At least give them the satisfaction of letting me down easy.

So I plaster on my most charming, easygoing smile and offer my hand, wishing I had my gun.

"Barry," I say, as if we're friends and not bitter rivals. As if we could even be called rivals, when he's got enough of a stranglehold to crush me at any moment. "Calypso didn't tell me you were coming to dinner."

Barry looks up.

He smiles his greasy goddamn smile like he isn't about to stab me in the back.

Like my girlfriend isn't on his arm and watching me with a smirk that says she knew this was coming.

She maybe even knew when she was in my bed last week.

"Holt," Barry says ever so warmly, taking my hand in a firm shake before gesturing to the empty chair. "Have a seat. They've already served the wine. It's a 1990 Chateau Margaux. I've heard it's quite pleasing to the palate."

Please, sit, he tells me.

Like this is his fucking rodeo.

Making sure I know who's in control here, rubbing his dick in my face.

Starting with a $1200 bottle of wine.

But I sit and play nice.

Though I'm already eager to throw that glimmering thin-stemmed glass of wine right in Barry's jowly, red, smug-fuck face.

"How lovely," I say, keeping up the illusion, even though everything in my body is *sinking* like a stone, because I know.

I know I'm about to lose everything.

And it leaves my gut as heavy as the rock in my pocket, fixed to a ring that costs more than most people's mortgages.

"So," I continue, "to what do I owe the pleasure?"

"Glad you asked..."

Barry picks up his wine glass by its delicate stem, swirling it before taking a deep, obnoxious whiff, his nostrils flaring.

I can't miss his possessive, meaty arm around Calypso's shoulders or the way she leans into it.

Like she's trying to get me riled.

Like she expected me to be angry and throw a storming tantrum, walking in to see her on another man's arm when she'd been in my bed just a few nights ago.

Fuck it.

I won't give either of them the satisfaction.

I'll just play the fool, and then I'll walk out forever.

"This isn't an easy conversation. I don't like to pussyfoot around things," Barry says.

"So don't." I'm trying to stay calm, but I can't help how clipped it comes out. "There's only one reason you're here, Barry, so let's get on with it. Then everyone can enjoy their dinner with the horseshit out of the way."

"I'm relieved you won't be difficult about this. You're a smart man, Holt. You truly are." Barry smirks. "Just not quite smart enough, I'm afraid. There could be a place for you at Hensworth Holdings, you know."

"I wouldn't need a place if my contract with the city was intact." I lean back in my chair, folding my arms over my chest. "But it's not anymore, is it?"

"No. Your investors, you see—"

"What about them?"

"Well, they decided to go with someone more battle-tested." He curls his lip, almost self-deprecating, as if it's just such a shame, not really his fault. "You know how these money people are. They like to bet on a sure winner, not take risks on a shiny new toy. And an unknown newcomer, well, that's a sizable risk."

"Mm-hmm." Somehow, I'm grinning, but it feels more like baring my teeth. "And it has nothing to do with the fact that half my investors are your lifelong golf pals? No handshakes at the country club, that sort of thing."

He lifts both brows mildly. Ever so shocked at the insinuation, of course.

Of course.

"With Hensworth Holdings' long-standing reputation in the community and our presence here, it's inevitable we'd know people," he says with a scoffing laugh. "You truly can't fault people for having friends, Holt."

My gaze darts between him and Calypso. She's pouty, lithe, and sensual in a silk sheath dress in pure white, clinging to her translucently and highlighting her long, leggy, perfect-ten body.

"And are you two friends, Barry?" I linger on her. "Is Barry your new friend, Calypso? Perhaps because her father's one of my investors, and you just happened to drop by the house for a visit?"

I guess that's the reaction she wants.

She finally smirks, rubbing her cheek on Barry's shoulder, nasty and catlike.

I take a little satisfaction in the fact that although Barry's wool suit probably has a higher thread count than my Egyptian cotton sheets, her foundation is currently ruining it, leaving colored, chalky smears on his expensive fabric.

"Don't be like that, Holt," she says. "You know how it goes."

Do I?

Do I really know?

Because this is a colossal amount of fuckery above my pay grade.

All I know for sure is I *fucked* her last week, and she screamed my name and held on like she loved me.

When she knew this was coming.

When she did nothing to warn me.

When she decided to stab at my soul just for fun.

In a twisted way, I get it, even if I'll never get the cruelty.

She's a pretty girl from a rich family.

She's just covering her own ass—barely, that dress is about to let it all hang out—and so she followed the money.

Leaving me in the dust.

The way they're both looking at me is textbook definition

smug. Conniving. Self-satisfied.

Like they're already done with this game, and I'm the only dummy who didn't know what was at play.

The bile rises in my throat, turning a sip of overpriced wine into poison.

This isn't my world.

I just wish I hadn't ruined myself to figure it out.

Not just my business, but my goddamn fool heart.

I thought I'd been in love with her, and maybe I had, but she never loved me.

Real love doesn't do this shit.

Maybe I don't know what real love is, not yet, but I know it can't be this.

I don't have to torture myself, staying here to let them watch me try to cling to my pride, while I crumble apart inside. That ends with me in prison after clubbing Barry over the head with his expensive wine bottle.

So I stand, offering Barry my hand.

"I won't be staying for dinner," I growl. "But thank you for being so kind as to inform me in person."

Like hell I'm letting him pay for my meal after he just took my livelihood away from me with a few casual words.

Barry looks at my hand as if it's somehow confusing, this gesture he can't process, before he takes it and shakes it again, tentatively.

"Don't take it personally," he says. "This is just how this industry works, especially in a city as big as this. You'll learn that with age and experience. Play your cards right, and someday you'll be on the right side of the table."

"No." I don't let go of his hand. Maybe I clasp it a little too tight, drilling my gaze into his until he flinches. "Matter of fact, I'd rather work with a little more integrity."

Calypso frowns and gives off a little sniff. "You, Holt? Integrity? As if you didn't ratfuck your way into every contract you've ever had."

That hits me like a knife to the gut.

Deeper than anything I've known.

Purely because she's right.

And I'm dizzy because suddenly, I don't want her to be.

I let go of Barry's hand, and for a moment I almost spill everything, turn into the raging bull Barry clearly wants me to be.

But looking into Calypso's perfectly made-up face, her gorgeous eyes, her soulless lips that tasted like candy days ago...

Fuck no.

I won't ever give her or anybody like her my soul.

I'm not letting go of my stubborn-ass pride.

Chin held high, I simply offer them both a sardonic smile.

Then turn and walk out, shoulders stiff.

I'll start over. I always do.

Next time, I'll build an honest empire no one can take away from me.

Present

I'VE TRIED like hell to forget that day.

Some days, the memory hits me harder than others, remembering everything I've lost.

Plus the things I never really had. The life I'd built was thrown together on a shitty foundation of grift and seduction and dirty backdoor deals.

The love I'd thought I'd won was with someone who breathed high society.

A place I never belonged.

I'm not sure where I belong, honestly.

Heart's Edge is a good place to start over.

At least here, I can make my own rules, and this time build those rules on trust.

Not just on what benefits me.

Fuck. Will Libby ever trust me at all?

There's nothing I can do...is there?

Then again, *what if?*

What if I found just what she needs to have her land declared a protected site that no one could intrude on?

There's got to be something.

I have to keep looking, but hell.

Maybe I won't tell her.

Not until I've got something concrete. I can't stand to get her hopes up, then dash them again—and if I do that, if I string her along when I've got nothing solid, then I'll give her every reason to never give me another chance.

To never trust me again.

I'll do my digging on my lonesome.

Scour through those survey maps, and if I have to, I'll take an excursion.

I'll find out what's down that old road.

She never has to know unless I find something worth knowing.

It's not the best logic, I know.

It's a little underhanded, even, trespassing on her place by going behind her back.

But she sure as hell won't let me do it to her face. Not now.

I just want to save us both.

Even if she hates me for it for the rest of our natural lives, it'll be okay if she gets to keep that ranch.

As long as *she's* okay.

"Boss?" Alaska thumps my shoulder lightly. "You zoned out again."

I shake myself from my thoughts as the world clears around me.

Shit. I'm still in the middle of the fabric shop, lost in my own head.

"Right," I say, forcing myself back on track. "Let's just finish this up, and then I'll buy you a beer."

* * *

THE SURVEY MAPS don't tell me much after poring over them all night.

Partly because they're so old they don't have much info that's relevant now.

Partly because they don't *match*.

They show different geographies, different land masses, which is pretty fucked.

Even with the same place names and distance markers, it doesn't add up. They're barely a decade or two apart, so it's not like some natural disaster erased the land.

Someone did shoddy work.

And I won't know who until I can see it with my own damn eyes.

Which is how I find myself parking my Benz about a mile away from the edge of Libby's property.

I need a better car, but right now, I'm glad for the quiet purr of the engine. It keeps from giving me away as I kill the headlights and the motor to settle into a hidden place in the scrub brush.

I'll be hoofing it from here.

My car isn't dressed for the wilds, but I am.

Back in USAF BMT training, they'd wake us up at two in the morning and send us jogging through harsh terrain, up and down gravelly slopes in full tactical gear.

I feel like I'm doing that all over again, even though I'm in sturdy jeans and hiking boots with solid soles. I've got gloves to protect my hands from thorny brush and a backpack with a flashlight, compass, emergency rations, plus several bottles of water banging against my back.

119

A man can leave the military, but it never leaves him.

I don't even need the flashlight as I set off at a steady run.

Right along the edge where tumbled rocks rise up into the mountain bluffs, the Milky Way and the moon lighting my way plenty.

In NYC, I'd forgotten how gorgeous a sky can look without all the city lights blocking it out.

Being out here, it's like standing in the middle of the universe.

I let that calm my thoughts as I hit that patch of brush marking the start of the mountain cut, picking my way through to find the trail.

It's slower going here.

Less flat terrain and more overgrowth so choked it's almost like someone—probably Libby, maybe even Mark—deliberately let it all go so the path would be harder to pass.

One way to discourage people from skulking around, I guess.

I frown, pausing for a sip of water.

There's something from the survey maps sticking with me.

Something about the flat elevation at the center of this cluster of mountains and bluffs, and this path leading right in.

All the old tapped-out mining veins marked on the maps around it, but nothing in that one clear spot?

Seems like the perfect place for mining.

There are tons of stories about little towns that started up and then petered out as their ore veins did. A lot of them lost to history with no one remembering their names or much else, nothing left behind but shanty houses crumbling to dirt, given back to the land.

Heart's Edge used to be one of those towns, but its location plus the deeper veins of silver out where the Paradise Hotel used to be made sure it stuck around longer than most.

Common sense tells me there's nothing amazing down this road.

But hope and optimism tell me I might just find something

worthwhile.

Especially when, after jogging forever, I almost trip over something unexpected.

A wagon.

The remnants of one.

It's old, the kind with the big old spoke wheels and timber framing that says it used to have a cover stretched over it, Oregon Trail style, though I doubt the owners died of dysentery.

The actual wagon bed's nearly rotted through, the whole thing a tilted and tumbled mess on the side of the road. The only things really intact are a few metal pegs and banding here and there.

I crouch down next to the wreck and pull out my flashlight, checking it over.

There's paint clinging to the wood, something that might've been letters once, but I can't make out a word. Old ragged bits of leather, too, though that's been chewed to hell and back.

I can imagine the cougars out here had a fine time using it for a scratching post.

I lift my head, squinting farther up the road.

No reason for a wagon to be going down there unless there's somewhere to go *to*.

No reason for a road that leads nowhere.

With a fresh charge in my step, I haul myself up and move.

Moon's starting to set. I must've gone some six, seven miles by now. I was faster in my military days, but I was also jogging on open terrain.

From the maps, this whole cut goes about twenty or thirty miles into the mountains.

Sunrise, I tell myself.

I'll go till sunrise, and then I'll accept defeat, turn back, and get the hell off Libby's property before she kills me.

I pass a few more things—more broken-down wagons, some rusty mining tools, even the remains of a fence, all things that get my heart racing and my legs pumping faster.

Finally, I stumble through a knot of trees grown over the road and—

And into an entire goddamn town.

What the hell?

I'd been expecting to find a few small shacks or the kind of old-timey gold-panning rigs they'd set up across streams to catch flakes and nuggets in the runoff from the springs that riddle this area.

This is a fuckton more than that.

There must be more than a dozen buildings—all of them constructed to last, and they're still standing so someone did it right. Proper framing and varnished boards, though the varnishing's worn off over time and everything's dirty as sin.

I glance around, taking it all in.

Church, houses, something that looks like it used to be a bank.

I think I even see an old police station, and inside some rusted iron bars.

This isn't some ramshackle settlement, but a proper town.

The crazy part is it's not on any damn maps I've seen.

How's an entire ghost town just sitting here, and nobody knows about it?

Back when I was a kid in the elementary school, they'd always tell us these old Wild West stories to keep us entertained.

Some crazy shit about bandits roaming the hills, full of half-truths. A name comes back to me, my seventh grade history teacher writing it on the board.

Ursa.

No one ever said where Ursa was.

Never saw it on a map.

This seems like it could be a good candidate, right in the middle of these tapped-out mining spots.

It's a perfect road through the cut for some outlaw screamers to come ripping out, howling like banshees and riding hard for Heart's Edge to raise hell.

Makes sense, too.

With the mountains and the road running through, there are only two narrow ways in and out, it's an easy place to defend.

Any white hat sheriff coming up here to take those boys out, they'd mow down that cop and every last one of his boys two at a time as they squeezed through the cut.

The scene plays through my head so vividly I can see it like I'm standing under the dusty sun watching it happen, six-shooters everywhere and bandits milling around.

Let's not get ahead of ourselves, I tell myself. *But hell, this might be it.*

If I can find anything that actually proves this town is Ursa and the home of those legendary gunslingers...

We've got this cat in the bag.

We could save Libby's ranch.

I flick out my flashlight again, making my way slowly through the streets.

Best place to start looking, I think, would be that big building right in the middle, with a hitching post—a real honest-to-God hitching post—out front and swinging double doors that are still on their hinges.

The construction man in me can't help but admire it.

Whoever put this place together did a beast of a job.

It's got to be well over a hundred years old.

The big building looks like a saloon.

If it's like any Wild West town I've ever heard of, it'd be the busiest place—and the most likely to leave behind some evidence.

I carefully push the swinging doors open.

I don't want to disturb anything, accidentally break or muck up anything that might contribute to this being considered a historical site.

My flashlight sweeps over rows of dusty, empty bottles with their labels long worn off.

They're lined up on shelves behind a bar that's mostly just a bunch of flat planks bolted to a long table, but it confirms my guess. It's a saloon.

Round ramshackle tables and chairs are scattered everywhere.

There's an upper level with stairs leading up to a railing. I can almost see pretty painted ladies leaning over with their bodices half-buttoned, flashing hankies and whistling boys upstairs.

As I sweep that flashlight over the bar again, I get the living shit scared right out of me.

There's someone there.

Sitting at the bar.

"Fuck!" I gasp, stumbling back with my heart zinging around my chest like it's on a zipline, fingers clenched around the flashlight.

For a second, my head fills up with flashes of haunted saloons and old cowboys stalking through the room.

A chill sweeps down my spine.

But I take a wary step closer, holding the flashlight steady.

Whoever it is, they're not moving.

My stomach fucking sinks.

I've found some evidence, all right.

Just not the kind I'm looking for.

Because I think this might be evidence of a fucking murder, and it's got nothing to do with Wild West bandits at all.

There's a skeleton slouched in one of the saloon chairs with its head propped up against the wall, held together by raggedy bits of skin and clothing gone dusty and frayed. Looks like he's been here a while, undisturbed by predators or people...but not *that* long.

There's still hair clinging to the corpse's leathery scalp.

I'm no expert on old-timey clothes, but I'm pretty sure that mottled suit holding him together is fairly modern, no more than twenty or thirty years old.

And Rolex damn sure didn't make 'em like the watch hanging

on his wrist a hundred years ago.

That watch is one of the things that's extra weird about this.

I flick the flashlight over the scene, barely even daring to breathe.

The old blood stains on his chest, his shirt are obvious—shot right in the heart.

Spent shell casing on the floor, looks like from a shotgun.

But he's still got his watch.

His very expensive-looking watch.

Gold cufflinks, too.

Also, a briefcase, dropped on the floor, resting against the leg of the tall chair like it fell from his hand when he died and went limp.

So this wasn't some kind of back country mugging gone wrong.

Somebody killed him, left his valuables, and ran.

There's got to be a story here, but I'm not sure it's one I should be privy to.

I'm not sure I should be here at all.

For now, I'm just glad I have gloves on, and I want to get the fuck out of here at lightning speed.

Still, I hesitate, then lean over and snatch the briefcase without getting any closer to the corpse than I have to.

That chill hits me again as my hand brushes too close to his skeletal fingers.

Then I back up, one step at a time, careful not to bump into anything else, before I turn and clatter down the steps of the saloon's front walk.

I take off at a jog for the trail with that briefcase dangling from my hand.

It's past time to go.

Fuck, if this is why Libby's been trying to keep me away from here, I've got a few questions.

And I'm gonna be asking, whether or not she owes me any answers.

VII: ALL OPPOSED, SAY "NEIGH"
(LIBBY)

One thing about running a ranch is that you almost never get a full night's sleep.

I'm used to being up at dawn, but sometimes I get woken up. Coyotes get past the fences and start messing with my sheep, or something spooks the horses, or I get a buzzard or an owl trapped in the rafters, just shrieking and flapping around everywhere.

This time, it's the damn coyotes again.

Sniffing around the barn, for once, but all it took was a single shot in the air to send them scampering off with their tails between their legs.

I've had enough of cowards for a lifetime.

But I'm not thinking about that right now.

Even if I'm tired as hell out here in my pajama shirt and ripped up jeans; even if it's after midnight...

I can't help but stop and stare at the stars, resting in the saddle with Frost's solid bulk warm and comforting beneath me, anchoring me to Earth.

It shouldn't hurt like it still does.

Tilting my head up to the sky, I look for the North Star first, just like Dad always taught me.

Find true north to orient yourself, and from there, everything else just sorts itself out.

From the North Star to the Big Dipper and the Little Dipper, Ursa Major and Ursa Minor. Aquila. Cygnus. Sagittarius.

I know them.

He engraved them on my heart and made them so important to me because they were important to *him*.

It was hard after Mama died and Sierra ran away.

Somehow, in a short space of time, we went from a family of four to just two lonely people sitting out here with no freaking clue how to make it work.

Falling apart.

Until one night, Dad took me outside, and we sat on the back porch and charted the night sky together.

It was something we'd done ever since I was a little girl, but that night was special.

It helped put our world back in place and reminded us we were more than our sadness.

That we weren't just two lonely people banging around inside a ranch house that was too big for us.

That out there were millions, billions, countless stars shining down.

And as long as we could reach up and spread our fingers to sift through the sky and name those lights, we weren't lonely.

We were gonna be okay.

Well, I'm not okay now.

I'm *so* not okay, gazing up at the sky and pressing my lips together to keep from crying. I clutch my Aries pendant like it can hold me together when I'm almost crushing the fragile silver threads.

No, I'm not gonna break. Not gonna lose my mind.

But I feel damn close right now, searching the sky for Aries even though it won't be visible until late fall.

I just want to see it so I won't be alone.

So I'll feel like Dad's with me, across space and time.

127

My eyes are still burning when something drifts into my vision. I squint harder.

Yep. There's a shape out there by the entrance to Nowhere Lane.

I sure as hell ain't imagining that dark silhouette moving through the brush like they're trying to be cute and not get spotted.

My pulse picks up.

I haven't spent half my life tracking cougars and vultures and God only knows what else for nothing. I can spot a grown-ass man under a bright, starry night sky.

My teeth pinch together.

Whoever he is, he's about to get himself a butt full of buckshot.

It's got to be Declan or Reid Cherish, I think, poking around where they don't belong. Acting like this land is already theirs.

Might even be prowlers with worse intentions.

Word gets around in this little town.

Some opportunists might be scoping the place out, looking to see if they want to buy once the bank's put it up for grabs, but knowing I'd run them off in broad daylight.

With my teeth bared, I tap Frost's side.

The Vanner perks his head up, shaking his mane like he's gearing up for battle.

That's my boy.

Even though I woke him up from a dead sleep to do the rounds, he's spry as he arcs forward in long, stretching leaps, his neck out. I pull my shotgun from the saddle holster, finger light on the trigger.

Frost picks up speed, thundering to a gallop, leaping the fence agilely and coming down hard on the other side, smart and quick enough to not even come near plowing into the ditch.

We go careening up the narrow strip between the fence and the ditch, surging toward that fleeing silhouette.

I swear, I'll run Mister Intruder right down.

"Stop right there!" I shout. "I can see you, and you ain't gonna scurry faster than a horse can run, you rat!"

The shadow stops.

Turns.

And devil-gold eyes shine right at me.

"You've called me a lot of things, but 'rat?' That's a new one, honey," a familiar, rumbling voice throws back.

It can't be!

Oh, but it is.

I pull back hard on Frost's reins, pulling him up short, almost trampling the man looking at me flatly with his arms crossed and a dusty briefcase dangling from his gloved hands.

Holt flipping Silverton.

And he's been down Nowhere Lane.

Crap!

* * *

I DON'T KNOW how I got him back to the house without having a panic attack.

Or killing him in cold blood.

I'd been ready to tear his stupid head off, erupting off Frost's back, demanding to know what right he has, what the *hell* he thought he was doing.

He's fucking lucky I didn't shoot him—that part scares me almost as much as knowing he's been down there.

That I'd almost shot him for real and hurt him bad.

It shouldn't bother me when a handsome intruder's still an intruder just the same. Of course it does, though.

One more reason on my long list of nearly a thousand to hate Holt Silverton.

I despise him for being the snake he is, angling to get in my good graces just for another attempt to buy me out.

For everything he's done to remind me he's nothing but a

conniving asshole who's just a little nicer about wanting my land than the rest of 'em.

For making me start to trust him...and then betraying it.

Freaking *twice* now, with him sneaking onto my property and going exactly where I never wanted him to.

I should be *glad* to shoot his face off.

Not scared out of my wits that I could've done him harm.

But I can't deal with these conflicting feelings, anyway.

Not when he's standing across from me on the other side of my kitchen table, a scratched-up, annoyingly sexy-rugged mess.

Leaves in his hair and sweat and grime on his tanned, toned neck. A familiar briefcase resting on the table between us like the Ark of the Covenant, waiting to melt our faces off if we dare open it.

I sure as hell haven't ever worked up the lady-balls to touch it.

I wasn't gonna leave my prints on that thing for the police to find.

I left well enough alone.

But if Holt's got the briefcase...that means Holt's seen the body.

Seeing that briefcase in his hand got me quiet when I'd been ready to slap his face right off his skull.

He just stood there looking up at me and babbling all kinds of excited crap I couldn't make heads or tails of.

Something about bandits, and historical sites, and Ursa—like the constellation?

I'm officially lost.

I just know I couldn't be standing out there with him waving that briefcase around where anyone could see. Maybe a dumb thing to be worried about at two in the morning, but when Holt Silverton comes stumbling out of the bushes in the middle of the night, seems like any dumb thing can and will happen.

Best not to take my chances.

Folding my arms over my chest, I cast a withering glare at him.

"You've got one minute to explain," I bite off. "Did I not tell you to back the hell off? Did I not tell you to stay off my land? You're lucky I didn't shoot you on the spot for trespassing. I'm still half tempted, Holt."

He raises both hands. "Libby, hold up. I was trying to help."

I narrow my eyes. "Explain to me how trespassing and," I pause, gesturing toward the briefcase, "whatever *that* is could possibly be helping."

"Still figuring that part out." He's breathless, his eyes too intense, glittering, deep and liquid as the finest whiskey, that color so ridiculously compelling it's too easy to want to believe anything he says—especially in his rumbling, earnest voice. "There's a whole ghost town at the end of that trail. You never knew about it?"

"Dad said it was dangerous to go down there, so I never went," I lie.

Oh, I know.

I know all about the damn ghost town.

And I know about the skeleton that was holding that briefcase, too.

But I'm waiting to see what Holt says before I show my hand. I can't let him spread that crap around. Not to Sheriff Langley or the rest of Heart's Edge.

I can't have him bringing people here who might figure things out.

"About the only thing dangerous down there is tetanus from all the rusty nails lying around," he says dryly. "There's a dead guy, but whoever shot him is long gone."

I arch a brow. "A dead guy. So, what, you just took his briefcase? And why are you so happy about it?"

"It's not the dead guy I'm happy about!" Holt fires back. "It's the ghost town, lady. You know the stories, right? From elementary school?"

I roll my eyes. "Old shoot 'em up crap like Louis L'Amour, yeah. I know. You don't actually believe in it, do you?"

"Look, it's silly, but all those wild outlaw stories are based on real legends. Some of those guys were real, historically documented and everything." Holt leans in urgently, planting his hands on the table next to the briefcase and watching me with his eyes alight. "What if that place is the lost town of Ursa where they say all these bandits set up camp?"

"So what if it is?" I shrug, glaring, hating wherever he's trying to lead me.

"Ursa might be your ace in the hole, Libby. A place with just enough historical significance to protect your ranch and get this place out of the bank's hands for good."

Oh, crap.

That's when I know I'm absolutely screwed.

Holt Silverton might actually be onto something.

My legs go out from under me. I drop down into one of the kitchen chairs hard enough to make it slide back with a loud scrape against the wood floor.

Then I just bury my face in my hands.

Jesus.

Salvation right there at the end of Nowhere Lane. It was there all along, and I can't have it.

Crap crap crap crap crap crap *crap.*

There ain't even enough craps in the world for the irony.

I don't know if I want to cry or start laughing hysterically.

Of course, the answer has to be right there, but if I let anyone into that town, if I let anyone down Nowhere Lane...

They're gonna find out my father murdered a man in cold blood.

They'll confirm something I've avoided staring directly in the face ever since Dad died.

I've always made excuses for him. Or excuses for myself, maybe, because I didn't want to believe it.

I always thought there had to be a good reason for that body, the briefcase, the words on Dad's deathbed. And that the man I loved, relied on, watched die with my heart breaking was still a good man. Not a liar hiding behind a smile just like everybody else.

I'm still just as trapped, but it's starting to feel like I'm cornered.

One way or another, people are gonna find that body as surely as Holt did tonight.

"Libby?" Holt asks. "What's wrong?"

"Nothing." I scrub my hands against my face, then against my tight, aching throat. "Not one word. Don't you say *one word* to anybody about that ghost town, Holt Silverton."

He sinks down in the chair opposite me.

That briefcase is still propped up between us, cursed as ever, but he's watching me with his brows knit together.

"Why?" he asks—then saves me the trouble of lying again by taking a wild guess. "Oh, shit. There's a lot of antique stuff out there, I'd bet. Looters would have a field day if they knew it was there."

"Yeah." I run a hand through my hair. I feel so tired all of a sudden, so defeated, but I can't give up. "Look, this might help, I gotta look some things up, but...it still doesn't explain what in the Sam Hill you were doing out there, Holt. You fucking snuck behind my back."

Holt ducks his head. There's that scorned little boy act, though the dimming in his eyes doesn't seem like it.

So maybe the devil can actually feel shame.

"I know," he says. "And I'm sorry as hell, Libby. I wanted to help, but I didn't want to get your hopes up with false promises. Not till I knew there was something out there. So I thought I'd scope it out, and if I didn't find anything, you didn't have to be let down. But if I did—"

"That's still sneaky, you ass," I snarl, holding up a finger.

I'm looking right at him to avoid the briefcase.

But it's just as dangerous when he looks so sincere. Every

time those golden-brown eyes lock with mine, it's this hot bolt right through me.

It knocks the angst and misery out of me and makes my toes curl and my palms sweat hot.

I jerk my gaze away, staring out the window, where it's gone so dark the sky's just a deep blanket of velvety blue-black.

"Even if your heart was in the right place...I still don't like it."

"I know," he growls—softer this time, his voice as dark as the night sky.

I try so hard to ignore the shivers when that electric feeling I get around him is what makes me ignore the common sense that says not to trust him any farther than I can throw him.

He rakes a hand through his dark hair. "I get it if you hate me, honey. It's okay. I just hope you can use this to do something good."

I let out a long, defeated sigh.

There's no ignoring the elephant in the room.

I can't let Holt go charging off doing something insane that will jeopardize everything I've worked so hard to protect.

Sighing, I gesture at the briefcase.

"That town's probably a crime scene." I have to phrase everything carefully. "That briefcase isn't a hundred and fifty years old, Holt. It's maybe twenty, thirty years old at the most. So what if the cops just declare my land a crime scene and shove me off it? Hell, what if the FBI gets involved?"

"That won't happen. We don't know what went on with the body or who was involved. They might just clean it up and file it shut. Cold case. But there's one way we can try to guess." His eyes glint. "We can see what's inside this thing."

"Holt, don't—"

Too late.

He reaches for the table and pops the case open, the snaps unlatching as easily as if they were brand new, the two halves of the smooth brown leather casing coming loose along the seams and the top side lifting a little.

My heart pounds.

I'm terrified of what's inside.

Especially when Holt lifts the lid with his gloved fingers, peering in, before the weirdest expression crosses his face.

"Libby?"

My mouth goes dry. I lick my lips.

I can't speak, but after a second I manage to croak, "Y-yeah?"

"Looks like a note."

He flips the case open fully, turning it sideways so he can lay it out flat with that piece of paper inside, curled with two creases like it'd been folded inside an envelope.

"It's got your dad's name on it," Holt says.

There it is. The whole world's just been yanked out from under me.

There's no floor anymore, no ground.

Just total free fall, and I'm plummeting when I haven't even moved off the chair.

I stare at the note.

It's handwritten, elegant and almost old-fashioned, but there's no mistaking that opening line even if my vision kind of willfully blurs on the rest.

To the esteemed Dr. Potter.

"I...I don't understand," I whisper. "Why would a dead man have a note for my father?"

"Let's see what it says." Holt watches me with those bourbon eyes dark with concern.

He plucks it out gingerly, handling it like fragile evidence and unfolding it with his thumb, smoothing it out.

Yeah.

Evidence my dad is guilty of murder.

Slowly, Holt reads it out loud.

"*To the esteemed Dr. Potter,*" he reads. "*You'll be pleased to know that the information is all here. I've spoken to the appraisers and can confirm total authenticity. This is indeed a rare find, and I'd be happy to work with you to find a buyer; this could well be the auction of the century! Please let me know how you'd like to proceed. We could finalize the deal tonight. I'd be delighted to pay you a deposit in advance of bidding. I'll be waiting to speak with you in the usual place. Yours truly and with utmost regards, Gerald Bostrom.* He's signed it August 14th, 1992." Holt stops, then, lowering the time-yellowed, thin paper. "Who the hell's Gerald Bostrom?"

"No clue," I say numbly, clapping a hand over my mouth.

I'm gonna be sick, and I can barely hold it in.

From the sound of that letter, Gerald Bostrom must be the dead guy.

That shotgun shell probably came from my dad's favorite rifle, hung over the freaking sofa on the wall rack even now.

Dad killed a man over money.

Money.

My eyes prickle.

No. I can't believe it. I won't believe it.

He wasn't that kind of man.

There has to be something more to this story.

I lift my head, setting my jaw. I won't cry in front of Holt. I swear to God, I *won't*.

Instead, I glare at the briefcase.

The *empty* briefcase.

"The letter says the information's all here," I say. "But there's nothing else. You didn't open it and take any other documents out?"

Holt shakes his head sharply. "Nope. So if there was something else in there, it came out before we ever had a chance to see it." He frowns, setting the letter down and stroking his thumb and forefinger over the neatly trimmed line of his beard, tracing down to the firm peak of his chin again and again. "I'm guessing Gerald Bostrom's our skeleton man."

Way to go, Sherlock.

"I don't know," I say. "But I—look, I can't deal with this right now. I've got to think about the ranch, and...and..."

And I'm about to break down.

I can't breathe. My chest is heaving, but there's no air coming in and I don't know what's happening, only that it *hurts*.

I suck in several wheezy breaths.

I barely hear Holt's panicked, "Libby?"

Pressing a hand to my chest, I curl forward.

Suddenly there's warmth wrapped around me—no, *heat*.

Heat that can only come from a large, firm body.

Heat that can only come from two enormous arms folding around me, gathering me close while Holt kneels next to my chair.

He holds me up effortlessly.

"Here," he murmurs, and his breath and voice are warm against my hair, his hands stroking over my back like he can tame my lungs. "Breathe with me and count. Inhale—one, two, three. Exhale—one, two, three."

He says it again, and I try to convince my rebelling, stupid body to listen.

Inhale. Exhale. Hold.

Holt...

My throat's so tight it's a miracle I can even get a breath out. But the more I do it while his dense, rhythmic voice rumbles in my ear and his warm body keeps me safely cocooned, the easier it gets.

"You'll be okay, woman. Won't let you be anything else," he says softly.

I close my eyes. My breathing calms. I catch myself leaning into him, melting, wanting to *hide* in Holt Silverton where I can pretend my problems don't exist.

"Holt..."

"Easy. We'll figure out a way to save your ranch. One way or another, I swear."

I lift my head to look at him.

That's a mistake.

Because when I do, it makes me realize how close he is.

How handsome, how caring, how perfect this devil can be.

His nose almost touches mine. I feel the warmth of every exhale from his lips, teasing against my mouth.

All I can see is *him*, taking up my whole vision with eyes that aren't so snake-yellow when I look closer.

They're the gold of a fox.

Wily, clever, gorgeous as sin.

My heart beats harder for different reasons, now.

He's the reason why I can't breathe, my chest seizing up. That electricity he builds up inside me goes off in these sharp zings that zip through me so hard it's almost painful, the *jolt* I feel as his hands flatten against my back.

We anchor there with me trembling for what seems like forever.

He's got to feel it too—that charge building, tension like thunder, threatening to explode any time and throw us both into the biggest mistake of our lives.

Just why?

Why is every bit of me aching to throw myself at a man I abhor?

At least, I think I still do.

Thank God he speaks.

His voice is husky, smoky, dark as he asks softly, "Better now?"

I nod slowly, but that's a mistake, too. Because when I do...our temples lightly touch, our noses brush, and...

Ugh. It would be so easy.

So freaking easy to tilt my head and seal my mouth to his.

And he's leaning closer, like he's got the same idea, the same wicked impulse.

My back arches as his fingers skim up my spine with a thrill that pulls me inside out, and then his hand weaves through my hair.

My gut catches wildfire with the subtle hint of a pull against my scalp. Then he presses his rogue lips to my forehead.

Um, what?

I want to enjoy it. His mouth is hot and sensuous and full, his scruff raspy against my skin, but after that sizzling-hot buildup, it's almost *insulting* that he just kisses my forehead and pulls back with a smile.

I'm about to light his ass up.

This teasing, this toying, this stinking—

But the next thing he says makes me go cold. "Give me time. I might be able to get leads on that body."

He's standing, pulling back from holding me, a little breathless and excited.

I'm almost pissed off that I don't think it's me that has him so keyed up.

But I'm more scared than before.

Worried that he's gonna unearth things nobody in Heart's Edge needs to know.

"You know, those Galentron bastards caused a lot of mayhem here," he says. "They might've had something to do with Mr. Bostrom never making that meeting with your dad. I'll ask my brother, see what he and the guys know since they're the ones who dealt with that mess more than anybody."

My eyes widen.

I just stare at him, speechless and frozen.

"I'll text you soon," he says, eerily calm before letting himself out, clattering down the front porch steps loud enough to wake the dead.

I let out the breath I've been holding in since that kiss.

He...he didn't even make the connection.

It never even crossed his mind that my dad might be the one who made Bostrom a pile of bones.

He just instantly jumped to those Galentron pricks who brought this town so much misery in the past.

Fine. That buys me more time.

But his brother and his friends ain't stupid. Once they rule out Galentron, they'll start asking other questions, and they might just figure some things out.

I've got to figure some things out, too.

Like whether or not I have the stones to try to hide a body on my own.

And then lie about it to Holt Silverton's face.

I stand up, reaching for the briefcase, meaning to close it up and hide it away.

But that's when I realize, with all the blood draining from my face, leaving me dizzy, I'm absolutely shafted.

Holt took that freaking letter with him.

VIII: THE RIGHT HORSE (HOLT)

*S*o much for hoping my brother would be any help.

I sit across from Blake in his living room while he reads the letter with his brows knit together. I've slotted the letter away in a plastic bag just in case there's evidence, prints, that sort of thing. It crinkles between Blake's fingertips as he turns the page over and squints at the blank back, then the front.

"I've got nothing," he says, shaking his head. "Never heard of any Gerald Bostrom livin' around here. And I can't imagine what Libby's old man would be selling that Galentron would be willing to kill over." He eyes me. "Where'd you find this thing, anyway?"

"You won't believe this," I say. "You know that old road leading off into the mountain pass on the far side of the Potter ranch?"

"Can't say I remember it, no."

"It's half buried in scrub, away from the old trails we used to ride. Not on any modern maps, either, but get this." I lean forward, propping my arms on my knees. "There's an entire fucking ghost town down there. I think it might be Ursa."

"Ursa?" Blake's eyes widen. "Shitfire, you mean the place from those old bandit stories they used to tell kids? The lost town that was like the evil twin of Heart's Edge way back when?"

"The one and only." I grin. "If I can confirm it, we might be able to get Libby's ranch a historical marker."

"Protected land." He latches on immediately and snorts. "You've been doing your homework, man. All this for Libby Potter, huh?"

I clear my throat, scrubbing a hand through my hair. "Don't you start, too. Trouble is, that dead body could throw a wrench in the whole works. So if we could get that cleared up..."

"I'll talk to Doc and Leo. See what they know. I was never waist-deep in all that Galentron crap like they were, but they might have some good intel. Hell, maybe they can even hit up old Fuchsia in Alaska."

"Thanks. Try to keep this quiet, though, okay?" I say. "If people find out there's a ghost town full of valuables, they might start looti—"

"Did someone say 'ghost town?'" A punky, purple-dyed head with an undercut hairstyle pops over the upstairs walkway railing. My niece Andrea leans over, practically doing gymnastics with the way she balances a few degrees away from falling over. "Where? I wanna see!"

I flop back in the easy chair, giving her a helpless look. "Both feet on the ground, young lady, or I'm not telling you another word."

She huffs but plunks her feet on the walkway floor, her socks scuffing the carpet. "You're as bad as Dad. What happened to being the cool uncle?"

"Since when am I bad?" Blake cuts in, muttering. But then he adds, "And your uncle isn't telling you another thing, period. You need to stay out of the shit for once in your life, girl. I'm not having another incident that winds up like the winter carnival."

"C'mon. You both know Peace would love it too." Andrea rolls her eyes. "I don't think cowboy ghosts are going to mess me up or try to set the town on fire, Dad."

"Maybe not, but you'd find trouble out there anyway. Or at least, hell, cut yourself on something and wind up with tetanus."

"I've *had* my shots." She rolls her eyes harder.

"Even so." He points a finger at her. "Go do your homework and quit eavesdropping."

With an annoyed face, Andrea stalks off to her room, muttering—and I don't think her dad sees the middle finger she flings back, but I do and bite back my grin.

I'll be the cool uncle and keep that to myself.

"Now you've gone and done it," Blake groans, rubbing the heel of his palm against one eye. "You realize this ain't the end of this."

"I know." I laugh. "God, I'm glad I don't have kids."

"You will one day. Then you'll get what it's like." He smirks at me. "Maybe a few little foul-mouthed, trouble-making half Potter kids running around will give you a taste of your own medicine."

"*Shit.* Don't go giving me imaginary kids with a woman who hates my guts."

Hates me.

Sure.

That's why she'd looked at me the way she did last night.

Because she hates me.

That's why we'd been so close I could feel her knock-me-down lips braising the air against mine.

Because she hates me.

That's why I could feel her heart beating so hard against my chest, her killer tits crushed between us, not even that heavy layer of plush flesh hiding the wild thump of her pulse.

...because she hates my dumb ass.

Fuck.

I've got to keep telling myself we're sworn enemies.

Or else I'll do something a whole lot more reckless than that cop-out kiss on the forehead.

I'll give her good reasons to hate me for the rest of her life.

* * *

Just because Libby hates me doesn't mean I can't try making peace and keeping her in the loop on what I've found.

Which is honestly a whole damn lot of nothing.

At least I've brought beer.

I figured she's a beer girl, after watching her nurse that can at Brody's like a lifeline.

Which is why I'm pulling up around mid-afternoon with a six-pack riding shotgun, still cold from the fridge at the store, condensation beading on the cans. Probably not great for my leather seats.

Don't care.

Just another reason to ditch the Benz soon.

But I've got other things on my mind as I park across the ditch from the main drive—and do a double take.

There's a big honkin' semi-truck in the driveway.

I recognize that truck because it's been parked outside my trailer too often.

Declan Eckhard.

Come to think of it...why the hell does a banker drive a semi when he's not sporting that Tesla? What's up with that?

It's always struck me as bizarre, but right now, I'm over-whelmed with odd things.

On a hunch, I dig around in my glove compartment until I come up with a pen and a scrap of paper, then write down his license plate number.

I just want to know more about our friendly banker man, the supposed love of Sierra's life.

That's all. I'll look it up later.

Right now, I'm worried about Libby, if Declan's got her cornered here alone.

I know she can take care of herself. I know she'd probably shoot him as fast as she'd spit on his polished leather shoes.

Still, I don't like the idea of her alone with him.

He's a big man.

Exactly the type to try to muscle a woman if he doesn't get his way.

I kill the engine, grab the beer, and step out, jumping the gate and heading for the porch. I stop just outside as I realize the door's open, hanging by a crack, but hell.

I can hear everything going on inside.

It doesn't sound good.

Sierra's there, too. I know it because she's the first voice I hear.

"You're still being unreasonable, Libby. I can't believe I'm wasting time trying to talk some sense into your stupid head," she hisses.

"It'd be easier," Libby bites off, "if we could talk alone for once. You don't know everything, Sierra."

"What don't I know?" Sierra scoffs. "Other than that you're being a controlling bi—"

"Now, now," Declan says. "No need to resort to fighting words."

My jaw clenches. I don't like his tone. It's like he's talking to kids, trying to referee a fight over a toy, instead of talking to them like they're grown women.

"Did I invite you to this discussion?" Libby retorts.

I almost grin.

There's my little firecracker.

"There's nothing you can tell me that you can't tell Declan," Sierra huffs, and through the crack in the door I can just make out her folding her arms over her chest. "In fact, if there's a ghost town out there, he's the best person to talk to. He knows *culture*."

Culture, my ass.

He's good at faking it, sure. But that man wouldn't know culture, class, or tact if it smashed him in the chin.

He proves it when he says, "If you're really interested in keeping your land, the town's probably crawling with priceless artifacts. Antiques and collectibles that could be worth more than the land itself. Sell it off, and you'll be in a perfect position to buy out Sierra's portion of the inheritance."

"Excuse me," Sierra says. "Anything in that town *is* my portion, too. It's just as much mine as Libby's, and if we're gonna sell—"

"*We can't sell*," Libby says, her voice rising furiously, then cracking. "Sierra...I have to talk to you alone. Okay? *Alone.* Not with Declan. Not with anyone else. Just you and me. Family."

I can hear the smirk in Declan's voice, even if all I can see of him is a burly shoulder in a pinstriped suit. "Tough luck, Libby. I'm not leaving unless Sierra wants me gone. This is her house, too."

Libby sucks a long breath, winding up. "You overbearing piece of—"

Shit.

I know that tone in her voice.

She's about one second away from murder in the first degree if her shotgun's anywhere in reach.

I know I need to mind my own business.

I also know I can't stand to let her make a fatal mistake.

Hoisting the six-pack of beer like it's all I've got on my mind, I throw the door open, stepping in and raising my voice. "Libby, hey, I brought beer if you—"

I stop just inside, where I can see into the open kitchen. Everyone's eyes whip toward me.

"Oh, hell. Didn't realize you had company. Clumsy me."

Libby's eyes are a little too wide, too stressed.

She looks like a spooked horse. Sierra looks guilty.

Declan, he just looks annoyed, and he draws himself up, opening his mouth like he's about to steamroll me.

I don't give him the chance.

I flash him my coldest damn smile.

"And by company, I mean I didn't realize some folks don't know when they've overstayed their welcome," I growl out.

"This may be Sierra's house, Mr. Eckhard, but it's not yours. Unless you want to get hauled out of here by Sheriff Langley, I'd suggest you move your ass wherever Libby wants it."

Declan narrows his eyes, sizing me up like he's trying to decide where to hit first. "I don't remember you being invited, Silverton. Never mind the fact we're still in a legal agreement..."

"I told you I can't fucking help you. And you know what?" I smile wider, showing all my teeth. "If you're so hard up for cash, you can keep the deposit I gave you for purchasing the property. Agreement's off. I don't want my money back after your grubby hands have been all over it, and as soon as I take this to the city council and file for historical interest, you won't get your paws on that, either. Now. Libby. You said you wanted to talk to Sierra alone, right?"

Libby nods slowly, faintly.

"Yeah," she murmurs.

The quietness of her voice tells me there's something severely wrong.

I was right to barge in when I did.

"You want Eckhard here?" I continue, while Declan glares goddamn murder at me.

"No." She shakes her head.

"There you have it." I gesture with my six-pack toward the door like I'm conducting a grand symphony, never dropping my smile. "Declan, you can go. I'll leave, too. Sierra, this is your home, Libby needs to speak with you, so you're obviously welcome to stay."

"Now you see here—" Declan draws himself up, puffing his chest.

"*No!*" Libby says, quiet but picking up strength.

She shakes her head, blue eyes snapping, blonde curls bouncing.

"No—you, all of you. Everyone. Everyone but Holt just...get out." Her voice is raspy like she's trying not to cry, but it still rises to a furious snarl. "Get the hell out before I make you!"

Declan goes still.

Doesn't leave me feeling any better.

It's his creepy-ass stillness that's made me question, time and time again, just what the fuck is up with this dude when there's violence brewing under his suit-and-tie exterior.

After a second, he offers Sierra his arm.

"Come, Sierra," he commands, lofty and aloof. "We've wasted our time. After negotiations broke down last time, this was pointless."

Sierra pouts but slips her arm in his, tossing her hair and turning a vicious look over her shoulder at Libby. "You'll regret this big time."

Libby just looks on solemnly.

"I regret a lot of things, sis," she says. "But not protecting our home. Get gone and don't bring that bastard here again. I'm willing to talk things out with you, Sierra Potter, but not with him trying to talk us both down."

"You're psycho," Sierra whispers, clinging to his arm, "Declan only has my best interests at heart. Unlike *some* people."

For a second, just looking at her, I see someone else.

Calypso and Barry Hensworth.

That same way of clinging to a man she thinks is invincible—powerful enough that she doesn't need to have any strength of her own.

I have an ugly feeling Declan's going to be a rude awakening for her.

Still, I keep my mouth shut as they turn and strut out like they own the place.

I'm pretty fucking worried that one day soon, they will.

Libby's a tense statue, standing in the middle of the kitchen, nearly vibrating.

She doesn't move until the door slams, slumping and hanging her head with a groan.

"Sorry," I say. "I know you hate it when I jump in and white knight—"

"Don't." She holds up a hand. "I...this time, you actually helped. I froze up. It was stupid of me, but you came at just the right second. I don't know what I'd have done."

"I overheard." I half-smile, taking a step closer. "I was trying to stop a murder."

Wrong thing to say, given the whole dead body thing.

She gives me a haunted, tired look, then turns away, drifting to the window and looking out over the broad expanses of fields fading away into scrub-covered, dusty land. Her voice drifts quietly over her shoulder.

"You paid them a deposit for the land?"

I shrug uncomfortably. "Didn't want someone else swooping in and grabbing that contract before me."

The look she turns over her shoulder is strange, watching me in this way I can't quite read, the blue fire of her eyes crackling. "You really needed that deal to keep your business going, didn't you?"

I'm silent, reaching up to scratch my jaw.

"And now you won't get it?"

"I wasn't getting it anyway, Libby," I admit. "It hinges on your land, and I told you, I'm hands off now and trying to help you save it."

She shakes her head. "I don't understand. You just...because I can't let my ranch go, you're gonna lose an awful lot, and you're actually *helping it* happen. And now you just gave up more money, too?" Her brows knit together. "Why?"

I don't have an answer because it's just like she says.

That's a hell of a lot to do simply because I want a chick to trust me. Even a drag-down sexy chick who electrifies my blood.

Truth be told, I don't have a good answer.

Not one I can put into words.

I just remember how hard I clenched Barry's hand, how I swore to that asshole and the demon harpy on his arm that I'd live with more integrity than either of them had in their pinkies.

"It's the honest thing to do," I tell her, the only thing that's true. "I'm betting on the right horse for once, win or lose."

Her lips quirk faintly, sadly. "Oh, my. The devil himself running his mouth about right and wrong..."

Those words should cut, but her tone's too soft.

Too confused.

Shit, too trusting.

I can't help chuckling. "I'm not Satan, honey. Old Scratch never repented."

"So you're mending *all* your wicked ways?" She lifts an eyebrow.

I take a step closer. Even when she's pensive like this, haunted, tired, she's magnetic.

"A man could be convinced for the right woman," I growl.

She turns to face me, leaning her back against the windowsill, just watching with that same strange look.

She's not dressed down for labor today. Her button-down shirt seems a little nicer, a pretty white thing with translucent sleeves that let the velvety tone of her skin shine through. Plus a pair of cutoffs that actually cover more than an inch of her thighs, the ends cuffed.

Her hair's been brushed so it pours over one shoulder, shimmering like captured sunlight.

Sweet hell, I can't stop myself from drinking her in, even if I'm being Captain Obvious.

Whatever her mood, whatever her worries, whatever her hate, this girl knots me right the fuck up.

She's asking for something, too, with those bright-blue eyes.

Then she shakes her head.

"Maybe you're not the one who needs to repent this time," she says, leaning forward and snagging the six-pack out of my hands. "But I can't have this conversation without a beer."

IX: REIN IT IN (LIBBY)

I can't believe I'm actually thankful for Holt damn Silverton.

Now I can't believe I'm about to tell him the truth. But I've got to, before this gets even more out of hand.

It's bad enough that now Declan and Sierra know there's something down Nowhere Lane.

I'd wanted to just tell Sierra, alone.

Try to trust her as my sister, make her understand why we can't let the land go and what it could do to Dad's legacy.

I was hoping we could come together as a family one more time.

When she showed up with that oily, smarmy ogre, I flipping lost it.

Said things I shouldn't have.

If I don't come clean with Holt, then it's only gonna keep getting worse.

We sit out on the back patio, watching clouds billow across the blue sky in little white puffs. Up there, it's cooler, and down here it's just heat and dead air and sweat dripping down my neck.

Makes the beer taste extra good, at least.

Another reason to thank him.

After struggling for words, I say, "This whole mess put me between a rock and a hard place, Holt."

He glances over. He's slouched in one of the deck chairs and looking infuriatingly fine in it—those jeans make his thighs look lean and hard, muscular and perfect.

They pull, riding low on his hips.

His belt draws attention to a place I wish it didn't.

Damn those translucent A-shirts, too.

It's like his uniform now, ever since he dropped the city suits.

Plaid shirts unbuttoned over those obscenely tight A-shirts that don't hide a lick of him. Somehow, it's *worse* than being naked.

Especially when his gold eyes drift to mine. He can probably tell I'm not looking at his face.

Can't blame a girl for needing the distraction.

My life, Dad's memory, my home...

It's all falling down around my ears.

Holt frowns. "What'd Declan say about antiques?"

"I don't know." I shake my head, pressing my lips to the rim of my beer can, letting the cold soak in. "I was thinking about the body. I didn't tell them, though. Not with Declan right there. So I said I thought there might be valuables. Heck, maybe there are. What do I know? Never spent enough time in that creepy place to see."

"Yeah. Something's off about that dude, if you ask me." Holt's hardly touched his beer, leaving it sitting on the patio table between us. It drips condensation on the frosted glass; he runs his fingertip around the metal rim, tracing slowly with the pad. "But why's that leave you stuck?"

"Because you said you were gonna file for protected status," I point out. "And now I have to, before they pull a legal gun against me to stop it. It's gotta go through quick or they'll block it, won't they?"

He winces. "Me and my big damn mouth. I'll see what I can do to push a request through the council ASAP."

Oh, crap.

Trouble is, that isn't really the problem.

I've gotta spit it out.

I want to believe things won't go south.

I've got to believe Holt won't do anything that would hurt me.

That beautiful idiot is practically giving up a small fortune to save my ranch.

That's worth trusting him again, ain't it?

I take a deep breath, nerve myself up.

Say it.

Say. It. Libby.

"You can't," I say, my tongue practically numb. "Because I think my dad killed Bostrom out in the ghost town."

Holt sucks in a breath, just staring at me. "Dr. Potter? Bullshit, he was such a—"

"I *know*," I say. "I know. He was like...like Einstein and Bill Nye had a weird love child. I know. I can't see him harming a fly —he never did growing up—but still..." I hate that stinging in my eyes, shaking my head. "He *told* me he did it, Holt. He confessed."

"Fuck. Oh, *fuck*." Holt slides a thick hand over his face, his gaze drifting away from me across the fields. "When? How?"

It's hard for me to say this out loud. "I always got lost down there as a kid, and then I just got so busy managing the ranch, I forgot about it for a while. But then Dad got sick, and I found out about the tax issues. I wanted to do a walk-through and take full stock of the property. That's when I found the town...the body...and that shotgun casing I know damn well came from Dad's gun."

"Shit."

"*Yyyep.* That just about covers it." I need a swig of my beer to keep going, wetting my dry mouth and giving me a little more liquid courage. "He was so far gone by then, Holt. Too far gone to tell me anything clear. But right before he died, he came back a little. He told me to find the man's gun, and something about a rock. He said he had to do it."

Holt drops his head.

I take a shaky breath, blinking my blurring eyes again and again, *hard*. "I just can't figure out *why*. So I've been trying to keep anyone else from finding out ever since."

"He must've had a good reason," Holt says. "Dr. Potter wouldn't just shoot a dude over nothing, Libby."

"I want to believe that so bad you don't know how much it hurts."

"I can guess."

Holt's looking at me fiercely.

I feel like he really *sees* me, right now.

And there's not a hint of judgment in his eyes.

"You've been carrying this around since he died," he says. "Haven't you?"

I nod miserably. "I never thought it'd come to this. He always told us not to go down there, but I always thought he was just trying to keep us from getting lost or hurt. And then when I found out the real reason..."

"It shook your world," he whispers. "He couldn't even clear his own name to you, once he died. So you'd rather live with not knowing at all."

I nod again.

It's too hard to speak this time.

But Holt offers his hand, stretching it across the table.

"That's not wrong, Libby," he murmurs. It's gentle. Sincere. Two sweet things I totally don't associate with Holt Silverton. "We all want to remember the people we love as their best selves. What the hell good would it do changing that now, after he's gone?"

"Y-yeah."

Don't take his hand, I tell myself.

Only, I need it.

My fingers slip into his, letting Holt's warmth and the roughness of his fingers envelop mine.

He doesn't say anything.

Just squeezes my hand gently, reminding me he's *here*, grounding me.

Maybe, just maybe, reminding me that people can start off not being all that great...but they can learn to be better.

I'm still tripping over words, but his grip makes it easier.

"He had to have killed that guy before I was born, or near enough. My whole life, I've grown up thinking I knew who Dad was...when he was someone else."

"Maybe he wasn't," Holt tells me. "Maybe he was the man you thought he was. Maybe he killed that man in self-defense or to protect somebody. Maybe someone else shot Bostrom with Mark's gun, but he witnessed it. He could've had a thousand reasons, honey, and a thousand reasons more for hiding it. Sounds like he regretted it all his days."

"Regret doesn't undo murder," I whisper.

"It doesn't," he concedes, tilting his head—but only holds my hand tighter, his thumb stroking along the back of my palm in long sweeps. "But protecting himself doesn't make a man evil. It doesn't change the way he loved you. You *and* Sierra both."

My lips quiver.

Nope. Nada. Not gonna cry.

"But that's just what I don't want," I force out. "Maybe he wasn't some big hometown hero like your brother and his buddies...but people remember him kindly. I don't want to ruin it. To turn that ugly. If the bank takes the ranch, or if people come out to inspect it—"

"They're going to find out, and without all the answers, they'll assume the worst," he finishes.

"Yeah. That."

With a small smile, he gives my hand another squeeze.

"We'll just have to get to the bottom of it ourselves. Prove your old man only fired under real duress, and then this whole thing gets sorted like it should. His name stays clear, the case closes, and you can save Potter Ranch."

I blink.

Again.

And then just one more time, like maybe if I just blink enough the world will clear up and what he just said will make sense.

"Pardon?"

He grins at me.

"Don't you 'pardon' me," he teases. "Talk like you know where you came from."

I kick him under the table.

Not hard, but he obliges me anyway, squinting his eye up with an exaggerated "Ouch."

Okay.

That gets a laugh.

I also realize we're still holding hands, and the inside of my chest goes molten-hot. I pull back quickly, clearing my throat, curling my hand against my beer, hoping it can help cool me off.

"Um," I say. "How the hell are we gonna prove anything? That shooting happened decades ago."

"Follow the clues," he says, shrugging like it's just that easy. "Your dad said something about finding the guy's gun and a rock. Right?"

"Right." I frown. "But I mean...I didn't see a gun in the town," I say. "And I don't have a clue what 'rock' he was talking about."

"Did your dad leave behind any stuff you haven't sorted through yet?"

"Boxes of it." I smile faintly. "He's kept every academic paper he's ever written since high school. Tons of stargazing stuff, old telescopes and lunar globes. I think he's even got a little chunk of moon rock. Probably illegal." My frown deepens. "You don't think that's it, do you?"

"Probably not. eBay sells illicit moon rocks these days." Holt snorts, then tosses his head toward the house. "C'mon. Let's have a look and see what we can find. Maybe there's something in his stuff."

I arch a brow. "Are you actually volunteering to help me clear out the attic? It's a big fat mess."

"A little hard labor never hurt a man." He grins. "Besides. I'm supposed to inspect another finished job on a building owned by a lady I slept with almost twenty years ago, and I think she's still sore at me. I'd rather be here and leave that shit to my man, Alaska."

I go flat. My eyes narrow.

"I'm gonna make you regret saying that."

Of course I mean for the boredom and hard work of cleaning out the attic.

Of course.

I'm not one bit piqued at the reminder that every woman over thirty in Heart's Edge had a piece of him back in the day.

Why would I care?

It doesn't matter.

I tell myself that a few more times as I get up and knock the screen door open, leading him inside.

But I swear it's like he's stalking me, amusement radiating off him with every step, his shadow falling over me as he trails behind.

It's like he knows.

And I kinda want to whack him for it—the usual reaction around him.

I can never figure out if I want to belt him or kiss him, so I just hold myself in check and don't do either, because both would be a bad idea.

Though they'd both feel pretty good, too, if I'm honest.

Right.

Focus on figuring out Dad's stuff.

The attic is more of an open loft, a kind of half-floor accessible by a ladder and filled with light from the bay windows. There's only standing room at the very center where the roof peaks, while you have to crouch down lower toward the sloping edges by the walls.

Holt's cramped, tall man that he is, walking half bent over. I show him the stack of boxes against one wall, all labeled **DAD'S STUFF.**

It's perched next to older boxes against the corner wall. They're marked too.

MOM.

Big black Sharpie strokes.

Angry adolescent lettering.

Ink blurred by tears.

It's old, but it's there. Not as many boxes, but...

I have to look away.

I freaking hate this.

Hate that it's like their lives are packed up in these sad boxes and put away.

Out of sight, out of mind.

Letting out a shaky breath, I pull down the first of the **DAD'S STUFF** boxes from the top of the stack and thump it down on the floor, then shove it at Holt.

"Start digging," I say. "I hope you're just as interested as he was in the hydrogen reactions of neutron stars."

"I..." Holt says cheerfully, "I have no fucking idea what you just said, but I guess I'll have fun learning something today."

I just roll my eyes and haul down another box. Together, we pull the tape from our boxes and start rummaging.

There's a lot in here.

A lot of things I hadn't really known about. Dad packed some of the boxes himself long before I hauled them upstairs.

Old journals with nightly observations on the stars he watched from this very attic window, his telescope still set up and trained toward the Hercules Globular Cluster, which he'd been documenting before he got sick.

But there's a whole lifetime's worth of star notations, near-Earth objects, comets, and so on.

You can feel the love in every page, every tiny scribble with degrees, trajectories, times.

I feel like I'm holding his hand again when I smooth my fingers over the pages.

And the way Holt handles the journals in his box, flipping through the pages gently, slowly, reverently...even if he doesn't know what it all means?

It's like he knows he's holding a man's whole life in his hands.

He's treating it respectfully.

That means something.

It brings a warmth that makes the hurt a little easier to bear.

There's more—snow globes full of glitter that makes them look like galaxies, silly little keychains with baubles in the shape of constellations. Dad was like a kid sometimes. If it had to do with stars and NASA, he'd want it, even if it was souvenir shop stuff.

Tons of books, too. University textbooks, paperbacks on the philosophy of the stars, even astrology.

If my dad wasn't looking up at the night sky, he had his nose in a book.

You'd think that would make him the kinda guy who never noticed the real world around him.

But he always saw us.

That's why I can't believe he was secretly a cold-blooded murderer.

No man who loved the sky and his family as deep and whole-heartedly as he did could do something so awful.

* * *

WE'VE BEEN DIGGING for what feels like hours and we're not finding anything useful.

Not until we get all the way to the back and hit on what I used to call the No-No Chest when I was a baby.

I called it that because every time I went wobbling toward it on my stumpy little legs with my chubby baby fingers reaching for it, Dad would swing me up with a laugh and shake his head and say *no, no, little one, those are Daddy's toys. You can't break them.*

I'd pout and whine, but he'd distract me with things I couldn't destroy.

Sooner or later the No-No Chest disappeared in the attic, where clumsy little hands couldn't sneak in when no one was looking. And I guess we all forgot about it.

It's lacquered wood, dark-stained oak with lighter trim, a rounded top and a simple latch. It's also covered in a layer of dust so thick I nearly sneeze as I brush it away.

The hinges creak when I lift the lid.

It's like opening a treasure chest.

Another ton of little keepsakes, most of them in clear plastic display containers with silver foil printed labels.

I can't help but smile as I lift them out, reading the labels.

It's the important stuff from his NASA days. A fragment of the last Apollo moon lander prototype. A tiny test component from the Viking probe. Bits of circuitry from too many projects to name. The scratched and dented lens of his very first high-powered telescope.

And yeah, right there, an ashy-colored piece of moon rock the size of my thumb tip.

Dad, you *dork*.

My smile hurts, but I can't seem to let it go, even though my breaths are choking.

There's more stuff here, too.

Little gold locks of hair tied with ribbons—mine and Sierra's. Photo albums with our baby pictures, family vacation pictures...oh. Baby booties, too. A dried bracelet of flowers I saw in one of the photos of Mom.

Also a little black velvet box with their wedding rings, little bands of gold, and a picture of them tucked into the top of it, a tiny wallet-sized photo of their wedding day.

They were so *young*.

They look so happy.

I wish I could've known them then.

I wish Mom hadn't died when I was so young.

I wish...

No. All the wishing won't bring them back or fix this mess I'm in.

"Hey," Holt calls over my shoulder, and I gasp so sharply I nearly choke. "What've you got there?"

"N-nothing."

Maybe it's because I'm so emotionally flayed open from going through these old memories, but I can't stand having him so close right now.

With a gruff sound, I pull away, hefting the chest up by its handles. It's not that heavy even though it looks like it should be.

"If there's anything special," I say, "it's got to be in here. Let's take it downstairs where there's better light."

There's plenty of late evening sun spilling through the window. I can see just fine.

I'm just after an excuse to put some space between us.

I refuse his help as I wrestle the trunk down the ladder. I need the distraction, something to keep my hands busy until my feelings calm down.

Downstairs I thunk the chest down on the kitchen table, then start taking things out, laying them in rows.

"All of this stuff is impressive, but it's not that useful," I say.

"So far. We're only at the top layer." He leans over the box, whistling softly as he picks up the chunk of moon rock and holds it up to the light to inspect it, before laying it down and reaching in to help me unpack more things. "Your dad collected a lot of cool stuff."

I half-smile. "'Cool stuff.' Now you sound like him. He never stopped being a big kid about space junk."

"Nothing wrong with that." Holt's hand brushes mine as we both reach into the box at the same time.

Sparks zip through me in a fluttery rush.

I jerk my hand to the side. He doesn't, continuing on like he didn't even notice.

"Is that why you and Blake got on so well with him when you were young?" I ask.

"Maybe so. It's good to keep a sense of wonder. You remember the first time you saw something beautiful when you were a kid? Don't you wish you could relive that feeling as an adult? Something that pure, that perfect, without all the ugly complicated shit that comes with growing up?"

"What would you know about anything pu—"

Oh.

Oh, *God*.

Lifting my head to look up at him was a mistake.

I thought he didn't notice the way our hands touched.

But from the way he's looking at me...

Crud.

I'm very, *very* wrong.

Holt looks at me like he sees something pure and perfect right here, right now.

Like he sees something that fills him with such wonder it makes his voice soft, his eyes dreamy and dark, and he can't look away.

No one's *ever* looked at me like that.

Usually it's a mixture of consternation, fear, and complete and utter disgust for my rude mouth. The way he's staring at my lips right now sure ain't foul.

Hot is the only word that comes to mind.

Like he's touching me without ever lifting a finger.

Like he can already taste my lips with his eyes and make it feel like a kiss.

Welp, I'm gonna spontaneously combust.

My fingers go limp on this small lacquered box I was lifting out. I nearly drop it—and it's the sudden feeling of it slipping that breaks the spell.

I suck in a breath, ripping my gaze from Holt's and grasping the box.

It's black, roughly the size of a grown man's clenched fist, fully opaque and shaped like a cube.

I frown, turning it over, fully distracted.

Can't remember seeing this thing before.

"What *is* this?" I murmur, running my fingers along the seam until I find the catch.

It pops open with a metallic *boink!*

Inside, nestled in a bit of foam that seems to be cut to fit it, there's an odd-shaped stone.

Maybe twice the size of a really big marble.

It's porous, almost like a pumice rock, and really light. The color seems strange, a kind of murky off-red shade that makes me think of the stones in my necklace, but not as polished.

Instinctively, I catch myself reaching for my Aries necklace, tracing the little red stars inside, while I turn the box so the rock catches the sun.

"This can't be it," I say. "Can it?"

"Doesn't look like much to me," Holt says before grinning. "Unless it's some old-timey fortune teller's prophet stone. Maybe Ursa had all kinds of weird shit going on."

I roll my eyes, flipping the box shut and setting it on the table. "Pretty sure that rock came out of someone's garden. Looks almost like the red rock they use for gravel filler. Maybe it belonged to my grandma or something."

"But why would it be in a case like this?" Holt picks up the black lacquer box, turning it over. "It's the only one without a label, too."

"It probably fell off," I say. "I bet if we dig around in the box, we'll find it crumpled up in there."

"Maybe." He sets it back down, then stretches, lifting his arms over his head until that flannel shirt rides up.

I get a glimpse of his tight, toned waist twisting against the paper-thin undershirt underneath. With a groan that borders on obscene, he drops his arms, rolling his neck, stretching.

Dear Lord.

"Think whatever we're looking for isn't here. We need a break," he says.

At least one of us does.

I need air to tame these hot flashes.

Swiping two of the four remaining beers from the six-pack in the fridge, I head outside like the devil's on my heels because he is.

But this devil seems oblivious to the effect he's having. He just thanks me with an easy grin when I pass him a beer before he flings himself back down in the chair he'd left before, sprawled there with masculine ennui and lazy strength.

Ass.

Yeah, I'm mad at him now.

Pissed for being so hot I can't peel my eyes off him for half a second.

But it's not grating like before. Mostly because my mind's on other things.

Sighing, I drop down in my own chair, cracking my beer and taking a cold sip to chase away the dust I'd breathed in up in the attic.

"So if we can't find this rock," I say, "what do we do?"

Holt taps his fingers against the side of his beer can with little *plinks*. "I'm not above helping you hide a body."

I snort, muffling a tired laugh against the mouth of my can. "Don't say that! I might take you seriously."

"Who says I'm not serious?"

"Holt." I tilt my head, glancing over at him, resting my cheek to my shoulder. "When you look at it straight, that's concealing a crime. Obstruction of justice and all that jazz. Only one of us needs to be guilty of that."

"You just basically admitted intent," he rumbles, half smirking, leaning across the table—and I'm suddenly too aware it's a damnably small table. "So now I know. If I don't go to the cops, I'm guilty of aiding and abetting anyway. Might as well get my hands dirty."

"First time I saw you, I wouldn't have believed you knew a thing about getting your hands dirty." I eyeball him, my lips twitching.

"Yeah?" Those whiskey-dark eyes drop down to my mouth. Holy hell, it feels like he's kissing me again with just his eyes. How does he *do* that? "Bet you believe I could get all kinds of down and dirty, now."

I groan softly, but it feels more like something luscious rolling over my tongue than the sheer exasperation I want it to be.

"Don't you flirt with me, Holt Silverton," I murmur.

"Why the hell not?"

"'cause if you do," I say, "I'm gonna do something dumb like this."

I'm moving before I realize it.

I feel drunk right now, but it's not the beer.

It's not even the dizzying summer heat that makes everything feel sluggish and hazy and slow and half-drugged.

It's him, messing up my brain, messing up my body, messing up my *everything* until somehow, I'm the one closing the distance between us, leaning across that stupid table, and pressing my mouth to his.

It's a kiss that shouldn't happen.

A kiss I can't resist.

And it's a kiss I lean into with all my heart and soul while Holt groans raw pleasure, reaching to fist a hand into my hair and pull me in.

Oh, he's got me hostage now.

Just enough for me to *feel* it with a little spark of pulling that makes the pleasure of his mouth that much better.

Maybe I'm the one who kissed him, but there's no doubt

who's in control when he kisses like he's got all the time in the world and he's gonna taste every freaking inch of me.

Holt takes over my mouth, caressing with these long, domineering strokes of his lips, his tongue just a tease darting around for half a second.

Half a breath, taunting me and making me want more, more, sweet hell, *more.*

For a second, I think I'd let him have everything.

Because the way he teases nice and slow says he knows what he's doing.

He knows how to wait.

He knows how to make it that much sweeter for every second delayed.

And when he finally slides his tongue against mine in a slow, deep thrust that slips past my lips to invade my mouth, I moan with a helpless little jerk of my hips.

My lips go slack against his. I feel that *thrust* deep down inside, the anticipation making it ring through me like he just hiked my hips up and wrapped my legs around his waist and slid his cock right into me.

Any man who can make a kiss rock my whole body like that, who can make me feel things he ain't even done to me?

Yeah.

I'm screwed without even screwin'.

God, I think I'd melt for him like a popsicle.

He's burning me more than the summer heat, leaving me struggling to breathe, my mouth wet and needy against his, my fingers rising to tangle up in his flannel shirt.

I pull him closer with a sharp jerk.

It's pissing me off how calm he is, how much he makes me want him, how he *does* this to me.

In a hot rush, I bite him, sinking my teeth into that cruel, sensuous lower lip.

Only for him to growl back.

A thrilling, deep animal vibration that says he's a man who ain't ashamed of his pleasure in the slightest.

Oh. My. God.

I need to hear that sound again.

So I bite his lip a second time.

My thighs get tight. My stomach gets hot and my breasts almost ache with the heavy, full, sensitive want in them. I—

There's a far off sound—one I recognize as buckshot.

Nothing to be worried about, probably.

Just Mendez on the neighboring ranch scaring rabbits out of his garden; he does it all the time.

But it shocks me back to my senses.

I fly backward, staring at Holt like he just gave me a lashing of current, my whole body trembling, every inch of me undone.

Of course he still looks like the fallen freaking angel he is.

Mouth red and wet, eyes molten.

Dangerous, sinful, masculine beauty that makes you want to just throw yourself at him and do anything he asks so he'll make you feel that way again.

Like he can reach down inside and twist you all up until you forget who you are.

Because there's nothing left under his flaming gaze but pleasure.

I can't lose myself so easy.

I can't forget who I am or what matters to me.

I swallow, thick and harsh, and dredge up some sane words.

"Holt. I think..." I whisper, "you should leave."

"Yeah?" That heavy-lidded gaze drifts over me before he stands. He's moving differently, like there's some kind of slick, sensual energy powering his muscles. "If that's what you want, honey. I'm gone."

I expected him to fight, maybe push me up against the nearest wall and *take* what I'm afraid to give him.

This almost makes the roaring ache between my legs worse.

Before I can call after him, he's already prowling away, a proud lion of a man.

I stand up and immediately tip over after I'm inside, sliding against the kitchen wall, burning the hell up, but shivering.

I *hate* that he doesn't argue with me about it.

Because it says one of two things.

Either he didn't feel that kiss the same way I did...

...or he did.

But he's oh-so-confident that I'll come crawling back for more. And he can just stroll away whistling and knowing he can wag his finger and have me any damn time he pleases.

Like hell.

No matter how divine that kiss felt, I'm not totally crazy.

I don't have room in my life for a tornado like Holt Silverton.

X: HUNG LIKE A... (HOLT)

I can't believe she bit me.

No, fuck, that's a lie.

I *can* believe it.

Just can't believe I liked it as much as I did.

Nah, that's another lie.

I liked it. I wanted it. Goddammit if I don't want her to do it again—preferably without as many clothes.

But I don't think that's happening now.

She asked me to leave, and over the past few days, it's been nothing but texting.

Dry exchanges of info. Checking in every day to make sure no one's been down Nowhere Lane. Updating her that I've made no progress on finding more that might shed light on skeleton man.

I'm thinking that's not likely, though.

Not when she said that shotgun shell came from her daddy's gun.

I'm still thinking about it as I sit at my desk in my trailer, reading through purchase orders for our next job. We've got a ton of these lined up right now—smaller contracts we can finish in a day or two, doing minor restorations on some damaged buildings—and honestly, they're the only things keeping us afloat besides the bigger Paradise Hotel cleanup job.

When you can't land the big contracts in a little town, sometimes it's smart to pick up a heap of smaller ones to pay the bills.

But if I don't score a six-figure something or other soon, that's not gonna be enough to keep my guys happy.

Exhaling slowly, I run a hand over my face.

Ninety-nine problems right now and a girl's about half of them.

It can't go on like this.

Boring messages. Not a damn thing about that kiss. No hints she wants me coming back to finish what I started.

She's pissed at me, probably. And when Libby gets mad, I'm realizing sometimes you gotta fight it out with her in the heat of the moment, but sometimes you give her time to cool down until she's ready to talk.

I'm not sure which one this is, but we need to sort this shit out.

Maybe I'm not holding back for her, though.

I'm holding back for me.

Because that hellcat turns me inside out and knocks my ass upside down.

I care what she thinks.

I want her to like me, trust me, believe in me, know she can rely on me.

That's a lot to process.

Because I can't do that shit again, only for her to turn around and drop me the second I slap my heart in her hands.

I'm mulling that more than wondering how I'm going to stretch a budget to cover a custom foundation adjustment to a pre-existing building when the door to my trailer rattles.

A single *hard* knock before it snaps open.

"Boss." Alaska leans in, his face grim. "Just got a call on the main line. One of the fire guys, Rich."

I frown. Blake's the fire chief, and if there's something I need to know, he's usually the one to call.

"What's up?" I ask, reaching for my phone—and realizing it's dead.

Well, that explains it.

I start to plug it in as Alaska says, "There's a fire at one of our sites. The clear-out and restoration at the old hotel."

Fuck!

Looks like I'm charging my phone in the car.

"Status on the site?" I shove it in my pocket, thrusting to my feet and whipping around my desk.

"They're putting it out now," Alaska says, falling into stride with me. "Blake said he'll meet you out there."

"Got it." I yank the door open, grim frustration rushing through me.

Damn it all.

Even with insurance, we can't afford a major setback.

This loss might be the nail in Silverton Construction's coffin, depending on how bad the damage is.

I start clattering down the steps.

Only to nearly stumble right over Libby Potter, who's just charging up them.

We both freeze.

She glares at me.

She's snapping mad. It's not hard to tell, but I've got to get to my site.

"Hey," she bites off. "I've had just about enough of this. You can't even be bothered to pick up your pho—"

"Phone died," I growl, ducking around her toward my Benz. It's not the right time. "Got to deal with something on-site. Sorry," I throw back over my shoulder.

She whips around to glare at me. "Can't it wait five minutes? You've been treating me like—damn it, Holt!"

"It can't wait, Libby!" I throw the door to the Benz open, sliding in, already kicking the engine up, barely waiting for Alaska to squeeze his massive bulk into the passenger seat.

I don't hear whatever she says in response.

Because I'm already pulling out, fishtailing across the lot, and hitting the street.

Libby's just a glimpse of hot, furious blue eyes in my rear-view mirror.

Damn, I hate turning my back on her like this.

But my whole livelihood is going up in smoke as we speak.

I've got to do everything I can to stop it.

BY THE TIME we get there, Blake and Rich and a few other people on the local volunteer fire crew already have the blaze under control.

It's not soon enough.

This was the big job that was going to shore things up while I worked on landing that mega mall contract.

We were clearing out the charred ruins of the Paradise Hotel and erecting a new commemorative tourist center.

Now, it looks like some jackass decided to reenact the Paradise Hotel fire from all those years ago that wrecked the place.

Not only are the building supplies we'd had stacked up torched, but the equipment we'd staged here has been scorched to blackened husks, too.

Mother *fucker*.

That shit cost a fortune.

I had to take out a small business loan to even lease it all at first after my New York defeat, and it took forever to pay off the loan. Even longer to finally lease out the equipment to full ownership.

Now I've got to replace it all when I don't have the cash. I'm not even sure I've got the *time*.

The insurance alone will be a nightmare and a half, if I can even get reimbursed in time before ruining myself in premium hikes.

Did I say ninety-nine problems?

More like nine fucking hundred.

Blake's standing at the edge of the ruined site, his fireman's coveralls pulled down and tied around his waist, his grey t-shirt covered in sweat and soot and grime. He's a dirty mess, but he always is when he's firefighting. It's how you know he did his damnedest.

I appreciate that he did his damnedest for me.

His expression's grim as I step out of the Benz and jog up to him with Alaska on my heels, taking in the smoking desecration. It's ash and cinders everywhere.

Rich picks through it to take the hose to a few more spots that are still glimmering with orange embers.

I just stop and stare, then drag my fingers through my hair, swearing.

"Fuck."

"Yeah," Blake says, growling under his breath. "That just about covers it, man. Tell me you've got insurance?"

"Not enough for this," I say. "But it'll be a start. Hopefully. What the fuck happened?"

"Smell that." He sniffs, demonstrating. "Take a good, long whiff."

I do—and almost choke.

At first all I get is this general burned smell, but then there's something else behind it.

Gasoline.

"...someone *did* this?" I choke out, rage igniting in me hotter than any fire. "Someone burned down my fuckin' site?"

"Unless you left any equipment running with a gas leak..."

"No," I snarl. "Everything here was brought in by truck. None of the big stuff was even fueled up. We drain tanks when we park equipment for the long-haul, and this was a slow job. Basic safety."

"Thought so." Blake folds his arms over his chest, staring fiercely at the site. "Real sorry, bro. If it's arson, it can't be worse than the last time—"

"Don't remind me," I growl. Like I could ever forget how *last time* led to me saving Blake's ass before he got turned into a charred mess himself.

I want to puke.

"Sorry," Blake mutters. "Bad memories. If we've got another spree starting—"

"Sure hope not." I shake my head. "Let's hope this was something personal against me."

"You? Who'd have a reason to set your shit on fire?"

"Uh, besides every scorned woman I've ever slept with in this town?" I snort. "I don't know. I could make a list, but it'd be long. Plenty of people who don't like me around these parts."

"Hmm." He goes silent for a bit, then grunts. "You find a dead body and start asking questions about it being connected to Galentron...then someone burns down your biggest construction site."

"You think there's a connection? Galentron's after *me?*"

He sighs, then shakes his head. "Honestly, nah. Galentron's got no stake in this. Warren and Doc couldn't find any dude named Gerald Bostrom ever involved with that company, and they dug deep. I don't think the stiff's connected to them. This is something else. It's you, Holt."

I let my gaze drift over the twisted ruins of what was my pride and joy.

"What does that mean?" I ask, a bitter feeling sinking inside me.

"Not sure," Blake says. "This feels personal, just like you said. Like someone wants to hurt you. Punish you. Get back at you for something."

"Yeah," I say. "The question is, *who?*"

A terrible knot in my gut says there's one good guess.

XI: OFF THAT HIGH HORSE (LIBBY)

*G*ood thing I didn't get my hopes up—or else I might've forgotten what a shit-stomping crapsack Holt Silverton is.

I can't believe his nerve.

Days of texting like I'm just some kind of client or something. Right after he kissed me half stupid and set my whole world on fire.

Not one word about the kiss, about...well, anything.

So I decide I'll take it to his doorstep. Have *that* talk.

Figure out why we kissed like that, and what we're gonna do about it.

Yeah. So much for that plan.

I'm fuming away so white-hot it's a minor miracle I don't start a brush fire with the heat simmering off me on the drive home.

See if I ever pick up the phone for Holt again.

Hell, I even tried calling him earlier today and he just let it go to voicemail.

I get it now.

I read him loud and crystal clear.

This man plays a certain kind of game.

Shame I'm not the kinda girl who likes being toyed with.

By the time I get home, though, I've got another reason to be furious.

Reid Cherish's decommissioned military Jeep is parked in my driveway.

It's his lucky day.

My fuse is about a micron long.

He's standing outside in one of his three-piece suits, so crisp and cool I don't think he even sweats in this heat. Gecko man just watches me with those flinty eyes, adjusting his cuffs as I pull up.

If he pushes my buttons, there's gonna be a second body in that ghost town.

I hop out of my truck, stink eye flying.

"The hell are you doing here?" I demand.

"Miss Potter," he starts, and I slice a hand out, cutting him off.

"Don't. I'm so not in the mood for your Jeeves shit today," I snarl. "Get straight to the point, and then leave."

He sighs. Long and slow. Like he's drawing it out just to annoy me.

My eye twitches.

"Miss Potter, you still haven't called to schedule a meeting about—"

"I haven't called, and I ain't gonna." I stalk closer, glaring up at him. "You came out here to try that old song and dance again? I told you. I'm not interested in anything that makes it easier for y'all to get your dirty fingers all over my ranch."

I know, I know, I'm being a banshee.

But now, more than ever, I can't let him find out about that body.

It's scaring me more because now Holt knows about it, too, and he's already proven he's willing to play games with my heart. Surely he isn't willing to mess with my secrets, too?

176

"I," Reid says primly, "am not trying to get my 'dirty fingers' all over anything. I'm trying to *help* you."

I almost laugh at the precise, formal way he lies.

But I'm still simmering, and it's enough to make me explode.

"Funny, I'm plain sick of you, and of every other fool barging in here trying to fix my problems," I spit. "If it's not you, it's Declan, or Holt—and all y'all do is make *more* mess!" I point at his Jeep, glaring sternly. "You get in that Jeep right now."

Reid actually looks pained. "Miss Potter—"

"I said *git!*"

I don't know if it's my grammar or my insistence, but his weird, strained look only deepens, like I flat-out belted him.

Don't think I ain't tempted.

Then he sighs his annoying freaking sigh again and nods. "Very well. However, you can't chase away your problems forever."

Maybe not, no.

But I can push some off a little longer.

I don't move until he's good and gone, backing his Jeep out around my truck and then taking off down the road. I pull my truck in and park it in the barn where it belongs, then spend a few hours working out my rage by washing stalls and lugging hay bales and doing all the chores that need doing.

I don't have any riding classes today. Nobody stopping by to check up on their animals, so I throw myself into making my barns as spotless as can be, sweeping and mopping until my arms want to fall off and I'm soaked with sweat.

Doesn't fix much.

Doesn't fix anything, really.

At least I feel better.

Wiping my brow, I head inside for a shower. After it, I dig out my laptop and flop down at the kitchen table, resting my sore body and sucking down a tall, cold glass of lemonade while I get to Googling.

I can't rely on Holt Silverton for this.

So I start researching how to apply for protected status. If that ghost town really is Ursa, I need proof.

What little record I can find online says Ursa was a town of Dutch settlers who migrated west and brought a lot of now-lost traditions with them. Could be a lot with archaeological value in studying the buildings, the tools, even the patterns on old faded blankets.

Trouble is, there's nothing that says how to get to Ursa, or where it was—only that it was in these mountains. Just like any number of tiny forgotten towns that had their boom and then went bust.

Maybe Holt got the town's name wrong in his memories.

No—no, I know I've seen it somewhere before.

I frown, thinking back to the boxes of Dad's junk.

That trunk. There was a leather-bound journal in there, real old.

I've seen it before.

I faintly remember Dad reading it when I was just a little girl, sitting next to him on the sofa and poring through my picture books of constellations.

I'd look over now and then with a child's curiosity, squinting at the lettering and tight script that my little eyes couldn't quite make out.

Do I remember seeing *Ursa* scrawled in ink?

Hmm.

Pushing the laptop away, I get up to dig in the chest, searching through all the little cases and foam padding until—

There it is.

An old-timey leather travel journal. It's all thick yellowed paper with crinkly, stiff edges wrapped up in portfolio-style binding and tied with a leather cord.

It's so old and feels so fragile I'm afraid it'll crumble. I peel it open carefully, undoing the leather knots and then laying the journal out on the table.

The old pages fan up stiffly, and I turn them over carefully so they don't snap right in half, reading through the faded ink that looks like it was scratched on with a quill.

It's the journal of a priest, I guess. That's what it sounds like, when it talks about reading services in the small towns he passes through. I guess he's a traveler, a wanderer...or maybe he was just on his way somewhere and doing his duty in settlements he passed through.

He signs every entry as *Father Matthew*, nothing else. Not even on the inside cover to say who it belonged to.

There's a peaceful, humble quality to the writing that makes it easy to get absorbed in. I page through his ruminations on nature and the beautiful things he saw, his thoughts on finding God in the skyline, in a hunting hawk, in the smiles of the kids in the towns he passed through.

When I'm almost halfway through, I stop.

It's a single entry dated almost a hundred and fifty years ago.

Arrived in Ursa today.

We shall see how well I settle in at my post.

I should pen letters to the Bishop at once, letting him know of my safe arrival.

He was right to send me.

There are many lost souls here in need of guidance.

Ursa, he said.

I don't think I've ever cursed a priest before, but damn if I'm not ready now.

I just wish he'd mentioned more places, some landmarks that would make it clear he charted a path right to these mountains and that ghost town.

The entries after don't help much, either.

They're day to day chronicles of people's confessions, their worries, the problems of the town. People suffering in poverty, wanting for food and basic needs as the silver—and the money—started to dry up. People doing terrible things to survive and falling in with some bandit guy named Danny as their leader.

And then nothing. A bunch of pages look torn out, just ragged edges left behind, and then blank space after that.

Shame.

At least I'm clear on one thing now.

Ursa exists where I think.

I just have to prove this journal came from there.

I've got to go back and get rid of Bostrom's bones.

Even if it means doing something crazy like dissolving him in lye to make sure there's not a single trace of DNA left.

It feels questionable, yeah. My belly tightens, I don't know if I could really do it.

Especially if an innocent man lost his life.

But is it that wrong for me to want to keep my home?

I didn't kill anyone.

I didn't hide it for years, though I'm hiding it now.

I just want my ranch, my horses, my life to be safe.

Why is that so wrong?

* * *

I WAIT until dark to saddle up and head out.

Most of the time I can be pretty sure I'm alone on my ranch, but right now that's no guarantee.

I've got too many people who want a piece of it—and me. I never know who might show up and catch sight of me disappearing down Nowhere Lane.

It's unfamiliar terrain beyond the first mile in.

It's been almost an entire year since I came down this path. But Frost is good, and I trust him to sense any predators, potholes, or other pitfalls long before I'd notice.

We take it slow, moving under moonlight that turns the grass silver and lights up the bluffs. They almost reflect back the sky from their cragged edges.

I can vaguely make out the path Holt made when he came through.

Doesn't seem like any fresh tracks since then, though, and that's a relief.

I'm jittery for the whole ride, and although we get through without running into anything scary...

That feeling doesn't fade.

If anything, it only sinks in deeper.

I feel like I'm being pulled around by Dad's ghost.

Like he wants me to find something, but I just don't know what.

Maybe I'm just carrying his guilt for him now that he's not here to carry it himself.

It's haunting as Frost takes one slow step at a time into the ruins. He heads toward the saloon like he knows.

The poor boy feels my tension, probably. I swear this place looks much creepier at night.

Like that dead man could jump up anytime and make me pay for my father's sins.

My heart thuds, my palms sweat.

I dismount and tie Frost up to a hitching post so old the Vanner would probably pull it out of the ground with one good tug.

But he's good—he always is—and only nudges my shoulder with his warm, velvety nose like he's reminding me he's always here for me.

I step through the creaking double doors, their scream too loud, too hollow, a terrible lament of the dead.

It's almost like the cry comes from the wide-open mouth of the skeleton slouched in the chair like he's been waiting just for me.

I know his name now.

Gerald Bostrom.

It just makes this worse.

I take a few tentative steps closer, but there's no sudden motion, no jump scare, nothing paranormal.

Just my own footsteps on brittle floorboards, which is bad enough.

My breathing thins.

When I look at the skeleton up close, he doesn't scare me.

He just makes me sad.

Sitting there with so many unanswered questions, haunting my life.

Dad told me to find his gun, but I throw my flashlight around everywhere and don't see it. There's nothing behind the bar but debris, a few fallen chairs around the tables, and an ancient piano in the corner.

Nothing catches the light but a spent shell casing I know too well.

Every gun's got its own kind of shell casing, and Dad's rifle...

Yeah.

I leave it where it is. I guess the bullet itself probably fell out of the mummified remains of Bostrom and might be hanging around inside that suit somewhere.

God, what *gun?* Where the hell is it?

I don't know.

I'm not thinking straight.

There's got to be something here that's key to burying this mess.

After taking a couple more long, nervous rounds, it's all I can stand. I head back outside and mount up.

Frost seems as eager to get the hell out of Dodge as I am, but just in case, I make one more run through the town.

I never really explored here much the last time I came, but there's a sort of quiet fascination to this place.

It really is a straight-up Wild West town like something right out of a movie set.

Just not sure if that movie's a western or a thriller flick.

It's eerie how it looks like the people just stopped what they were doing and left.

Plates are still on tables when I peer through windows. Tools left lying around, half-finished horseshoes next to a dead forge at the blacksmith's, ledgers left open at the bank, though from what I can see the weather's gotten in the windows enough to make the ink illegible.

One day soon I'll pick through every building until I find something, anything, just one scrap of paper that says this place is *Ursa*.

As I get to the far side of town, though, I'm caught by the church.

It's as run-down as everything else. Sturdy and standing, but dirty and with some shingles torn out. There's a small graveyard beyond it, mostly wood markers crumbled into bits of kindling and a few brave stones still standing.

Was this Father Matthew's church?

Could this be the key, linking this church with that journal?

Another thing catches my eye as I start turning Frost away, though.

And it chills my bones more than any skeletons or spider-web-clogged churches ever could.

Tire tracks. They're there on the road leading out the far side, toward the exit of the mountain pass.

Fresh ones.

Someone found where the road lets out and the pass opens up on the other side of the mountains. They came in from the opposite direction so I wouldn't catch them skulking around and chase them off for trespassing.

Despite the melting heat of the summer night, I'm frozen with dread.

Just staring at those tracks.

Frost picks up on my unease and prances restlessly under me.

Someone else knows about the ghost town, now.

183

Someone besides me and Holt.

Which also means...

Oh, no.

Someone knows about Gerald Bostrom, too.

Shit.

XII: LOOK A GIFT HORSE IN THE MOUTH (HOLT)

*G*otta say, it's a lot easier to track an arsonist down when he's conveniently spewing fire everywhere.

That's what happened the last time things blew up in Heart's Edge.

Turns out, it's a whole lot harder when all I have is guess-work about who might be pissed off at me, plus a little detective help from my brother.

Whoever set the blaze knew what they were doing. It's easy enough to rule out any random jealous boyfriends, husbands, or lovers, or angry ex-lovers themselves.

I'm good, but I'm not worth burning six figures in equipment and inventory good, and possibly going to prison.

Rival contractors?

Nah. Most everyone in town with any construction experience is an independent contractor.

Before I came back to town, they'd form a small crew to raise a barn or take on odd jobs. Now I've got ninety percent of the local guys employed on my crew, and they're happy for the work.

So that knocks competitors off the list.

Which means my chief suspect is somebody furious at me for getting in the way.

One guess.

A good old banker like Declan Eckhard wouldn't stoop to arson, would he?

He'd besmirch his company's *good name*.

Still, nothing else adds up, even if Eckhard seems tricky to pin down.

And I've got more shit to worry about than whodunnit. I've also got to pick up the pieces, pay my crew, and start over.

I've already filed my insurance claim, but that'll only cover part of it. They're going to want to investigate and make sure I didn't set fire to my own stuff so I could take the money and bolt from a failing business.

I don't have time to wait for that.

Looks like I'm selling the Benz sooner.

Which is how I find myself in Spokane for the day.

There's a car dealership in Heart's Edge, but not one big enough to pony up the kind of cash I want for a Mercedes-Benz that's less than a year old and has less than ten thousand miles on it.

I think I might've bamboozled the car dealer in Spokane with a little slick talk, though.

I walk away with a decent five-figure chunk of cash, plus a trade-in on one of those sturdy old Ford pickups that doesn't ever die even when you try to kill it.

Good for hauling shit around.

Not a bad deal, and now I can pay my crew.

Replacing my equipment on the fly, though...that's harder.

Time to bite the bullet.

I wince, pulling into Confederated Bank & Credit Union.

I don't want to be here.

As far as I'm concerned, between Declan and Reid harassing Libby, these people are the goddamn enemy. But I need a small business loan, and maybe if I play nice, I can coax them into taking some heat off her.

I won't lie.

I'm also curious about Declan and hoping to get a glimpse of him in his natural habitat and see if I can figure him out.

There's no sign of the rat when I push the glass doors open and step into the tidy little space.

It's an open floor. There used to be an ice cream shop here, and funny thing is it's right next door to the Menagerie.

The place actually got fixed up before the vet practice did, though I didn't know who'd be buying it out and moving in once we were done with our repair.

The place looks patched together, redecorated, but serviceable.

Bright, too.

Somebody put some big ass bulbs in overhead.

I'm squinting after coming in from the natural sunlight outside. Not so much that I don't recognize Reid Cherish behind one of the desks. He taps away diligently at a laptop with his posture so straight I think he's got a yardstick shoved down the back of his pants.

When he sees me, his lips turn down at the corners.

Hello to you, too, pal.

I guess the best customer service smile he can manage is forcing them back up into a flat, neutral line as he stands to intercept me, stretching out one hand.

"Mr. Silverton," he says smoothly. "What can I do for you today? Are you here to insult me again?"

I grind my teeth.

Yeah.

This stings like a cigarette burn to the nipple, swallowing my pride to ask this guy for a loan.

I glance at the other desks, but the people behind them suddenly seem extremely interested in what they're doing—and not in meeting my eyes.

Goddammit.

Sighing, I shake Reid's hand.

"I'm here on business today, not busting your balls." I say. "Relax. Looks like you're working, so how about we keep it professional?"

"Certainly," he says, like it's perfectly natural, and gestures toward the chair opposite his desk as he takes his seat again. "Please, sit. Tell me what I can do for you today."

I settle down in the chair and tell myself to relax.

We can do this real friendly-like, and then I can get the fuck out.

For a second, I hesitate, but there's no use in prolonging my torture.

"I'm here about a small business loan," I grind out.

Reid studies me, his eyes half-hidden behind the overhead lights reflecting off his glasses. "I assume this has to do with the recent fire damage to your worksite and equipment. Pity, that."

I smile, though it feels bitter. "Hardly here a month and you're already tuned in to the town gossip mill, huh?"

"Word about disasters gets around." His brows knit together. "Rather often in Heart's Edge, it seems. This town has broken quite a few mirrors."

"You don't seem like the type to believe in superstitions." I can't help barking out a laugh.

"We all have our foibles." He adjusts his glasses. "How much are you looking for?"

"About two hundred thousand," I say—and before he can start in, I raise a hand. "I know. I know it's a lot. Construction gear isn't cheap, and I've got to start off leasing to own all over again. I already traded in my car for the cash to sign my crew's checks, and the insurance company's going to cut me a pittance in maybe a week, maybe a year. Thing is, I have to replace my supplies and break ground now, so I can't wait that long."

He thins his lips, musing.

I want to be mad at him, but right now he doesn't seem like a bad sort.

Sure, he works for a bank that's after Libby's land.

I'm not too fond of him, but if he deals me fair...

"I can't guarantee approval. However, what I can do is submit the loan for that amount, and then negotiate to find out how much I *can* get you. Can you work with that?" he asks.

I tilt my head, then give him a firm nod.

I don't have a choice.

And once I find out what my budget will be, I can start making plans from there.

"Excellent." Reid pulls his desk drawer open and, without even having to rummage, plucks out a stack of blank paperwork. "If you'll fill out the application, I'll get it submitted for review and be in touch shortly."

He slides the stack over and sets a pen on top of it, then promptly ignores me to turn back to his laptop, continuing to tap away at a speed that turns his fingers into a blur.

I raise a brow.

Guess our conversation's done.

It doesn't take me long to fill out the loan paperwork. Dot my I's, cross my T's, and then sign away my life for however goddamn long it takes me to pay this back.

Too bad I gave up on the mall contract, even if I haven't informed the city yet.

That payout would've solved a lot of my problems.

I can't believe I'm being this stupid over a woman again, jeopardizing my entire livelihood.

Well, sometimes dumb don't learn.

And Libby Potter makes me triple dumb.

While Reid takes a look over my paperwork to make sure I didn't fuck it up, I take another look around the room.

"Where's your boy, Declan?" I ask. "Out harassing more ranchers while there's still daylight?"

Reid glances up from my paperwork with a puzzled frown. "Declan?"

"Eckhard," I snap. "You know?"

His frown only deepens.

I cock my head, staring at him.

"I'm afraid I don't know anyone at this branch or in the main Chicago office by that name," he says. "Are you certain you're remembering it right?"

"I'm sure," I say, and that sense of unease I've gotten time and time again becomes a stabbing under my skin. "Well, maybe I'm confused."

"I should hope so." Reid sounds almost offended. "Declan Eckhard may be someone from corporate, but I should think if corporate assigned someone to work over me in the Potter case, they would at least have the courtesy to let me know."

"Rude," I agree, but keep the rest to myself. "I'm probably just misremembering. No need to get your panties in a twist."

"I," Reid says coolly, "do not wear panties."

"More than I needed to know, my man." I chuckle, rising to my feet. "Anything else you need from me?"

"No," he says absently, lowering his eyes to skim the pages again. "Thank you. I'll call you within forty-eight hours about your loan approval, Mr. Silverton. Thank you for doing business with us."

"Sure. No problem."

Our parting handshake confirms my problem isn't here.

Not with Cherish or Confederated Bank.

It's with a damn liar with an agenda, who suddenly seems more dangerous than I thought.

I NARROWLY MAKE it back into my room at the Charming Inn without getting caught by Ms. Wilma.

I'm just lucky it's late, and she's in her kitchen at the big house harassing Warren and Haley and the kids over dinner.

I love her just as much as anyone else in Heart's Edge adores her, but I don't want to find out just how much she's heard about me mooning around Libby and doing stupid stuff for that woman.

I get enough crap from Alaska and Blake.

Libby's on my mind right now as I tuck myself into the cozy two-room suite overlooking the daffodil-filled inner courtyard of the main house, settled at the window with my laptop.

Looking up *Declan Eckhard* doesn't give me much.

I have that scrap of paper with the license plate on his semi tucked into my pocket. I dig it out and search.

Finally, some serious pay dirt.

Forum posts, all by long-haul truckers. Looks like there's an online community for everything—in this case, multiple communities.

All of them send the same message: *watch out for these plates, he'll fuck you over.*

Dozens of stories.

Everyone saying the trucker with those plates is a big time gambler, a swindler, and a con artist who'll cheat a man out of his money and then take the next job that gets him on the road, ahead of any pissed-off people who want their cash back.

Plus a few anecdotes about towns where he's ripped businesses off, too.

Declan's entire history is full of bad loans, flashy bling, and debtors on his heels.

Him using sob stories about how he got conned himself. He talks folks into being his muscle to go shake a target, only to disappear with every damn penny after getting others to do his dirty work.

They describe him like those old-school riverboat gamblers.

Fine clothes, likes nice things, puts on the illusion of refinement, but underneath it, he's a brawler.

Dark hair. Cold eyes. Oily smile.

That's the Declan I know, all right.

Fuck.

Sierra's boyfriend isn't with the bank at all.

He's a liar and a cheat who must've seen the public notice about the lien and saw an opportunity to get in good and pull one over on some small-town rubes.

Only, I've been around real con men. Big city millionaire con men.

Declan's a guppy.

I doubt he's tried to pull a con job this big before, and it's showing in how he's getting fidgety around the edges and heavy-handed.

What if that heavy-handedness means violence?

Shit, fuck, *damn.*

My mind zips back to Libby in a heartbeat.

It's been days since I heard from her, I realize.

Days since she was trying to talk to me at my trailer in a huff, but I was so focused on the fire I just breezed right past her with my heart in my throat.

It's a miracle she hasn't hunted me down and set my hair on fire yet.

But the silence alone tells me I'm probably in a fuckton of trouble, if she'll even speak to me.

I pick up my phone and pull up her contact—and that's when I notice the missed call from the day my site got torched. It must've come through when my phone was dead.

With the way things have been, Libby probably thought I was ghosting her.

She's gonna shoot to kill the next time she sees me.

I know she is.

If she's *able* to shoot me, and somebody hasn't shot her first.

Hey, I text. *I'm coming by to talk. Found some stuff you need to see. It's important.*

I wait a good fifteen minutes while I scroll through more stories of the nameless trucker with those plates.

No call. No cuss-filled texts. No rude emojis.

Nothing.

That shouldn't worry me.

Libby's a busy gal. She might be up to her elbows in shearing sheep right now, or God only knows what else.

Maybe she's just ghosting me right back for spite, but hell.

With the stakes here, you'd think telling her I found important stuff would get a response.

Snarling, I try calling again.

It rings a good seven times before it goes to voicemail.

So she didn't deliberately shunt me, unless she let it ring out.

I sigh.

Goddamn my meddling and my paranoia, too.

I need to know she's okay.

Because Declan's the snake who burned down my construction site, and next he might just go gunning for Libby with more than threats.

I barely keep it together enough to get ready.

Then I haul myself up, make sure my Colt is tucked under my shirt, and go barreling into the dead of night.

Tell me I'm being stupid again.

Whatever.

I'd rather be dumber than hell than be right about this.

XIII: MAKING HAY (LIBBY)

*I*f everybody could stop making my life difficult for one freaking day, I'd never ask for anything else.

I've got ten voicemails from Reid Cherish. Every last one asking the same thing in his robotic monotone: *Please call me at your earliest convenience.*

Holt Silverton has vanished off the face of the Earth.

Oh, I'm not done with him. Not until I can rip him a new asshole.

If he thinks I'm gonna let him treat me the way he treats every conquest, he's got another thing coming. It's shaped a lot like a searing slap to the face.

The cherry on top must be Sierra refusing to answer her texts.

I know she's guilty.

She was the one who drove out to Ursa with Declan, I'm sure, and helped him navigate.

Worst part is, I can't even legally get her for trespassing because it's her property, too.

Needless to say, I've *had it*.

When my phone buzzes while I'm making a late dinner, I whip it out of my pocket, ready to yell at Sierra. But it's not her.

It's King Idiot himself.

Holt, yammering on about how he found something and it's oh-so-important and I—I just can't.

Maybe later, but for now?

I'll keep stabbing this spoon into my big old pot of pot roast stew until it's ready to eat and I can finally sink my teeth into something that doesn't taste like rage and disappointment. The savory smell of meat so tender it's falling apart is a nice distraction.

Then I hear a noise outside.

A clatter.

A barn door swinging, squealing on its hinges.

Not the kind of noises a coyote makes.

One day.

All I ever asked for was one flipping day of peace.

I grab my sawed-off shotgun and make sure it's loaded with a good scatter of buckshot, but just in case, I tuck a few proper slugs into my pocket if I need 'em.

Shotgun propped on my shoulder, I kick the porch door open and stomp out.

The motion sensor lights by the barn are on.

That alone tells me something ain't right. They're calibrated and sensitive enough not to go on from the movements inside the stalls, only outside.

Creeping closer, I catch a shape moving in front of the lights, silhouetted.

"Hey!" I shout, slinging the gun down and jacking it sharply. "You're gonna want to come out real slow. Hands up. I've got no chill tonight and a barrel full of buckshot."

Nothing. The silhouette disappears, and I creep closer, wary and on my guard and definitely pissed off.

There's no one in the barn, though the horses are restless, unsettled.

But one of the stall doors is open—and Plath isn't inside.

Crap!

I don't know if it's horse thieves or vandals, but you never, ever touch my mare.

There's a flash of motion again just outside the barn door. I make sure I've got a firm grip on my shotgun and go darting out.

I'm not letting these freaks get away.

I'm not expecting to walk into an ambush, either.

I'm ready for one or two half drunk kids from town daring each other to do something stupid—but suddenly I see how wrong I am.

My heart climbs into my throat.

Roughly ten tall men in black with masks all come charging, slamming me up against the barn wall.

I manage to get one good shot off, sending buckshot spraying.

One of them howls and staggers away, clutching at his arm and his face with a muffled cry.

I hope I made ground beef out of something on that guy.

But I'm horribly outnumbered. The others grab my wrist, overwhelming me and slamming my hands up over my head.

The shotgun slips out of my hand. I hear someone else grab it and toss it away.

Oh, God.

I know how screwed I am, but if I'm going down, it'll be kicking and screaming.

Making it hard to keep a grip on me, I shove one foot out and hurl a boot right in one of those fucker's guts, slamming him back.

He doubles over with a roar.

Then I whip my head to the side and crack another intruder in the skull. Makes my head ring, but my daddy didn't call me hardheaded for no reason.

Even with my vision blurring from the blow, I manage to drive an elbow into someone else's face before they get me.

Ten against one, and I knocked out three.

Not bad, but...

I think they're ready to even the score.

Suddenly I've got brutal hands on my arms, pinning them to the barn wall. Another hand on my neck, men all crushed in on me so I can't move my legs.

Cowards.

If they really had balls, they'd show their faces when they came to beef with me.

I don't recognize any of the eyes scowling at me through the masks.

Which means I don't get quite as much satisfaction when I haul back, wet my mouth, and *spit* right in the closest one's face.

I'm half expecting him to go the cliché movie villain route and backhand me for my efforts. I'm braced for it, even.

But all he does is wipe his face, growling, his mouth moving beneath the mask.

"Can't blame you for that, bitch," he sneers. "You fight real good. But listen, I got nothing against you. I'm just here for the treasure. You talk, and this doesn't have to get any uglier than it already is."

I stare at him, blinking slowly.

His voice doesn't sound familiar, and I definitely don't know those blue eyes staring at me.

But I realize there's some big blocky shapes silhouetted past my fence, on the road. And they sure as hell look like big rig semi-trucks to me.

"Treasure?" I'm not bluffing when I say I'm lost. "What fricking treasure are you on about?"

"Don't play dumb!"

Now he starts the movie villain crap, squeezing my windpipe because I gave the wrong answer.

Only, the dumbass is wearing thick padded workman's gloves.

And he's not very experienced at this because he's not squeezing the right place to smother me.

All I really feel is a dull pressure that doesn't do much but make me uncomfortable.

"You suck at this," I say.

He blinks. "What the fuck?"

"You can't even choke me like a man. You're out here about to give yourselves heat stroke in winter gear and ski masks on a hot summer night. How dumb. And you're supposed to be scaring me into giving up some treasure?"

One of the boys in the back snickers.

It's a small relief these aren't real dangerous people. But it's a bigger worry that things could get reckless real fast.

Seriously.

Treasure?

When did pirates invade Heart's Edge, looking for their flipping booty—

"Enough!" he roars.

Crack!

There it is.

Finally.

The rough backhand snapping across my face.

That whiplash jerk of pain twists my neck, my head slamming to the side, my whole skull ringing. I taste blood and feel the burn where my teeth cut the inside of my mouth.

"*Ow,*" I rasp out.

Those blue eyes go stone-cold.

"Am I doing better now?" he mocks.

"B plus for effort," I slur around my swelling lower lip. "But I still don't know what the hell you're talking about. What treasure? Someone forget to tell you Talk Like a Pirate Day is in September?"

From the back of the cluster, that snicker comes again. "Think you hit her too hard. She's talking crazy."

"*You're* talking crazy," I spit back, thrashing against the hands holding me down, squirming my body against the barn wall. "Look at you. Ten men against one little girl, and you've got me pinned down while you yack about some treasure? You call yourselves adults?"

I know.

I *know*.

My smart mouth is about to get me killed, probably.

Never let it be said I didn't go out brutally defiant.

These losers don't scare me.

Not until Blue Eyes stares at me flatly and says, "I'm done playing games. You know what we're talking about, girl. You know about the ghost town. You know about the antiques. We know about the dead fuckin' body." I can see his mouth moving under the mask in an ugly sneer. "So unless you want an anonymous tip to the cops about a real nasty murder...you might want to start talking."

The sarcastic retort on my tongue just dies.

Holy hell.

I'm about to be sick, but I'm still not petrified by these devils.

I muster up a smile, baring my bloody teeth, and spit as hard as I can.

Right in old Blue Eyes' face again.

He was nice enough to get my mouth all messy, so he'll reap the rewards.

This time I hit him right in the opening of the mask. He jerks back, closing his eyes, and takes a deep breath. For a minute his hand loosens on my neck.

Time to risk a concussion.

I snap my head forward, ramming my temple into his like a bowling ball.

If he wants whatever he's after, he's gonna hurt for it, and hurt good.

Roaring, he staggers back, clutching his head and letting me go.

The other men jerk in surprise, enough that their hold weakens, and I start kicking and thrashing again, squirming, dropping down into a tangle of legs.

For a split second, I think I actually see sweet freedom.

The tiniest sliver of space between their milling bodies.

I dive for it.

Only for that blue-eyed dick to shoulder me to the ground, hitting me in the gut so hard I'm instantly winded.

He slams me down like a rock. Pain rattles through my bones as I hit the ground with bruising force, and he tumbles down on top of me.

"You wanna play rough, dummy?" he snarls. "Because I can get real rough and real ugly, if you don't want to start talki—"

An engine noise cuts him off.

Headlights sweep over us a second later.

His head jerks up just as a gunshot rips through the air, loud and deadly and sharp.

I manage to get a glimpse of a truck I don't recognize, or maybe it just doesn't look like a truck to me when I'm seeing double and triple and a few colors I don't think actually exist in the visible light spectrum.

I recognize the man standing next to it, though.

I'd know Holt Silverton anywhere.

Even in the dark, even with a probable concussion and the wind knocked out of me, I see him.

Colt held high, his jaw set tight, and absolute murder in those devil-yellow eyes.

If there was ever a spitting image of a modern knight, it's here, him glowing like a savage ghost under the moonlight.

"You're gonna want to think real fuckin' hard about what you're doing right now, boys," Holt drawls, that Heart's Edge country twang coming out in his voice *hard* when he's angry. "'Cause I don't see a single guy here with a gun but me."

He grins, then dips to pick something up off the ground.

My shotgun.

So now he's double-armed, smirking like the cocky fiend he is.

"Now I've got two. Who wants to play?"

Oh. My. God.

I've never been so happy to see someone in my life.

I must be the only one.

Those creeps scatter like panicked chickens.

Leaving me groaning alone on the ground—and covering my head when Holt fires one more warning shot.

You never know where that bullet's coming down.

I guess they're thinking the same thing. They get moving quick, shouting at each other to *go go go* and suddenly I hear truck doors slamming and engines grinding and tires screeching, kicking up mud.

Two against ten doesn't seem like fair odds anymore.

And when Holt fires a parting shot after them, scattering buckshot from my rifle, that gets them moving even faster—and I think I hear a tire puncture, too.

Good!

Holt stands tall until the last of them peels away. Then he holsters his Colt with a sharp look over his shoulder, vaulting the fence to race to my side.

He drops down on one knee, setting the shotgun down and touching my cheek, concern darkening his features. "Fuck, Libby, what'd they do to you?"

"Nothing they didn't bleed for," I mutter, closing my eyes with a wince. "It's not as bad as it looks. Bit my cheek. That's all the blood. I'm just dizzy. Help me up, would ya?"

I'm expecting him to slip an arm behind my shoulders and lift me a little.

I'm not expecting him to give me a fierce look, then pick up my shotgun, crack it open to activate the trigger block, and set it on my stomach.

Right before he scoops his arms under me, lifts me up, and draws me into his warmth, his strength, his overprotective growl.

I can't help it.

I *yelp.*

The world's already spinning, and Holt's way tall.

For a minute, I think I might almost dump my pride and *pass out*. I grab at him, wrapping my arms around his neck with a gasp.

Only to freeze, shoulders hunching as he looks down at me with those hazel-fire eyes so lit and his brows drawn together.

"You okay?" he growls.

"Y-yeah," I breathe. "Just hit my head a few times."

Holt frowns. "They threw you against the barn that hard?"

"Nahhh. I sorta smashed my head on theirs." I smile weakly. "Dad always said I was stubborn and hardheaded as a goat. Thought I'd try a little ram action."

"*Libby*." He chuckles. "Let's get you inside and patched up, honey."

"No, wait!" I kick a little. "They...they let Plath out, I need to—"

"You need to sit still. If you fight with me, I'll take you to the hospital," Holt says, already turning to carry me toward the house. "I'll find Plath."

Sigh.

I hate that he knows me well enough to know that'll make me hold still.

I'm not a fan of hospitals. Don't need a bunch of nurses nannying me half to death.

So I make myself relax and hold still.

And maybe, just maybe, I lean against him a little.

He's so warm, a kinder heat than the sticky summer air. His arms feel solid, safe. They lock out the pain throbbing through me until all I can feel is Holt.

His heartbeat, too, seeming to tick to the rhythm of his steps as he hauls me inside.

He elbows the door to the house open and, once we're inside, makes a beeline for the big ratty sofa that's been in our living room for as long as I can remember.

It's been patched a few times and covered in quilts to hide

how ugly it is. But that just makes it that much softer when he sets me down on it.

Kneeling in front of me, he smiles, tucking my hair back behind my ear.

"Hold still for a few," he says. "I'll get Plath so you won't worry, and then I'll come back and take care of you. Just do me a favor and don't close your eyes. Not till we're sure you don't have a concussion. You get tired, you call me, okay?"

Maybe it's the head injury.

Maybe it's him being soft and gentle and *asking* me these things.

Maybe it's me spending all my anger on those bumbling idiots who attacked me, and I don't have any left for him.

But all I can manage is a nod and one meek word.

"Okay," I whisper, scrubbing the back of my hand against my mouth to wipe some of the blood away. "You've got three minutes before I start doctoring myself."

That just makes him grin.

"Challenge accepted." He braces his hands against his thighs and pushes himself up in a fluid movement.

I watch until he's gone.

Then curl up in the corner of the couch and let myself *hurt*.

When I take stock, it's not too bad.

Bruised stomach, lower lip's a little swollen, but not even split. It's just that cut on my inner cheek, metallic and a little pulpy. It stings like a hornet when I probe it with my tongue.

Probably got a few other bruises, but I've had worse falling off a horse.

Bashing my head against two guys, though?

Yeah.

I should probably be worried about that. The lights still have halos around them and everything's still got a double edge.

I don't know how long Holt's gone.

He's back faster than I expect, shouldering the door open and walking inside. I push myself up against the arm of the couch, frowning.

"You couldn't find her?"

He stops, brows drawing together. "She was right behind the barn. Good girl, she didn't run far. Just waited and let me coax her back inside with a couple of sugar cubes. She's bedded down and fine now, and the rest have calmed down." He grins. "Gave Frost a sugar cube so he wouldn't get jealous. I think he's mad I'm in here with you and he isn't."

I manage a tired smile. "He knows he's my favorite."

"Might make me jealous." That smirk of his is almost wistful, though, and he jerks a thumb toward the hall. "First aid kit in the bathroom?"

I nod, hugging my knees to my chest. "I might not even kill you for patching me up."

"So gracious."

With a chuckle, he ducks away and reappears with the little box I made when I was a little girl. It's popsicle sticks with a big red cross painted on it.

Even when I was barely knee-high to a cricket, I had to do things for myself.

Holt starts to approach, but stops, looking me over, his brows lowering.

"Hey," he says, settling down on the couch next to me, the box propped up on his knee. "You scared? They didn't hurt you bad, did they?"

"No," I growl, glowering over the forearm I have draped over my knees. "They just made me *mad*. Where the hell do they get off?"

"I was hoping you could tell me." The look that slides over me is warm, almost approving. "What'd they want, anyway?"

I hesitate, then curse, closing my eyes. "They were talking about treasure, the ghost town...and they know about Bostrom. Threatened to go to the cops if I didn't tell them where to find the artifacts or some shit."

"Damn," he says grimly—right before something wet and burning presses against my lower lip. "Thought so."

"Ah!" I flinch, opening one eye and glowering at him. "The hell do you mean, you thought so?"

He's still holding a cotton ball dipped in peroxide. "You gonna hold still? I'll tell you."

"You'll tell me even if I don't."

"Yeah, but then we're gonna argue, and let's not tonight." He raises both brows. "Hold still and I'll explain."

I wrinkle my nose at him, scowling.

Finally, I sigh and lift my head, jutting my chin and giving him my swollen mouth.

Holt chuckles, this rich, deep, strangely soothing sound.

"Brat." He presses the peroxide-soaked cotton ball to my lower lip again, his smile fading as he studies me solemnly. "You saw they came in trucks?"

I start to answer—but I'm not allowed to talk, so I nod.

"And who else do we know who drives a rig?" he asks.

"Declan." I suck in a gasp.

"Mouth closed, honey," Holt says, pulling back the peroxide swab until I comply. With another wrinkling of my nose, he presses the swab against my cut. "Declan. Right. Makes sense, don't you think? He knows about the ghost town, and he was talking about priceless antiques. And that's not all."

What now? I wonder.

Holt swabs at my lip with a surprisingly tender touch, and I know if I try to talk again, he'll just wait for me to stop.

So I just glower some more, holding my tongue.

He better enjoy the reprieve.

"I wrote down his license plate number a few days ago," he says. "Seemed weird to me that a banker drove a semi like that. What was even weirder, I stopped by the Confederated branch the other day, and your pal Cherish said he'd never heard of Declan Eckhard. He sure as hell doesn't work at the bank in Heart's Edge."

205

My eyes widen.

Forget seeing halos.

Now I'm seeing ragey *red*.

"Jesus. That lying, two-timing, conniving piece of chicken—"

I actually stop mid-sentence, waiting for Holt to chide me.

Instead, he just moves his hand to let the swab dangle, watching me with a sort of cynical amusement.

"Go ahead," he tells me.

"—chickenshit son of a *fuck!*" I finish, balling my fists. "He's been faking it this whole time. Trying to swipe my land and Sierra's money all in one go! God, we have to—"

"I doubt he wants the land," Holt says. "I Googled his plate. He's got a nasty reputation in the long-haul community. He doesn't do long cons. Short swindles are more his style. Then he hits the road and leaves a lot of angry mobs in the dirt."

"I'll put *him* in the dirt," I snarl. "And Sierra too. Ugh, I can't believe the two of them...I'll turn her and her boyfriend in to Langley myself."

"Not so fast," Holt growls. "There's still Gerald Bostrom."

Oh.

A lead weight pools in my belly, dragging everything down.

"You mean the dead guy everyone and their grandma knows about now?" I whisper, flumping back against the couch and folding my arms over my chest, wincing as the movement pulls on my bruised stomach. "Eff my life. I hate this, Holt. All of it."

He nods, empathy shining in his gaze.

I glare at him from the corner of my eye. "I still hate you, too."

"Still mad at me, huh?" There's a sheepish smile on his lips.

"You know what you did."

"What it looked like, you mean. I didn't brush you off, Libby," he says. "When you came by the office, my main worksite was on fire, the Paradise Hotel—and I think Declan's the prick who set it."

I blink.

Then flush, scrunching down into my shoulders.

Okay.

Crap.

Okay, maybe I jumped to the wrong conclusions.

"So, what?" I mutter, avoiding his eyes. "You didn't just brush me off because you're a kiss-and-run playboy who likes playing mind games with women?"

"Not lately, no." I'm not looking at him, but I can hear the grin in his voice.

"...and you weren't treating me like a client in our text messages just so I'd come begging after you?"

"Nope," he says mildly, restrained laughter edging at his voice. "Shit, I thought I was treading lightly until you were ready to talk about the fact that you kissed me and then told me to get out, but now I'm wondering...would you have come begging, honey?"

"No way!" I shoot back.

If I'm honest, though...I'm not so freaking sure.

If I knew he wasn't playing games, I just might've embarrassed myself.

Though I don't know if anything can be more shameful than how I feel now, when it hits me like a whirlwind.

"I was a brat, wasn't I?" I huff out. "I'm sorry. God. Your whole site burned down?"

"Yep. I'm surprised you didn't hear, what with the never-ending small-town gossip stream."

"I haven't been to town in a few days. Been kinda busy trying to figure out the process for that whole protected site thing. Then there was..."

I flick a tired arm toward the door, all I need to say about the incident outside.

He nods.

"This whole thing is totally messed." Then I let my arm drop, wincing. "*Ow.* Dammit. Why do my arms hurt?"

"Because you took one hell of a bruising." He leans forward, angling to catch my eye. "Libby, seriously—you need a doctor? I'll drive you."

I shake my head firmly. "Just need some painkillers and some rest. I'm not even bleeding anywhere else. I'm more mad than hurt."

"Sounds about right," he grunts.

But it's not mocking.

It's soft. So is the look in those flaming gold eyes, mingling with something else.

Oh, no.

Holt Silverton's *worried* about me.

"Libby," he says, catching my hand gently—and it's amazing that even as battered as I am, I can still feel the zing that cuts through me when he touches my skin. It's lighter now, breathless, and it's not just my body getting too hot. It's my heart when he tugs on my hand and says, "Come here. Just for a little bit."

Maybe it's the concussion.

Maybe it's the blinding fact that I've had a really rotten night.

Or maybe I don't need an excuse, and it's okay to want this because it feels good.

Whatever it is, I don't resist when he pulls me into his arms.

I just let him wrap me up, and burrow into him with a rough, achy breath. I won't let it become a sob because even now, I've got too much damn pride.

That pride could've gotten me killed tonight if Holt hadn't saved my bacon.

"You were brave," Holt rumbles, resting his chin on top of my head. His hands are so steady, so sure, just like he's made to hold me together. "Don't think I didn't hear your smart-ass mouth before I got my warning shot off. I'm amazed they didn't flee from your tongue."

There are a thousand snarky comments on my lips.

About my tongue.

About *his.*

But I don't have it in me tonight to snipe back and forth.

"Stop trying to soothe my ego," I mumble, burying my face in his chest. "...and thank you."

A simple *thanks* shouldn't be so hard.

He takes it with a soft, appreciative sound that casts a wonderful shiver down my spine, like thunder felt at a distance, vibrating on the air.

"What're you thanking me for?" he asks.

"Ummm..."

He wants me to say it?

But I can't just say *I was afraid I was about to die* out loud.

"For having good timing," I whisper.

That makes him chuckle, his big shoulders shaking, bouncing us both. "It's not a proper white knight rescue if I don't come riding in at the perfect moment."

"Yeah, well, drama's your middle name, dude." I tentatively loop my arms around his torso, though I can barely reach, hugging him tight. Holt just smiles and holds me closer while my heart somersaults. "Holt...what are we gonna do?"

"Don't know yet, Libby. If we can't go to the cops, our hands are tied."

That's when I realize I said *we*.

Like we're in this together.

Then again, if a perfectly lickable man chases off masked bandits for you...

...that's enough to earn a few trust points.

I bite my lip, turning my head to rest my cheek over his heart. "I can't believe I'm giving you another chance. So much for thinking you were just another deadbeat playboy."

"You know my reputation. And you know I earned it." He's speaking honestly, frankly, even if it's with regret.

I'm not sure what to do with it.

Especially when he continues. "I thought that was the life I wanted, turning over beds. I know now I was wrong. I ran from this town because I was afraid to admit that everything I ever wanted was here all along...and I damn near ruined myself in the process. I'm starting over. New life, new me. I'll claw myself up from the muck if I have to, just as long as I can build something honest and real."

I try to tell myself he means his construction business.

A self-made man after honest work.

But some secret, longing part of me feels like he's talking about me.

Hopes he's talking about *us*.

Like I could be that girl who tames the wild stallion.

It scares me a little.

Just thinking he's a stallion who can't be broken. If I'm starting to feel something for him, then this ends in something magnificent or a heart-stompy cataclysm.

I'm quiet for so long I guess he thinks I don't want to talk about it.

In some ways, he'd probably be right. I'm too tired and beat up for this kind of heavy conversation right now.

"I don't think you should be alone here for a while," he finally says.

I smile faintly. "What? You think I'm ever alone? The animals are better than any alarm system."

"Sheep and horses can't knock a man out cold or call 9-1-1." He pauses, keeping one broad hand warm against my back, holding me close to him.

"You underestimate how well I train my horses." I wink.

"Libby. Be serious for a minute."

Uh-oh.

He's looking at me that way again.

That way that gets me all riled.

All quiet and gentle and concerned. All sexy and heroic.

Maybe I'm steel wool on the outside, but just like any girl, I've got a million soft spots. But it ain't so often we meet a man who shows his, too.

Men don't like to show their weaknesses 'cause other dudes make them feel like shit about it.

But this man, right here, twists me up inside.

All because he's making it pretty undeniable that one of his soft spots is *me*.

"I'm gonna crash here tonight," he says. "Maybe for a few nights. Don't even start."

My mouth hangs open.

Ohhh, he knows me too well. Because I'm about to shove him off with a comment about his libido, but he heads it right off.

"Don't think I'm up to no good. I'll sleep on the couch like a choir boy. Scout's honor," he says. "I'm only here to keep an eye on you, Libby. I just need to know you'll be okay for an hour or so while I go get my stuff from the inn."

That gets my attention.

I snap my head up, bracing my hands against his chest to glare at him. "Holt Silverton, are you telling me you've been back in Heart's Edge this long and you've been living at the Charming Inn? You couldn't have rented a freaking apartment or stayed with Blake?"

"My choice."

"*Why?*"

"Shit." He coughs, exaggerated and deliberate, turning his face away, rubbing the back of his hand over his beard. "I don't want to bother settling in proper until I can find a real home. Just haven't had the time to buy or build."

"So you're living like a typical bachelor? Out of a suitcase, with a stranger cleaning your home and washing your underwear." With a growl, I shove at him playfully. "Go. Get your stuff. *All* your stuff. You're staying here until further notice."

He stares at me, his eyes wide. "I'm what? Obviously, I want to stay to protect you as long as it takes, but—"

"But nothing!" I snap, like this was my idea to start with when we both know it wasn't. "I'm not having you living like that, even if the Fords run a tight ship. Go get your stuff."

He stares me down, his eyes narrowed.

"You heard me." I snap my hand out, pointing at the door. "*Go.*"

He just keeps looking at me for a few more dumbfounded seconds before a slow smile curls his lips.

"Yes, ma'am."

"Don't make me regret this. I will kill you."

"And I'm being ever so obliging by giving you plenty more chances." He's laughing as he stands, holding his hands up in mock-surrender. "I'll be back soon. Call me if anything else happens and I'll turn right around. Phone's fully charged this time. No more missing your calls."

Missing calls?

Oh.

That's why he hadn't picked up, and I'd been so mad I could've spit nails.

Dear Lord.

I *cannot* let this man get under my skin this much.

"Out!" I jab my finger at the door again.

"I'm moving." He turns and swaggers out, giving me a glimpse of a butt built like a god, pure devil-may-care smirk on his lips, which he throws back over his shoulder.

I don't stop glaring until the door closes in his wake.

Then I rock forward, bending over my thighs, and bury my face in my hands.

Oh, my God.

What did I just do?

I practically begged the man who kisses me like wildfire to move on in.

Indefinitely.

He drives me up the flipping wall and through the roof.

And *he* comes marching right back through my door.

I lift my head, a question on my lips.

One that I never get to speak.

Because in one fluid motion, he drops down to his knees in front of me, captures my face in his palms, and kisses me like the whole world is ending now and this is his only chance.

Out here in Montana, in the dry season, we worry about wildfires constantly.

All it takes is a stray spark.

A little dry grass.

The right wind.

In seconds, you can go from a single orange ember to a roaring blaze that lights up sprawling acres like nothing, consuming them completely.

That's how I feel when Holt attacks my mouth.

Every square inch of me lit to burning intensity in a single instant.

From nothing to this twisting inferno of heat that rips me apart as his tongue slips deep and hot, as he teases my mouth with suggestions of what he can do with other parts.

My hands clench into helpless fists.

I'm a panting wreck in no time, my lips slack and greedy and begging against his.

I can promise you this: there's no dry season right now.

Not for me.

I'm wetter than the Pacific.

I'm ready to throw caution to the wind and let him burn me down by the time he's done ravaging my mouth.

I don't even care that it hurts when his tongue teases my swollen lower lip. The pain and the coppery taste of blood between us only makes me hotter, wilder, gasping and clutching at his hair, pulling him into me.

I'm *hungry.* This frantic urge rips through me that I know won't be sated until he fills me with those piston hips.

It's wicked.

It's wonderful.

And just as addictive as his kiss.

Then that bastard stops. Slowly, but I feel it coming.

I have just enough dignity not to cling to him when he pulls away with a smile that reminds me of the first time I saw him. I thought of Lucifer, fallen right out of Heaven and into sin and then onto his ass in the mud.

"This time I surprised you," he growls. "Now we're even."

He stands, and I can't miss what's at eye level, thick and hard and ridiculously huge against his jeans. His bulge tells me I'm not the only one burning to death right now.

"Back soon," he promises, and even though he said he was going to sleep on the couch...

There's so much suggestion in those two words, it makes me shiver.

I'm left staring after him, frozen, as he turns and walks away.

My face hits my hands again the instant the door slams shut.

I let out a despairing little moan.

I'm not gonna fall for this demon that's possessed me with his sexy voodoo.

I'm *not*.

Only trouble is, now that I've tasted him—the real him, not just his slick act and polished smiles, I'm worried.

If I've already fallen, I'll never get up again.

XIV: FROM THE HORSE'S MOUTH (HOLT)

*M*y custom heated king-sized bed in my penthouse apartment in NYC was luxurious.

The cozy, plush beds at the Charming Inn are nice—soft, if not particularly high-end.

Tonight, I've never been more comfortable, sprawled out on Libby's lumpy, misshapen old couch with a quilt draped over my hips, listening to the soft sounds of her sleeping upstairs.

I'm staying up all night.

I've even got a book to keep me awake—an old read I used to love as a kid called *A Canticle for Leibowitz*. I wasn't surprised to find it tucked away in all the fantasy and sci-fi novels left behind on Dr. Potter's shelves.

I barely make it past the second chapter before I'm out like a light.

So much for all night.

It's been a long week, and I'm no good to anyone half dead.

If anything happens, I'll hear it, though—and spring up like a watchdog, ready to lunge.

Thankfully, it's a quiet night.

This is the best rest I've gotten since I moved to Heart's Edge.

Amazing because I can't even see her.

I just feel Libby, up in her room, picturing her cozy little sleeping area with a tight body tucked in and a hint of gold hair splashed across her pillow.

It's even better in the morning with slender arms draped around my neck. Soft curves press against my chest, her tits plush against me, a round hip fitting into my waist.

A slow, shy kiss flutters over my lips.

Talk about one fuck of a wake-up call.

All it takes to get me up in more ways than one, too.

I open my eyes to Libby's mouth teasing mine with full lush lips and a touch that makes every bit of me *throb.*

The second she realizes I'm awake, she stops.

Then pushes herself up with a hand braced against my chest. Hot damn if I'm not aware of her naked skin on mine, her palm pressed between my pecs, her fingers flat against my chest.

There's a curious smile on her lips.

She watches me with those blue witchfire eyes stirring.

"So that's what it takes to get you up," she drawls, quiet laughter in every word, before she leans away to pick up a steaming coffee mug. "Thought the smell of this would do it, but you just kept snoring away."

"I don't snore," I mumble drowsily, yawning around a huge smile.

Shit, yeah.

I could get used to waking up like this.

Maybe do one better, waking up next to her.

And if she's waking me up like this with those sweet-as-pie lips and that bonbon body, maybe, just maybe, Libby might be interested in getting used to it, too.

Can a man go from uneasy truce to claiming her as hard as every inch of me wants?

Right now, she's giving me her skeptical look that says I'm walking a mighty thin line between making her laugh and stepping in horseshit.

"Okay, sleepy. And I'm sure you've had a couple dozen ladies verify your snoring habits, huh, cowboy?"

I grin and sit up, plucking the mug out of her hand and setting it back down on the coffee table—before hooking an arm around her waist, reeling her in, daring her to just *try* that kiss again.

She'll see what happens.

"Little early to start calling me cowboy. I haven't done much riding in years."

"Probably," she teases, leaning in closer, her nose brushing mine, "because any time you try, you'd get bucked off. Plath's just a softie," she says with a wink.

"Just like her owner, honey." I tilt my head, ghosting my lips across hers, feeling how they curve into a warm smile with every word. "You never really forget how to ride. Just gotta fall off a few times before you remember how to stay on."

She chuckles, walking two fingers down my chest. "You'd better be talking about horses."

"And if I'm not?"

"You're setting yourself up to get laughed at. I don't know if I'm ready to be your practice ride if you're just gonna end up on your ass."

"Sweetheart," I say, leaning in to nip her lower lip, "if anyone's bucking and riding around here, it better be *you* riding me."

While she gasps, her eyes widening and oh god *damn*—there's that perfect rosy blush on her high, gorgeous cheekbones—I tease my lips against hers in a light kiss.

"See? Now we're even again," I growl.

Her startled look tells me she's not quite as experienced as her brash little mouth suggests.

With a huff, she pulls back and shoves the mug of coffee at my chest so hard it comes one tiny splash away from spilling all over me.

"Oh, we're counting kisses now?" she asks.

"That, and possible third-degree burns." I can't stop grinning, though, as I clasp the mug and take a sip. It's a nice rich brew that shocks the senses awake. "I might owe you another kiss just for this. Damn good coffee."

"It's Felicity's Arabica. She wouldn't let me buy it until she taught me the right way to make it." With a snort, Libby pushes herself up from kneeling next to the couch and settles in on the cushions next to my feet, watching me with her arms folded over her stomach. "I haven't started breakfast yet. Don't know what you like—and don't get any notions about me trying to please you, mister. I just don't like wasting food if you're gonna refuse to eat my grub with that finicky big city palate."

I burst out laughing, shifting to sit up and swinging my legs over the side to the floor, stretching them out.

"I'm hardly picky. Hell, I missed good home cooking. Beats paying fifty bucks a plate for an inch-wide square of tuna drizzled in some sauce on a fifteen-inch wide plate."

She blinks at me. "You're kidding...right? I'd slug the waiter."

"Not the waiter's fault, honey." I smirk. "You'd be better off punching the chef."

"Damn right I would."

There's something *off* about her. The more we talk, the more I sense it.

She's preoccupied, and I can't help giving her a careful once-over. Can't see her bruises under her cute pajama top or the little shorts that go with it.

At least Little Miss Stubborn's actually awake after insisting on going to sleep with a possible concussion. Her lower lip's still red and plump, even if a lot of the swelling's gone down, and it doesn't look as bad as it did last night.

Still.

"Something's wrong." I lean forward and set my coffee cup down. "What's on your mind, Libby?"

She bites at her lip.

With an irritated look, she mutters, "I think we have to go to the cops, Holt."

I tilt my head. "Last I checked, we were on the same page about involving Langley being a bad idea, what with Gerald Bostrom's dead body and everything."

"Yeah, um...that was before somebody, probably Declan's cronies, broke in here and assaulted me last night." She wrinkles her nose. "I don't like it, but this is getting to the point where if I have to shoot someone, I want documentation. Proof I've been threatened and assaulted, and anything else is definitely self-defense."

"Smart," I say. "But that still leaves a dead body to explain."

"And the fact that we're dealing with Sheriff Langley," she groans, rubbing at her cheek. "He's not exactly a crack CSI team. Then again...it wouldn't be hard to keep him around the crime scene and nowhere near Nowhere Lane."

"He does keep the Mayberry in Heart's Edge." I prop my elbow on my knee, resting my chin in my hand and watching her. "You sure about this? I agree, it's gotta be Declan. Those guys were incompetent, too. I'm guessing they're the latest crew he's scraped together, and he's talked them into the noble task of roughing up a lonely lady for a shakedown to get their money back. I'd love to see him cuffed for it, but it's still a risk."

"What's life without risks?" she asks, though she looks a little pale.

I hold my hand out. "You've got me for backup."

"What're you gonna do?" She slips her hand into mine, curling those calloused fingers that I admire so much against my palm. "Put on a clown suit and dance a jig?"

"If I have to." I chuckle, squeezing her hand tight, hoping I can offer reassurance.

Shit. I'm not used to being in this position.

The women I've been with just wanted hot nights but were always afraid of showing me their anger, their vulnerable side, their needs.

Fuck that.

I want real.

I want to protect.

I want to own what's right in front of me.

Libby's not afraid to need me, and I love it, especially if I can bring her comfort.

I just hope I can truly sort her shit.

"I've got a few other ways to distract the sheriff besides calling the circus into town. Like my own case with the fire out at my site. If I tell him I think Declan's linked to both, that'll get his head so knotted up he won't think about anything else like a trip out to Ursa."

Libby frowns. "You really think Declan set that fire?"

"Who else would?" I ask. "I made it pretty clear I'm playing for the wrong team now. Burn all my shit, leave me in debt and desperate for money, and he's hoping I'll change sides again and get you to flip so I don't lose my business."

Libby goes pale. "Holy crap, I didn't—Holt, are you gonna go under? Because I'm being stubborn and won't sell on top of him wrecking your stuff?"

"No." I hold her hand firm, reassuring, and look at her steadily. "Libby, I'll be just fine. I'm a brawler and I don't quit. Hell, when I die they'll have to bury me face down or I'll dig my way out, even if I'm a hundred and too decrepit to move."

That actually gets a faint smile out of her, but I hate how she looks guilty, her eyes dark with worry.

Libby's a fighter, too.

I don't even want her thinking about surrender because she feels bad for me.

"I'm already taking care of things," I say. "I sold the Benz. Needed to anyway; truck's better for hauling construction supplies. That deal gave me enough liquid cash to cover pay for my crew, and I've put in for a loan at the bank. I leased my equipment to own once. I can do it again. Once I've got my gear and supplies back, I'm good to go."

She stares at me. "You went to that bank for help?"

"Didn't have a choice. After everything that went down in this town lately, they're the only game in town. A bigger bank wouldn't take a gamble on me, either. You can bet on that." I shake my head. "They can't do much to me over a small loan. And I'm glad I did, because talking to Cherish is how I found out Declan doesn't work there."

"Yeah, you mentioned that." Libby presses her lips together in a disapproving line. "I still don't like it. You'll be in trouble without the mall contract, won't you?"

"I wasn't getting that contract either way, but now no one is. They need your land, and we're going to keep that out of anybody's hands but yours." I grin real wide and give her hand another squeeze. "Now c'mon. Let me help you with breakfast, and then we can call old Langley and do what needs doing."

* * *

IT'S BEEN a long time since I worked in a country home kitchen, but it's surprisingly easy to fall back into it.

Years ago, it was helping Blake and Ma make dinner every night after school. Later it was nights off base, roughing it on deployment and cooking over propane ranges. Can't say I ever fully settled into New York's fine dining scene, either.

Nah.

Give me a griddle full of hash browns and cheese, enough bacon to make a whole pig, gooey dripping cheesy scrambled eggs, and a pretty girl any day.

I still don't know what I'm doing here with Libby.

In one breath we went from screaming insults to screaming desire.

Right alongside this sort of quiet thing where we're partners in crime.

I'm here to keep her safe, no question.

It means I get to enjoy the way her body brushes against mine while we move through the kitchen together.

The way the sunlight falls through the window over the range lights her up and turns her into gold with sparks of blue-eyed mischief.

The way she smiles like it's a secret when I almost burn myself grabbing at a cast-iron skillet without a pot holder. All because I got too used to fancy stuff with no-heat handles.

I can damn well *tell* she's biting back a snarky comment about city boys being useless or something like that.

It's almost like she enjoys having me here, and that's got me seeing the world flipped upside down.

Breakfast is quiet. We go over what we remember from last night—what I saw that she couldn't with those bastards swarming her, what happened before I showed up. We also agree to be careful firing guns in the air. Those bullets could've landed anywhere, including punching through the roof of the barn.

Being heroic is always harder than it looks in the movies.

By the time Sheriff Wentworth Langley shows up, I've got a pretty clear picture of what happened.

Libby heard noises outside. She found the lights on and Plath missing from her stall because they'd probably let her out just to draw Libby outside and jump her.

Then they all ganged up on her, and she fought good, but with that many on her, she didn't have a chance. They threw her up against the wall, started threatening her about the ghost town, the "treasure," the dead man.

That's the part we'll leave out for Barney Fife.

We'll say they didn't get the chance to talk because I showed up, but we're assuming it's something related to the land dispute. Probably thanks to that prick Declan pretending to be a bank employee so he can pull one over on Libby and Sierra both.

Sierra might be in on it, too.

Libby's gone quiet. I can get not wanting to turn her sister in to the police, no matter what she might've done.

That's the point where I showed up and chased them off, and possibly shot out one of their tires.

That's the story we tell Langley.

Close enough to the truth without being absolutely true. At least it covers the parts that matter.

He strokes his mustache gravely as he listens to us, writing a few things down in that notepad he always carries around in his breast pocket.

"Sounds like a right mess, Miss Potter," he says, putting an extra-gravelly *oomph* in his voice so we know he's taking this right serious. "Why didn't you call it in last night?"

"I just..." Libby wraps her arms around herself. "I was dizzy and freaked out. I just wanted to be safe, and I had Holt here."

That makes something hot course through me, knowing she trusts me to protect her.

We follow Langley as he does a walk-through around the house and the barn, and then the driveway outside. Signs of a scuffle linger everywhere, dirt torn up, tire tracks. Libby said the guys were wearing gloves, so no hope for prints.

There's a little spatter of blood we hadn't noticed before, out in the dirt by the barn.

Could be hers, sure. But considering how she smacked those fucks up hard, I hope it belongs to one of her attackers.

It's a little weird, if I'm telling the truth, to see Langley being a real cop for once and kneeling down to study the bits of blood caked into the dirt.

He uses the edge of a piece of paper to lift them carefully into a small plastic evidence bag without contaminating anything with skin-to-skin contact.

Wonder if he learned that trick on TV.

Sure, I'm being a little unfair.

He's a good guy. It's not his fault that all the weirdness that keeps coming to Heart's Edge is far beyond a small-town sher-iff's skill set.

Maybe I'm still a little sore he locked me up in the drunk tank after people thought I was the idiot setting fires last winter.

Then again, if he'd been a better cop, I wouldn't have been able to break out in less than half an hour.

He's taking this seriously, though, and promises he'll put out an APB for a semi with a blown-out tire, though that lead's gonna go cold fast.

There's no way in hell that asshole wouldn't change his tire ASAP.

Langley promises to keep an eye out for Declan Eckhard, too, and says he'll run Declan's plates and see if he can pull up any warrants and past criminal records.

"Since y'all didn't see any faces and can't ID vehicles," he says, adjusting his hat brim, "I can't keep him long, but I can at least bring him in for questioning."

"It's something," Libby says with a smile. "Thank you, Sheriff. Maybe if we can be there to watch the interrogation, we might catch something he says that'll incriminate him?"

"Well..." Langley rocks on the heels of his cowboy boots, moving his mouth like he's chewing on a mouthful of his own mustache. "We don't have those kind of fancy interrogation rooms here, you know. The ones with the one-sided mirrors, where you can see in? Maybe you can stand in the other room and listen through the door."

Fuck me.

This is one thing I don't miss about small-town life.

Even after Galentron, a drug ring, and a serial arsonist, Lang-ley's boys still aren't prepared for worse than someone stealing ice cream from a kid or the odd drunken brawl at Brody's.

If we're looking for competent help, I don't think we'll get it here.

That leaves me, Alaska, and Blake to get to the bottom of this.

We could bring in Blake's buddies, too, the other so-called Heroes of Heart's Edge.

I smile grimly to myself.

When I was a kid, I always wanted to be part of the older boys' group with Blake and Warren, but I was always just the runt tagging along.

This wasn't what I had in mind when it came to playing with the big boys. I wish I didn't have to call on them like this, especially when they're all men with families now.

Still, if it keeps Libby safe, I'll swallow my pride and enlist all the backup I can get.

We watch Langley make one more round by the barns, then wave him off in his cruiser.

Standing next to each other beneath the bright morning sun, squinting at the dust plume left behind by his wheels, Libby and I grimace.

"That's not gonna do a lick of good, is it?" she asks.

"Nope."

"So what now?"

"Now," I say, "we call in the cavalry."

* * *

THE CAVALRY CONSISTS of Blake and my niece at the moment.

Andrea's in the kitchen messing around with Dr. Potter's old chest of curiosities, whispering to herself in fascination as she picks up one thing after another, reading the labels with wide, curious eyes.

She's a smart girl, too smart for her own good sometimes.

Which is why we're out of earshot while we lean over the coffee table like we're plotting a conspiracy, talking in low voices while Libby and I give the dirty details to Blake.

Honestly, once we're done telling him about the whole thing, he looks at us like we sprouted second heads.

Who can blame him?

"Let me get this straight," he whispers, darting a look at his sharp-eared daughter. "There's a lost ghost town up through the mountain pass. You," he points at me before continuing, "think it might be the lost bandit town of Ursa. And you think it's the key to saving Libby's ranch."

I nod firmly.

"Okay. But shit, hold up." Blake points at Libby now. "You think your daddy killed a man before you were born, and his body's rotting away in the saloon in maybe-Ursa. You don't want anyone to find out it's there because Mark's name will be mud and the cops might seize your land as a crime scene. Plus, your sister's entitled to half of it and she's up your ass to sell, and she's being pushed around by this skeevy asshole who's been pretending to work for the bank. The same damn bank that's playing tax collector, breathing down your neck."

"Yep," Libby confirms.

"Hell, people. And here I thought all that Galentron shit was complicated," Blake growls.

"That's where you come in, brother," I say. "Declan sent some muscle around to scare up information about the ghost town. He wants to raid it for valuables and sell them since he can't get Libby to sell the land. You get me?"

"Man, there's one thing I don't get," Blake says.

I cock my head. "What's that?"

"Sierra grew up here, too. She knows about Nowhere Lane, and she ain't stupid," Blake points out. "If she's with Delcan, she'd just tell him the town's down there. You said you saw fresh tire tracks out there, so obviously they've been there. They saw the body and threatened you with it. So why the hell do they need to muscle you for this 'treasure' when they've already got a town there ripe for the picking?"

Libby looks puzzled. "I don't know. I never figured out what they meant by treasure. Don't think they're after player pianos and wagon wheels. There must be something else."

"I didn't really see anything big worth stealing when I was

there," I say. "Except the dead guy's Rolex, and I can't blame them for not touching that."

"What are we missing?" Libby asks. "There was this old journal from Ursa in Dad's junk. A diary by a priest named Father Matthew with a lot of pages torn out. Maybe Sierra told Declan about it, so he thinks there's something hidden in the town?"

"Hm." Blake raps his knuckles against his chin. "We ought to take a day trip out there."

"Maybe," Andrea calls from the kitchen area, "you should take me with you. It's no fair you get to see this ghost town and I don't."

"Maybe," Blake retorts sternly, raising his voice, "you should stop eavesdropping on the grown-up talk, Little Violet."

Andrea wrinkles her nose at the nickname and sticks her tongue out. "Grown-up talk? Are you three years old? Jesus."

Slowly, Blake breathes in and out, closing his eyes and pressing his hands together, then burying his face in them. "Never have kids, you two. Just don't."

"Aw, she's a lot like me at that age," I tease.

"That's why she drives me so damn nuts." Blake groans again.

"Uh," Andrea calls. "Guys?"

"The adults are still talkin'," Blake mutters.

"Yeah, well, the grown-ups might want to get their grown-up asses over here and have a grown-up look at what I just found," Andrea retorts.

"Language, darling," I say mildly, if only because I'm trying to be the good uncle.

"Uncle Holt?" Andrea answers in the same mild tone.

"Yeah?"

"Shut the entire fuck up."

Blake's head comes up sharply. "Andrea!"

Libby bursts out laughing.

"I like her." Standing, she tosses her head toward the kitchen area. "C'mon. Let's see what she found."

Together, we get up and gather around the table.

Andrea's taken everything out of the box, including the foam padding nesting things in place.

Apparently, that includes the bottom, too.

Only, the bottom isn't really the bottom.

It's a wood panel over the real bottom, more than an inch of space, a hidden compartment. And inside, in the bottom of the box, there's a thick stack of papers.

The ones on top look printed out, but there's handwritten stuff on legal paper underneath.

What looks like old parchment paper, yellowed until it's nearly brown and torn on one side.

Libby stands on her toes to peer in, then lifts the documents out, scanning the top ones before her face goes white.

"Holy *hell*," she breathes. "Does this say what I think it does?"

"Let me see," I ask, and she passes the top layer of stuff over to me.

They're from some kind of...appraising service?

It looks like they do scientific analysis of minerals or something. There's info detailing percentages of volcanic basalt rock, trace elements of potassium, sodium, magnesium, and chloride.

I'm smart, but I'm not Dr. Potter smart.

I don't get it.

Until I read the signed notarized paragraph underneath the numbers.

It rocks me so hard I have to read it out loud, whispering the words in something of a hush.

"*Dear Dr. Potter,*" it says. "*Thank you for entrusting the Seattle Institute of Minerology with such a valuable sample of your find. On analysis we can confirm with almost absolute certainty that this specimen dates to approximately 187 million years old. Its composition is analogous with that of Martian rock—specifically, the basaltic shergottite group. As you know, scarcely more than one hundred meteorites on Earth have been labeled successfully as Mars ejecta. Since most Martian meteorites have been discovered in northern Africa, south*"

Asia, and the Middle East, discovering one in our own Pacific North-west region makes this a fascinating find. Considering the composition of the terrain around your sample, it appears likely that this meteorite broke off from a larger object that disintegrated in the atmosphere during the Jurassic period of the Mesozoic era, and created the depression in the mountains where it was found on impact. I would love the opportunity to further study this Martian artifact, if you can ever find it in your heart to part with it." By the time I get to the closing and the notary's stamp, my mouth is so dry I can hardly talk. "*Signed, Norman Danford, Ph.D. of Extraterrestrial Minerology.*"

I'll just sign it *holy fuck.*

Libby, Andrea, and I all stare at the little black box on the table with that porous red rock inside.

Blake's the only one out of the loop, and he scratches his head, frowning. "What the hell's that all about? Sounds like some sci-fi shit."

"This," Libby says breathlessly, picking up the black box with that innocuous-looking bit of rock inside. "This is the only thing that matches that description."

"Wow," Andrea whispers, staring at the rock with her eyes bugged out.

Libby starts to reach inside the box, then stops, shaking her head and pulling back like she's afraid to touch it now.

"This thing can't be that special, right? It's just a big red rock. It can't really be..."

"I mean, Mars itself is just big red rock," I say. "It might be worth a few thousand bucks to the right buyer."

"Maybe," Libby says, and that's when the tone in the room turns dark. "But if this is what my father shot a man for...is it even mine to sell?"

Andrea's head snaps up sharply. "Your dad did *what?*"

"Ah, shit." Blake groans, smacking his face into his palm.

Libby winces. "Oh! Crap. Sorry. I...I didn't mean to mention that in front of the kid."

"I'm not a kid!" Andrea grumbles. "Look, I've seen enough of

NICOLE SNOW

the crap that happens in this town. A psycho almost gave me a bad case of frostbite, remember? I'm not gonna freak over a dead-ass body!"

"Violet!" Blake yells desperately, before I hold my hands up, clearing my throat.

"Could the clown car stop for a second and everybody just breathe?" I ask. "What we need to be thinking about is if this is the treasure Declan thinks he's looking for."

"Could be," Libby says somberly, holding up the pages still in her hand. She's flipped past her father's handwritten notes on legal paper, and to those older parchment pages. "Because these other papers...looks like a few of the missing pages from Father Matthew's journal."

* * *

TODAY'S BEEN a day for some serious goddamn *revelations*.

We've got a Martian rock worth murdering over, a priest's confessions totally linking Ursa with its legendary bandits, and no frigging clue what to do about Declan until he shows his face again.

Blake suggests having someone post watch at the town to make sure Declan and his crew don't start looting.

It's not a bad idea.

Trouble is, *who?*

It's one thing to ask Blake, Warren, Doc, and Leo to step in for quick things, but overnight guards are for single men—not married guys with children, businesses, and lives of their own.

Which basically leaves me and Alaska.

And I don't want to leave Libby alone at night when those thugs might just come back.

Guess I'll be owing my foreman free beer for life.

After Blake and Andrea leave, Libby and I sit in the living room, silent and facing each other across the L-shaped couch

230

with the rock and the stacks of papers on the coffee table between us.

Libby presses her clasped hands against her mouth, her brows knitting. "I'm still not quite buying it. It's just a freaking *rock*. It can't be from Mars. And it can't be...I mean, Dad loved astronomy, but he wouldn't kill someone over a meteorite. He wasn't that kind of guy."

"I know he wasn't," I say, trying to keep my voice low, soothing. She's had a rough enough day. "There's got to be more than we're seeing. Bostrom said he had buyers lined up from that note in the briefcase."

"So something went sour between them." She stares blankly at the table. "But what?"

"We're not going to figure that out tonight, honey. No use in turning ourselves inside out until we're stressed to death and still don't have any answers." I flash her a quick smile. "How do you feel about getting dressed up?"

"Huh?" Libby lifts her head, blinking at me quizzically.

"Well." I drape my arms over my spread thighs, leaning across the table toward her and dropping my voice to a conspiratorial whisper. "Just so happens the Nortons are having a big shindig tonight. Half barn raising, half barn dance."

It's not hard to tell she's locked up inside her own head. She's staring at me like I've lost my mind. "And?"

I chuckle. "Libby Potter, I'm asking if you want to go out with me. We've been stressing over so much shit we're fixing to give ourselves an aneurysm. You ask me, we both need to take our minds off it and shake loose. It'll still be there in the morning to sort. Tonight, let's get messy."

It dawns on her slowly. Then her eyes glitter, wicked blue and bright as she leans back on one hand, throwing the tempting curves of her body into stark, enticing relief.

The worst part is, she doesn't even know it.

"I take it," she says, "you know about this barn dance because

231

the Nortons' twenty-one-year-old daughter invited you after your crew put up their new barn?"

"It's a possibility," I concede. "She didn't tell me I couldn't bring a date."

"Because she was hoping to *be* your date. She's too young to know not to mess with men like you," Libby points out with a smirk.

"You, too?"

"Huh?"

"Are you too young to know not to mess with dudes like me?" I tease.

She leans forward, folding her arms over her thighs, drawing close to me across the coffee table.

Shit. It gives me a damn nice view down the plunging neckline of her tank top, distracting me with creamy tan lines against gold skin.

"That depends what you mean by 'mess with,'" she drawls in a husky whisper. "'Cause I can promise you, Holt Silverton, I'm *old* enough to mess around plenty with any man I please."

Those words stab lightning right through me.

The girl's a grade A tease, I'll hand her that.

While I'm staring, my mouth practically half open, she just pulls back with a pixie smile playing at her lips and stands. The switch of her hips draws my gaze down over that tight ass and those toned, pretty thighs as she heads for the stairs and the bedroom.

"Hope you've got something nicer than that to wear," she throws back over her shoulder. "Even if we're raising a barn, you shouldn't dress like you were raised in one."

I look down—another flannel over an undershirt, jeans. Typical work duds lately if I'm not in protective coveralls, but it does just fine for casual wear, too.

"What's wrong with my outfit?" I ask.

"Nothing, if you're mucking out stables," she calls down, and I laugh.

"I can do that, if you want me to."

She doesn't answer, and I tilt my head, looking upstairs where I can just make out hints of motion.

"Libby? You want your stables cleaned so bad, I can make myself useful around h—"

Her head appears over the railing—and a few other tempting glimpses.

Tumbling golden hair falls down over the edge, lacy bra straps, hints of bare flesh through the latticed wood.

But it's her smile that fucking does me in.

Wicked, wild, bright, and sinful.

"Holt?" she says sweetly.

"Yeah?"

"You just asked me out on a date. In case you didn't notice, my answer's *yes*. So go get in the shower and make yourself presentable. We'll talk about putting you to work tomorrow."

Laughing helplessly, I stand and snap off a proper Air Force salute. "Yes, *ma'am*."

But from the way she's looking at me?

Goddamn.

Is it wrong to hope she'll be putting me to work *tonight?*

I wasn't lying when I told her it's been a while.

My dick is so blue I think I'm part Smurf, and I might plow her clean through the wall if she gives me half a chance.

Ever since the shitshow that killed my career in New York, I've behaved. I've held back.

But where Liberty Potter's concerned?

I'm fucking *starved*.

And tonight, she looks like dinner.

DELECTABLE CAN'T EVEN DESCRIBE Libby when she comes downstairs.

I've cleaned myself up a bit, trading work boots and worn

jeans for a pair of my nicer designer denim and a pair of square-toed boots with a buckling strap.

The boots are another expensive, showy gimmick I've kept from my New York days, but tonight they work with the clean, pressed black button-down I've swapped with my flannels.

I must pass muster because her eyes glint with approval as she flits down the steps, looking like a goddamn dream.

She's wearing a peasant dress, off the shoulder with a ruffled bodice. It's this pretty semi-translucent fabric that's off-white with subtle patterning in tiny red dots and stripes.

The chest bells hang loose, offering suggestions of her sweet curves in ripples and a flared skirt.

She's wearing sandals like a flower child, cork soles with lace-up pink ribbons that crisscross her ankles. Draws me right in to the deep golden tan of her skin.

For now, just a sexy tease, but *dammit,* those tan lines on her chest are still there, peeking above the bodice's trim.

She's gorgeous.

Especially with her hair brushed into a golden tumble, pouring over one shoulder, calling like a siren in every movement.

Her lips curl into a smile that's both shy and defiant as she stops halfway down the stairs with one hand resting against the railing.

I've never met a woman who hollows me out with a glance.

No bull, no coy mannerisms, no quiet games.

When she fucks with me, I know it up front.

Libby doesn't play at being anything but herself.

Turns out, *real* is damn hot on a woman.

"Well?" she teases, arching an eyebrow, her eyes glimmering like wicked twilight. "You just gonna stare at me all night, or tell me I look nice?"

"Thought this look told you plenty." I grin, offering up my arm. "You look a lot better than nice, woman. You could wake the dead. Prettiest cowgirl in Montana."

"You could've stopped with 'better than nice,' but I'll accept the flattery." She descends the last few steps lightly and slips her arm into mine, her hand resting against my forearm.

She leans against me.

Just a little bit, but enough to make it feel like I'm walking on air.

"You found your balance between small town and big city, I see," she says, casting me a sidelong glance. "I *suppose* I'll let you escort me."

"You're too good to me."

I can't stop smiling at her shit. It's practically hurting my face.

Fuck, I haven't felt this giddy with a woman on my arm since...*ever*.

Don't know how to explain the difference. This feels purer than the easy conquests that came with winning over high-class women with rich families and born power.

There'd been real desire sometimes, sure.

Maybe that's it.

This is something more than dumb desire.

Something so *much* more it makes me freak to put a name on it.

It's a little scary how something this powerful could grow so fast with this pint-sized powerhouse of sass and determination.

"C'mon," I say, giving her a little tug. "The party's going to start without us."

She laughs, and I lead her outside to my truck—where she stops, staring.

"Oh, wow. You went full country, huh? Dropped the Benz for this?"

"These trucks never die. Great for construction." I thump the hood, then hoist her up into the passenger seat. "Besides, who'll take me seriously driving around this town in a Benz?"

She pulls a comically straight face. "You could have tea with Mr. Cherish."

"I'll pretend you didn't say that."

She just laughs her head off while I climb in and take the wheel.

We don't say anything else as we drive out under the stars, the night lit up as bright as I feel inside.

We don't need to.

It's just us, and the charged glances full of promise that we give each other with every mile that passes.

The Nortons' farm isn't that far.

Heart's Edge is one of those towns where half the population lives outside the town itself, sprawled out on little ranches and homesteads throughout the valleys and rolling hills.

The Nortons are one such homestead with a ranch house older than Libby's and a few barns, surrounded by pens full of healthy, shaggy sheep and goats.

The brand-new barn we put up a few days ago glows bright red, lit up everywhere with string lights and lanterns.

There's music busting out of the open barn doors, too.

Rockabilly in full swing, loud and energetic.

We can make out dozens of shapes moving around, people strolling among the refreshments set out outside on picnic tables or slipping off for what looks like more private...conversations.

There's barely room to park on the road outside the fence, but I find a spot and hurry to help Libby before she tries to climb out on her own.

I know she can.

I just want the excuse to get my hands all over her. Helping her down, I steady her waist as she jumps down off the footboard, into my arms.

I've only been to two other barn dances in my life. They don't happen as often as those down-home country movies would make a person think.

Usually it's just grown-up parties with wine in people's dining rooms or kids having awkward dances in the school gym.

Barn dances are one of the only times adults and kids get to mingle in the same place. There's something nice about seeing teenagers swinging it out on the dance floor while their folks embarrass them slow dancing to the exact same music. Meanwhile, plenty of bystanders sit on hay bales stacked all around and chat over drinks.

I can't explain why, but seeing faces both familiar and strange, all here together laughing and dancing and talking...it makes me feel like I'm *home*.

Nowhere has felt like home since I left Heart's Edge.

I'm starting to think nowhere else ever will.

All I want, right now, is to drag Libby out on that clean-swept floor and dance away our woes—dead bodies, thieving assholes, and debts—but I can't quite get clear without talking to the hosts.

The second Keith Norton catches sight of me, he raises his hand, hollering out "*Holt!*" at the top of his lungs. He tumbles down from a stack of hay bales, nearly crashing into me.

What follows is the most embarrassing damn display of back-thumping, thanks, and praise for my crew's hard work.

The whole time Libby watches with a smirk.

One that says she knows how awkward this is for me, so much that I'm fucking red-faced while Norton talks like I hung the moon instead of built him a barn.

After I've had my hand practically crushed from shaking over and over again, we're alone.

Finally.

She folds her arms over her chest, tilting her head up at me, her hip cocked.

"Look at you," she teases gently. "Mr. Respectable. What happened to being the pariah of Heart's Edge?"

"I lost that crown when I stopped sleeping with anything that moved and started offering good work cheaper than they could hire out of Missoula or Spokane." I laugh breathlessly. "God-damn, though. That was a little much."

"What, don't like having your ego stroked?"

I bite my tongue. No sense in detailing a few other things I'd rather have stroked.

Then again, the gleam in her eyes and that catty little smile says she *knows* it, anyway.

She knows, and she set me up.

This little screamer loves testing my self-control.

Chuckling, I sweep an arm around her, pulling her close. "Hey. How about we forget my ego and dance?"

"I wouldn't say no to that."

Her hand slips in mine.

A low growl burns up my throat.

I tug her close in a single pull, her body pressed so light to mine, and shit, it feels good to rest my hand on the small of her back, the curve of her spine against my palm.

She's hot tonight, burning me through thin fabric. I feel her body printed against mine from the swell of her immaculate tits to the just-right curve of her belly to the softness of her thighs.

I don't even care what song's playing.

I want to hold her with those blue eyes looking up at me all starry and dazed, that pretty red mouth parted, her cheeks all pink and warm.

She's so fucking lovely it *hurts*.

The speakers start pumping out some fast-paced Molly Hatchet, and there's my cue.

Spinning Libby into my arms and a quick-step dance, we twirl in brisk rhythm. Her skirt spins around in a pinwheel flare and her face ignites with laughter.

We test each other with intricate steps.

There's an energy here that makes me feel like lightning.

An energy to *her* that feels like I'm taming a storm.

Every time her body brushes mine, I tense up.

I'm on the verge of straight-up combusting, breathless and animalistic and hot.

We're both misted in a thin skim of sweat by the time the song ends and we tumble together, laughing.

The night's warm, but we're on fire.

Her scent rolls off her real lush, sweeter than even the earthy scent of hay all around us.

She drapes her arms around my neck as the music melds into a slower song, and *fuck,* she's so pliant and smooth against me.

Libby molds to me as we fall into a sway, still panting to catch our breath.

"You're not half bad at this," she whispers, tilting her face up to mine with unvoiced laughter sparkling in her eyes.

I settle my arms around her waist.

Fuck, yeah, she fits just right.

"You know what they say about dancing," I tease, and she smirks.

"Do enlighten me."

"It's just sex with our clothes still on." I grin. "So if I'm good at dancing..."

"Oh, I've heard enough rumors about your prowess, Holt. I don't need to hear your bragging, too." She giggles, though, and her body stays close to mine, moving with me as we turn in slow circles. "Besides. I said you're not bad. I didn't say you were good."

"*Ouch.*" I lean down, nudging her nose with mine, pouring warm breath against her lips. "C'mon. Admit it. You're having fun."

"Maybe." A little tilt of her head, her mouth teasing over mine. "But half of it's 'cause that Norton girl is glaring bloody murder. I think she's sulking."

I try not to be obvious about glancing to one side, where Charity Norton leans against the wall, pretty as a picture in a little button-down jean dress with a painfully short skirt.

Another day, another time, another *life...*

Yeah, I might've been tempted by the sullen pout on those lips and those long farmer's daughter legs.

239

Tonight, the only woman tempting me is already in my arms.

I chuckle, pressing my hands just a little harder to the small of Libby's back. "She'll get over it. Leave her to pout at her friends. They'll tell her the rumors about me, and she'll realize she had a near miss with disaster and she's better off."

"So that's the verdict now?" Libby's silent laughter makes her body move against mine in ways that make my cock jerk as her tits press against my chest. "Women are better off without you?"

"I'm a heartbreaker and a devil, you know." Without even thinking about it, I'm leaning harder into her.

Just the two of us in our own little world. Not an inch of space between us, all heat and body language and slow, signaling movement.

"I hear one woman even calls me a snake on account of my eyes. Or maybe my tongue. Not quite sure," I growl.

She sucks in a sharp breath, then narrows her eyes. "*Felicity.* That traitor. She told you I call you that?"

"Didn't take much coaxing, either." I drop my voice to a whisper. "It's almost like she wanted me to know you're hard up for a little Holt."

Libby scowls. "Who says I am?"

"You," I say. "The fact that you're still holding on to me even though you're glaring."

Her breath sucks in and she shoves back, pushing at my chest. "I hate you."

I let her go, but I can't look away from the snapping fire in her eyes.

"Try again, honey. Don't think *hate* is what you're feeling right now."

Hell no.

Not when she's flushed thermonuclear, still breathing so hard her chest heaves even though we've been slow dancing for a few minutes now and my breath's all caught up.

Not when I can see her nipples riled hard against the fabric of her dress, pressing in clear outlines and making my mouth burn, imagining how they'd feel on my tongue.

Libby's brows draw together in a fierce line before she looks away sharply, folding her arms over her chest.

"I just need some fresh air," she says. "I'm going for a walk."

"You want some company?"

She darts an almost wary look at me.

Then looks away stubbornly before offering me her hand, slim fingers outstretched.

Fuck, she's hardheaded to the end.

Leading her outside, we pass beneath the starry spangles of the string lights and move into the darkness beneath the real stars. The Milky Way's a wild thing of beauty above us, breathtaking lights in a thousand pale colors.

I tilt my head up, looking at the sky as we walk hand in hand, the music fading behind us. We move along one of the pasture fences.

She's not scowling anymore, but her expression's pensive, withdrawn.

"You're thinking about your dad, aren't you?" I say.

She smiles weakly. "Sorry. I know we're supposed to be having fun and forgetting things for a while, but...I can't help it."

"He was everything to you," I tell her. "Now we're standing out here under everything bright and spinning. Probably feels like those stars are him watching you right now."

She inhales, darting me a wide-eyed look. "How'd you know?"

"Because it's how I'd feel, too. If everything I grew up with was suddenly thrown into question." I squeeze her hand. "It's fine to have doubts, Libby."

"I don't *want* to. That's what upsets me the most." She bites her lip, drifting to a halt, resting her free hand on the wooden fence railing and looking up at the sky. "I want my faith in him to be so damn unshakable not even a whole graveyard of bodies could change anything. It hurts that it's not. Scares me. Makes me feel like a bad daughter."

"You're not a bad daughter. You're human, honey, and so was he." I settle in next to her, leaning my arm on the fence—but while she's watching the sky, I'm eyeing her. "It's okay to realize our parents aren't gods. Even if you're having doubts, even if you're scared...you're looking for answers. Just asking questions doesn't mean you've lost faith in who he was."

Her throat works in a tight swallow, and she touches her fingertips to that pretty, delicate silver necklace she always wears.

"You know," she whispers, "I think maybe he'd like who you are now."

"I'd like that. But I've got a bigger question on my mind." I watch her intently, the way the night shades her in delicate colors. "Libby, do *you* like who I am?"

"Aw, *hell.* You gotta go and ask me something like that?" But she's smiling, no matter how shaky.

I grin back. When she looks up at me, her eyes are gleaming.

"I think...yeah. Maybe I do. Maybe I like you an awful lot, and that scares me too, Holt."

"It's okay." I curl my fingers against her cheek, stroking along the high, soft crest of her cheekbone. "We're both freaked, woman. You do the craziest shit to me."

Her laugh comes gently.

"*I* scare you? What's your score?"

"It doesn't matter. I'm not keeping score with you any day, sweetheart." I shake my head. "Promise you, the way I get being around you is a first for me every time. There's nothing to compare with that."

She wets her lips, that red tongue so tempting. "Tell me how you get around me, Holt Silverton."

"So pissed off I can hardly see straight," I say, and she laughs again, stronger this time, that glint in her eye less sad now and more amused, and it warms my heart. "So frigging spun up all I can think about is you. The madder you make me, the more I want you. You mess me up."

"Yeah, well, funny how that works," she whispers.

"I'm not done. The more I want you, the more I want to be someone you can respect just like the way I respect you. You push all my goddamn buttons. You make me want to be a better man...and that's fucking nuts, Libby." So crazy my heart pounds like mad, but I've got to say these things. "Because trying to be better means failing. But being afraid of failure's no reason not to try."

Her lips quirk, one-sided and sweet.

"All of that, huh?" she says, tilting her head to press her cheek into my palm.

"All the hell of that and more," I growl back. "I've said enough, though. If I say anything else, you'll think I'm just buttering you up."

"Probably. I got no use for sweet talk. You know that." She rests her hand to my chest and looks up at me with her eyes as clear as the wide Montana sky. "So kiss me, Holt. 'Cause I'm done talking."

"Honey," I murmur, "anything you say."

Curling my fingers in her hair, I pull her in close—but she meets me halfway, rising up on her toes to press in close and slant her mouth against mine with an eagerness that's almost defiant, pushing back against her fear of this heady thing between us.

It's hot. Wild. Perfect.

Every whipsaw sweetness I could ever want, her lips hungry and working at mine like she's trying to quench a desperate thirst.

I get it.

I get it fucking *deep*.

Libby burns me up so hot I'm desperate for anything to ease the pain of it even as I crave her more and more and more, devouring her mouth.

I'll show her with every needy, scorching kiss that this is *real* for me.

More real than anything I've ever known.

When her lips part on a gasping moan, letting me into her, letting me taste her, I let myself sink into this feeling rushing through me until I'm a fucking mess.

I'm hard as goddamn steel. My jeans are a necessary evil to keep me under control, pure torture when it *aches* every time her body sways against mine.

Our tongues twine.

Her arms slip around my neck, her fingers buried in my hair.

With a ragged groan, I grip her waist, lifting her up to sit on the fence, pulling her up to my height so I can taste her.

Shit, it's like there's ambrosia inside her.

The deeper I search, the better she tastes, hot and wet and luscious.

Her knees part, her thighs flanking my hips. I lean into her with nothing left between us but that dress falling between her legs, but it's so thin I can feel her heat through it.

Her pulse sears my hips, making my cock throb and jerk with a surge of pure lust.

Skimming my hands up her thighs, I push the dress up around her hips.

Yeah, I know we've got people not that far away. For me, right now, there's nothing but us and the stars overhead.

Plus, the thrilling way she whispers my name.

"Holt," she murmurs against my mouth, needy, and I've never heard my name sound better.

My lips hurt from the crush of our mouths, bruised and sensitive.

It's the best feeling in the world—almost as good as the heavy weight of her tits on my chest, her nipples hot points against my skin.

Almost as good as her panties dragging against my jeans, and maybe the denim's too thick for me to feel how wet she is, but fuck.

I can *smell* it, creamy-tart and alluring, making my mouth water.

My tongue aches like hell to find out if she tastes as good as she smells.

"Holt." Her knees grip hard at me, then her thighs, quivering and tightening, and I can *feel* the desire rushing through her in the tautness of her body. "Take me home."

If I could, I'd have her right here, right now, naked under the night sky in all its glory.

But the lady wants home, so I'll take her.

Then I'll keep her up until dawn.

Reluctantly, I pull myself away.

Walking hurts when I'm struggling with a hard-on that could do riot control.

I take her hand and lead her through the fields, toward the truck, lifting her up over the fence at the edge of the Norton property before jumping it myself.

We'll just have to be rude and leave without saying goodbye to our hosts.

I can't stand sharing Libby Potter with anyone else right now.

Not when she's sure as hell already mine.

It's a tense drive back to her ranch, the air between us crackling with anticipation.

We don't say a word and don't even look at each other.

It's like there's a live wire stretched between us, passing this charge back and forth, building more intensity with every mile we cover.

It's a miracle I don't break the speed limit.

The moon's high and bright by the time I pull into her drive and park outside the gate. She's out of the truck before I can even come around to open the door for her, taking my hand, pulling me up the walk and toward the golden glow of the porch light.

Underneath that light she's all honey and soft tones.

Libby stops and looks up at me with her hand resting on the door.

"You're coming in...right?" she asks, nearly breathless.

"If you want me to," I tease, smiling wickedly, drawn by a heat that puts the summer night to shame. "My stuff's here, after all."

Her lips twitch. "I did kinda bully you into staying here. But if you really want to go back to the inn..."

"Fuck no."

Can't even think about a hotel room again.

I sink down and capture Libby's mouth with mine, pushing her back against the ranch house door, pinning her there with my hands on her shoulders.

She's right there with me, sliding her hands over my arms, arching back, biting my already-sore mouth. Hot twinges echo in sharp, bucking jerks of my cock, impatient and hungry.

She's wilderness. She's wildfire. She's everything that's beautiful and bright.

I'll let her fucking sear me to cinders if that's what she needs tonight.

This woman kisses me with equal love and hate.

Like she wants to punish me with every extreme we pull from each other—a bruising battle of warring tongues and teeth.

We damn near assault each other with heat and hunger.

I can't keep my hands off her, dropping them down from the door to clutch her thighs, her ass, pulling her into me hard.

I let her feel everything she does to me, everything she draws out, from the heat of my lust to the gut-deep groan spilling out as she bites down *hard* on my lower lip. I give it right back, snarling like a beast.

She holds me tight with one arm, the other fumbling behind her for the door.

Then we're spilling inside, nearly tumbling to the floor when we don't let go of each other for even half a second, practically devouring each other whole.

Somehow, I manage to kick the door shut.

Somehow, we get up to the loft without killing ourselves.

Somehow, we end up on the bed.

And somehow, she's underneath me now, her body sinking into the bed, a perfect fit for mine.

I push myself up on my knees over her, struggling to catch my breath, drinking my fill of Libby Potter.

I fling my shirt off, dragging my undershirt up over my head.

She's hot perfection under me.

All radiant color, gold and silver and sky, her hair tumbled across the sheets in coils of shining yellow sweetness and her eyes so darkly dilated they're almost all pupil.

Her gaze smolders, taking me in with a hunger that makes me want to swallow her up.

The top of her dress has come down, baring the upper curves of her cleavage and those tan lines that make my cock insane, daring it to bust right out of my jeans.

I could fucking die.

I could die fucking *her*.

Especially when she reaches out, running her fingers over my stomach, following the light line of hair down to my navel and then lower, skimming over the waist of my jeans.

"You just window shopping?" she teases—but I can tell now it's a defense mechanism, the way she's blushing like she can't handle how I'm looking at her. "Or are you gonna buy?"

"Trying not to get greedy, honey," I tell her. "Believe me, I want everything."

Yeah, I'm gonna take my sweet time.

Take it slow.

Draw it out.

Keep complete control and tease her until she's buck wild and begging. And I'll still be denying her just for the pleasure of making her writhe.

But the second I hook my fingers in the frilly edges of her top and tug it down, baring the fullness of those tits, I'm gone.

It's like something possesses me.

Some monstrous, obsessive thing that just wants *her*.

I can't help seizing her tits with my hands, spreading my fingers, feeling everything. Their shape, her hot, smooth skin, the lace edges of her bra, the pressure of her nipples.

My tongue screams with the need to taste her.

While she makes restless whimpers and squirms under me, I roll her tits against my palms, feeling the soft flesh yield, focusing on them with such wild abandon I could drown myself.

Libby makes a hot noise in the back of her throat, lifting her hips against me, bucking hard, and it's not doing anything to help my raging erection.

She's got her fingers knotted up in the sheets, dragging at them, clawing like the tiger she is.

"Holt!" My name sounds like music on her lips.

When I press her breasts together and dig my fingers in, tracing my thumbs over the peaks of her nipples, dragging the lace against her skin, she throws her head back.

A cry rips out, and she grinds her hips against mine so hard it's a damn miracle I don't come in my pants.

I'm so hard it hurts—the best kind of pain.

I was gonna torture her, but every second I'm not in her tortures me.

Still, I keep teasing her, slowly kneading her tits, stroking her nipples, watching her twist and gasp, her face so gorgeously flushed and hot, her lips parted real sweet for me.

"Enjoying yourself?" I growl, barely able to get the words out with the way every breath scorches me.

Her eyes open, and she gives me a fierce, glaring look.

"You assho—*ah!*"

Libby cries out sharply as I cut her off with a flick of my thumb against one nipple—and I do the other to match as she rewards me, snarling out "*Holt!*"

"Goddamn, girl," I say. "Love the way my name sounds on your lips."

I show her how much, bending down, brushing my mouth over her searching lips like I might kiss her deep. But my mouth goes lower, finding the upper curve of her breast.

I know what I'm after.

Those *tan lines*.

They're a hot fucking target.

I taste her, sucking over her skin hard enough to leave little red marks, nibbling and teasing and dragging my tongue along her swells.

It's like I can taste the difference between pale flesh and dark, like cinnamon and sugar.

Again and again, my tongue lashes, leaving my mark all over her skin.

Finally, I catch her jostled bra with my teeth.

Tug it down.

Claim one plush nipple with my mouth.

The sound she makes is wild, raw, and suddenly I've got nails in my back, on my neck, digging into my hair.

She grabs me hard and holds on, arching her back, practically pushing that honey-sweet flesh into my mouth.

This girl's demanding, wanton, and I like it.

The more she begs, the more I give.

I lavish her nipple with heat, with friction, lapping and sucking and toying, gently rolling it in my teeth before drawing it between my lips in a soft pull. Never quite doing the same thing twice.

It's fun keeping her on her toes, keeping her guessing, always reacting to every sensation like it's this new and shocking thing.

The whole time she's dragging fire down my scalp, my back, her nails digging in—and the pain just makes me harder.

I'm gonna burst.

I'm gonna fucking burst, and I've never had problems holding back.

Too bad I've never met a woman who turns me on like Libby.

If this is torture, I'm enjoying the suffering, shifting my hips in agony while my dick throbs lightning.

I ignore it, save for the willpower it takes to keep me contained while I tear her dress down around her hips and start finding out how she tastes everywhere else.

There's not an inch of her I don't mark with my tongue and my teeth.

The crests of her ribs, the dip of her waist, the swell of her belly, the indent of her navel.

Lower, dammit.

That last bit of dress skims down her body and I toss it away, leaving her in just that lacy little shell-pink bra yanked down below her breasts. Plus matching panties that barely cling to her by the thinnest of strings.

Those strings catch between my teeth.

Jerking my head sharply to the side, I snap them clean off her in a single movement.

No apologies.

I'm fucking carnivorous when I find out how wet the lace creased between her folds is.

When I also see how her hips melt into her thighs.

Those curves all flow together, and *fuck*, I'm out of control, biting her again, nipping that tender place that creases soft flesh down toward her pelvis, pushing her thighs open, grazing the very points of my canines down the sensitive flesh of her inner thighs.

She's never stopped crying out even once.

Like she can't process how she's even feeling, writhing and helpless in my hands, holding on for dear life.

It feels good to be able to do that to her, make her completely lose herself when she's always trying so hard to keep control.

I know how to break her chain.

I pause, waiting just long enough for her to come down enough to look me in the eye.

Then I smile slowly, dip my head, and let my tongue do the talking.

I flick it against her clit, finding that little bead of flesh against the peak of her folds. First teasing it lightly, then pressing the tip of my tongue to it and working it in a slow, deliberate circle.

It's like someone put fire to dynamite.

Her legs fold around my shoulders, her voice rising to the rafters, back arching to thrust those beautiful tits in the air, pink nipples jutting out *hard*.

All while her nails sink into my shoulders.

It just turns me on more, like the scent of the hunt, salty-hot and as delicious as her taste.

She's slick and glistening. So wet, pooling and threading on my fingers as I stroke them over her folds just to feel her clench.

Just to hear her curse and make more of those ruined sounds.

It's fucking fascinating ravishing this woman.

And I take my time learning her, dragging my lips against her clit, against her folds, delving my tongue inside her.

I trace her from the inside out, always coming back to her clit. Drawing it into my mouth, I suck ever so gently at the tender, sensitive flesh when she least expects it, playing her body just to heighten her high.

Rhythm does the job.

Letting her get used to soft, gentle strokes, something melting and slow and easy...

...right before I shock her with the raw intensity of sucking lips and the subtle threat of teeth and a deep, deep thrust inside her.

Shit, I could get addicted to this woman.

To the taste of her, the sight of her, the smell of her.

Everything.

If this is foreplay, I damn well can't wait to claim her pussy, too.

Still, I take my time, lingering until she's crying out like it hurts, tasting her in swirls of my tongue until she's drenched, listening as she calls my name over and over again in complete and utter desperation.

Holt.

Holt.

HOLT!

Hell, yeah.

There's something special about seeing a woman as controlled as Libby completely undone.

She digs her heels into my back, her entire body convulsing with an attempt at restraint, slim limbs tensed and straining and so gorgeously graceful.

That's when I know she's ready.

I tease her one last time with the flat of my tongue over her clit before pushing myself up to look down at her. She's flushed and gorgeous, sprawled under me in a mess of passion.

"Ready, honey?" I whisper.

Her eyes flutter open, blue whirlpools eager to consume me.

"I'm gonna hate you for this in the morning," she says, her voice so throaty, so raw, and she half-smiles as she trails her fingers down my throat, right over my beating pulse. "So you better make it good."

I grin.

Then I lean down to kiss her, sealing my mouth over hers and giving her a damn good reason to hate me for every slow, lingering kiss.

Libby moans, sliding her body against mine.

I worship her mouth, stroking my hands up her arms, caressing until I find her hands, lace our fingers together, and hold on tight.

After a moment, I reluctantly pull one hand away, moving it

between us to find my jeans and drag them open. I bare myself with a snarl as some of the brutal pressure releases.

My cock practically burns my palm, agonizing to the touch, so close to driving me utterly insane that I can't stand the contact but crave more.

I'm on the prowl with every kiss.

I spread her thighs wider.

My cockhead rubs against her folds. Groaning in the back of my throat, my breath hitches while she tenses and shudders.

The *noises* coming out of her.

Fucking hell.

They're sounds that climb into high, drawn-out cries as I rock my hips forward, pushing into her softness, her heat, and sink in deep.

Shit!

She's so wet for me, so tight, so damn giving.

It's incredible burying myself to the hilt in this slick, pink flesh that parts for me so smoothly, so sweetly, wrapping around me in this layer of stroking softness.

I shudder, my fingers tightening against hers, my kiss plunging deeper when I need to have *all* of her, every depth branded with my touch.

We're perfect together.

Tangled up like this, flesh on flesh in a layer of misted sweat.

I officially can't hold back any longer.

Growling like thunder, I arch my back and rock my hips, throwing myself into the sweet friction of her body.

Every last second of claiming her feels better than the last.

From the way she tightens around me, gasping frantically and biting at my mouth, to the wonderful sexy desperation shining in her eyes.

It's slow, at first, but there's honestly no such thing as slow with Libby.

Not when she's holding on so tight, her thighs pinching my

hips, her body convulsing around me so hot, so tight, that she brings me to a frenzy.

Biting her back, snaring my hand in her hair, I drag her head back and open her mouth to me more, snapping my hips hard.

I drive into her just to feel her around me.

Just to make her arch and jerk and shudder.

Just to feel that fire of her nails playing down my back until she tears my skin.

I don't fucking care.

This burn, inside and out, is everything I need.

She's everything I need, and she's got me in rut like an animal.

We fuck like it's a fight to the death, passion and combat inextricable.

I'm losing my mind.

She wrecks me as I plunder her with every thrust, and soon we're a mess of snarls and writhing and hot tandem rhythm.

Faster, faster, until I'm not even sure if I'm pushing her or she's pushing me.

Only that we're speeding toward something that could split me in two.

Destroy me and remake me anew.

My mind goes blank until there's nothing but pleasure.

Her nails in my flesh, her teeth savaging my lower lip, the sound of her voice rising as she comes on my dick for the third time, the crushing sweet pressure of her body locked around mine.

"Come for me, honey. Come with me!" I snarl, almost out of time.

A second later, I'm gone.

My cock balloons. An electric charge goes off in my spine, ripping up my body.

Then I'm all roar, driving in deep, balls pressed against her ass and wringing every last drop of me into her.

We never calmed down long enough to even say a word

about protection, but when I'm spilling every bit of myself deep inside her sweet cunt, I can't be fucked to care.

"Holt!"

Last thing I hear before she loses herself again, joining my ecstasy, burning me up with her bright-blue witchfire.

I can't take my eyes off her even as my vision blurs.

My cock jerks in harder bursts, straining against her clutching walls.

She's torn me to pieces, and I don't care.

After having her once, I'll never be the same.

And I don't know if I can survive without having Liberty Potter on demand.

XV: A LITTLE HORSEPLAY (LIBBY)

So this is what it feels like to be one of Holt's conquests?
Can't say I mind it too much.

Sure, I expected to *feel* conquered, ravaged, even a little sore. And there's all of that in spades, but there's something I don't expect, too.

I actually feel...

Cherished.

If this is how he made every woman he ever slept with feel?

No *wonder* they hated his freaking guts when it turned out to be a charming lie.

He sprawls in the bed next to me, watching me silently, skin starkly tanned against the white pillowcase. The shadows make those whiskey eyes glow with their own light.

He's pure sin stretched out in my bed like this, all hard muscle so gorgeous it's obscene.

He keeps those rough fingers buried in my hair like it's some kinda fix for him.

Even after it's over I can't quite come down. Every inch of me is aware of *him*.

More than I want to be.

For all I know, this is just another of his one-night things.

Maybe I just played right into his hands.

Believed all the sweet things men say to get a girl in bed, when they don't mean a single word.

"You're giving me a funny look," he says. His lips quirk, his gaze drifting over my face.

I pull the sheets closer against my chest. "I'm just...picturing you in bed with other women. Lovely, I know."

I don't think I've ever seen a grown man actually go pale.

"Oh, shit," he says, slipping his fingers out of my hair and pushing himself up on one elbow to look down at me with his brows furrowed into an almost comically deep line. "Am I in trouble already?"

I can't help but laugh, turning to muffle it in the pillow.

He's like a little boy in a grown man's body, sometimes.

It's ridiculous and cute as hell.

"What?" He actually sounds worried. "What'd I say that's so funny?"

"*That.*" I hide another snicker against the pillow, then clear my throat and turn my head to rest my cheek to the cool pillow-case again, looking up at him. "I'm not mad. I was just wondering if you were like this with other girls."

Holt looks straight-up confused. Then he sinks back down on the bed slowly.

"Like what?" he asks.

"Making them feel..."

I frown, trying to find the words for it. For the way I felt when he looked at me like I was the only woman in the world, touching me like he knew me better than I know myself.

Yeah. That.

Every bit of that.

"...special. Treasured. That's why they hated you, because they realized after it was over it was all fake." I bite my lip. "A dream. One that made them wish they could never wake up—only you're already gone, leaving them dreaming away all by their lonesome."

Something I can't quite figure out flickers in his eyes.

It's dark, strange, and it might almost be sad.

"Is that how you're feeling now?" he asks softly.

"I don't know." I don't want to hurt him, but I don't like lying, either.

I've had e-damn-nough of that for a lifetime.

"I don't know if you're really here with me," I say.

"Oh, I'm here, honey," he promises, his voice deep and hot. "If you're dreaming, then I'm dreaming right the fuck with you, woman. And I'm not keen on waking up."

The way his words come out kills me.

This rough, heartfelt thing, hitting that much harder when his gritty voice has this sensuous quality that just makes my knees butter.

About as weak as the roughness of his palm gets me.

He presses it to my cheek and strokes down my jaw, holding me captive with those eyes.

I'm back to thinking they must be the devil's again.

He's got me *that* spellbound.

"Truth be told, I've never been like this with any woman in my life. That's not just pretty talk to make you believe me, either. It's...fuck." He makes a low sound in his throat, brows lowering. "Women always wanted me to be dirty. So I was. You're the first woman who wanted something else."

He stops.

Dead *stops*, staring at me like I'm something he's never seen before in his life, something that confuses and enchants him all at once. My heart trips over wild beats.

"You wanted me to be real," he finishes in a whisper. "So I was real for you, Libby."

God, it almost pisses me off, the way I flutter up when he talks like that.

I want to *believe* him, instead of thinking it's just some slick act so I won't put him out on his ass before he's gotten a good night's sleep out of the deal.

But something about what he said bugs me.

I actually hurt *for* him instead of bracing for him to hurt me.

"What about for you?" I ask.

His mouth quirks quizzically. "What do you mean?"

"You were dirty for them and real for me. I mean, you were plenty dirty, too, but you know what I mean." I press my hand to that huge, rough hand against my cheek, turning my head to kiss his palm and inhale his scent.

He smells like hot summer days and the mountains and a hint of raw, wild sex.

"What do you ever do that's for you, Holt?" I ask.

"Tough question." Holt smiles, and there's that completely disarming boyish sweetness coming out again. "A whole lot of what I used to do was tied up in my ego. So even if I was being filthy for those girls, I was also doing it for me. To prove something. That I could make them crave me, make them want me. So in a way, doing what they wanted was all for me. I wasn't some martyr."

"Yeah?" I whisper.

He lingers on me, stroking his thumb against my cheek, tracing just beneath my eye.

"Being real for you, that was all about you. About wanting to make sure that if you were gonna give me a shot, actually be with me..." The more he talks, the more that Heart's Edge drawl comes out, lazy and purring. "That you wouldn't regret shit. Even if we never do this again, I don't want you to regret tonight."

God, I want to believe him.

Hard not to when he touches me like this is his only chance, and he's making sure he remembers it for the rest of his life.

Making sure I remember it, too.

Even if he walks out that door in the morning, I don't think I'll ever forget Holt Silverton.

"And if we do it again?" I ask tentatively.

Uh-oh. This cocky bastard *grins*.

Dark, wicked, a slow smile that tells me exactly what's on his mind.

"If we do it again, I'll show you what dirty *really* means," he rumbles.

Everything inside me quivers. "Like what you did to me already wasn't filthy."

"Honey," he says, "That's just the tip of the iceberg." He leans in close, and I think he's about to kiss me, but instead he brings that dark, dirty voice right up against my ear, making me shiver. "If you'll let me, I can..."

What he says next makes heat, then chills, then fire blast rip through me so roughly my whole body snaps tight. With a gasp, I shove at his chest, my face on goddamn fire.

"Holt Silverton!"

He lets himself be pushed back, smirking wickedly. "There's the small-town girl. What happened to the tiger who clawed my back up?"

I freeze. "Oh—oh, crap. I didn't even realize—are you bleeding?"

The smirk on his face and the light in his eyes makes me want to crawl under the bed from sheer mortification.

I can't believe I lost myself so much that I left *marks* on his back.

Now he's never gonna stop being smug about being that good.

And he sure as hell sounds smug now as he purrs, "Nothing I can't handle."

Nope.

I'm checking out of here before his head gets too big for the room.

I should put something on his back, anyway, since human nails are dirtier than any animal claws.

I gather the sheet up as a makeshift robe and sit up, starting to swing my legs over the side of the bed. "Let me—"

"Libby." He stops me with a hand curled around my wrist, that smug look softening into a warm smile, a lingering gaze. "It's fine. Stay here with me. Talk."

I'm tempted to yank loose and run.

I could. He's not holding me too hard.

That touch isn't a demand. It's a question. A request.

But I think that's why I stay.

Because it's like he knows me that well already.

Try to pin me down, try to push me, and I'll just kick back, shake him off, and fly away.

Ask me, though, give me a choice...

I'll choose to stay.

And I stay now, even if it's giving me the shakes, settling back against the pillows and letting go of my death grip on the sheet.

"O-okay." I don't think I've ever sounded so nervous in my life. "About what?"

"You. Me. Us," he says, still looking at me like he can't see anything else. "And if you want this to mean anything."

I kind of hate him right now.

Just because it was a hell of a lot easier to hate him when he was smarmy in that stupid suit, smirking at me and saying dirty things that curled my toes.

When he's like this, it's not so easy.

His eyes reach down inside me so deep, reminding me how he can make me feel with a single kiss.

I look away, folding my arms over my chest and curling up against the pillows.

"Do you want it to?" I ask.

"Nice deflection." He makes an amused sound. "What if I do?"

"I don't know. I don't know what that means."

"Well, for starters..."

I hear his body moving against the sheets, his skin hissing

261

against fabric, like its roughness is a whisper reminding me how it felt against my flesh.

His warmth presses against my side. One hot, heavy arm drapes around my shoulders.

"For starters, you can try not shutting down and hiding from me," he finishes in a low rumble.

Some stubborn part of me wants to resist. To pull away.

I'm a little tired of being stubborn, though.

Uncurling myself, I tuck in against him, burying my face against his chest so I can be close to him without having to meet his eyes.

"There," he growls, both arms around me now. "You feel damn good, Libby."

"Um, okay," I mutter, but then after a moment, my face burning, I add, "so do you."

He chuckles. "Don't know about you, but I think we got a chance at something real here. I don't know what else to call it...if you want to give it a shot, I'm game."

"I...yeah. I think I could."

It's hard to say, hard to admit, but I'm so tired of fighting everything.

I feel like the whole world's against me, trying to take everything I love.

Right now, Holt's the only one trying to give anything back.

Trying to be here for me.

Trying to cherish me.

"Honestly, it scares me to trust you," I whisper. "It feels like all the people I've ever trusted turned out to be awful."

"Not true," he soothes, stroking his hand down my arm. "Your father wasn't awful. We'll get that cleared up. I bet your mom wasn't awful, either. Sierra, well, she's a mess, but she's got her own pain to deal with. The problem is, she's making it your problem, too."

I smile faintly and shift my head to his shoulder, curling my fingers against the taut, honed strength of his upper arm. "I just barely agreed to let you be my sort-of person. Now you're stepping up to be my therapist?"

"I'm not your shrink, just your listener." He kisses the top of my head, his beard a lovely rasp. "How often does anyone ever listen to you instead of expecting you to take care of shit by yourself?"

That hits harder than I expect.

So hard it's like someone punched me right in the sternum, socking the breath right out of me.

I don't want to cry.

I don't want to, but it's prickling my eyes, and it makes me realize I never really mourned Dad.

Not for real.

Not when his death came with so many other things to deal with, too many responsibilities that couldn't be ignored. Other than that first burst of tears, I've been too busy running.

"Dad used to listen," I whisper. "Before he got sick and just disappeared into himself, he'd...he'd listen to me. We'd talk about everything." I swallow, but it won't make the tightness in my throat go away. "It was us against the world sometimes. Family. We could always lean on each other."

"And," Holt whispers, "you feel like he betrayed you by leaving you alone."

"You're not supposed to *know* that!" I gasp, curling up tighter.

But this time, when I try to retreat into myself, he's right there.

Sheltering me with this quiet strength it's taken me too long to figure out he has.

There's a lot with Holt that's just surface deep.

Not real.

But you scratch past that, underneath?

There's a loyal, kind, powerful man who's a bit of a lunk, sure.

But a lunk who'll hold me while I fall apart and put me back together in one solid piece until I feel like I can hold myself up again.

No denying it.

Not exactly the sexiest pillow talk ever, but here we are.

It's not just Dad I'm mourning.

It's me.

Because I want to be able to lean on Holt, to have something where we trust and hold ourselves up and take care of each other.

But what if I have that with him, what if I want that with him...

...and something just snatches it away from me again?

For now, he stays where he is.

Holding me while I have the ugliest of ugly cries ever, until I can finally breathe again and I'm not just making a mess of myself all over him.

"Sorry," I mumble. "I don't think this is how you imagined tonight ending."

"I wouldn't say that," he answers lightly. "Thought it'd end with you in my arms. It did. And I'm hoping me being here made that easier for you to deal with. If it did, sounds like a win for me."

"I—you—" I scrub at my nose, then scowl up at him. "Quit being so *nice*."

He just grins unapologetically, gold-brown eyes nearly glowing with satisfaction.

"You really want that, honey? Because I can be plenty mean."

"Goddammit, Holt." There's no winning, especially when that wicked grin just makes me want to smile right back.

I compress my lips, trying to hold it in, but it doesn't work.

After a second, I sputter out a tired laugh and thunk my head on his chest.

"I still hate you. A little less, maybe," I tease.

"I know you do, sweetheart. I know." He kisses my hair again. "You want to shoot the shit some more?"

"I don't even know." With a sigh, I let myself go lax against him. "I just wish I knew more. The first time I went down that road and saw that guy's body, suddenly it made sense why Dad always kept us away from Nowhere Lane. But realizing that means he was hiding it all this time...it makes me look at my whole life with him in a different light."

"Should it?"

"How can it not?" I ask. "All this time, knowing he was lying, hiding it from me..."

"Protecting you," Holt adds. "Listen, I don't think the love he gave you growing up was a lie. His love doesn't have to be different just because you know something new about him."

"It'd help if I knew more." I lean my head on Holt's shoulder, letting my eyes drift to the window, a little arcing bay thing that gives me a perfect view of the stars.

I've been tracking the whirl of the constellations through that window for years. It hurts to think that gift Dad gave me is tainted.

"I can't see it," I whisper. "No matter how I turn it over in my head, I just can't see him as this cold-blooded killer."

"We'll find answers, Libby," Holt promises, his hand stroking up my spine, soothing and soft. "And when we do, you'll rest easy again."

I want to believe him.

But right now, there's only the darkness and silence.

Too many unanswered questions between me, Holt, and Dad's secrets.

They're there, haunting us like a ghost I can feel in every floorboard and rafter of this house.

* * *

FALLING asleep next to Holt shouldn't be this nice.

It took me a while to drift off with my brain going in circles, but the nice thing is that Holt knows just how to let a girl *be*.

265

He didn't pry at me, didn't push me.

He just held on and let me tire myself out.

It felt safer, somehow, to do that in his arms.

Knowing he was lying there awake with me, guarding me from my own bad thoughts.

Maybe he was having bad thoughts, too. But at least we were having them together, and I kinda hope being so close helped him the same way he helped me.

Still, it took far too long to fall asleep last night.

I'm a sleepy wreck come morning.

A little too sore to be riding much today. I swear, it's with complete disgust that I crack one eye open and watch him roll out of bed like it ain't nothing.

He's full of energy, moving with this sinuous grace that makes him as impressive as he is gorgeous.

"Oh, *nooo*. Don't tell me," I groan, dragging a pillow over my face against the rising rays of the sun flitting through the window. I can't resist peeking at him, watching how the light flows over his body. "If I'd known you were a morning person, I'd have kicked you out."

"As opposed to fucking?" Holt snorts back a laugh as he steps into his boxers and jeans, hoisting them up around those delicious V-hip crests designed to make a girl insane.

"Why you gotta say it like that?" I snag the other pillow and toss it at him.

He ducks, still laughing, and rakes a hand back through that sin-black hair, smirking at me.

"'Cause that's exactly what happened. We fucked real hard, honey. Your legs wrapped around my waist, and..." He turns his head, glancing at his own shoulder, where a fading red mark digs into his skin in two neat oval-shaped arcs. "Yep. Sure enough, you bit me."

"Oh my *God*." I scrunch down, pulling the covers up over my head. "Get out. Get outta my house, you dick."

Mortified, I'm still laughing.

"Kind of have to. I've got work. We've got a shipment of new equipment coming in today so we can pick up clearing the Paradise Hotel site."

His weight pushes the bed down then, and he catches the covers and drags them down.

Then he kisses me, kneeling over me until all I can see is him and the light and then nothing at all. I close my eyes and sink into it with a soft, hungry sigh.

He makes me feel too good.

Like I'm just liquid in a lady-shaped skin, slowly heating up until I'm ready to boil over with every caress of his mouth, every slow taste he takes of my lips.

He knows how to kiss a girl, all right.

That perfect mix of sweet and naughty that makes me tingle in all the right places.

He uses his tongue in soft suggestion, slipping into me until I'm moaning, going loose, forgetting I even meant to hide from him and kick his stupid, arrogant, sexy ass out of my house.

I'm a lazy mess by the time he lets up, my defenses burnt to a crisp. He pulls away with a self-satisfied smile that says he's got me right where he wants me.

Ass.

But I can't stay too mad when he gives me that smile and tucks my hair back with coarse fingertips.

"Stay in bed a while longer," he says. "You work hard enough. I'll make you breakfast."

"You're just trying to spoil me so I don't put you out."

"Not quite, but the thought might've crossed my mind." His smile fades, though, his eyes darkening, concerned lines criss-crossing his brow. "You going to be okay on your own here today?"

"I'll be fine. Those assholes won't come back. Not in broad daylight."

"Only if you're sure."

I shove my hand into his face, laughing. "Go make my breakfast already."

"Will do," he rumbles, his lips moving against my palm and making those hot sweet tingles slice through me.

Damn him.

Damn him all to hell.

I'm still damning him by the time the smell of hand-griddled blueberry waffles drags me out of bed and downstairs.

He's not a bad cook.

It's nice sharing breakfast, quiet and easy in between a few jabs at each other 'cause we just can't resist.

But it's also different now, not all anger and salt in open wounds.

It's like a kiss with a sting of pain, that sweetness from the nip of hungry teeth against sensitive lips.

I think I kinda like it.

I'm still thrown off guard at how weird it hurts to watch him walk out the door with an arrogant wave over his shoulder.

Even knowing he's coming back tonight.

Even knowing the second he walks in that door...he's going to tumble me onto my back and make me beg for it.

* * *

I⊤'s an antsy day without Holt, but I keep busy.

I've got kids to teach, and if a few of them ask why I'm riding sidesaddle, well, I tell them I just messed up my back a little and this way's easier for now.

They don't need to know my nethers are twinging like I've taken a bad jump on horseback, and they sure as hell don't need to know why.

I get through the lessons, mucking out the stables with the help of the part-time hands I can still afford to pay, then check the sheep's legs to make sure nobody's come up wrong on some gopher holes.

It's good work, satisfying work, despite the heat of the sun making me drip sweat, but the day drags on longer than usual.

I can't deny the wash of heat that rushes through me—not a damn thing to do with the sun—when I see a beat-up old truck heading toward me in a cloud of dust, framed against the setting sun.

Holt gets out battered and covered in construction grime.

Just how I like him.

We don't say a single word, drifting toward each other like we're magnetic.

We barely get a foot inside the house before my clothes are flying off and he's got his hands cupping my ass, lifting me up to straddle his hips.

Holy hell.

He takes me just like that: mounted on him, standing up, those big hands swinging me up and down on his massive length while he wants to break me.

I grab tight to his shoulders and ride hard, pushing him faster, desperate for more when it's so *good* I could scream, losing myself and biting him all over again, leaving love marks up his neck and jaw.

Holt gives it right back, bringing his devil's tongue to my nipples, pulling softly with his teeth and then grazing his stubble up my throat.

I'm. So. Gone.

And I show it with my hips swiveling, the hot whimpers pouring out of me, the way I say his name.

Yep, the man's got me begging again.

If I weren't so far gone, I might be ashamed. But when he drives into me so deep and hard, when he looks at me with *that* glint in his eye?

Shame isn't in the makeup of the desperate, sex-crazed creature I become.

He asked for this storm.

He brings out this manic wildness I didn't know I had.

He makes every part of me clench, burn, and melt into bliss. Oh, God.

I can't even last that long before I forget who or what I am.

For now, I'm just a steaming hot puddle for Holt damn Silverton as he growls *honey, fuck* right in my ear, grinding his pubic bone sweet against my clit.

He brings me off just like that.

It's all frantic rhythm and sharp hissing through my teeth before I blow apart. Then it's just ecstasy, raw and real and overwhelming.

My body convulses like I've been hit with a current.

Coming!

"Holt!" My fingers sink into his shoulders and my hips might break, ratcheting down on his fullness again and again.

He snarls back. His hands crash against my hips, just the right tart *whack! w*ith both hands, and then we're colliding together in a chain reaction that might rival an atom bomb.

His seed pours into me, so hot and deep, it sets me off again.

I can't stop until we're both a spent mess on the sofa, gasping and sweaty and tangled up in a daze before we catch enough air to burst into laughter.

I don't even know what's so funny.

Don't think he does, either.

Maybe it's just having a reason to feel good for once.

HOLT GIVES me more reasons to laugh as the days pass by.

For a while, it's almost like I can forget what's happening to my life, my home, my memories, my family.

It fades in our own secret nights spent defiling each other, tired mornings over breakfast, and now and then when I give in to that urge to see him in the middle of the day.

It's not like I'm falling for him, okay?

I sure as hell ain't his little woman.

But hell, we're sharing space.

He's keeping an eye on me. I can't help but want to make sure he gets a good meal while he's working his britches off day and night. Almost literally.

Not like I'm planning to make it a habit.

So that's why I'm washing up after I finish a morning run with a few of the horses folks send here for me to train, putting them through their paces on a long lead. I'm sweaty and dusty for my troubles.

I'm *not* making myself look cute or any crap like that for him.

That's what I tell myself as I shower off and then brush out my hair.

But maybe my little off-the-shoulder ruffled blouse shows an inch more cleavage than it needs to.

And maybe I'm fine driving out to the Paradise Hotel site in the valley in my little cutoff jeans.

Holt hasn't been the least bit shy hiding his feelings about my legs.

Maybe I'm a bit of a tease.

When I pull up outside the site, though, with a wicker basket piled full of good home cooking, I'm surprised at all the activity going on. Holt's always made his work crew out to be a small thing, but I see a good two dozen men swarming around the crater where that charred-up hotel used to be.

I hardly recognize it now.

They've cleared out the mess and even ripped out the foundation, starting over from scratch. Men climb high on scaffolding as they erect framing, cranes moving big beams into place.

Holt stands on the edge of it all, somehow managing to radiate authority even though he's as dirty and gritty as the rest of them, wearing the same workman's coveralls.

I linger in my truck, watching him.

It's the first time I've ever gotten to look at him without him knowing I'm watching, taking him in on his home turf.

Dear Lord. If we'd met this way first...

I'd have fallen for him a lot sooner.

He's got this way about him.

His body language is calm, confident, strong.

Not arrogant, just plain reassuring. Like you can trust him to have your back.

I'm not sure when I started trusting him to have mine.

But watching him like this makes my heart beat just a little too fast.

It takes me a second to pull myself together and stop acting all fluttery before I grab the basket and slide out of the truck.

As I do, his head comes up, and his eyes lock on mine.

Even over the distance, I *feel* how his gaze warms.

How he rivets me in place like I'm in a spotlight, captured in his eyes.

I'm not gonna blush, dammit.

I'm not.

It's this dumb summer heat, that's all, swarming around me as I tread over the dusty ground.

Holt's with a big, older guy, the kind of thick-bearded, long-haired behemoth that makes you think of Viking warlords, though his hair's black.

Never caught a name other than "Alaska," though I know he moved here around the same time as Holt and it seems like they're friends.

He offers me a friendly smile now, completely at odds with the smoldering way Holt's eyes dip over me, lingering on the low neckline of my blouse and trailing down to my legs.

"Afternoon, Miss Potter," Alaska says. He's got one deep old voice all right, and this slow, kind way of speaking. Almost fatherly. "Not expecting to see you on-site today."

He elbows Holt then, and Holt blinks, clearing his throat and tugging at the neck of his coveralls before offering a grin. "Hey, Libby."

"Hey yourself," I answer, holding up the basket. "Lunch. 'Cause for all I know, you're greasing up at Brody's every day."

That grin turns sheepish. "Shit, you're psychic?"

"Nope. I know men, and I know you. You're hopeless." I dip my head to Alaska. "Present company excluded. You seem like a decent sort. Better than your boss, anyway."

"I'm plenty decent." Holt laughs, but he's still looking at me, mischief dancing in those whiskey eyes that won't stop drowning me in heat.

"You don't even know the word," I retort, while Alaska grins.

"So now I know why you keep showing up with your coveralls zipped up to the neck." He hooks a finger in the high collar of Holt's coveralls and tugs it down, revealing a line of marks I left behind. "Looks like you two had fun duking it out, huh?"

"Goddammit, Alaska!" Holt swipes his hand away.

I clear my throat and studiously avoid the giant's eyes.

Look, I ain't ashamed that I get a little rowdy in bed.

But I don't wanna have a *conversation* about it with a man I just met.

Holt makes a half-annoyed, half-resigned sound and steps closer, his hand curling against my arm as he nudges me a few steps away.

"Don't mind him," he says. "He means well. He just spent so much time around fucking polar bears and arctic wolves up in Alaska that he never socialized like a human being."

"I heard that," Alaska grunts.

"You were supposed to," Holt tosses over his shoulder before turning his smile on me again. "So what's for lunch?"

"Chicken salad and fresh-baked bread with homemade cheese." I pull the cloth back over the basket to reveal the saran-wrapped containers inside. "Nothing fancy, but I figured it'd keep until you have time to stop."

Holt lights up like a little boy as he leans in to peek. "You baked me bread?"

"Um, yeah. And the cheese has been curing for a while. Horses aren't all I do, *honey.*"

He grins at the pet name I throw back at him.

"A woman of many talents." He whistles softly, then nudges my arm. "Stay and eat with me?"

I blink. "Sure, but do you have time for that? Y'all seem pretty busy."

"We are, but it's about time to call it anyway. Don't want anyone having a stroke in this heat." He leans away from me and slips two fingers between his teeth, then lets out a piercing whistle before raising his voice.

"Lunch break, boys!" he calls, his clear, strong voice ringing over the site with a warm authority that just makes him seem like a different person. "We'll pick up in an hour and a half."

The atmosphere instantly changes—from the ordered, methodical movements of men at work to a flurry of casual activity.

People shut down machinery and stow tools, moving in friendly clusters to get their lunch kits. A few pile into their cars, probably heading into town to Brody's, no better than Holt himself.

Eh, not my problem.

I'm only here for one man.

And he gives me an easygoing smile, tossing his head toward my truck.

"C'mon. Sit and have a bite with me." His eyes sparkle. "I'll grab us drinks from the cooler."

A minute later, I'm sitting on the tailgate of my truck, snuggled against Holt's side and nibbling on little slices of sharp orange cheddar while he swigs from a condensation-dripping bottle of lemonade.

The sun's bright, the sky's clear, and Holt feels too good.

Especially when he's flattering me over the bread.

It's nothing special, but maybe it is to him because I made it for him. Or maybe that's just my wishful thinking.

We're quiet as I lean my head against his shoulder, sharing the basket.

I wonder...am I seeing what I want to see with Holt?

Am I so desperate for some stability and hope in my life that I'm seeing him as someone he's not?

Am I already praying after we've gone back to normal, maybe he'll want to stick around for more than a few hot nights?

XVI: FOUR HORSEMEN (HOLT)

*I*t's more than a little intimidating walking in through the back of Ms. Wilma's kitchen and coming face-to-face with all four of our hometown heroes.

It's late on Friday, long after the old woman's gone to bed. A plate of dangerous smelling oatmeal cookies she's left out casts a strange contrast with four huge guys who've got their war faces on.

Sure, I'm used to them individually, but like this?

Goddamn.

I'm lucky that the last time they were saving Heart's Edge, they were only up my ass as a suspect for a little bit.

"I'm thinking Blake already gave you boys the rundown?" I say, sliding into a seat next to Leo, an overgrown beast who looks like he could pick up Alaska with one hand.

"We wanted to hear it from you," Warren tells me, taking a loud chomp off a cookie. "Haven't seen hide nor hair of this Declan fuck or any of his buddies. Hay told me he checked out of his room the other day with Sierra, and nothing since."

Fuck. I don't like it.

Doc Caldwell notices the way I stiffen, clearing his throat, those emerald eyes of his as sharp as jade knives behind his glasses. He shoves them up his nose in this way he has.

"We're wasting precious time," he whispers. "Every day that slips by with this man missing could mean he's bringing reinforcements. You said he had a full crew the night they paid Miss Potter that unsavory visit?"

"About a dozen men. All dudes he probably charmed into service if the stories I dug up online are true." I scratch my chin, blood going hot because there's zero doubt about what I read.

This asshole's repeatedly proven he's dangerous. It's just a question of how long his fuse is before he blows up again and hurts Libby, hurts Sierra, hurts the town.

"What about the tax problem? The bank?" Leo rumbles, taking an earth-splitting bite out of *two* cookies pinched between his thick fingers.

Warren gives him the stink eye. "Easy. Grandma's trying to sleep, and so are my wife and kids next door. Bet folks can hear your shit across town when you're eating like a bear."

I resist the urge to play peacemaker in a damn cookie feud between two guys I wouldn't want to take on any day.

"We're working the protected land angle to stall things out. I've got the papers drawn up, just as soon as we have some supporting documentation for the city council and the governor's office," I say. "Trouble is—"

"The dead dude. I filled them in, bro," Blake says, flashing me a not-so-helpful wink across the table. "Your bigger problem's dredging up enough proof to get the request taken seriously, like you said. Let me ride out there. Take a look around. A fresh set of eyes could turn up something."

"I don't like it," Leo growls, flexing with his arms crossed. That mess of ink and scars stamped on his skin forms fierce dark whorls like storm clouds. "While you're digging around in this ghost town playing detective, the trucker and his men could hit us anytime. Catch us with our damn pants down. We need defense so you've got time."

"You're certain you don't want us on guard duty, Holt?" Doc asks, ninja swiping a cookie off the still-warm pile and taking a civilized bite compared to the others.

"Libby wouldn't have it, and neither would I. You guys have been through the grinder more times than anyone can count. I'm not pulling you away from your women and kids to watch over a pile of bones and some dusty buildings."

"Better there than on our doorstep," Leo says. Those strange violet-amethyst eyes of his glitter in the dim light. And people think *my* eyes are weird. "We sit around waiting forever, he's bound to go after something or somebody in town. Hit hard and create a ruse before he comes for Ursa."

Fuck.

My jaw tightens, my brain sifting through the many ugly possibilities he's conjured up.

"He's right. We've made the same mistake too many times, sitting back and manning our fort." Warren strokes his chin, looking past me, out the window at the sleepy, idyllic night grounds of Charming Inn. "We need to flush his ass out."

"Can't be that easy, War," Blake chimes in. "Holt said this guy's crafty. If he's really that sly, he'll see it coming from a mile away."

"No, wait," I say. "There's one way we can do that, and one way only—Sierra Potter."

Four heads swivel toward me, eyes tense in the moonlight, slowly blinking.

"You really think she'd flip on him?" Blake asks weakly. "From what you said, the poor girl's smitten with this clown. She'd—"

"She'd be sorry if she fucked her sister over," I say, sitting up straight in my seat. "She may be confused, reckless, desperate, and misled. But mean-spirited isn't the vibe I got from Sierra. She doesn't want to hurt Libby, not really."

"It's not crazy." Doc nods firmly, his keen mind in overdrive. He senses it too. "She's been lied to, not unlike the rest of this grifter's little army. I only fear she won't have a chance to figure it out, much less escape."

My blood goes cold. It's a real possibility, even if by some miracle Sierra figured out her boyfriend's a dumpster fire and walked out on him tomorrow.

"We won't let that happen," I say, without a clue how I mean to make good on that promise. "I'll find her, have Libby talk some sense, and get her to give up that fuck's location."

Doc leans back in his chair, sneaking another cookie under the table.

"We'll keep our ears open and draft a few more, then," Leo says, looking at me and his friends, one at a time. "The girls hear and see all sorts of traffic, seeing how busy they are. We're lucky men. We need our wives for this shit. Help them help us find Sierra, and then we can turn her over to you and her sis. I know how the bond with sisters goes, no matter what comes between them. It's freaky shit, too strong for any asshole to sever."

Heads nod all around. I bite back a grin.

It's honestly a bit touching to see these bruisers looking all starry-eyed when they talk about their women. I'm also humbled at them bringing in Haley, Ember, Clarissa, and Peace. Their girls are as sharp and battle-tested as they are beautiful.

The fact that they wound up with these guys at all means they did their fair share of suffering, too.

"I'm grateful," I tell them, trying to keep it short and sweet. "Not just because you're all doing your thing keeping Heart's Edge safe. Again. When I first came back here, I didn't have a friend in the world with the arson thing and all...now, I'm just happy somebody's got my back. I won't let you down."

A big hand slaps my back. I look over to see Blake grinning like the big dumb weirdo he is.

"No need to get these guys all teary, man. We'll figure this out. You just keep Libs and her horses safe."

We break up then, and I clasp four powerful, sincere hands as everybody clears out. Can't resist stealing a couple cookies myself for the road.

Blake trails me to my truck, keeping pace better than he could months ago, that trademark limp of his down to a barely-there cowboy swagger.

The crickets are loud tonight, our background track for every word.

"I still feel like an asshole for burdening everybody like this," I tell him, leaning against my tailgate. "If it weren't for the body, I'd go to Langley and the Feds, but...damned if you do, damned if you don't barely cuts it here."

"Hmm. Can't decide whether or not I like this," Blake says, sweeping his coppery brown hair back.

"What?"

"You having a conscience and all. Seems like now that you've got one, you don't know where to point it, bro." He grins his usual insufferable shit-smile.

"Yeah? That more of your sage radio wisdom when you're not taking on callers who want to talk about alien butt probes?"

He chuckles. At least he's used to me giving him crap about his ridiculous Coast to Coast AM meets love doctor radio show.

"That's me helping you pull your head out of your ass, Holt. I told you what you need to worry about," he says.

I fold my arms, quirking an eyebrow, waiting for him to enlighten me.

"Libby, Libby, and also Libby. You know your shit, man. You've been through active service and busted a few heads like everybody else. Protecting her from bodily harm ain't the hard part." He pauses, glancing up at the stars. "You've gotta do her heart right, too. If it were me, I wouldn't be wasting another second here while she's in bed waiting. So go tuck her in. Take her on a real date, too."

I start to open my mouth and fling something back, but it's in his smile. He's being serious.

It's like he's speaking from experience with Peace, and I can actually believe him.

I just nod, mutter another thanks and goodnight, giving my brother a parting handshake.

They say good help's hard to find, and maybe it's true.

Here in Heart's Edge, it's closer than I ever thought, and only a royal pain in the ass about *half* the time.

XVII: DARK HORSE (LIBBY)

*B*y the time the weekend rolls around, I'm almost ready to chase his ass away.

Listen.

Otherworldly gravity defying monkey-sex every night is cool.

But you try functioning like a normal human being less than eight hours after you've been cored out like a freaking apple, left sore and sated and not remembering how to curse the man who did it?

Yeah.

It's a little much.

It's even more disgusting when, come Saturday morning, he's bouncing out of bed with that same endless energy while I'm just dead in the covers.

Well, he can run the farm today.

I'm sleeping in.

"What do you want for breakfast?" he asks, nudging my side and leaning over to gently bite the back of my shoulder.

"Solitude," I mumble, reaching back to swat him. "Are you an incubus or what? Where do you get the *energy?*"

"You. So maybe I am." Snickering, his beard scrapes against

my oversensitive skin, he nips down over my shoulder, toward my shoulder blade, while I push my face into a pillow. "You make me happy, Libby. Guess that gives me all the pep I need."

I push myself up on my elbows and give Holt a disgusted look through the mess of hair falling in my face. "It's way too early in the morning for sweet talk."

"Not sweet talk. Truth." He brushes my hair aside, tracing his lips over mine gently. "Get some more shut-eye. I'll cook and then start on what needs doin'."

"You're gonna work? On my ranch?" I arch a skeptical brow.

"Why not? The crew's out for the weekend, the site's packed away, and I'm not looking to sit in the house and do nothing while you slave your butt off." Holt steals another kiss and nearly gets bitten for his trouble when I snap my teeth at him, making him laugh. "No fussing, lady. If I help, you can finish early, and then maybe we can go on another date."

That sparks my interest. "Where?"

"Anywhere you want." He raises his brows. "Is the old drive-in still open?"

"Only sometimes. But we can see if they're showing anything tonight." I sit up, yawning and stretching, enjoying the way his eyes fall over my naked body.

He's gonna make a girl vain at this rate.

Can't really complain.

But I fish around until I find the shirt I ripped off of him last night, stealing it to wrap myself up, the warm flannel saturated in his scent. Swinging my legs over the side of the bed, I flick his arm as I stand—and bite back a wince as my thighs protest.

Nope, I won't give him the satisfaction.

"I'm up now," I say. "I'll help you with breakfast, then we can let the sheep out."

Seems like I'm in for an easy day.

Or so I think.

I swear to God, if I didn't know it, I wouldn't believe Holt grew up in Heart's Edge.

283

I've never seen a clumsier man on a ranch in my life.

All that confidence I'd seen at the construction site?

Gone.

He's hopeless. Dropping stuff, tripping over everything, almost ending up ass-first in the ditch again. It's cute as hell but also slows me down.

I give up around the time he manages to spook the sheep into nearly breaking out of their pen.

You'd think sheep couldn't stampede.

You'd be wrong.

I don't even know how he did it.

Next thing I know, Plath's pitched him off and gone charging off on her lonesome to cut the sheep off, tossing her mane with something almost like annoyance.

A good horse is as awesome as a sheepdog, if you train her right.

Turns out, horses train way easier than men.

I leave Holt rolling in the dirt for a few while I kick my heels and send Frost charging forward with a challenging snort. He moves at an angle to Plath so we can stop the sheep from ramming the fence. It's all upset *baa*-ing and stomping and clouds of dust.

Total chaos.

But after a few wild minutes, I get them under control and settled back in their pen.

Plath's a little harder to contain.

She's a bit like me.

Feisty as hell, and once her blood's up, she's ready to go hoof to hoof with just about anyone.

Thank God for Frost.

She's got this thing with him where she just can't bring herself to lash out at her buddy—and when he trots me over to her and lays his head across her neck, she stops her snorting.

I swing down out of the saddle, looping my arms around both their necks and stroking their manes; their big heads hang heavy against my shoulders, hot horseflesh against my skin.

"There we go, guys," I soothe. "Everything's okay."

Holt comes loping up, chagrin written all over his face as clearly as the dirt streaked all over him.

"Sorry," he says. "Don't know what happened. It's like the sheep just hate me."

"Animals can sense pure evil," I say dryly, and he belts out a laugh while I snort. "Look, you obviously can't be trusted not to destroy this place if I let you do anything hard. Why don't you put Plath away, give her a good rubdown and a carrot or two, and then muck out the stalls?"

He blanches. "I fucked up so bad you're putting me on horse-shit duty?"

I smirk, nodding. "Yep. That bad. It ain't glamorous, but at least it's hard to screw up."

"Fuck, fine," he growls out an exaggerated sigh and hooks an arm around my waist, pulling me in close with an easy strength that makes my stomach flip. Leaning down, he buries his face in my hair, breathing in deep. "Just let me get a smell of you first for the road."

Tangling my fingers in his grubby shirt, I choke on a laugh. "Aww, c'mere."

I don't need to ask him twice.

My lips hit his and we go hard.

He kisses me rough, makes me forget everything but the feel of Holt Silverton completely taking me over in shivers and gasps. I'm nearly rubbing my body against his in rhythm with the deep, teasing stroke of his tongue.

There's a sweet friction to it, slick and velvety as our tongues duel.

I feel every caress, warming me up so hot I know I'll be feeling him for hours.

God, I'm letting him in too deep.

I know it.

I just can't seem to help myself.

Finally, I break for air, shoving at his chest.

"Go," I say. "Get gone."

"Getting gone," he says, saluting me with that unrepentant grin. It's made all the worse by the fact that his mouth is so red.

I watch him storm away on those long, muscular legs, looking like walking sin.

Yep, I *hate* that man.

...if only because I love how he makes me feel.

It just ain't fair.

* * *

THERE'S a lot that goes into running a ranch, and with Frost for company, I head out to mend a few fences that've been left neglected for far too long.

Don't even go there with the Sierra metaphors.

It's twilight by the time I'm done.

When it's over, I'm sweaty, scraped up, sore, and working out a few splinters.

Still picking them out, I mount up and head back to the barn. I'm so in tune with Frost's gait that I can ride without even holding the reins, busily focused on tugging little bits of wood out from under the skin of my fingertips.

I find out real quick that's a mistake.

When as I draw up to the barn, I catch a hint of motion.

Holt, standing there outside the barn with the hose held over his head, water pouring down him in glittering sheets.

Crap city.

He's shucked his outer shirt, leaving one of those ridiculously tight undershirts and his jeans, both of them soaked to his skin until he might as well be naked.

The fabric clings, outlining every chisel of his abs, every hard edge of his pecs, every ripple and bulge of the gorgeously toned muscles in his thighs. His bare arms glisten, the water running into the sharp-cut channels between stark ridges of biceps and forearms.

He sloughs off dirt from the barn like he's *trying* to tease me to death.

It's like one of those pinup calendars with half-naked cowboys come to life.

And I'm so busy watching I don't even realize I'm squeezing my hot, aching thighs against Frost's flanks so hard the horse jolts forward.

I'm not sure if the lurch in my gut is vertigo or a sudden flare of twisted desire.

He doesn't even see me yet.

Doesn't realize I'm watching this lion of a man with a ruthless hunger building up inside me.

But I can't hold back.

I'm swinging down before I realize it, looping Frost's reins around the closest post and striding across the space between us like I'm being pulled on a tether.

He lowers the hose, bowing his head down just as I close in.

There's a second where his head tilts.

His eyes widen.

His lips part.

He's about to say my name.

I don't give him half a chance.

My hands move, grabbing wet handfuls of his shirt. Steaming with his body heat, we go down *hard*.

I don't know if I'm kissing him or it's a freaking attack.

All I know is, I'm gonna die if he doesn't touch me right the hell now.

It's like striking a match to a lake of gasoline.

First one spark, and then everything bursts into flame.

Next thing I know, we're stumbling back toward one of the empty stalls, first me pushing him and then him pushing me, fighting for it—and my back slams hard against the wall.

Yes!

Be rough with me.

Make me feel it, make me fight for it, make me scream for every second.

He reads my mind.

His hands rake every bit of me, dragging at my clothes, and I'm ripping at him, too.

We race to unwrap each other.

God, he feels good when he's steaming wet and sultry to the touch underneath that slick water, hard muscle glistening and burning against my palms.

"Fucking hell, Libby," he gasps out, his fingers digging hard into my ass, lifting me up against him until I wrap my legs around his waist.

He's the only thing holding me up, my body grinding tight against his.

I love how his weight shadows mine, my breasts dragging against his chest, my nipples puckered.

I also love his hardness against my stomach, already so stiff it gives me a thrill to know he gets like this for *me*.

And I definitely love the challenge in his eyes as he lifts me higher, dragging my panties down, ripping them off, burying his face in my neck.

It's almost a game.

How long can I torment him before he has to be inside me?

Today it's a game with one round.

The second my bare flesh presses against the denim of his jeans, hot friction making me scream like a cat in heat, dragging against me and getting me so, so wet...he curses, biting at my neck, tearing his jeans open, freeing his cock.

The head presses against me—right *there*—his thickness making me squirm.

Oh, baby, I *do*, twisting my hips, trying to take him inside me.

But he's got me tight, keeping me on the edge, and I scream, cursing and shoving and biting his shoulder.

"Holt!" I hiss, and he chuckles against my throat, licking the stinging bite mark.

"Let me have my little pleasures, sweetheart," he whispers, voice like booming thunder.

Then he catches up a handful of my hair, pulling my head back gently—but still hard enough to make me thrill, hot and burning and begging.

My scalp prickles and my whole body ignites with a ripple of wild heat.

He's got me pinned against the wall.

I stare up at him, smoldering with need, with something that feels like hate, but I know it isn't even close.

A second later, he crushes his mouth down on mine.

Make no mistake: this is a kiss that *claims*.

Probably for life.

His rock-hard cock pushes into me, piercing me and filling me in a single smooth stroke.

He gives up everything I've been demanding, everything I crave.

It's quick. It's hot. It's rough.

I don't care what it is as long as it puts out the fire burning me alive.

I'm greedy, shameless, and every time he slams into me, I'm ready to *kill him* when he pulls back out. It leaves me feeling so alone, so empty, dying for his fullness inside me, slamming deep and touching this spot somewhere that makes me lose my ever-loving mind.

Leave it to Holt to discover parts of me I didn't know existed.

The best part isn't even the scalding feel of him fucking me against the wall.

When I'm like this, I get to stop thinking.

I just *feel*.

Feel him rocking me from head to toe in hard-pisting rhythm.

Feel him grasping my hair, fisting it like he can't even stand to let go, and he's hellbent on leaving his marks.

Feel how hot his entire body gets, this forged steel thing burning me alive everywhere we touch, inside and out.

Feel my heart beating fit to break with every savage swipe of his tongue and the graze of punishing teeth.

I need this.

I need it so bad.

I'm just scared of him finding out how much I need *him*.

But I can't hide it in how I hold on tight, in how I kiss him back just as viciously, or how I gasp out his name as he takes me deeper, *deeper*, throwing me over the ledge and into white-hot bliss again and again.

I'll never know how many times I come. One O blurs into the next.

This is what shattering means.

Falling apart.

Falling for Holt.

Falling in love.

Yeah, it scares me, but it's the nicest fear ever—and it turns my senses up, makes everything hotter and more intense.

More irresistible.

That overwhelming moment comes when he drags me down on his length, roots in me so deep it's like I can feel him in my belly, joining us so tight we'll never be apart.

I come again instantly, and so does he.

It's terrifying, honestly, losing every last shred of self-control.

Pleasure drives me out of myself, rolling through my body like an earthquake until I scream so loud it spooks the horses.

Holt roars, pouring himself inside me, pumping so deep and so hard it claws at his soul.

My nails go to work again, ravaging his back until I can't take how good it feels, until I just dissolve.

Like I said.

Terrifying.

...but God if I don't want it again and again and again.

I scare myself a little more coming up from the frenzy, thinking what this means.

An uneasy truce isn't enough anymore. Not with a man who pushes every last button in my manual.

I want to keep Holt Silverton messing me up for a long time.

* * *

I'M KINDA glad I got everything out of my system earlier.

Makes it easier for me to be calm, snuggled up against Holt on the hood of his truck at the drive-in theater. The stars blaze bright overhead while an old Greta Garbo flick plays on the ginormous screen in black-and-white.

It's a loosely held summer tradition for Heart's Edge.

The town doesn't do this every weekend, not when it's spendy to run the big projector, and there's something about movie licensing in the mix.

Nobody really cares what's playing.

It's about the atmosphere here, being together like this.

All of us just silhouettes, faceless, but part of the town, held together in this silent communion.

I haven't been in a long time.

Not since I was little and used to come here with my parents and Sierra. We'd spend half the time watching the movies and the other half looking up and counting stars.

It's almost bittersweet to be back here now, remembering happier times with a sister who wasn't threatening my whole life.

I'm a little surprised, though, to see Reid Cherish here.

His Jeep's parked a little ways off from dozens of vehicles.

For once he's not done up in his suit, though he looks like he just came from work. No suit coat, his button-down shirt loose at the collar, tie off, sleeves rolled up.

Hell, his hair's even mussed up, a bit of it falling in his face.

His gaze is locked on the screen, but it's like he doesn't quite see it from the way he's glazed over.

Like he's seeing something else, and he's got this weird, melancholy look on his face.

I don't want to feel sorry for him.

I don't want to see that banker man as human.

But I know that look he's wearing too well.

It's twin to the feeling inside me, remembering how once I had a family to share nights like this, and now I've got nothing.

I tear my eyes away from Cherish and bury my face in Holt's side.

No, not nothing, I think.

I've still got my ranch. I've got my dignity. I've got Frost and Plath.

And I've got Holt for however long this lasts.

Why the hell am I worried about Sierra or Cherish right now when they're the people trying to take everything away?

At least Cherish is here. I shouldn't be thinking about Sierra, but I can't help it.

Not when I can still hear her girlish giggles and remember how she'd hug me like a real sister then.

Dad would let me pick out the stars on my own, but when I said them wrong, sometimes Sierra would patiently repeat them, one syllable at a time, until I said it right.

Ugh.

Part of me actually misses that annoying backstabber. Misses her being my sister and not my sworn enemy.

She's vanished. Totally off anyone's radar.

I haven't seen her or Declan anywhere. Not even that big old truck of his that's hard to miss.

No one's tried to come sniffing around Nowhere Lane or the ghost town, either. I've ridden out every day, and found no new tracks. Ditto for Holt and Alaska going on patrol.

Holt told me about his meeting with the guys, how they said

they'd keep their eyes and ears open. He also mentioned Declan and Sierra checking out of Charming Inn.

That should be good news.

Maybe they realized the jig was up, got smart, and left town.

That'd be a huge weight off my shoulders.

One less evil to contend with while I try to get everything sorted with the ranch. Maybe, just *maybe*, after things are secure, I can work out the will. Maybe I can pay Sierra something so she can get her life back on track without needing these shit-awful men.

Something's still eating at me, though.

And I guess I'm ruining the night because Holt squeezes his hand against my shoulder, gathering me closer.

"You're tense," he whispers. "Something on your mind?"

"Just bad memories," I say, practically crawling into his lap. "Sorry. I don't mean to screw up our date."

"Nothing's screwed up as long as I get to be with you." He makes an amused sound, nuzzling my hair. "You want to talk about it?"

"Nah. It wouldn't help tonight." I tilt my head back against his shoulder, looking up at the sky. "Just hold me, Holt. Let me watch the stars."

* * *

FOR THE FIRST time in a few nights, Holt and I head home and sleep like the dead.

It's nicer than I want to admit.

The safety and security that comes with being able to slip into a man's arms and know he's not there for anything but my company, my warmth.

There's this thing I've started realizing about manipulative people.

They can also be really empathetic.

It takes empathy to realize what people want, but what

NICOLE SNOW

matters is how you act on it. Some people use it to jerk others around. They're sensitive to what you want, sure, but they only care as far as it takes to get what *they* want out of you.

Then there are people who use it the right way.

Guess which one I thought Holt was.

Now guess which one he *really* is.

It's still strange, looking at him with new eyes, but I like what I see.

I think he'd listen to just about anything I told him, too, and I'm not used to having that anymore.

So I'm quiet as I slip into bed with him and we turn out the lights. He gathers me up like he's gonna use that tall, strong body to wall off all the things messing with me.

In that silence, where the only thing I can hear are his slow, soothing breaths, I let it out.

"Y'know...I miss having a family," I whisper.

Holt stirs slightly, then tightens his grip, his hands firm and sure.

"Nothing wrong with missing that," he says.

I smile.

Then that wicked insight that makes me want to kiss and slug him simultaneously comes out. "Nothing wrong with missing Sierra, either. Even if you're missing the sis you wanted and not the sis you got."

"How, Holt?" I squeeze my eyes shut, looping my arms hard around his neck.

"Come again?"

"You just take all these jumbled up things inside me and sort them out with a few little words," I tell him. "How do you see so much?"

"Because we're not so different, honey." He sighs heavily, but it's not a sad thing. More thoughtful. "I never got the family I wanted. Blake, yeah. He's all the good things you could ever want in a brother, and I'm glad we're making up and figuring out our shit. But I never knew who my father was, and my ma was...not who she should've been. Not right in the head, pitting her boys against each other for favorites. So I miss the family I never had."

I murmur softly.

He dips his head, rubbing his jaw gently to my hair, his beard scratching lightly. "Doesn't mean I can't make that family one day, once I'm settled down."

That thought cuts deep.

Not just the idea that one day, I could *make* the family I've craved too...

...but that maybe me and Holt want that same thing, deep down in our feeliest of feels.

I don't wanna be that girl.

Miss Reads Too Much Into It.

Thinking that because he's willing to tell me what he wants, he might just want that with *me*.

If I were in my right mind, being my mouthy, brazen self, I'd just ask him what he means.

But I don't want to ruin this tonight.

I need him close right now.

So I don't say anything at all.

I just cling hard enough that he's almost got no choice but to hold me until morning.

While I slip away into sweet dreams, hoping everything looks better with the dawn.

* * *

I CAN'T SAY things look better, but they're not looking worse.

It's an easy, warm morning with Holt again. Another day where he doesn't have to go back on-site with it being Sunday, but I've still got work around the ranch.

Animals don't take days off.

Of course the lunk insists on helping again.

We work quietly in a tandem I really enjoy, hauling hay bales and feed troughs and letting the sheep out to graze. Before long we're mounting up to ride the property, checking the fences yet again and watching for gopher holes and fox burrows.

Nature doesn't respect fences. We can at least negotiate a truce where we can.

We head out to Ursa, too.

Those old tire tracks are still there, damning evidence that someone's been snooping around, but there aren't any new ones.

Maybe Declan and Sierra really did realize they were in over their heads and just got the hell out of Dodge.

Even if I got a lucky break, that leaves the bank and Dad's legacy to worry over.

I make myself dismount and head for the saloon.

Gerald Bostrom hasn't moved, no surprise.

Even the skeletal hand resting on the bar, outlined in years of accumulated dust, remains totally undisturbed.

I focus on the skull, that empty, hollow face.

If I just stare long enough, could I see what kind of man he was?

If he had a story to tell?

If he was innocent?

Or was he so bad, right down to his rotting bones, that Dad had to kill him? Had to leave him here decaying, a sight so awful the scavengers won't touch him?

There's not even a coyote tooth-scratch on his bones.

I press my hand to my mouth.

Is this what I'm doing now? Convincing myself he was a bad man because I can't believe my father was?

"Libby," Holt says, and I just about leap out of my skin.

He comes up behind me, resting a hand on my shoulder, moving in his silent prowling way that spooks me sometimes.

"Could you knock or something?"

"C'mon, Libby," he says softly. "Nothing for you here. You're just going to make yourself crazy."

"There's got to be *something*," I whisper, glancing around the saloon, the old wood turned yellow in the afternoon light. "Dad said find the gun. So where is it? There's all that crap behind the bar, but I'm scared to start digging. It's...it's like some kind of shrine. A Schrödinger's box, maybe. As long as I don't disturb anything, I don't have to know, one way or the other."

Holt walks behind the bar to the mess I've seen there before. Several huge boards, tangled up in a heap of other nameless objects coated in dust. Crates, maybe?

If the gun's in that mess of stuff, I'll never find it. Nobody will without leaving evidence someone was here recently.

He gives the biggest board his best push, but even a big, strong man like him can't move it more than an inch or two. I watch him fling off his jacket and roll up his sleeves, gritting his teeth, like he's ready to throw real muscle into it, but I see the dust he's kicking up.

"Holt, no. Don't do it. You'll leave footprints. We can't have anybody knowing we were here..." A breath sticks in my lungs.

After a second, he shrugs, then steps back around it to my side, carrying his jacket and dusting himself off.

"Let's get out of here," he says, tugging gently at my arm.

I follow him quietly with one last look back at the dead man.

Gerald gives up nothing as usual.

Nothing but more questions and a formless sense of dread.

I don't wanna be scared like this.

One fine day, I'll have to face down what happened here, and the fact that Dad's part of it.

For now, I mount up on Frost, and together we head back, riding side by side down the trail through the mountain cut with our knees bumping, Frost and Plath so close their tails practically melt into each other as they lash away flies.

When we get to the mouth of the cut, Holt surprises me by veering off along the cliffs.

I frown, tugging lightly on Frost's reins and turning him to follow.

"Holt? Where are you going?"

"Just c'mon," he says with that devilish grin.

I sigh, rolling my eyes.

I'll probably regret this later, but for now I'll *c'mon*.

If only 'cause I'm curious as hell.

We ride slowly along the edge of the tall cliffs and mountain slopes that give Heart's Edge its name, but I don't realize where we're going until the Charming Inn is a distant silhouette high at the top of one bluff.

Below it all, the massive meadow of summer flowers blends into the trees covering several hills nearby.

Every summer, the meadow below the half-heart cliff behind the inn blooms like an artist's wet dream.

We're talking wild colors everywhere, a carpet of pink and blue against verdant green.

All kinds of flowers, lavender and peonies and even violets, crowd their heads up against each other.

I haven't been out here in forever.

Haven't thought about the local legend—a story I'm sure changed a hundred times in the telling.

It's about a farm boy in love with a mayor's daughter, and the mayor wouldn't let them be together—so they jumped over the cliff and became some kind of spirits.

They blew away to live together in the mountains, forever watching over the town and answering the wishes of new lovers who toss flower offerings over the cliff and swear their love.

My practical side always wonders if they killed themselves like Romeo and Juliet.

Maybe folks romanticized the story over time until it was forgotten and no one ever thought it might be real. Just a fairy tale.

Then there's my hopeful, sappy romantic side.

I like to imagine them flying over the cliff is just a metaphor for skipping town together.

Flying the nest and being free to love each other, wherever they wound up.

"Woman," Holt says, "you've got the dreamiest damn look on your face right now. What's up?"

I laugh, glancing over at him.

He's almost out of place in this bright noonday sun when he's all night colors. Mostly, this dark leather jacket that's thin enough for summer, but leaves him looking perfectly imposing.

He's dressed for prowling around in the shadows. Not sitting on my mare under a high, bright-blue sky.

At least he's easy on the eyes.

Who am I kidding?

He's divine. I can't stop drinking in that chiseled face, those wild amber-brown eyes, the way he makes everything look easy with his endless, casual, calm strength.

Holy flipping potatoes.

I might be falling a little bit in love with Holt Silverton.

I wanted to tell myself it was lust.

Just me getting myself all wired up over a pretty face and mistaking that enchantment for love, but now?

I don't think that's all it is by a long shot.

Because it's not just his face making my heart thump so hard.

It's the gentle, curious, *knowing* way he's looking at me.

It's the fact that he brought me out here. He knew I needed something sweet to take my mind off all the bitterness.

"Libby?" he calls me again.

I smile. "You know what's up. You brought me out here so I'd get all starry-eyed over the flowers."

He grins. He's sitting in the saddle with his hips slouched forward and his thighs spread in a way that just punches my gut.

"Worked, didn't it?" He looks away, his gaze drifting across the field. "I don't know how many times I've stood on that cliff and thrown flowers over it with some chick."

"You...what?" My breath stalls, nervous anger licking my ears. "So that's why you brought me out here? To see the legacy of all your broken hearts?"

"Nah. But you took the bait, hook, line, and sinker." He

smiles that shit-eating grin. "I never did anything here. This place is serious, too sacred for games. I just wanted to see it for myself." He turns his head back to me. "I'm not coming back here again until I mean it one day."

Oh, now that ain't *fair*.

It ain't fair that he's looking at me like he's thinking all those things that've been running through my head since last night.

It ain't fair that with one hot look, he gets me all flustered, my breaths tight and my face burning.

It definitely ain't fair that I want him to come here and throw flowers over the edge with *me*.

I tear my gaze away with a snort. "I think I'll only come back here when I'm ready to throw you over the cliff."

He bursts out laughing. "Don't think the legend said anything about human sacrifice."

"Maybe I'm not looking for love. Maybe I just want a pact with some devil to solve all my problems."

He's quiet then, smiling at my side, though I won't look to see what his eyes can tell me.

"Not looking for love?" It's there in his voice.

I can't answer that. But I can distract us both.

It's a good thing I trained Frost well. He doesn't even balk as I edge him over next to Holt.

Then lever myself out of Frost's saddle and into Plath's.

There's a jolt, a bit of a side step, Holt's soft grunt as I land across his lap, straddling him, facing him.

His hands fall to my hips, steadying me.

Soon we're just eye to eye, lips to lips, form to form.

A frozen second.

Those hazed, dark eyes of his pour into mine.

God. There's something sad there I can't quite make out, but something just as hungry as the wildness in me.

There's barely another breath that passes before we crush into each other with a scalding heat.

If you've never kissed a man on horseback, you haven't lived.

We spend a good long while kissing each other's faces off.

Best part is, I get to watch his sinful beauty the whole time.

Holt Silverton, my own fallen angel.

My secret wish, even if nobody chucks any flowers over the cliff today.

XVIII: A HORSE IN THIS
RACE (HOLT)

I'm starting to think fate had something in mind when it threw us together.

Maybe that's just wishful thinking, but I can't help wanting this to be real as I settle into my days with her.

Weekdays on the site end with coming home to Libby's cooking. We fall into bed together, pass out, and I wake up in the morning to whip her up some breakfast.

Weekends on the ranch, putting in some hard labor to help her out and getting a feel for the place all my own. I start to get why she's so attached to it.

Her sweat's in this land.

Her blood.

Her life.

Her love.

She'd rather die a thousand times than let anybody steal this place away.

Yeah, I know I'm only temporary.

I know I'm just here to keep her safe until we're sure Declan's hyenas aren't coming back.

Still, with every day that passes, I'm starting to feel like a part of me belongs on the Potter ranch, too.

I'm starting to feel like it's home.

I'm also starting to feel like this place is too damn quiet.

It'd be nice to think a tough-talker like Declan was actually a chickenshit, a coward who ran when he realized his easy mark wasn't so easy after all.

I've got a bad feeling, though.

This silence feels more like the crackling ozone in the air right before a mother of a storm splits the sky in two.

Which is why we're back in Ursa today.

Inside the old saloon.

Standing over that fucking body, side to side with our hands on our hips, trying to figure out what to do with him.

I cock my head to the left.

She tilts hers to the right.

Then she says, "Um, I hear if you put bones in lye—"

"Libby, no!" I can't help a tired laugh, dragging a hand over my face. "Look, buying enough lye to dissolve human bones is gonna leave a paper trail. The easiest way to do it without being *noticed* is through a purchase order with my company. Trouble is...paying for stuff in bulk leaves a cash trail even when you try to do it through back channels. You don't want to leave evidence? No lye."

"Oh, fine. Don't think I could dissolve a dead guy into nothing anyway. I don't have it in me." She sighs, folding her arms over her chest. "Jesus, I just want him *gone*."

"I don't know. I still think there's a story to tell, if we can figure out what went wrong here." I stroke my fingers through my beard, frowning. "Leave him be. Blake's gonna be here soon, anyway."

Libby grimaces. "You're sure it's a good idea to have them out here?"

"If we want Blake's help, yeah. Andrea and Clark are an unfortunate baggage to make it look like an ordinary family outing. Plus, the more he sees it, the more he can pull some answers out of the ether with his boys."

"Yeah, well, it's not them I'm worried about. The kids might talk."

"Not if we don't talk too much in front of them." I shrug. "Andrea already knows too much, anyway. Trust me, she's a good kid. She knows when to keep her mouth shut."

"I'll have to trust you on that. But we keep the kids *out* of the saloon, okay?"

"Agreed," I say, then lift my head as I hear clopping hooves and Blake shouting. "We've got company."

Libby looks less than pleased.

She's had a puzzled scowl on her face ever since we rode out this morning.

I guess she's thinking about her old man again and this mess he left her.

But she tosses me a faint smile anyway, and we turn to push through the saloon's swinging doors, where Frost and Plath wait patiently by the hitching post.

We get treated to the sight of Blake and the kids riding in on horseback.

Naturally, my brother looks like he's forgotten how to ride, shifting his ass from side to side in the saddle of a big stocky gelding who just plods on patiently while Blake squirms, clutching the reins every few steps like he's about to fall.

The teenagers look fine, though, perched on two leggy young mares who could be twins.

Andrea and Clark lean over their saddles, murmuring to each other.

I think somebody's in love.

And Blake's probably mighty pissed about it.

As they pull up and Blake swings down with a wince, I can't help a bit of real concern.

"Hey," I say. "Your leg holding out okay, man?"

"Yeah. You'd be surprised what this old boy can handle now that I'm hitched to a massage therapist." He thumps his thigh.

I nod. He's got an old war injury there, one that used to

plague him pretty bad before his miracle of a wife got through to him about regular therapy.

"Mostly just a pain in my ass. Don't have the saddle skills to hold up well anymore." He grins, holding his hand out to Libby. "Hey, Libs."

"Blake," she says dryly and reaches out to shake his hand. "I'm just glad you weren't on my horses with how you were riding."

"Nah, borrowed these guys from the Carters. Put out a grease fire at their place a month or two back, so they owed me one. They said it'd be good to let the horses get out and stretch their legs. No way we were driving up through all that brush." He whistles softly then, letting his hand drop and turning around slowly to take in the town. "So this is it, huh? Looks like a set from one of those old Wild West films. Perfectly preserved, almost."

"It's eerie," I say. "You'd think weather and wild animals should've done the whole place up, even if nobody knew it was here to loot."

"Nah, see?" Blake lifts a hand, pointing at the mountaintops and bluffs ringing the little depression where the town sits. "Got a lot of overhangs here. These high cliff walls...the whole place would miss the worst of it. Winds, snows, storms. Pretty arid, too. Creek bed looks dried up, no wind means no seeds dispersing down here, so not much in the way of grass or trees to attract herbivores, so nothing that eats them, either." He shrugs. "It's like a time capsule, and we just dug it up."

I glance at Libby dryly. "As you can see, he's the smart one in the family."

Blake snorts. "I just know this shit because knowing how weather affects dispersal patterns helps with knowing how weather affects brush fires, they—*hey!*"

He breaks off sharply, head swiveling around, and fixes a fierce glare on Clark and Andrea.

They're still in the saddle, leaning closer, their lips almost touching, acting like we're not even here.

But that holler from Andrea's daddy bursts them apart real fast.

They break back so sharply their horses kick.

Clark lets out a startled sound. A blush lights up his face around all those punk piercings. Andrea gently pulls on the reins and pats her mare's neck, her mouth thin and her face red.

Blake glowers. "You two wanna get down and tie your horses up instead of trying to suck face on my watch?"

"God," Andrea mutters, rolling her eyes. "You're so embarrassing."

They oblige, though, swinging down from their saddles.

I glance at Libby, whose lips are twitching almost uncontrollably.

"You thinking about having kids? 'Cause this is what you're in for."

Andrea hisses at me. "Don't embarrass me, Uncle Holt."

Libby doesn't say anything.

She's just giving me a weird look, oddly wide-eyed and stricken.

What'd I say?

I don't get the chance to ask. She just turns away, flicking her fingers and stepping off the saloon porch.

"Let's take a look around and see if we can find anything new." Then she points a stern finger at Andrea and Clark. "Saloon's off-limits, guys. Stay where I can see you. If I catch you trying to go in there, I'll get your daddy to ground you."

"You're just making me more curious," Clark says. Little punk to the core with his blue-tipped hair and ripped-up black clothes. "And Blake—uh, Mr. Silverton's not my dad. He can't ground *me*."

"Bullshit, boy. I've got your Uncle Rog's number on speed dial," Blake growls.

Clark blanches, then wrinkles his nose at Blake.

"You still suck," he says.

"I could've said you can't even come," Blake mutters. "Shut up and try to have some fun."

I smirk while the kids cluster together and wander off toward the old church, holding hands the whole time.

It's almost a bonding activity, having a common enemy.

"I don't really think that's how it works," I say mildly, and Blake groans, dragging a hand over his face.

"Maybe not, but they're too distracted being mad to think about disobeying me, so that works for now." He tosses his head. "Give me the grand tour, bro."

"Sure thing."

Libby's walking ahead of us, not looking back, her shoulders tight as we wander through the town, looking into the various buildings: shanties, the bank, a boarding house, the old sheriff's station.

I want to ask her what's wrong, but not now.

She's too proud.

If I ask her, she won't tell me in front of Blake.

Guess I'm being kind of obvious, though.

While Blake walks next to me, he nudges me with his elbow.

"Well?" he asks, his voice low, but just to be safe I drop back a little. I know what he's about to get into. "What's going on with you and the firecracker?"

I stuff my hands in my pockets, shrugging. "What makes you think there's anything going on at all?"

"Aw, don't even fucking try it." He smacks my arm. "Everybody's seen you two around. At the barn dance, at the drive-in..."

Shit.

I don't know why I'm defensive about this, but all my hackles go up.

Maybe I'm so used to everyone having a say about what I do, who I sleep with, that I want this to be private. Don't want other nosy townsfolk prying.

My business is with Libby and nobody else.

"What about it?" I snarl. "We're dating. That a problem?"

"Not for me." Blake holds his hands up. "Hey, man. Cool it. I'm not judging. This just seems different than usual for you. I just wanna know if you're happy."

I eye him. "Shouldn't you be asking if she's happy? Since I'm such a loser gigolo who fucks everything that talks?"

"Think that's between you and her." My brother chuckles, watching me with eyes that seem to know me too well after being estranged until recently. "But is that what you're doing here? Being a loser gigolo who fucks around with everyone? Who's fucking around with her?"

"Enough." It comes out of me in a seething growl, my voice pitching louder.

Libby turns her head as she stops on the porch of a little mini-barn up ahead that looks like it might've been a craftsman's place, judging by the horseshoe hung over the door.

One blue eye flicks over us curiously. "Everything okay?"

"We're fine," I say, forcing my mouth into a smile and lifting a hand. "Just arguing like we always do. You wanna check that out while we look in over here at the..." My eyes land on the nearest building, the wooden shanty with a faded red cross painted over the door. "Hospital, I guess. Or what passes for the nearest thing."

"Sure," Libby says, but she sounds skeptical.

She never has wholly bought my bullshit.

Still, I flash her another smile while she disappears inside, then grab Blake's arm and steer him toward the building, glaring at him.

"How about we not have this conversation in earshot of her?"

That asshole just smirks. "What? You afraid of her hearing that you actually damn well like her?"

"Maybe. Maybe not."

We step through the half-broken door of what's less a hospital and more like...I don't even know what to call it.

Makes me think of the old medic's tents set up on deployment more than a real hospital or doctor's office. All the old equipment and supplies are scattered on tables on the far end of the large single room, one big slab of an operating table, rows of cots with old, mouse-eaten sheets still stained.

Blake and I move from bed to bed, checking the windowsills, under the mattresses, places where sick or injured people might've kept little journals or keepsakes that might be just what we need to put this place on the map.

Something more significant than a few antiques that might fetch a nice price at auction, but won't do much else.

Blake glances at me now and then.

"You really do like her, don't you?" he grumbles.

I straighten from feeling the bottom of a lumpy mattress to see if there's anything stitched into it. Gold, even. Might be useful.

"Is it that obvious?" I ask, lifting my head and scanning the room. "She gets me going, yeah. Makes me want to be..." I search for words, shaking my head. "Better than I am, that's for sure."

"You really think you were that bad a guy?" my brother asks.

"Don't know about bad, but maybe just...fuck." I shrug, moving on to peer over the exam table and the racks of tattered bandages, old cloudy bottles with dried residue inside, ancient tools I don't even want to think about being used on a human body. "I was focused on the wrong shit. Libby makes me focus on what's right."

"You talk different now, you know."

I blink, squinting at him. "I do what now?"

Blake grins. "You sound more like me. Pure country. No more of that New York city slicker shit."

I snort, rolling my eyes. "Shut up. Look, you can't take the country out of the boy. You know that."

"Yeah, well..."

There's a pause, and then Blake mumbles something.

I frown, eyeing him.

"What was that?"

He clears his throat, pretends to cough, turning his head to muffle it against his shoulder and talking in a low mumble. "I said...*itsgoodtohavemybrotherback.*"

That's how it comes out.

One long word.

Now it's my turn to fake clear my throat, looking away, scrubbing a hand over the back of my neck.

My face feels warm.

It reminds me of why I keep going back to see him, Andrea, and Peace.

To be Uncle Holt, not just this drifter.

"Yeah, well," I mutter, "it's good to be back, Blake."

We don't say anything else after that, picking through everything.

I find what looks like an old doctor's logbook. Ragged black leather, faded pages in a sort of weird pale green with thin blue lines printed in grids. Looks like names, notations of dosages, dates.

"Damn, man. Doc would have a field day with this old stuff," Blake whispers.

I flip through. It dates as far back as the eighteen fifties.

This could be good.

Especially if we cross-check the names and come up with anyone famous like the legendary bandits.

I set it on a shelf carefully, mentally noting where it is. I don't want to touch it any more in case the acid in my skin messes with the paper.

Just as I move over to check out some dried-up test tubes with a thin skim of flaky rust inside, a call comes from outside.

The kids.

I don't even hear what they're saying, don't even think.

My heart nearly slams out of my chest, and I go rocketing toward the door. Blake's ahead of me, off like a gunshot.

You don't get between him and his little girl when she's yelling.

Just as we bolt out, Libby comes leaping out of the horseshoe place with her ponytail bouncing.

The three of us stop and stare.

Andrea and Clark stand in the middle of a little fenced yard in front of the church, blinking at us like they're wondering what the hell our problems are.

Brats.

They're just fine, oblivious to scaring the living crap out of us.

Blake stops, wheezing, bending over and bracing his hands on his thighs. "Andrea? What's wrong? What happened?"

"Dad, calm down." She rolls her eyes. "We found some stuff. Thought you might want to see it."

Blake closes his eyes with a deep, long-suffering breath.

"The next time you start hollering like that," he says, "you better be in trouble."

Andrea arches a brow, pursing her lips and folding her arms with a sassy little switch of her hip. "I thought you told me to stay out of trouble. Now you're telling me to get into it?"

I flick Blake's shoulder. "She's got you there."

"I knew there was a reason I liked her," Libby snickers.

"Y'all done?" Blake straightens, growling at all of us.

"We are now," Libby says firmly. "Let's go see what's inside."

We follow the kids into the church.

It's a small place, looks like it's barely one room, but there's a rustic charm to it.

It's not made of the same weathered pine wood as the other buildings. Looks more like pale oak, polished to a shine that's gone dull.

The interior rafters are carved into an arch, not just slotted up there with planks.

There's real care in how this building was put together.

Not much left of the pews besides crumbling planks, and same with the pulpit.

But I'm wrong about the place being a single room.

There's a small door in the back.

That's where Andrea and Clark lead us.

Right to a tiny room I'm guessing used to be where the priest slept, but someone else has been here more recently.

The old iron bed's been fitted with a mattress that's definitely worn, but too modern.

The dusty equipment on the table's not anything from the eighteen hundreds.

Little collapsing telescopes. Compasses. Microscopes.

Stacks and stacks of journals, books from the eighties about astronomy, cosmology. Even some philosophy texts. The old shit, the classics, Plato and Aristotle and the like.

Libby draws the same conclusion I do.

Judging by the crack in her voice as she whispers *"Dad"* and steps forward, brushing her fingertips over the top of one small journal, it hits her a lot harder than me.

She swallows like she's got her heart up in her throat, staring down at the scattered things.

Even in the faint light trickling through the one tiny, high window up on the wall, her face goes pale.

I think we've had enough for one day.

"Hey," I say, touching her arm—and giving Blake a significant look.

Blake turns to the kids. Whispering, he ushers them out of the room.

The second they're gone, I pull Libby close.

She's almost limp as she falls against me, but there's nothing weak about the strength of her grip as she knots her fingers in my shirt and clings tight, clings hard, burying herself into me.

I wrap her up tight and bend over her.

"It's okay," I say. "If he was researching something, it makes sense he'd spend some time out here. Must've been before...you know. Bostrom." I stroke my hand over her ponytail, hoping I can soothe her. "Let's head inside. We've seen enough for today. I found a medical log that might be helpful later, but we need to come back with the right equipment to handle it. Gloves and plastic bags and shit."

Her laughter is weak, forced, making her shoulders shake. "So you're a forensic anthropologist now?"

"I Googled what not to do to ruin everything if we found anything worth preserving." I laugh, too, but it's tired. I pull back, grasping her hands, looking down into exhausted, worried sky-blue eyes. "Let's head back before it gets too hot."

"Sure," she says, but then looks at the stack of mess on the table.

I know her mind's got to be reeling.

* * *

WE DON'T GET to talk more until later in the day.

The kids don't want to leave the "cool-ass ghost town" yet, but it's getting hot, and I'd rather not put my niece in the hospital with sunstroke.

We all mount up and head back to the ranch for lunch and some cold drinks. After hanging around and talking for a bit, Blake mounts up and takes the kids to return the horses.

Libby and I need to get to work, too. We've already put Frost and Plath away, but we've still got things to do around the ranch.

Right now, though, we're just sitting on the back patio, taking in the day, both of us with our condensation-dotted cans of cold beer parked on the tiny table between our chairs.

The tiny table where both our hands rest, fingers interlaced so she knows I'm *here*.

For whenever she wants to unravel that knot between her eyebrows and spool it out, tell me what's going on in her head.

It takes a while.

A few more pulls of beer.

"What was he *doing* there?" she asks, almost out of nowhere.

She sounds so quiet.

So lost.

So young, more like a confused little girl on the verge of shattering than the brassy, confident woman I know.

It's her old man's secret place.

She's been holding on to her memories of him for so long, and now they're conflicting with reality.

I capture her hand.

"Remember what that report said? The geographic formations of the area around town are probably an impact crater? Probably what drew him out there," I say.

She tears her gaze from the horizon and looks at me, nodding mutely. I squeeze her hand and offer an encouraging smile.

"Your Dad always loved learning, right? He knows star shit, knows all about meteors and craters, and maybe he noticed the shape of the depression where the town is and realized it looked like one. What if he went out to study it?" I hold her eyes. "That's all it has to be, Libby. It was a quiet place with stuff he enjoyed. He started messing around Ursa and the hills beyond and found that rock."

"I wish he hadn't." She bites her lip. "Oh God—what if it's radioactive? What if his cancer—"

I'm out of my chair in an instant, rounding to hers, dropping to my knees so I can gather her close.

"Stop right there. The rock didn't curse him," I say firmly, rubbing my hands against her back. "And it didn't give him cancer. If it was radioactive, those people at the lab place would've said something in their letter. And he wouldn't have had it in the house with his girls all these years."

She makes a soft, whimpering sound and buries her face against my neck.

"Okay. I'm being ridiculous. But how is it you have less doubt about my dad than I do?" she asks with a half-hearted laugh.

"I don't have a horse in that race, honey," I tell her. "Your old man and his memory mean so damn much to you that you can't even look at stuff head-on to parse it. I can. What I'm looking at tells me he wasn't a bad guy, and if we had all the facts, we'd see there was an explanation for everything."

"I hope you're right," she murmurs, wrapping her arms around my neck. "I hope we find answers in time to save the ranch."

I smile then, tracing her jaw nice and slow.

She never had any intention of hiding Bostrom's body. We both know it's not the right thing to do.

I just wish I knew what the right thing *was*.

Because that clock keeps ticking, and our little break in paradise hasn't slowed it down one bit. With half the summer gone, we're down to a couple weeks at most in Reid Cherish's tax countdown.

Time waits for no one.

My phone buzzes in my pocket, and I stiffen.

Even though it's Sunday, it's the ringtone I set for work calls.

Libby and I both groan before she laughs, shoving at my chest.

"Go on," she says, smiling sweetly. "Answer it. Duty calls, Mr. Builder."

"You come first," I remind her.

I'm rewarded with a sugary smile that does my insides in before I reluctantly fish my phone out and check the name.

Alaska.

My mouth turns down at the corners.

Dammit, he wouldn't call unless there was something important. I'd trusted him to handle some deliveries coming in today, too.

I swipe the call and lift the phone to my ear. "Silverton."

"Hey, boss," he says. Normally slow-talking and blunt, right now Alaska sounds ready to strangle someone, a harsh edge in his voice. "Can you get down to the site? I've got a trucker here with an entire semi full of our shit—won't sign off on delivery because it's marked COD, like any damn body would ship out this much rebar COD. It's already paid, but he ain't listening."

315

Cash on Delivery? Is he joking?

"The fuck?" I growl, frowning and already standing, then grasping Libby's hand for one more squeeze. "I'll be there in a few. Don't let him leave with our rebar."

I hang up quickly, pocketing my phone.

Before I can say anything, Libby smiles and rests her cheek to my hand, her soft skin so warm.

"Gotta go be an adult, huh?"

"Unfortunately." I grunt but let myself smile just for her, resting my knuckles against the high crest of her delicate cheekbones. "I shouldn't be gone long. Some invoicing and supply crap, probably. Alaska needs me to come be an asshole with authority over contracts instead of just an asshole in general."

Libby lifts both brows mock-innocently.

"Hey, when you've got natural talents—"

"Don't you even start." Chuckling, I lean down and steal a quick kiss, then disentangle myself and head for the door.

"Back soon," I throw at her.

But I'm not sure I will be.

Something smells fishy about this.

That trouble that's been brewing like a far off thunderhead?

It might be about to break and rain down hell.

* * *

I WAS RIGHT to be suspicious.

Funny how this tough-talking trucker was giving Alaska hell, but when I show up he's all contrition. Some kind of mix-up in the paperwork, everything's fine, here's your rebar.

I've never seen the man before in my life, but he looks at me like he's seen a ghost.

I can't help lingering on the faded bruises peppering his burly forearms.

Sure, bruises aren't much reason to accuse anyone of anything.

Being a trucker is rough work, and they get banged up all the time.

Still, something seems weird about it, especially when he avoids my eyes and practically hides in his truck while my crew offloads everything. Most truckers would help so they can get back on the road quicker.

All those stories about Declan swindling other truckers into doing his dirty work...

Nah.

They can't be dumb enough to try something like this, right?

Scamming me out of money with a fake-ass invoice mess?

By the time it's over, I've got a headache from working in the glare of the hot Montana sun. Once we've got everything secured, I send the guys home to enjoy the last of their weekend and head back into town myself.

I'm not quite ready to go back to Libby. I'm pissed off, irritable, and wondering if I'm being overly paranoid about this shit with the oddball delivery.

Don't wanna give her more to worry about.

I also don't want to keep her uninformed if Declan's still skulking around, planning to make a move, either. She can't find Sierra soon enough.

On a whim, I stop by The Nest to grab a coffee. Felicity's brew should ease my headache and give me time to think before I go back home.

Home.

Shit, I'd always wanted to build my home from my own blood and sweat.

Now there's something appealing about putting my blood and sweat into helping Libby make her home stronger.

I'm still brooding as I order up, hardly even noticing Felicity's pleasantries. Though I manage a smile for her and ask how she's doing when she calls me up for my cup of thick black double-caff.

I'm so preoccupied by all this shit running through my mind

that I don't realize there's someone standing behind me. Not until I turn and bump into her, nearly splashing coffee over both of us.

"Dammit, sorry," I growl out, grappling at my cup.

It's not really clicking who's in front of me, my focus more on keeping scalding hot liquid off my skin and hers, until she speaks.

"So I finally run into you," she says. "I'd almost think you were hiding from me, Holt. That's so cruel."

I blink. What in the...?

I look up from my coffee cup at the woman in front of me.

Sally Jenkins.

Oh.

Shit.

I haven't seen Sally since high school. She was a pretty girl then, and she's a pretty woman now. Tall, curvy, with wheat-blonde hair and soft, curious brown eyes and a delicate, almost pixie-like face with long lashes and a pert little strawberry of a mouth.

I know that mouth a little too well.

I know *all* of her.

She's the girl my brother crushed on in high school.

With how fucked up things were between me and Blake back then, I just had to have her because he wanted her first.

I'd been having wet dreams over Jenna Ford, Warren's sister.

But Jenna was older and never looked twice at me, so it wasn't a big deal to keep dating Sally off and on during the feud with my brother—for attention, for status, for anything we could turn into a fight like the juvenile hotheads we were.

Back then, Sally was catching feelings like the kids say now.

I just hadn't really thought anything about it because I was a callous little teenage bastard.

From the way she's looking at me now, though, I think one of my oldest chickens is coming home to roost.

"Hey, Sal," I say, offering a neutral smile. "Long time no see. I've been real busy since I've been back in town."

"So I hear, rebuilding half of Heart's Edge, aren't you?"

She arches a pointed brow, folding her arms over her ample chest.

Deliberately, I realize.

Plumping up her tits and pushing them up against the low-cut neckline of her tight-fitting shirt.

I nod slowly, numb to her charms.

Funny how just a year ago, I'd have pounced on all that cleavage and the clear display meant to pique my interest—among a few other things.

Not anymore.

I feel like I'm doing something wrong just by noticing it.

And I keep my eyes fixed firmly on her face as she continues, teeth toying at her lower lip. "A man of few words, huh? Guess it comes with the territory when you're trying to be a hero builder. And sleeping around with everyone, of course..."

I start to growl, to tell her I haven't been *sleeping around* with anyone but one sweet girl, period, but she's still talking.

"...everyone but me," she finishes.

There it fucking is.

Right between the eyes.

Hell.

That spidey-sense that told me I was in trouble the second I saw her was too right.

I try to hold on to an awkward smile as I glance around the coffee shop helplessly. There aren't too many people around. Most folks are out enjoying their sunny evening, but there are enough.

Gossip spreads like fast-moving poison ivy in this town.

Which is why I can't believe she's choosing to pull this crap right here, right now.

Okay.

Fuck.

I take a deep breath, then say neutrally, "I'm not really looking for a hookup, Sal. I'm not on the market right now."

She rakes me up and down with a cat-like look, toying with her lower lip in a sulky pout.

Sally remembers the little things that get to me, my own personal kryptonite in a woman.

They're just not working anymore.

All I can think about is Libby.

"Oh, stop. You're always on the market, Holt Silverton," she says, and although it's whiny, there's a bit of justified accusation, too. "So, what? Suddenly you start hooking up with Libby Potter and you're a changed man?"

"If you really wanna put it so bluntly, yeah," I admit.

It's making my face burn something fierce to say that out loud, but it's true.

Libby's changed me.

Made me realize the man-whore I was before isn't who I want to be.

A complete dick like Sally wants.

I stare her down.

Sally snorts, rolling her eyes. "You'll come to your senses. You ain't a one-woman kinda man," she says, stepping closer.

I lean back instinctively, but I can't go far with the coffee bar at my back and a cup of hot black coffee steaming in my hand, waiting to scald us both with any sudden movements.

Smirking, Sally reaches out to run her fingertip along my forearm. "I bet I could accommodate you. Don't you remember how good we were?"

I grimace. "That was high school, Sal. Twenty damn years ago. Everything seems better than it was with that much time passing."

She lets out a flirty laugh. "Not for me. I remember everything." Stepping closer still, until I can smell her light, floral perfume, she looks up at me through her long lashes. "I remember how you made me feel, Holt. I remember every day. I don't know how you did it, but you ruined me for anyone else. And when I heard you were back..."

No. My eyes pinch shut. *Don't fucking say it.*

She nibbles at her lower lip, her fingertip against my wrist, hooking the curl of her finger over the wrist bone. "Well, I was hoping you'd come see me. Hoping you thought of me as much as I thought of you."

Oh.

Oh, *fuck*.

Sally Jenkins has been in love with me since high school.

And she's still in love with me now.

Funny thing is, I'd rather kick my own ass a hundred times than hers for this tease.

I'm worse than a player leaving my mark on half the women in town. I'm a reckless douchebag who deserves everything he has coming.

Now it comes down on me like a fucking avalanche.

There's no denying, all those years ago, I *used* her.

Used her to get at Blake by making her love me. Making her need me. Making her think we had something special so she'd always choose me over Blake.

Sure, there was always collateral damage from the way Blake and I used to fight, always competing for our screwed up mama's love.

Thing is, nobody's heart should ever be collateral damage.

Not from two broken, bitter boys trying to duke out their way to adulthood.

I gotta fix this.

I gotta make this right, but I don't know how.

Not when, beneath the coy look she's giving me, I can see hope there, too.

And that's not even touching the hurt.

I think deep down, she knows.

She knows what a shit I was, and I think she sees I can't feel anything for her now.

I just don't want to hurt her even more.

Turning, I sigh and set my coffee on the counter, freeing my hands from the threat of second-degree burns.

Then I capture her hands in mine, pulling them away from her reaching for me.

I can't let her do it.

Not if I want to keep from hurting her.

Not if I want to be the sort of man Libby respects.

I take hold gently but firmly. From the expression on her face, I think she can tell I'm about to let her down, her brows crumpling slightly, her mouth going soft.

But I've got to say this, once and for all, even if everyone in the whole damn Nest is licking their chops, ready for a week's worth of gossip.

"Sal," I open my mouth—and stop the second I realize it.

Oh, I've got an audience, all right.

And it's not just the nosy townsfolk.

Aw, *shit!*

XIX: HORSING AROUND (LIBBY)

Minutes Earlier

DON'T PANIC.

Do *not* panic, I tell myself again and again.

Easier said than done.

I stare down at my phone, and the recent call listing Sierra's number, over and over again.

One inbound call.

Five outbound calls that I let ring and ring and ring until they went to voicemail, only her voicemail box was full. I can't reach her.

She'd called me.

And even though I told myself I was so angry at her I could spit, the second I recognized the name on the caller ID, I'd scrambled for the phone like my butt was on fire.

I just needed to hear her voice.

Whatever's gone sour between us...

I just wanted to know my sister's still safe.

But there was nothing on the line but dead air.

Not even breathing.

Just silence, weird and ominous, that left me struggling to breathe as it stretched on while I said *Sierra? Sierra, you there? Talk to me!*

I must've repeated it five times.

Then, with a sharp digital *click*, the call went dead in my hand.

Left me practically hyperventilating, imagining the worst after weeks and weeks of radio silence and that abrupt way she took off from town with a demon.

I know men like Declan.

They might be physically big, but they're small inside—and the only thing that puffs them up is hurting other people.

Hurting women like my sister, who'll come back for more because there's something in her searching for a peace she thinks she'll find with a wolf.

Even if that wolf savages her.

God.

I can't stop worrying.

Pacing.

Scowling.

I try her number a couple more times, only to get that *voice-mail box is full* message that makes me want to strangle whoever made those recordings in their semi-mechanical, overly polite voice that sounds so pleasantly disinterested in my mini panic attack.

That voice is a total asshat.

I growl to myself, glaring at my phone, and then try Holt.

He's not answering either.

Dammit, is everyone in my life trying to drive me nuts right about now?

Sierra could be in danger. I can't wait for Holt to finish work and come back.

I shove my feet into my boots and climb into my truck, heading straight for the construction site in the valley.

Except as I pass through town on my way to the feeder road that leads out there, I go by The Nest and see a familiar shape.

Holt's new—well, new-ish, beat-up and dusty—truck in the parking lot.

I turn around, whip in and park next to him, then climb out and shove the door to the café open.

The moment I walk in, I know something's up.

There's a thick tension in the room, like everyone's watching a show that's building up to this big climactic finish and getting people all breathless waiting.

As soon as I lay eyes on Holt, I realize I ain't wrong.

He's squared off with Sally Jenkins.

Sally and I haven't ever gotten along much.

She's not a bad gal, just...clashing personalities.

Plus, I don't ever want to get tangled in the he-said-she-said mess that seems to follow her around. She's got a tendency to not want men unless they're with someone else, and I know at least three marriages that ended because of her.

I get that she's lonely.

There's some kind of void she's trying to fill.

But I ain't happy to see her zeroing in on Holt when I know damn well the rumors about us have been going wild around town.

Now she's right here with her hands in his.

And I'm standing in the doorway frozen but simmering.

I don't think anyone even notices I'm there. They're too focused on Holt and Sally, waiting to see what's gonna happen. There's a vulture greed to it that I hate.

Like they know Holt's reputation is set in stone.

They think they know what's about to happen here.

I don't want to believe it.

I want to believe in him.

And that's when I realize, *he* knows I'm here.

His gaze flicks to me over Sally's shoulder, those sunset-dark eyes pleading, like he's asking me to stay back.

To let him handle it.

I don't know what there is to handle, but hell.

I feel like I'm making a big decision here.

To not butt in or get all stompy and territorial because I'm trusting him. And that scares the ever-loving crap out of me.

But I don't say anything.

I just nod subtly, clenching my fists, holding my ground. Holt's got his lips parted like he was about to talk and I stopped him, but now he starts again.

"Sal," he says—and he's talking to her that same gentle way he talks to me when I'm hurting, that way I didn't even know he could, except instead of intimate it's just sad. "I know we had a thing a long time ago. It was just that, a thing. We were kids. We didn't know what we were doing, who we were, or what we were feeling. I'm sorry if I made you feel like I was leading you on. Like I could be the man you need." He shakes his head, squeezing her hands. "I can't be the one to help you find it. I'm the dude who hurt you in the first place. All I can say is, I'm sorry. And all I can say is no because I won't hurt you that way again. You deserve better."

It's not something I'd ever thought would come out of Holt's mouth.

It's mature, thoughtful, kind, and restrained.

Sally's right there with her cleavage so far out you can almost see nipple, throwing herself at him when I know damn well he's got a libido you can spark with an inch of bare skin.

But he's choosing not to respond to it.

Instead, he's thinking about what's best for her.

I'm realizing now I never knew Holt at all from my first impressions.

I'm also realizing I'm proud of him.

Sally still hasn't noticed I'm here, watching the whole thing go down.

Hell, she doesn't seem to care that she's got an audience and people are gonna be talking about her like a dog. I feel a little bad for her with the way her shoulders slump and she just stands there, quiet as a mouse with her fingers loose in his.

Until she smiles, this heartbreakingly sad face that makes me kinda wonder if she's a lot like Holt.

There's more to her than her reputation says, but sometimes she just gets fed up and decides to be who everyone thinks she is.

"I get it," she says softly. "I do. Maybe more than you realize. I think I'm just wishing..."

"Wishing for what?" Holt prompts gently.

Sally lets out a soft, cracking laugh like she's on the verge of tears.

"To be innocent again," she says. "To be innocent enough that when a man says he loves me, I can trust it."

"I'm sorry if I'm the first asshole who broke that trust." Holt lets go of her hands slowly, offering a rueful smile and touching her cheek. "You'll be okay, Sal. You don't need me for that. And you don't need to try to rekindle a bunch of teenage craziness."

"Maybe not." She bites her lip, steps back, but then leans in, slipping her hands up over his chest and curling them around the back of his neck, rising on her toes. "Maybe one more kiss for old times?"

His face goes cold.

Holt grasps her wrists and pulls her arms back, bending at the waist and out of reach of her puckered lips. He darts me a desperate, wide-eyed look that'd be hilarious if this whole scene wasn't so bitter.

I've seen enough.

Clearing my throat, I lurch forward from the door, acting like I just moseyed on in. "Hey, Holt. I was just looking for you!"

Over Holt's shoulder, Felicity catches my eye from behind the bar and winks, mouthing *Nice one.*

I roll my eyes at her, but then offer Holt a smile before looking at Sally like I just noticed her. "Hi, Sally. How's it going?"

NICOLE SNOW

Sally looks between me and Holt, stricken, while Holt slips an arm around my waist and pulls me pointedly close.

I don't blame him.

And maybe I'm feeling a little possessive, too.

Because I snuggle against his side, just looking at Sally innocently, while she blinks again and again before offering a wavering smile.

"Everything's great," she says, her voice cracking—and oh shit, here come the waterworks. "Just *great*."

Before either of us can say anything, she stumbles back, shaking her head. There's a frosty look, like we did this just to hurt her.

Then she turns and scrams right out of The Nest.

With everyone staring after her, the café bursts into noisy chatter, like the movie just ended and everybody wants to talk about what it means.

We're the only ones keeping quiet as I bury my face against his side with a soft, satisfied sound.

I know what Holt was like before, but he did it.

He turned her down for *me*.

"I didn't mean to upset her," I mumble, hating how guilty I feel. "But you told her no, and she was still trying to kiss you."

"Honey, I'm grateful." He kisses my temple, his breath warm and smelling like good coffee. "I'm the one who hurt her years ago. It's my fault. She was clinging to something unrealistic. I'm happy you helped me help her get through that shit."

With a half-smile, I tilt my head, looking up at him as I wrap my arms around his waist, though it feels like trying to span a giant tree trunk.

"Maybe I've just got a jealous streak," I tease. "And since it's illegal to brand human beings—"

"Yowch!" Holt mock-winces, but he's smiling, the haunted look in his eyes fading to amusement and warmth that curls my toes. "Seriously, Libby, were you worried I'd hop into bed with her?"

I clear my throat. "Not *worried*, so much...but maybe wondering if you wanted to."

"Not even for a second."

Oh my God.

This man has no sense of shame.

Here we are in a coffee shop with my best friend watching, and he's stroking his fingers in little circles over my back fit to make me melt, looking at me like I'm the only woman in the entire world.

His fingers bury in my hair, bringing that hot thrill I always get with a little pull on my scalp, igniting a reaction that sure ain't fit for public consumption.

"Sex doesn't mean anything if there's no heart in it," he whispers, husky and hot and so sincere. "Not anymore. Sally doesn't have my heart. There's only one woman who can make that claim now."

Everything inside me twists into knots as I stare up at him, my breath going still in my chest.

It's instinctive to want to doubt him, after watching a woman fly out of here in tears because she believed his pretty words so deeply that she's been ruined since high school.

But that was then.

This is now.

And the Holt Silverton I know makes me laugh day in, day out, and quietly does everything he can to hold me up, so I don't have to carry everything on my lonesome anymore.

That Holt wouldn't ever play me.

He wouldn't stand here in front of all these people and tell me I'm his.

Not if he didn't mean it.

I don't know what to say.

People keep watching us like they're waiting for me to answer a proposal or something.

Then I remember what I came here for.

Sierra.

Even if Holt's making me feel like I'm glowing, I can't stop worrying myself sick.

So I press tighter into him, hiding my face against his chest, closing my eyes with a shaky sound as I hold on even harder.

"We need to talk, but not here," I whisper, because people have had enough of my business to chew on for a month. "Let's go home."

* * *

WE DON'T GET to talk on the drive back in our separate vehicles.

Probably for the best.

I'd probably crash the truck trying to fumble words out while driving, and I wouldn't even know whether to start with Sierra or this burning, lovely butterfly storm in my belly.

But the choice gets taken away from me as we pull up to the ranch.

That ugly-ass Taurus is waiting.

My heart leaps into my throat.

It's like all my worrying brought her to my doorstep.

I know Sierra has a key, so if she's nowhere in sight...

She's either inside or down Nowhere Lane.

I go from focused to fighting mad faster than it takes the needle on the truck to drop as I kill the engine.

Girl goes and gets me all scared for her, then just shows up here after ignoring her phone?

Oh, she's getting an earful.

Holt looks puzzled as he climbs out of his truck. I join him at the gate, scowling.

"Sierra?" he asks.

"Yeah. I didn't get a chance to tell you, but I came out looking because I was worried. She sent me a dead call this morning, then wouldn't pick up." I shove the gate open. "So her showing up here now, after all that?"

"Damn fishy," he agrees.

I stalk up to the front door and sure as shooting, it's unlocked.

When I push it open, there she is.

Sitting there on the sofa looking all mournful.

For once she's not dressed to her version of the nines in too-tight thrift shop attire.

Today it's just ripped, tight jeans and a white shirt splattered in artistic rainbow bits of paint, tied up over her midriff to bare her stomach.

She looks—I don't know—weird?

Like the color's been drained out of her, her hair's gone lackluster, her cheeks sunken in, hollows under eyes that look a little more washed out than before.

Dammit, I'm worried about her.

Especially when she offers me a wan smile.

"Hey, Libby," she says, glancing past me. "Oh, hey, Holt."

I freeze next to the bowed up wall of a man next to me.

He senses it too.

Something ain't right at all.

"Sierra," Holt answers carefully.

I don't say anything at all, at first. Then it just comes out.

"Where's Declan?" I hiss.

Sierra flinches, fidgets her hands together.

"Not here," she says. "He...he doesn't matter. I didn't come here to talk about Declan, Libby."

Warily, I eye her, folding my arms over my chest. "What did you come here to talk about? Couldn't get you on the phone earlier. I've been worried."

"I know. I came because...well, Nowhere Lane." She swallows, her mouth working in a soft, upset twist. "I know what's out there, Libby. I don't know why it's there. I don't want to know. It's just...too much."

"You're damn right it's too much."

I want to snap at her, but I don't get it.

I've been carrying this *alone*, the weight of that dead man ever since our dad died.

And now—*now*—she wants to poke around?

It's tempting to lay into her, but I can't.

Not when she looks so sad, so emptied out.

I know I'm a sucker for my sister.

Sue me.

I sigh, unfolding my arms and stepping into the living room, dropping down on the opposite arm of the couch from her.

Holt follows, settling next to me, this silent, warm weight anchoring me down.

"Listen," I say. "You don't have to get involved with all that. I'm taking care of it. But what prompted this? Last I checked, your boyfriend was sending his boys to threaten me with jail time over it."

Sierra ducks her head, grimacing. "I'm sorry about that. I didn't know he'd..." She waves her hands. "Any of that."

I blink, studying her closely.

"I'm tired, Libby. I'm just tired, that's all." She draws in a shaky breath. "And honestly, I don't want to make a bigger mess for either of us."

"Making messes has kinda always been your specialty," I point out dryly.

She actually gives me a real smile for once. A smile that lets me see my sister, and not the two-faced creature she's become.

"If I ever had a talent, it was that," she says before abruptly asking, "Hey...did I ever tell you why I stole Mom's stuff?"

That's enough to get me flashing hot—instant ice to fire, a scowl hurting my face. "Huh? Now you want to tell me?"

"Better late than never, right?" She looks away. "I never said it was a good reason. But since...since I feel like that's all you think I am, that bitch who stole Mama's stuff, I can at least tell you why."

Narrowing my eyes, I lean back against the sofa, folding my arms.

"I'm waiting."

"If my talent's making messes, yours is being judgmental," she says bitterly.

I start to snap back—but Holt's hand on my arm stops me.

It's gentle, but it's enough to ease me back without a word.

He's not wrong.

Sierra may be pissing me off, but she's trying to do *something* here. I can try not to turn it into a battlefield before I know what's up.

And maybe she ain't wrong about me.

I am pretty bad about snap judgments.

"Just tell me why," I grind out through my teeth.

"You know how it is with me," she whispers. "Always a guy. Always the *wrong* guy. And I always think I'm in love."

"So you stole her stuff to give to some jackass?"

"To pawn," she admits shyly. "He was hot, but then I found out he was a drug addict...and he'd get real violent sometimes. Said he'd hurt me if I didn't get him money. I didn't want to get hurt, so..." She shrugs. "I was seventeen. Didn't have my own money. I did the only thing I could."

My heart twists into a hot, hurting knot. "Sierra, why didn't you tell me?"

"How could I? You and Dad were always in your little bubble, off counting stars, or running this place and I just...I was always on the outside looking in."

It hurts.

I never realized, but I should have.

Sierra was a mama's girl. I was a Daddy's girl.

So when Mama died, maybe Dad and I had each other, but I guess Sierra felt like she didn't have anyone left, even if Dad tried his best with her.

Sierra's been a mess her whole life, but I think maybe I made mistakes, too.

Like not knowing when my sister truly needed me.

I don't know what I'm thinking with these thorny feelings erupting and only Holt at my side keeping me from exploding.

I lean forward, watching her intently. "Is Declan threatening to hurt you now, sis? Is that what's going on here?"

"I don't want to talk about him." She shakes her head quickly —*too quickly.*

Holy hell.

She might as well have said *yes.*

"I just wanted to lay things to rest, okay? I won't keep pushing about the ranch. I won't try to get you to sell. I can't help with the taxes, but we'll leave you alone. Me and Declan both. He's already left town, and...I'm leaving, too." She smiles her tired, bitter smile again, the one that makes me worry. "See? Didn't even have to go to court."

"I never wanted a legal scrum with you," I say, watching her worriedly. "And I don't want you to run away with that viper."

"Oh, I'm not running." She shrugs, standing up, smoothing her hands fretfully over her jeans. "It's just time to move on. You know I don't stay in one place long."

But I don't think she wants to go.

I don't think she's safe.

All my intuition screams *don't let her leave.*

This is too sudden, and she seems too scared. Plus, that part about leaving me alone sounded too rehearsed.

"Sierra." I stand, reaching for her. "You don't have to go. Stay here with us. If Declan's hurting you—"

"Jesus, I tried to keep it real. Can you stop bringing up Declan?" she snarls, her voice cracking, and she whips out of my reach. "This ain't about him, okay? I'm just sick of fighting, and this piece of crap house isn't worth fighting over. You're gonna lose it to the bank anyway, so there's no goddamn point."

I stop in my tracks as hurt cuts through me.

But she's staring at me with something like desperation.

Like she's trying to drive me back, pleading with me not to

push her. And before I can say anything else, or fight words out around the knot in my throat, she's gone.

Bolting out the front door and stomping across the porch.

With a wordless cry, I stumble after her, but by the time I hit the door, she's already in her car.

Wheels spinning, she backs out in twin clouds of dust, that Taurus racing down the road like she's fleeing something.

Maybe from me?

Or maybe from the things I've started to figure out about her and Declan.

I don't move until Holt comes up behind me and wraps his big arms around my shoulders, anchoring me with his warmth.

"You okay?" he asks softly.

"No." My mouth feels numb, my tongue thick. "I don't know what the hell just happened. If that was real, or something else. Why didn't you stop her? I thought you said we needed her to get to him."

"We do. Still, you don't push a hurt cougar up in a corner to make it do anything useful," Holt says. "No doubt here, she was real upset. Whatever's going on, I feel for her, and I'm willing to wait for her to come back on her terms."

"If it's not too late." I sigh, slumping against him. "No matter what crap's between us, she's still my sister, Holt."

"I know." He's all sweetness, gently drawing me back into the house. "You believe her, about leaving town?"

"About as far as I can throw her."

"Honestly, I think you could throw her pretty far, honey," he teases, getting a weak laugh out of me. "But c'mon. If she's still in town, someone will spot her."

"So?"

"So let's use the whisper tree of Heart's Edge to our advantage," he says, and I can *feel* his wicked grin against my skin, right where he kisses my neck. "Time to get on the phone."

XX: HORSE OF A DIFFERENT
COLOR (HOLT)

*I*t doesn't take long to make a few strategic phone calls —mainly to Ms. Wilma and the guys.

Ms. Wilma Ford, the wise old owl of Heart's Edge, hears everything from everyone.

Warren and Haley overhear almost as much when they've taken over running Charming Inn.

Doc and Ember get more gossip at The Menagerie than he'd ever like with women chatting him up at the vet's office right in front of his wife until she chases them off, while Blake's always got an ear to the ground with the fire department plus his dumbass radio show.

Same for Clarissa Regis, too, running Sweeter Things, which is always bustling. And her hubby, Leo, he's a big damn man, and yet scary good at skulking around, seeing and hearing things he's not meant to because he knows how to melt into the background.

Sooner or later, they'll turn up something.

I trust them after our late-night meeting.

Later, Libby and I settle in on the sofa, her looking totally deflated.

I'm worried. She's always carrying so much.

Don't know what I can do besides hold her tight and promise it'll be okay.

So I do—pulling her into my lap to sit cradled sideways across my thighs.

Sometimes it's startling how light she is.

How small.

How fragile.

Yet she's got this larger-than-life presence that takes up a room in all the best ways, overwhelming it.

If she drowns me with her light, then maybe I don't want to come up for air.

She seems almost shrunken now, curled against me with one hand resting over my heart and her head on my shoulder.

Her eyes are closed.

Up this close, I can see details I never quite caught before. Most of the time when we're pressed up on each other like this we're hungry, grasping, seeing who can rip each other's clothes off the fastest.

Her eyelashes are thick and dark—but they're actually a dark, shimmery bronze, so dense they look black all clustered together.

She's only got a few freckles, sunspots on her cheeks.

I count them, six total, each one adorable against her suntanned skin.

There's a tiny scar cut through one eyebrow. The sort of thing you don't really pay attention to at first, thread-thin, and so old I can imagine her as a rambunctious kid, falling on her face.

She's got another one, too. Newer, but still a few years old, a delicate line crossing the crest of her jaw.

Right where those assholes bruised her up.

And though her bruises are faded and she looks like she's never been hurt, I can't help but hold her tighter as this protective urge churns in my gut.

I keep watching her with silent fascination.

Think I could love this woman for hours with my eyes.

Dammit, but I think I'm *in love.*

We stay like that for so long I think she's drifting off, her breathing slower.

Until she cracks one eye open, peeking at me and biting her lip.

"Hey, so..." she starts uncertainly.

"Yeah?" I shift her weight a little, settling her deeper into my lap.

"You, um, you said some pretty heavy stuff at The Nest."

"Sally?" I raise a brow.

"No, you jerk." She lightly swats my chest. "That stuff you said to me. About me. At least I think it was about me. I'm gonna be mighty pissed if it *wasn't.*"

I grin. "You want to enlighten me, honey? What'd I say, exactly?"

She scowls, and now that I've seen it, I can't help but notice how that tiny scar draws up clearer when she does. "You know what you said. Don't make me repeat it."

"Why? Does it embarrass you?"

"*Yes!*" she growls, glaring. "You said that I..."

"That you have my heart," I say bluntly, and she makes a strangled sound, swatting me again.

"You can't say stuff like that out loud!" she hisses. "That snake charmer stuff doesn't work on me."

"No snake charming here, or snake oil." I shrug. "I wasn't just running my mouth, Libby. I'm not into anyone but you. Turns out, I do have a monogamous bone in my body."

"Don't even talk to me about your *bone.* I'm too familiar," she mutters, biting back a smile.

Then she darts me a shy look, before looking away, folding her arms over her chest. Makes quite the picture, sitting there perched in my lap but all riled up.

"Did you mean it, Holt? Really?"

"I did," I promise. "Look, maybe we crashed into each other

like two speeding trains. Maybe we fell headfirst in the weirdest way possible, but hell." I gather her closer, resting my chin on top of her head. "You feel good. You feel right. And I'm not denying it. I'd like to stick around, if you'll have me."

"Oh my God. Why are you like this?"

She burrows into me, practically hiding.

Amazing how my shameless, brazen girl gets so flustered when we talk feelings.

You get her mad and she'll cuss you blue, but tell her you care?

Well, hell, she'll probably *still* cuss you blue.

I'm not wrong.

After a sullen moment, she slips a hand up, her hot little palm against the back of my neck, and pulls me down toward her.

"Enough, you sentimental ass," she says, lifting her head enough for me to catch sparking blue eyes that snap hot. It's not real anger no matter how much she pretends. "Just shut up and kiss me."

"Woman," I growl, "you don't need to ask me twice."

Normally we kiss like wildfire, two forces of nature coming together.

Right now, I kiss her like she's delicate, tender and soft and slow, even if I'm half expecting her to rip me a new asshole and tell me to stop messing around.

Instead, she just melts, sighing as her lips part and press real sweet to mine.

Eventually I gather her up and carry her upstairs.

It's so careful, so slow as I lay her down on the bed.

She twines her arms around my neck and traces her fingers down the back of my neck, touching me gently. The heat between us is no less intense than when we rip at each other and leave each other bruised.

Still, there's something different this time.

It's unspoken, and the way she touches me is something else too.

Need, I get.

Need is this intense thing, a compulsion that can't be denied.

It's a whole different thing when your girl touches you like she *wants* you.

When it's not a compulsion, but when she's deciding she wants it and wants *you*.

It'll fuck a man right up in all the best ways.

And she's got me completely scrambled as her delicate, calloused hands caress my jaw, stroking my beard, slipping down my neck, onto my chest—moving with the rhythm of our lips as we kiss with a slow-burn intensity.

Time stops existing.

There's no rush.

We own the moment.

Just *us*.

I take my sweet time kissing her, exploring her mouth, touching her, tracing the curves of her shoulders, her cleavage, the dip of her waist, the swell of her hips and belly, the toned fullness of her thighs.

One inch at a time, I tease every little bit of clothing off her, baring hot flesh like I'm trying to memorize her, to imprint her on my palms.

Her skin's velvet. It's a pure pleasure just touching it, feeling how she grows tenser, then melts all over again when I find a sensitive spot, playing my fingers against her flesh.

She gives herself up and lets me lead her through soft, sighing gasps until she moves like liquid fire under me—tossing her head from side to side as I explore my way down her body.

The way she moans is fuck-hot.

Utterly addictive.

My face winds up between her legs.

I've had her sweet cunt more times than I can count, but today I fucking *devour* her nice and slow.

Her plush pinkness, her taste, her scent, every little bit of

Liberty Potter becomes property of my tongue. It's so intense I can't tell if she's begging for more or for a reprieve by the end.

I choose wisely.

Pull her clit between my teeth, lash it with my tongue, and bring her off like a shrieking rocket. My hands drag her hips into me, making her ride my face, dousing myself in her cream while I glorify her sweetness with my beard.

She comes so hard I bet she sees her stars tonight without any sky.

I'm rock-hard and ravenous as hell by the time I come up, still licking her off my lips.

Her tan lines greet my eyes as she sinks against the mattress, still panting.

They make me throb like with a devil's fever. There's something about the color in this woman, the contrasts, that fucks my eyes.

The mellow pinkness of her nipples, the shadow of her inner thighs, the wetness of slick flesh. I slip my fingers back in her and as she spreads her legs, loving how she sucks in a breath.

There's nothing about her that isn't fascinating.

Entrancing.

Beautiful.

And I feel like I worship her for hours again with my tongue and my fingers, slipping in and out of her in slow, deep thrusts, guiding her toward her peak one shuddering breath at a time.

Until her shoulders jerk—until she closes her thighs against my hand, trapping it, reaching for me with splayed fingers.

I reluctantly drag my hand away and watch as she flips over, ass up and prone.

"Holt," she whispers, practically begging. "Come with me! I want you to come in me."

With me.

Good goddamn.

Doesn't she know I'm always with her?

I get what she wants because it's the same for me.

Growling, I lace my fingers with hers and cover her body with mine.

"Give me those lips," I whisper.

Fisting her hair to help her along, I drink her sigh from her lips sideways while the rest of me pounds her into submission.

We fuck together nice and hard in a smooth, gliding stroke, trembling as I own her heat and wetness, letting her envelop me, making her clench down hard on every thrusting inch of my cock.

That timeless feeling falls over me again, a river of flesh and heat.

Also a rhythm guided by my pulse, the rising whimpers pouring out of her.

After she comes on me again, balling up the sheets in fists tossed over her head, I know I can't go much longer. So I flip her around, push into her, and go the fuck to town surrounded by beauty and the hellfire tearing up my spine.

I can't stop kissing her, biting her, raging heat building in my balls.

My eyes slip open to watch her as so many expressions flicker across her face each time we meld together in perfect, rolling movements. Mutual pleasure that belongs to *us.*

And it only feels right that it takes us both together.

Libby tightens at the same time it crashes through me, this sudden sharp bolt skipping up my spine, igniting every inch of me.

I don't know who screams whose name first.

I just know it's my turn to see stars under the ceiling, watching her combust, and coming myself blind in searing, bone-deep heat.

* * *

LYING in bed with my hellcat afterward always feels better than even the best afterglow cigarette or shot of whiskey.

Coming down is pure bliss, melting my thoughts away and just leaving me blank and boneless. I can't remember the things I'm supposed to be stressed over.

All I can remember is that I've got the only thing that matters here in my arms, naked and sweet and soft against me.

We drowse in bed, watching the sun set through the window, the light turning a rusty red. Makes me think about that rock at the root of this shit.

How much could a meteorite from another planet really be worth?

That reminds me...

"Hey," I say, jostling Libby with a shrug of my shoulder. "You awake?"

She moans softly, then opens one eye, peering at me. "Am now."

I offer an apologetic smile. "I just remembered something. You know how I went down Nowhere Lane for a checkup yesterday?"

"Mm-hmm." She's already drifting off again.

"I brought some more of your dad's things back. The journals from that room in the church. They're in the back of my truck. Have you ever looked at any of them?"

Her eyes snap open.

She looks at me oddly, then pushes herself up to lean on one hand, her gold hair cascading down over one shoulder and coiling against the curve of one full, heavy breast.

"Oh, crap. With everything else, I just totally forgot," she says.

"You want to have a look now? If he was studying the town and the impact crater, we might find something useful."

"Hmm. Okay, sure."

"You don't sound so sure." I cock my head.

She presses her lips together, curling a hand against her chest, her eyes lowering. "It's just the same old thing. I always feel like pushing to know things one way or another opens me up to finding out the worst."

"It's a chance to find out the best, too," I point out. "If you don't want to, it's all right. I don't want to bring up bad memories."

"No, no, it's fine. Let's look at them together."

I reach up to brush my knuckles against her cheek, hoping to be reassuring.

I lever myself out of bed, snagging my jeans from the back of the chair under the window. "I'll be right back."

I step into my jeans, then drop downstairs and head outside barefoot and shirtless to fetch the small box I'd packed the journals into, hidden safely under a tarp in the back of my truck.

By the time I'm back inside, Libby's gotten up and come downstairs, dressing herself in one of my flannel shirts that's so big on her I can barely catch a glimpse of the tiny denim shorts she's wearing under it.

Yeah, maybe there's something stereotypical about a man getting all hot and snarly possessive, seeing his girl wearing his clothes.

Don't care about being a stereotype.

When I see her like that, it punches me in the gut.

I try to ignore it as I thump the box down on the dining room table and toss the flaps open, exposing a small stack of leather-bound journals.

"Here we go," I say.

The journals are dusty enough to make me sneeze. I brush a layer of grey off one and flip it open, while Libby takes the next.

The moment she opens the cover, though, she lets out a soft, warm laugh.

"Uh-oh. I don't know if we're gonna find much useful here."

"Eh? Why not?" I look down at the first page of the one in my hand, then blink when I realize what I'm looking at.

"Holy shit. Is this?"

"Poetry," she confirms. "*Bad* poetry, but Dad never cared about how awful his literary writing was." She cocks her head, then laughs. "No, that's not true. I remember him saying he took up astronomy when he was young because he couldn't write to save his life, and the next best poetry was right up there in the stars."

"That's actually not half bad poetry itself." I skim down the short lines, then laugh softly. "The swell of her mossy dell makes me feel like a ne'er-do-well...oh, *fuck*."

"Ew!" Libby looks horrified. "Close it. I don't even want to think about my dad writing nasty poems about *mossy dells*. Especially if he meant my mom."

"Right, then. No mossy dells." I clear my throat, suppressing my smile and flipping to the next page.

"Just keep looking to see if there's anything else."

We spend a little while longer digging through the pages.

It's more poetry, a few observations on shooting stars, nothing all that incriminating or exonerating. But as we go through journal after journal, I pause when I get to the back cover of one.

The leather binding is folded in at the corners, glued to the hard interior cover, and then the inside all papered over to cover up the workings.

There's writing on that paper.

There hadn't been on the others.

I'm not sure what I'm seeing at first.

It's just two lists of numbers, what looks like calculations based on...weight? Mineral value? And something to do with rarity and classification, or maybe I'm reading the abbreviations wrong.

What I'm not reading wrong, though, is the fact that those numbers have been run twice.

And they come out to dollar values in rough chicken scratch writing.

One number somewhere just over a million dollars.

Another not too far south of eight million.

And underneath, no, I'm sure as hell not misreading anything.

345

Big, bold, angry letters.

*You lied to me, **Gerald.***

"Shit," I whisper. "Libby, is this Mark's handwriting?"

She leans over, peering around my arm. "That's Dad's handwriting all right. It—oh no." She goes pale.

"Yeah," I say reluctantly.

Libby closes her eyes, her shoulders sagging. "So we just found a motive. The value of that freaking rock—"

"Maybe, maybe not," I tell her. "We don't know the whole story here. Look." I run my finger down the page. There's a phone number, a local area code. "Someone at this number might be able to tell us more."

"Yeah," she says listlessly. "But do we really *want* to know?"

"We should," I say as gently as I can. "If you want, I'll make the call."

"Sure, if you want to."

She doesn't sound too enthused.

Can't really blame her.

I start to say something comforting, if I can, but then I'm distracted by another set of numbers, dashed into the corner of the page.

1831-1869.

Looks like years.

What could that mean?

I really don't know.

But for Libby's sake, I'll try to find out.

* * *

I WAIT until I'm at work the next day to call the number.

If it's bad news, I don't want my expression to give me away in front of Libby before I can figure out the right way to break it that'll hurt the least.

I kick my boots up on the desk in my office and tap the number in, waiting with my throat so tight I feel like I'll choke.

This matters to Libby, so it matters to me.

My phone keeps dialing forever before a voice clicks on.

First that weird three-tone sound and then a lady's voice. *"We're sorry, the number you have dialed is no longer in service."*

Figures.

Only one thing left to do.

I flip open my laptop and type in the number. It's definitely a Montana area code, and there's a listing on Google Maps for a business marked *Closed.* Looks like it's been shuttered for years before Google Maps even existed, but hey, gotta give them points for data completion.

Oddities and Antiquities.

And the owner?

G. Boston.

Gerald damn Bostrom, misspelled.

I pull the right name up a minute later in a state business registry, it's LLC long since expired.

Hmm.

Unfortunately, there's nothing else on a business this old. I sure as hell don't remember an *Oddities and Antiquities* around here growing up, so they probably closed up when I was too young to give a shit about stuff like that, or before I was born.

Lucky for me, I know people with long memories.

I think it's time Libby and I paid a visit to Ms. Wilma Ford.

XXI: BEATING A DEAD HORSE
(LIBBY)

*T*ime for a silly confession.

    I've always been a little scared of Wilma Ford.

It's not 'cause she's mean or anything.

She's one of the nicest old ladies ever.

It's because she's *formidable*.

She's seen, done, and lived through everything.

When I was younger and an even bigger hothead than I am now, I figured out early on that she wouldn't take any bull from a brat like me.

A long time ago, one of our horses got out. Thoreau.

It was my fault. I didn't latch the barn door tight enough because my head was scattered everywhere.

I'd tracked that horse to the edge of Ms. Wilma's property by dark.

Back then, she'd been a bit more robust, her hair iron-grey instead of silvery-white.

She'd looked pretty terrifying when I'd snuck onto her property and turned around only to bump face-first into her, asking me if I knew what the criminal charges were for trespassing.

She wasn't serious, but I was fourteen and didn't know that.

I tried to lie and bluff my way out of it.

She just looked at me and didn't have to say a word to tell me she knew I was full of it.

And when I burst into tears and told her the truth, she took me inside and wiped my face until I stopped snotting everywhere, then hugged me and told me she knew how hard I had it with my mom and all.

Then she cleaned me up, took me out to go find that stupid horse, and tied him up to her front porch while she pulled me back into the Charming Inn. We sat down for some cocoa before she sent me home on Thoreau's back.

That's the kind of woman she is at any age, and it's made me admire her a hell of a lot.

But that's the thing with people you look up to.

You end up wanting them to think well of you, and it makes you kind of a fidgety, awkward mess in their presence.

That's me, right now, as Holt parks outside of the Charming Inn.

Like I said—it's silly.

But I'd rather focus on being a bundle of nerves over Ms. Wilma than think about the reality of why we're here.

That info Holt found on the disconnected phone line.

The fact that it decisively ties Dad to Bostrom and something real bad going down...

Does that mean they pulled guns on each other because the guy lied to him about a Mars rock?

It just doesn't make sense.

That's the sort of thing Dad would take him to court over.

Sue him for fraud, deception, whatever, but killing him in cold-blooded revenge?

It doesn't add up.

Ms. Wilma welcomes us into the Charming Inn with open arms and a promise of cold lemonade and cookies.

I'm less intimidated by her, and more afraid of what she'll say.

She ushers us inside her kitchen, which is kind of like every-

349

one's daydream of the perfect grandma—homey and sweet and comfortable, clean and neat and welcoming, warm without being stifling and full of light.

There's a long wooden table there with ladderback chairs, and she shoos us into our seats.

Next thing I know, Holt and I are sitting there like kids being served up treats, exchanging wry looks.

Even when I'm scared as hell, Ms. Wilma knows how to make people feel at home.

"Now," she says, settling across from us and lacing her thin fingers together on the yellow-and-white-checkered tablecloth. She's got smart, piercing blue eyes, just like her grandson. "What brings you here? I can already tell by those long faces it's not for tea, or I'd have brewed some already."

Holt starts to speak, but I hold up a hand, stopping him.

"First," I say, "I need to know everything we say here *stays* here."

"Dearie, I hear everything but say very little." Her eyes twinkle, though her smile's sticky sweet. "Now. What seems to be the trouble?"

I elbow Holt.

Now he can talk.

I don't wanna be the one to ask this.

Holt jolts a little, giving me an amused look before clearing his throat.

"We were wondering if you knew anything about an old place here in town. *Oddities and Antiquities*, and a guy who owned it, supposedly. Gerald Bostrom."

Ms. Wilma's eyebrows lift up into her neatly swept silver hairline. "Gerald Bostrom? That's a name I haven't heard in ages. Wherever did you hear about him?"

"Old records," Holt says grimly. "We're just hoping to learn a little more about him."

"He was quite a walking scandal, you know." She leans across the table conspiratorially, like she's telling us a secret. "Practically fancied himself the Gatsby of Heart's Edge once upon a time."

I blink. "Scandal?"

"Oh, yes," she says merrily. "He was about to be indicted on a number of charges by several angry people before he disappeared."

The way she says *disappeared* makes my stomach drop.

Like she knows.

Like she knows he's dead, and my father had something to do with it.

But she doesn't even seem to notice that I'm sitting here with my glass of lemonade frozen halfway to my mouth, clutched tight in my hand.

With a wave of her hand, she continues, "He was this antiques dealer who blew into town in the eighties, but that's not *all* he was. He was always entertaining, putting on these lavish parties with some rather interesting guests. Thought he'd be a big fish in a small social pond. He was a rather small man of petty airs himself." She sniffs, her aristocratic nose wrinkling. "I suppose he thought he'd get on well with these small-town rubes, never noticing what he was up to."

"What was he up to?" I finally make myself speak, taking a sip of my lemonade to wet my parched mouth.

"Well...you didn't hear this from me." She leans closer still, her voice dropping to a stage whisper. "Illegal art dealings. The kind of thing you see in those absurdly delightful heist movies. Why, he'd have flipped the Mona Lisa if he could've gotten his hands on it, but as it is, I've heard he ran quite a few stolen artifacts through Heart's Edge and sold them in secret auctions at his home. There were *wicked* rumors about those auctions. Things like Hitler's personal art stash, spell books from the middle ages, missing gold...oh, and of course, the orgies."

"The what?" I blink, glancing at Holt to make sure I heard her right.

She sniffs again and takes a ladylike sip of her lemonade.

"Oh, people always think whenever there's wealth and secrecy, there must be orgies. Rich people seem to have nothing better to do."

Holt chokes on his own lemonade, spluttering on a laugh. "I hadn't really thought about it, ma'am. That's pretty interesting, if he was brokering stolen stuff. Where do you think he got it all?"

"I certainly wasn't involved in his dealings, so that I can't say." She tilts her head. "I imagine the usual means, though. Thieves looking for someone to fence their stolen goods without exposing them. Perhaps swindling people out of their personal effects, when they aren't educated enough to know the value."

Holt and I exchange somber looks.

That note.

Those numbers.

Bostrom probably tried to swindle my dad one way or another.

It's all making sense and it's not looking pretty.

Ms. Wilma clucks her tongue. "The two of you look as though you've just seen a ghost. Why so terribly glum?"

I offer a hasty smile. "It's nothing, really. We're just digging up info while we try to figure out some property zoning stuff."

"Well, I can't imagine what Gerald Bostrom might have to do with that." She folds her hands on the table, watching us shrewdly. "You haven't touched your cookies, dear."

Holt and I are like chastised kids, both of us dutifully taking a bite of our cookies.

I'm not sorry I do. Ms. Wilma's baking is legendary, and the still-warm, gooey chocolate chips practically melt on my tongue.

Maybe it's enough to clear my throat and give me enough of a sugar rush to clear my head so I can ask another question.

"Ms. Wilma, have you ever heard of a place called Ursa?"

Her face goes pale. Now she's the one who looks like she's seen a ghost, and I can't help but wonder why.

"My, my," she says, sitting up straighter in her chair. "There's a name I've not heard for ages. They say it wasn't far from here, but I wonder...even by my grandmother's time it was just a wild story. Everyone acted like it was cursed."

"Cursed?" Holt echoes, his brows pulling together.

She stops, shaking her head with a sigh.

"It's less that, and more..." Trailing off, she tucks her silvered hair behind her ears, her eyes unfocused as she looks somewhere past us. "...more like they didn't want to invoke bad luck. Like summoning an evil spirit. Say its name, and it might bring you grave misfortune."

The place is creepy enough, isn't it?

I could definitely see that.

"What did your grandma tell you about it, if you don't mind me asking, ma'am?" I prompt.

She blinks and gives me a look, offering a polite but sheepish smile.

"Old, far-fetched stories, mostly. Half legends she'd whisper mostly at night to scare us kids into bed, or else Danny the Rattlesnake and his magical blood stone would come out of the mountains to take me." She wiggles her fingers with a smirk before trailing off into a ladylike laugh. "All these tales of cults and crazy outlaws, surely you've heard them?"

"Grade school stuff, yeah," Holt says. "Never heard of Danny or cults, though. They'd tell us all those stories to keep our attention so we wouldn't riot like the sugar-filled little monkeys we were. I always figured they were just exaggerating, making it up as they went to keep us entertained."

"Exactly," Ms. Wilma says, her eyes twinkling. "But there's some truth, you know. Danny the Rattlesnake was real. So was Ursa, I believe. It was an early silver town, before Heart's Edge, back in the mid-eighteen hundreds. Sadly, it didn't survive. The veins tapped out, and Heart's Edge just proved to be more stable when our founders broke ground here. So as Ursa started falling apart...the bad folks moved in. All sorts of thieves and lunatics and con men. Danny was the worst of them."

"What'd he do?" I whisper.

She tilts her head. "He played the people of Ursa, they say, the ones who didn't pull up stakes when money and mining work dried up. He said he'd make them rich because he had a vision, and claimed he had proof—a blood-red stone he pulled out of the ground."

Proof.

Like an ancient rock that sent him messages, and he used it to turn the entire town of Ursa upside down.

Just like Father Matthew's journals said, always talking about how the town fell to sin.

It's real.

Oh my God, it's all real.

There's no other way Ms. Wilma could know about the town at the end of the mountain pass or the journals we found or the maybe-meteorite.

Any chance that this is all a weird hoax or misunderstanding vanishes.

I can't breathe.

But I can't let her know what's going through my head, so I take a quick gulp of my lemonade to try to settle myself, kicking Holt lightly under the table.

I need him to keep talking while I can't.

He needs to keep Ms. Wilma from asking questions that might make her connect why we're asking about Ursa.

Never mind why we're asking about a man who's long disappeared.

Holt jumps a little and gives me an odd look before his expression clears with understanding. He switches his gaze back to Ms. Wilma.

"So that's it then?" he asks. "Were they just straight up having some strange religious sect up there in the mountains?"

"Oh, I really doubt it was as much as all that," she says, waving a hand. "Honestly, I think the prophecies and their blood stone were just an excuse. These were unclean people, my dears. Bandits, killers, and men so desperate they'd do anything. They merely wanted an excuse to plunder as they pleased. Danny claimed his blood stone was meant to guide them to riches hidden in Heart's Edge and gave them a mandate to murder."

"Hell." Holt's dark brows lift rather sharply. "That's pretty creepy."

"People do terrible things when they can find a reason," Ms. Wilma says with a sigh. "Granny said they'd ride in during these terrible night raids. Come swooping down from the mountains on horseback and pillage the town, slaughtering and stealing loads of silver, claiming it was theirs by right. They'd take over the road into the town, too, so no one could ever follow them back. It came to be that just speaking the name 'Ursa' or mentioning Danny made folks tremble, fearing they were summoning another raid, so no one ever did."

"A local superstition," I fill in. I've had a few moments to breathe. I'm feeling a bit clearer-headed. "That's why nobody talks about it. Sooner or later, people died and the raids stopped, but everybody kinda forgets Ursa existed. It just fell off the map."

"Not quite." Ms. Wilma smiles again, and there's a touch of pride there. "You see, someone actually put a stop to Danny's reign of terror. I'm proud to say my own great-great-uncle Jubal Ford—partnered up with the great grandfather of our own esteemed Sheriff Langley."

"Langley?" I choke on the next sip of my lemonade and cough, thumping my chest. "No *way*."

Holt smirks. "You're telling me this town used to have a competent police chief?"

"Holt Silverton, you watch that devil's tongue," Ms. Wilma chides with a repressed laugh. "Poor Sheriff Langley puts up with quite a bit for us."

"Ever so sorry, Ms. Wilma." Holt clears his throat, putting on his best good-schoolboy smile.

"Hardly, you devil of a boy. You never have been," she says fondly, shaking her head. "But yes, back then those two men decided to play hero. They gathered up the strongest men in Heart's Edge and rode out to Ursa. It was a twilight duel, they say, between Uncle Jubal and Danny himself. The whole nest of snakes scattered after my ancestor shot the rattlesnake prophet. But the superstition held on long after Ursa didn't. You're right about that, Libby. Perhaps people feared the ghost of Danny long after everything else was forgotten. I do believe it's somewhere north in the mountains, if any part of it still exists—not so far outside of town."

No, not so far indeed.

Holt and I exchange another heavy glance.

Then he asks, "You know anything about what the numbers 'eighteen-thirty-one to eighteen-sixty-nine' might mean?"

"Sounds like a grave marker, dearie, don't you think?" Ms. Wilma asks. "And, well, I do believe eighteen sixty-nine was the year Danny would've died in the shootout. If my grandmother's stories happened just as she said."

I think they did.

And I think we've already said too much.

Especially when Ms. Wilma gives me one of those mild looks that says she sees a lot more than anyone would want her to.

"Tell me, why this sudden interest in old legends?" she asks.

"We just found some old books in the library, and we were curious," I say quickly. "Notes in the historical zoning records and stuff like that. Figured it couldn't hurt to know a bit more about local history."

"Is that so?" she says shrewdly.

Yeah.

For now, it'll have to be.

* * *

THERE'S a little more small talk, and we don't leave without her pressing some more cookies on us, still warm and wrapped up in a plate covered in a paisley cloth.

We're both quiet on the drive back to my ranch.

There's a lot to think through here.

All those weird stories aren't just guesses and half-truths anymore.

They're real.

There's a history in this town I never knew about.

That history is sobering as hell, but it's also the one chance I have at saving the only place I've ever called home.

I just have to prove it and whip up enough interest to earn heritage protection status.

Danny's weird reputation might be enough to satisfy any historians, along with the freakishly well-preserved scraps of ghost town.

Now I just have to figure out Gerald Bostrom.

Having Holt here helps me feel grounded, like I'm not alone.

We both settle into the evening routine of maintaining stuff around the ranch like we've been doing this together for years. He's not even half as clumsy as when he first started.

Looks like there was a cowboy underneath the big-time real estate boy after all.

Later, when we're done, we saddle up and head out.

We don't even need to say a word to know where we're going.

Where we *have* to go.

Ursa's waiting, and so is that dead man.

* * *

IN OTHER CIRCUMSTANCES, it'd be a lovely ride.

We take it slow, letting the horses find their way in the dark with instincts we don't have, trusting them not to trip as we amble along beneath the stars.

As I look up at the sky, I finger my necklace and let the rhythm of Frost's plodding steps lull me into peace.

Now and then, I catch a glint of whiskey-gold as Holt glances over at me.

I don't know what to say.

I just know I'm glad he's here.

The town—Ursa, *Ursa*, I feel like knowing it for sure is a curse—isn't any different when we get there, but something feels off.

Like there's this dark cloud hovering over the place.

This specter of an outlaw prophet, promising there's more pain around the bend, just waiting to stir up all the sleeping ghosts here.

I stand inside the door of the saloon and peer inside, watching that unmoving skeleton. It's worse in the shadows, like he's fixing to jump up and come after me.

I shiver, folding my arms around my sides.

"You holding up all right?" Holt says, his hand falling to rest on my shoulder.

"Yeah," I say. "Just wondering what we do next."

"I have an idea, but it's probably not legal. I dunno, it might be. I mean, technically you own this land, yeah?"

"It's part of the acreage my grandfather passed down since the old homestead days, so yes." I smile grimly. "Feels a little weird to say I own mountains."

"Better than it being public land, 'cause that means whatever's on this property is yours by right." He shrugs. "I hate to say it, but that Declan asshole might've had the right idea."

I eye him suspiciously.

Anything involving *Declan* and *right idea* is instantly suspect.

"Uh, how?" I whisper.

"Quit giving me the stink eye. I'm just saying, there's a lot of stuff here that may be valuable. Sell it off bit by bit in auctions, assess the antiques one at a time..."

"Nickel-and-diming won't beat the bank's countdown, Holt. Dad was way behind in taxes thanks to his medical bills stacking up." I shake my head. "And we're up against the same problem selling stuff off piecemeal. Anything from here won't be worth much unless we can verify its authenticity, and that means experts."

"Which means letting people on this land."

"And letting people find Bostrom's body."

"Shit, yeah." Holt narrows his eyes. "You know what I don't get?"

"What?"

"Declan giving up with his tail between his legs. I know his type." He shakes his head. "Why hasn't he used that dead body against you yet?"

I sigh. "There's no way he can pin this on me in a way that'll get me in trouble. Only compromise the land with a crime scene. You can't call me an accessory for not reporting it. Really, Declan's got more to lose by going to the police and having to explain why he was snooping around on someone else's turf. Plus, I bet I'd need more hands than I've got to count the number of warrants that man has out for his arrest."

If it were just Dad's reputation and no risk of losing everything, this would be my too-stupid-to-live moment.

All of this is about more than keeping my home and happy pastures for my horses.

It's about me not wanting to let go of the memory of the man I loved, the man who raised me.

Shaking my head, I step back from the door.

"Let's go," I say, turning away. "I gotta think."

We barely step off the saloon's rickety porch before there's a loud buzzing in Holt's back pocket and a square of light glows under his flannel.

He frowns, fishing his phone out and squinting down at the screen to read the texts.

In the night he's all shadows in his black jacket, man-shaped darkness in graceful slashes and angles fit together, centered by those animal-gold eyes. But even on a moonless night, it's not hard to see how he goes pale.

"It's Blake," he says, a harsh edge in his voice. "He says somebody broke into The Nest."

"What? Oh my God." My heart stumbles. "Is Felicity okay?"

"Seems like it." He glares fiercely at his phone. "Dunno. May or may not be connected to this mess, but—"

"We have to check it out! She's my friend."

"Right." He shoves his phone in his pocket, turning his head, scanning over the horses tied to a post, then beyond, checking the perimeter. For a moment, I can see the soldier in him, in his alert posture, the sharp tension in the set of his jaw, the clarity of his gaze. "Let's move. I'll scope things out, see what I can find."

"I'm going with you."

Together we mount up fast, untangling the horses' reins from the post and sending them jostling toward the trail.

As we pass the old church, I pause.

I can't help lingering on those little graves, stone and wood standing the test of time.

1831-1869.

If those are dates, someone's life...

Maybe I'll find a name on those worn markers.

Maybe I'll catch a slam dunk piece of historical interest like the psycho Rattlesnake's final resting spot.

But there's no time to check now.

Holt's already moving.

Felicity might need me.

I only hope my crap hasn't wound up on her doorstep.

With one last look at the church, I nudge Frost around to follow Holt.

FELICITY'S HAD plenty of straight up rotten luck.

I still remember back when that mess was starting to heat up with the Galentron company that used to have a secret lab around here. She got in the thick of it with her cousin, Ember, and wound up with her life on the line.

She's always kinda taken things in stride. Fel's just got this way about her.

Sweet and kind and open, but she's kinda sad, too. Like she's seen too much and nothing surprises her anymore.

Probably no wonder, then, that I'm more freaked out than Felicity is when Holt and I pull into the parking lot of The Nest.

She's standing outside talking to Sheriff Langley, her expression almost dead in the light of his police car. Her eyes are empty. Off somewhere, maybe, either far away or long ago.

I don't know.

Something's up with Felicity, but I learned a long time ago, ever since we got to be friends, that she doesn't talk about herself all that much, and always finds a way to talk around the questions people ask.

But if I were her, I'd be fighting mad at what those assholes did to the café.

The whole front and side windows are smashed, floor to ceiling, so it's like no walls left on two sides.

Glass everywhere, inside and out.

They ripped a couple booths out of the back wall, leaving the stucco exposed to show the wiring and underneath.

Chairs kicked over.

Glass display cases with the bakery stuff shattered.

Equipment crumpled in like it'd been hit with a big old sledgehammer—and we're talking that expensive commercial stuff, too.

Metal all dented up like crunchy aluminum foil.

Like a sick joke, they left the glass door intact.

I'm gonna fucking kill them if she doesn't.

I'm already steaming as I push out of the truck and beeline right for Felicity.

Blake's here, too. I guess doing the whole fire chief's job of inspecting the damage and making sure the building's not an active danger, but I don't pay a bit of attention to him—or Holt, who heads straight for his brother.

I just cannonball myself into Felicity, cutting her off mid-sentence and hugging her tight.

"Oof!" She doesn't even tense up, though she does flail her arms a little awkwardly before settling them around me with a tired laugh. "Hi to you too, Libby. Sorry, Sheriff."

"It's all right, Feli—er, Miss Randall," Langley says. "But, say, if you could finish describing the assailants? You said that you were cleaning when they broke in?"

I pry myself halfway off Fel but still lean against her side, listening while she nods and continues. "I was in the back when I heard a big crash. Just looked out in time to see what was happening before I locked myself in the storeroom." Her brows knit, and she tucks a lock of her dark hair back. "They didn't even try to get in. They totaled the place, emptied the register, and left."

"It's likely they didn't realize you were there," Langley says. "If the register was the target and not you, it was just a smash and grab. No time to go lookin' around for anything else."

My temper flashes hot, and I squeeze Felicity tighter. "They sure took their sweet time beating up the place! It's a goddamn mess. That had to take like half an hour or so."

"Fifteen minutes," Fel whispers. "I was counting."

"Did you get a look at any of them?" Langley asks.

Felicity nods. "Won't help much, though. Just a quick glimpse. There were four of them, all men, all of them wearing black with ski masks. I think they had crowbars."

I go still.

Wearing black with ski masks.

That sounds too familiar.

But I keep my mouth shut, letting Fel talk. Blake and Holt walk by, heads together and deep in conversation. I catch Holt's eye.

He slows, lifting his head, glancing toward my friend.

"Most of them just seemed ordinary, but the one in charge, or at least I think he was...he was big," Felicity says. "Real huge. This brick of a build, even had a square head."

I stare at Holt.

Jesus. I don't want to say anything out loud here, but...

Who the hell do we know that's built like a tank and prone to violence?

He's giving me the same look.

Declan Eckhard.

But why would he target Felicity to get at me?

Or was it not about me at all, and he was just looking for another way to get some dirty cash?

If those other truckers were getting impatient, ready to kick his ass...he could've muscled them into helping with a break-in. Felicity wouldn't have had a fortune in the register, but probably a couple thousand or so after a solid day's work.

All gone now.

Along with the hellish amount of work she put into keeping this place afloat, from fundraisers to bake sales to anything and everything else she could ever think of.

It makes me so stinkin' mad.

When I find that prick, I'm gonna make him eat a mouthful of my fist as an appetizer for the teeth I'll shove down his throat.

I just hang on to Fel while she gives Langley a few more details.

I can't help but notice how tense she gets when Langley looks at her again.

"Can you think of anyone who might've had a motive to do this, instead of just a crime of greed or opportunity?" Langley asks.

Remember how I said Felicity never gets shaken by anything?

She looks pretty damn shook right now.

It's just for a second.

Her face goes blank, her eyes dull.

Hugging her is like hugging a steel mannequin.

Then she just shrugs it off like nothing and smiles, tucking her hair back again. "Unless I ever served a cup of coffee *that* bad, no, not really."

Langley gives a little chuckle, scribbling something else down in his notepad, then flips it closed and tucks it in his breast pocket.

"All right then," he says. "I'll get some police tape up to cordon this place off, and in the morning we'll take some photos once we've got better light. You gonna want them for insurance purposes?"

"Yes, please." Felicity flashes him a grateful smile. "Is there anything else you need from me?"

"Not tonight." He shakes his head, hooking his thumbs in his belt and hitching it up a little. "You should go on home, get some rest. If you don't feel safe, call a friend. If you remember anything else, you know how to reach me."

"Only one who ever answers 9-1-1," Felicity teases, earning another laugh—more of a guffaw—from him.

She's the only girl I know who could keep laughing in a situation like this.

Langley shakes her hand, then drops into the driver's seat of his patrol car, immediately picking up the radio on the dash and muttering into it.

I let out a long sigh.

Our town's so small we don't even have a proper dispatch officer. But we sure do have our fair share of trouble.

I look up at Felicity. She's looking over my head, her eyes misty as she stares at the wreckage of her coffee shop.

"Hey," I say, bumping my head against her shoulder. "You okay? You want to scream? Break something?"

"Nothing left to break," she says wryly. "Looks like they got it all."

"Rat bastards," I hiss. "I don't know how you can be so calm."

"I guess because getting angry won't undo it," she says.

364

"No, but getting angry feels real good sometimes." I search her face. "You really don't have a clue who did this?"

There's a pause, giving something away, before she shakes her head. "Nah. Probably some assholes joyriding through town, thinking I'd be easy pickings."

Assholes joyriding through town don't come prepared with ski masks and crowbars, though—but I keep that part to myself.

I can't help watching her, wondering what she's not saying.

"You sure?" I ask. "You went kinda funny back there. Is something up, Fel?"

She gives me a strange look, like she has no idea what I'm talking about—but then looks past me and arches a brow. "Your boyfriend's looking at you."

I actually flinch. More out of surprise than anything else, hearing it out loud.

Boyfriend.

Holy crap.

I know what we are, technically. I just feel like the town's latest soap opera after that dramatic scene with Sally Jenkins. Now everyone's waiting for the drama that'll break us up.

I look over my shoulder.

I can't help it.

I know Felicity's diverting me like she always does. She doesn't let people get past the surface.

But bring up Holt, and it's second nature to look.

He's standing under the café's outside canopy in one of the few areas that isn't covered with broken glass.

He's talking to Blake intently, Holt gesturing with his hands in jerks that catch my eye.

His hands are big but graceful, like they're made for hard work—sculpting raw granite and marble into works of gorgeous art or wrenching metal into fine filigree sculptures.

Maybe he doesn't do anything that fancy, but there's a style I've noticed on the sites he's built, this detail and craftsmanship that turns something rugged into something as elegant yet strong as the hands that made it.

And Holt's *such* a hand talker, always gesturing to make his point. It's a second language adding another dimension to his words.

While he's talking to Blake, he's glancing at me.

Intently. Deeply. And it's not those hot, wicked gazes he gives off when we're working around the ranch, either, but it doesn't mean there's no heat in it.

Here, it's more like warmth.

Heat and warmth may seem pretty close, but let me tell you...

When a man's looking at you like he's reaching deep down to caress your trembling heart and watch you sigh with all the gut-clenching feeling of it?

There's a hell of a big difference.

I gotta look away before I embarrass myself.

Ducking my head, I run my fingers through my hair.

Felicity cracks another knowing grin.

"He's not my—well, okay, so what if he is?" I huff at her. "So damn what?"

"Girl, men don't look at women that way unless they're thinking about staying." Fel leans against my truck, watching me curiously, then glances past me at Holt. "Never realized how much he looked like Blake until now. For half brothers, they aren't much alike on the surface, but there's something in their expressions." She smiles slowly. "That's exactly how Blake looked at Peace, y'know—right before he married her."

Ahh!

I make a choked sound, and I swear the air temperature goes up some fifty degrees.

Suddenly, I'm boiling.

"Felicity Randall, don't you dare put thoughts like that out in the wild. We're just fooling around. Nothing crazy."

Ha ha, right. I'm such a bad liar.

"Are you?" she asks mildly. "Then why are you blushing like a beet?"

"Because you're being ridiculous," I spit.

And because Holt already said I've got his heart, and I want to believe him so bad, but I'm scared to admit that to anyone else when they'll just look at me with pity for being another dumb little girl falling for his wicked ways.

They'll just look at me like I'm a fool.

For falling in love with him.

Ugh. I can't think about this right now while we're standing outside Fel's livelihood in shambles and one big, threatening, MIA asshole still breathing down our necks.

So I just give her a little shove, and she pushes me back, grinning.

Seriously.

I still don't know how she's smiling after the night she's had.

"You need a ride home?" I ask. "You're not too shaky to drive, are you?"

"I'm fine," she promises. "You worry too much, Libby."

"You're my friend. I'm gonna worry." I bite my lip. "Listen, just in case, how about I follow you home in the truck? Never know, they might double back. Or if it was personal, they might've hit your house, too."

There's the weirdness passing over her again.

It's like, whenever I say certain things, she's remembering stuff she doesn't want to.

Sometimes I wonder what happened to Felicity when she left town.

Ever since she came back, she's been different.

All those nasty rumors that she was sleeping around with Dennis Bress for money before he passed, and then the close calls with her cousin and an untimely end only added fuel to the fire.

I can't put my finger on it since I didn't know her too well before then, but she changed somehow.

And I wonder if this break-in is my crap raining on her parade...or her old chickens coming home to roost?

She only shakes her head, smiling. "No need. I'm fine. But if it'd make you feel better, okay."

"It would." I squeeze her arm for a second, then pull away. "Be right back."

Holt smiles when he sees me coming, leaning in to murmur something to his brother before stepping away.

"Felicity okay?" he asks as I draw closer.

"She's taking it pretty well, considering. I'd be ready to commit a freaking homicide." I smile tiredly. "But I'm gonna shadow her home just in case. Make sure she's safe and locked down tight. You wanna come?"

Holt glances over his shoulder at Blake, running a hand through his thick black hair and ruffling it up. "I'm gonna stay here with Blake and see what I can suss out. He'll give me a ride back. Don't worry about me."

"Okay," I say—before letting out a startled sound as he hooks an arm around my waist.

Holt gets me with that easy strength every time, the way he just casually pulls me in like I don't weigh more than a feather, pressing me against his tall, firm body, letting me feel every hard edge of his frame...and there's a lot of hardness to go around.

I make a flustered sound, pushing lightly at his chest.

"*Hey*," I protest. "People are watching."

That just makes the smirk cut across Holt's face like a sword. He leans down, smothering me in his warmth, raking his scruff against my cheek.

"What, you embarrassed to be seen with me now?" he teases, and I grumble.

"Little bit."

"You should be. I'm about to get real damn embarrassing, honey."

That's the only warning before he covers my mouth with his, silencing my protest.

Nah—more like I lose the will to protest at all.

The second his lips touch mine, I start to go off, all adrenaline and heat, gasping as he parts my lips with a firmness that isn't one bit shy about stealing into me.

He kisses the way most men fuck.

Slow and hard and deep and urgent.

The way his tongue glides in and out of my mouth makes me remember him with every single sense—how he smells when we're sweaty and tangled together, the way his beard rakes against my skin as he licks all over me, the clever circles rough fingers work against my flesh, the taste of his salty skin when I bite his shoulder, the way his eyes gleam in the darkness with heat, need, urgency, the sound of the bed creaking as he surges into me hard enough to make the headboard slam against the wall.

God.

Holt Silverton makes me relive all that and more with just the plunge of a deep, needy tongue and his hands on my back, reminding me I'm so flipping *his.*

By the time he lets my lips go, there's one more hard thing pressed between us.

Sweet Lord.

If it wasn't for Felicity and Blake, we'd barely get out of sight before I mounted him right there in my truck.

He does the worst things to me.

I just hope I'm not letting my body override my heart, when his touch gets me so deep for reasons I don't want to name just yet.

But I feel like the gasps he pulls out of me are speaking those things to the stars above, anyway.

Making it true.

Finally, I can breathe again, our lips parting as I look up at him.

For a hot second, all I can see is Holt against the backdrop of the stars, the sinful beauty of a fallen angel, forbidden and entrancing, his mouth still wet from our bomb as hell kiss.

I gotta talk to him. After tonight. Tell him how I feel.

With a shaky smile, I press my fingers to his lips.

"Save some for later," I tease, then pull away, my knees weak. "See you back home."

"Sure, babe," he says, and I can feel his eyes on me, watching me so close, like a tether stretching between us as I step toward my truck. "See you real soon."

* * *

IT'S NOT a long drive to Felicity's place.

She lives in one of the town's inner suburbs—well, really the *only* inner suburb. Even with all the growth lately Heart's Edge isn't much bigger than a postage stamp.

Her little cottage-style house looks clear when we pull up outside. Doesn't look like the door's been forced, no windows broken, yard is neat and clean.

I still wait in my truck, headlights flooding her porch, until she unlocks the door and peeks inside.

When she waves back a minute later after a walk-through, giving me the go-ahead thumbs up, I wave, then back out of the drive.

She'll be okay.

She's surrounded by good neighbors, and she's a tough, smart cookie.

She can take care of herself.

But I can't help but worry over her anyway, playing through wild theories in my head as I head home.

It's a long, lonely drive.

I remember taking this route with Dad so many times back when I was practicing for my license, or even when I was younger, falling asleep in the seat next to him and hanging on his arm while he drove.

He'd play soft music on the radio, low so it wouldn't wake me up.

That man was a total sucker for Patsy Cline.

I guess it's nostalgia that makes me turn the radio on, searching through stations, looking for some oldies. I don't really expect to find any Patsy, but I get Billie Holiday, and "What Is This Thing Called Love?"

Good question, Billie.

With mellow jazz playing, I let myself sink into the lulling quiet of the drive, just half watching the stars and half watching the road.

It'd be peaceful as hell.

A great way to clear my head.

If only it wasn't for the grinding sound of engines and the rumble of siding metal.

It's that highway noise when you're passing one of those big eighteen-wheeler rigs. Even though the sides of the freight box in the back are made of solid metal, it booms and shakes in the wind over the rumble of its own speed.

That's what's coming up on me in a roar, snapping me out of my daze.

I check my mirrors, just as a huge semi-truck comes ripping up the road behind me, veering in from one of the small feeder roads.

It's speeding like a missile on wheels.

Faster than rigs should go, way over the speed limit, its engine howling like a rabid dog in my wake as it comes charging up at my rear end.

"Holy shit!" I whisper.

There's barely time to get a bad feeling about this.

I slam on the gas, making my truck leap forward, but I feel like I'm already outgunned.

Being smaller and more maneuverable doesn't cut it. Not when that thing's got an engine made for long haul power.

My pulse punches my throat, hot fear-sweat and even hotter anger rushing through me.

I grind down hard on the gas and beg for just a little more speed out of my poor truck. I'm a fighter, but I'm not stupid.

That rig could splatter me like a honeybee.

I just gotta get to the little lane that dips off the road, down the palisades of the highway, toward my ranch.

It's a tight curve, no way in hell that truck can barrel down it without tipping over.

And it's less than two miles.

Go, Libby!

It almost feels like Dad's voice in my head, telling me to get the lead out my ass and floor it.

I lean into the steering wheel, clutching it so tight my hands hurt, punching the gas pedal until the needle creeps up over eighty, ninety, and all I can hear is the gunfire of my heart. Plus the roar of that semi creeping up like a hungry bear, so big its shadow falls over me.

No headlights, either.

He's driving with them off, and when I steal a desperate glance in the rear-view mirror, I can't see who's behind the wheel. But I've got a good guess or two.

He's almost on my bumper.

For a second, we flirt just inches away from a crash, before he veers left.

What the?

Oh, crap.

He's trying to block me, wall me off before I can make the turn.

I've got my shotgun here somewhere. I fumble under the seat, but if I don't wanna crash, I've gotta slow down.

Maybe that's the smart thing.

He's pulling up alongside me and won't expect it.

Yeah.

I don't slam on the brakes, but I do ease off the gas—and

suddenly I'm dropping back while he surges ahead with a grinding of gears. A split second later, I risk dipping down to feel around until I find the holster and rip my shotgun out.

I jerk myself back up, propping the barrel on the steering wheel, blowing my hair out of my eyes as I take aim and—

And nearly knock my own dumb teeth out, slamming my head on the window as the semi angles over with all the grace of a hippo and slams into me sidelong.

He'd fallen back, too.

In the flash it took me to get my gun, he's taken me by surprise.

Now the inside of my cab crunches inward with a metallic squeal, my head bouncing off the window in an agonizing *thwack!*

The shotgun skitters from my fingers and drops down between the dash and the passenger seat.

Crap, crap, crap.

With a cry, I grab at the steering wheel.

My gut lurches and twists as the truck goes up on two wheels, then crashes back down.

I just barely wrench the whole damn thing away from the shoulder before it can plunge through the guardrail and into the valley.

Breathing hard, I take a second to orient myself.

My poor truck's limping. I can hear its front axle squealing, and I'm having to fight to keep it in a straight line.

But that semi's still running alongside me, going a hell of a lot smoother—it's like swatting a fly with a flipping tank, and as the whole rig goes easing over to the left, my breathing just stops.

Bastard's gearing up to do it *again.*

He's gonna hit me harder, and this time I won't be able to stop him if he slams me over the guardrail to God knows where. This is almost like what happened with Warren and Haley Ford when they took down that drug lord—except the one man who could save me doesn't even know what's happening.

My heart turns over.

Terror becomes my state of being.

Thing is, I'm also too pissed off to die like this.

No, I'm not gonna make it if he hits me again. But I've got a few more aces up my sleeve.

Before he can wrench his semi over like a wrecking ball again, I slam on the brakes and swerve my truck to the left, cutting over behind him as I drop back.

I was gonna let him cut ahead of me while I did a swift U-turn and hauled it back to town. Only, I didn't count on my truck's age catching up with it, plus whatever damage he did from nailing me the first time.

One of my front tires just pops right off.

And that's the end.

I'm dropping down in a sudden twisting jolt, sparks flying and metal screeching, the truck starting to spin while my tire goes bouncing merrily away.

Hissing, swearing myself blue, I wrench the wheel and hit the brakes as hard as I can, forcing the truck to a halt with its ass fishtailing across the road.

It finally swerves to a stop, completely blocking the highway.

Up ahead, the semi's brake lights flash neon red.

Crap crap crap crap *crap*.

Diving down, I grab under the seat until my hand lands on the smooth barrel of the shotgun.

Snatching it up, I kick the driver door open and tumble out, then duck down behind the bed, using it as a shield.

That semi's coming right at me, charging like a bull.

I brace my hip against the rear wheel guard—discover one of many bruises in the process, *ow*—and prop the shotgun's barrel against the edge of the truck bed, bracing as I take aim.

I still can't quite make out the driver's face, but I can see enough to shoot his windshield out.

And if that's not enough to slow him down, I'll run.

Straight down the hill, into the brush, get myself out of here.

I'm no coward, but I know when to stay smart to stay alive.

Breathing hard, every sense ratcheted up to a thousand, I lay my finger on the trigger, letting him get closer and closer...

Until I realize he's slowing down.

Until his engine quiets, then stops, easing to a stop just a few feet away from the side of my truck.

Swallowing hard, my entire body prickles with nerves.

I hold, watching suspiciously, waiting to *fire*.

The semi's driver side door swings out with a squeal.

Then that silhouetted body emerges into the light.

Big.

Bulky.

With a face as hard as stone and a smile as slick as oil, Declan Eckhard casually aims a pistol my way.

It's one hell of a question who'll shoot first.

I'm trained right on his heart.

He's aiming right between my eyes.

But my finger goes numb on the trigger as he speaks, calm as you please, his voice just as slick as his smile.

"Good evening, Libby," he growls. "If you'd ever like to see your lovely sister alive again, would you be so kind as to lower your gun?"

XXII: CART BEFORE THE
HORSE (HOLT)

*L*ibby didn't come home last night.

I still feel weird calling it *home*, but dammit, that ranch means something, almost as much as she does.

When I'd texted last night, she replied back almost instantly.

Felicity doesn't feel safe. Staying over. See you tomorrow, champ.

Champ?

She's never called me that before. Part of me wonders if she's cooking up new pet names.

It's weird, impersonal, a little mocking even for Miss Sassy herself.

Not like the way we usually are where sarcasm is half the lead-up to a fight and half foreplay.

Maybe kissing her like the ship was sinking in front of Felicity and my brother last night was a little too much, and she needed some space.

I overheard her conversation with her friend at The Nest, even if I wasn't supposed to.

Am I really looking at her the way my brother looked at Peace?

Shit.

I remember watching them together back in the winter, marveling at how fast that redheaded hippie girl poached my brother's heart.

If that's how I look at Libby, can you blame a man?

And can you blame me for being in the only frigging jewelry shop in Heart's Edge, blundering around like a moose, looking for something I can give her?

Not a ring.

It's too early for that, even if a psycho part of me says *do it.*

No—I want something that'll make her think of me when she touches it, the same way I know she thinks of her old man when she touches that little constellation necklace she always wears.

Something to remind her I picked it out just for her.

"I don't know," Alaska drawls at my side, rubbing at his thick, dark beard as he looks down into the jewelry case. "It's a flower. Don't girls like flowers?"

I eye the gaudy rhinestone orchid he's looking at and snort.

"Alaska, I don't know how you can be so damn smart, but this damn stupid."

"Hey," he grunts. "Look, I—"

"Yeah, yeah. More experience with polar bears than with women. Ain't that always your line?"

He scowls at me. "You gotta tell the whole town that?"

From behind the counter, the clerk—Cindy Northman, another of my old high school classmates—tries not to laugh, covering her mouth politely. I'm glad she's married off with a family, not still pining away for yours truly.

"Holt Silverton, are you really in here buying jewelry for a lady?" she asks. "For Liberty Potter?"

Sometimes it's actually helpful having everyone in a little town knowing all your business.

Still, I make a face at her.

"Might be. You want to try being more helpful than *this* lunk?" I thump Alaska's arm.

Cindy clears her throat around another laugh. "Well, what kind of stuff does Libby like?"

"Stars," I say immediately. "But that's more her memory with her dad. I want something for us. She loves horses, her ranch, and she's always wearing red and yellow. Maybe something gold, or something with a ruby?"

Cindy clucks her tongue. "That's a little simple, Holt. Favorite colors? Horses?" She shakes her head. "Let's try something else. Tell me about the first time you kissed."

I eyeball her. "If I hear about this from anyone else..."

"Oh, I'm not asking for gossip!" she says with a snicker, her cheeks flushing. "Really, do you think I'm that bad?"

"Yes."

"Maybe just a little." Her smile turns impish, but it's actually sweet, not flirty.

It feels like I've turned a corner.

Maybe some folks around here are starting to believe I'm not the scoundrel I used to be.

And maybe they're rooting for me and Libby, too.

Not just waiting to see how I muck it all up.

I shake my head. "The first time, she actually kissed *me*. There've been a lot of kisses since then, but I could tell you about the night I kissed her. Right when I realized I was falling in love with her."

"Please do." Cindy's eyes light up like she's got a million stars in them.

Alaska nudges me. "Boss, did you just tell this nice lady you're in love with Libby? I'm pretty sure you ain't even said it to her yet?"

I wince, nodding.

"Never mind that," Cindy says. "Tell me about the kiss!"

"All right, all right," I say, laughing and rubbing the back of my neck. "It was at the Norton's barn dance. She was all dolled up in the prettiest dress, and she just looked like a flower drifting every time she moved. We danced together until it was

378

too hot to breathe. Then we went for a walk under the stars. We were talking about her daddy, about *us,* and I told her how she gets me all messed up inside."

I can still see her that night.

Looking up at me with those sky-blue eyes that turn me inside out.

"I remember how all her colors turned silver in the moonlight, bright and pretty as you please. She looked like goddamn *magic,* Cindy." I can't stop smiling.

Cindy mouths a silent *wow.*

"That's when it hit me. I knew I could look at Libby and want to kiss her for the rest of my life. She lit up my world like she was the moon and all the damn stars a man could ever need."

There's silence.

I realize I've been shooting my mouth off like some purple prose spewing kid with a crush. I look away sharply, clearing my throat.

"Think that's how it went, anyway," I mumble.

"Damn, boss," Alaska says in a soft hush. There's something like respect in his voice, though I don't really understand why. "You're serious about this bird."

"Holt," Cindy sighs, and Christ her voice is practically *dripping* with all this dreamy emotion. "That's lovely. I think I know just the thing."

Finally.

I'm ready to start cursing with relief.

It's so embarrassing I want to get this done and get the hell out of here.

I'm also aching to be with Libby.

I think after a quick stop on-site to make sure the new framing is going okay, I'll head back to the ranch and surprise her. Spend lunch with her before we both get back to work.

Cindy guides me away from that hideous case of rhinestones and over to another display, where delicate pieces are laid out against black velvet. They sparkle under the lights without overwhelming with too much glitter—letting you appreciate the more finer bits.

The moment I lay eyes on it, I know exactly what Cindy wants to show me without even being told.

It's a bracelet.

At first, I'd have scoffed at it for Libby. She's a rough and tumble girl who'll break something so light in a heartbeat. That's the thing with her, though.

She's rough and tumble to her core, but she's delicate, too.

She never breaks, and I know she won't break this.

The chain is figaro-style, thread-thin, crafted so fine with tiny diamonds no bigger than seed pearls. They're interspersed between the large links and the small ones, glittering like tiny stars.

And dangling from it, I smile when I see it.

A crescent moon.

Its framing is silver with crushed diamonds inside.

Fine as powder, like moondust itself, making that crescent moon shine as bright as the real moon did overhead while I looked down at Libby, all silver and gorgeous and breathtaking.

Yeah, fuck.

I can feel it in the swell of my chest, in the slow smile growing on my lips.

That's the one.

"It's perfect," I say, and Cindy lights up with a pleased smile. "How much?"

"Three thousand dollars even," she chirps.

Alaska lets out a soft whistle, giving me a troubled look. "Boss, with the cashflow issues lately..."

"Don't worry, big guy. I've got it covered."

That's when I slip my hand into my back pocket and pull out a small velvet box.

Once, the same box held my hopes and dreams before they were pulverized in a New York minute by Barry the fuck and that banshee Calypso, hanging on his arm.

Now?

Now it's just a protector for an overpriced piece of useless jewelry.

I set the ring box on the counter and flip it open.

The five-carat Bulgari ring inside nearly blinds poor Cindy in the shop's lighting.

The diamond is obscene, marquise cut and set inside a concentric frame of white gold. It's an antique, one of those things you buy as much for the prestige as the size of the ridiculously large rock.

I'd bought it for Calypso because it suited her.

Like hell I'm going to recycle something picked for another woman for Libby.

She'd probably just laugh her head off at the sight of the thing, anyway.

Cindy stares, though.

So does Alaska, and he gives me a wide-eyed look. "Boss, is that the same—"

"Yeah," I tell him. "Trust me, I don't need it anymore."

Cindy bites her lip. "You want to sell this?"

I nod. "I've got the papers and everything. It's over sixty years old, used to belong to some big Italian opera guy. Paid a small mortgage for it. Different times."

With a sharp gasp, Cindy tears her wide eyes away from the ring and back to me. "Oh, my. I don't think we can..." She swallows. "I'll have to talk to the owner, Holt. We-we need to get an appraiser, you see, and—"

I chuckle. "Deep breath. I'm not expecting full price. How about you hold that for me, lock it up in the safe, and write me the paperwork so you can hold it for appraisal? When you've got the owner's approval and a price, you can call me, and we can trade off for the sale and the bracelet."

"S-sure," she says, looking a little pale.

I think it might just scare her a little to have that kind of responsibility on her hands.

There's probably never been a ring this expensive in Heart's Edge in her life. She's probably too young to even have been a sparkle in Gerald Bostrom's eye.

Thinking of Bostrom is sobering, though.

As much as I'm riding on cloud nine, we still have trouble.

While Cindy bustles away to open the safe and draw up the paperwork, Alaska gives me an amused look. "You sure you want to be selling off that ring? Seems more like you should be buying one?"

I snort. "She'd kill me if I popped the question this soon. That's moving so fast she'd push me *off* the cliff if we showed up by the valley to do the flower toss all the locals do."

Not to say I'm not thinking about it.

Thinking about it way more than I should be.

"Love doesn't run on schedules," he says gravely.

I give him a flat look.

"That some mountain man wisdom you learned up there in the wild?"

With a long, patient sigh, he just eyes me. "One day, boss, you're gonna stop giving me a heap of shit."

"Not today, pal," I tease, before frowning as my phone goes off in my pocket. "One sec."

I step away from both Alaska and the jewelry counter as I pull out my phone and check the number. It's one of the guys on my crew, Steve, who keeps an eye on the office when I'm not there.

I swipe my thumb over the screen and lift the phone to my ear.

"What's up?" I say.

"Hey, boss," Steve says, but I can already tell from the tone of his voice that something's very wrong. "You might want to get down here quick. You've got company—and she's real upset."

* * *

"She" turns out to be the wrong Potter.

I was so worried about Libby I went tearing back to the site like my ass was on fire, leaving Alaska to wrap up the transaction and get the paperwork finished so I can either get my ring back or get paid—and I may or may not have broken a few laws, both speeding and texting while driving.

It scares me to think why Libby would be in my office, but she isn't answering her phone and didn't call me first.

It fucks with me even more when I go busting into the trailer and see the state Sierra Potter's in.

She's hunched in the chair opposite my desk like she's cold even though it's blistering hot out—curled in on herself with her arms wrapped around her like she's trying to hold her heat in, damn well shivering.

Her arms are bare.

They're covered in bruises.

Her sleeveless pink blouse is ripped and dirty. Same for her white denim capris, and where her legs are bare, she's covered in scratches. Some of them deep, the blood drying but still wet enough to be bright red.

Her hair's tangled, straggling out of its ponytail, dirty and littered with grass and leaves.

And her face.

Holy fuck, her poor face.

Her mouth looks swollen like she's been hit with a brick, all split with dried blood, a black ring around her eye, her jaw a purple lump.

I don't care what she's done to Libby.

If Declan did this to her, I *will* fucking slaughter him.

You don't treat a girl like this.

Not fucking *anybody.*

Especially not the sister of the girl I love.

"Sierra," I blurt out, stepping in—and she flinches, looking up with haunted eyes. "One second, let me get the first aid kit—"

"There's no time!" she gasps. "I barely made it, Holt. I barely got away, and if he notices I'm gone and figures out I came to you..."

Her lips are trembling frantically, her eyes wet.

I go still, staring at her.

"Declan?"

She nods miserably, staring at me, guilt burned all over her face.

"I...I tried to save her," she whispers. "I tried to save Libby, but I couldn't. You have to go to her. You *have* to, before he hurts her any m-m-*more*—"

Any thought I have that this might be a trick breaks off when Sierra bursts into deep, rasping sobs, tears pouring down her face as she buries her head in her hands.

She's not that good an actor.

Fuck.

I curl my hand against Sierra's shoulder, gripping tight, the only reassurance I can offer right now when my mind's on Libby, my thoughts racing. I grab my phone and try texting her again—and then stop, staring at the text she sent me.

"She said she was staying with Felicity last night," I say. "Was she?"

Sierra shakes her head miserably before grasping my wrist like I'm her only lifeline.

"I'm the one who...who s-sent that. He made me. I tried to give you a hint—*champ*."

I close my eyes, swearing, but then tap out another text just to try anyway.

I have to, instead of relying on someone else's word.

Libby. If you're safe, tell me the name of the horse I used to ride when I'd come by your place as a kid.

Even a wrong answer would tell me something.

Nothing comes back.

Nothing again when I try to call, either, all while Sierra watches me with woebegone eyes.

While I swear for the hundredth time, she shakes her head slowly.

"He took her phone," she says, rubbing at her nose. "And her truck. It's all banged up. I saw them bring it in last night. He's...he's trying to make her show him where the treasure is."

I stare at her, bewildered.

"*What* goddamn treasure? There's nothing in Ursa but some old antiques that might not even be worth all that much."

"I don't *know!*" she bursts out, almost wailing. "He's been obsessed, ever since he realized Libby's been hiding something down there. The dead guy just makes him think it's something priceless enough to kill over. I...I couldn't tell him, I didn't know."

She touches her face then, right below her black eye, and that's when it clicks.

Declan thinks there's a secret fucking treasure in Ursa.

Not realizing the treasure *is* Ursa, and possibly that stupid rock.

He thought Libby and Sierra were hiding it, and he beat Sierra, trying to get it out of her.

Then, when she didn't cough up details, he went after Libby.

My jaw clenches alligator tight.

Death is too good for that fucker.

I take a slow breath, trying to clear the red mist of rage from my mind before it's too late. I have to calm down before I get Libby killed, charging out there unprepared.

"Are they in Ursa now?" I ask. "Is that where he took her?"

Sierra nods slowly. "Last night, him and a bunch of guys. Those trucker thugs he owes money to, they set up camp. Said they weren't moving until they found something big out there."

I could almost smile, if I didn't want to snarl.

History's repeating itself as tragedy and farce this time.

Looks like Danny the Rattlesnake found himself a successor.

"Give me your phone," I demand.

Sierra gives me a blank look, her hand hovering near the pocket of her jeans, but she hesitates. "Wh-why?"

"I'm calling Declan," I tell her. "He'll pick up for you."

Her eyes widen, and she shakes her head frantically. "You can't! If...if you use my phone, h-he'll know I went to you, Holt. I won't be able to go back and—"

"Sierra, listen." I pull the other chair over next to her and sit down, propping my elbows on my thighs and leaning forward, watching her intently. "Why do you *want* to go back?"

She bites her lip, looking at me with those glistening eyes that are so much like Libby's, and yet so different.

I feel like under their dullness, there's a spark.

If she can just remember how to ignite it.

"I...I still love him," she whispers.

I hold in a breath, remembering she's been abused.

I'm no shrink, but it's classic Stockholm Syndrome, falling in love with her asshole captor. Knowing deep down she's dependent on a monster, but not knowing *how* to leave him.

"Tell me one thing. You love him more than you love your sister?" I ask calmly.

She glares at me, hugging her arms closer to her chest. "Libby and I hate each other, we—"

"Bullshit, girl," I interrupt her as gently as I can. "If you hated her, you wouldn't be so desperate for me to save her." While she stares at me, her swollen lip quivering, I continue. "Things happen, Sierra. Bad blood. Scars to the heart. At the end of the day, you're still sisters. Look at me and Blake. Family love's real, and it holds—and real love would never hurt you like Declan."

Reaching out, I lightly touch her arm, just below the creeping bruises.

They look just like fingertips.

She flinches and won't meet my eyes.

"That's not love, Sierra." I let my hand drop away. "He's using you. And you're so used to being used that you mistake it for love."

"No!" She closes her eyes tightly, pressing her lips together. "That's...that's cruel of you to say."

"I don't want to hurt you," I say. "I get it, he's all you think you have. But if you help me save Libby, then you've got her for life."

Sierra doesn't say anything else, her shoulders hunching.

Then she curses softly under her breath, thrusts her hand into her pocket, draws out her phone and shoves it at me.

"Six nine one seven," she chokes out, her voice breaking. "The unlock code. Declan's in the contacts under Hot Stuff."

"Thank you," I say with everything in me, giving her shoulder another squeeze as I stand, swiping her phone and unlocking it.

I don't know what I'll say.

I've got a few ideas.

Pacing the office to keep myself calm, Sierra's head turns to follow me. I tap the speed dial and then wait, listening to the ring.

If he doesn't pick up, I don't know what I'll do.

It'll likely get me arrested, and I won't feel the least bit sorry.

Just as long as Libby's safe.

On the third ring, the bastard picks up.

Gone is that slick, silky-talking menace, replaced with the growling, snappy prick he truly is.

"For fuck's sake, girl, where the hell did you run off to—"

"Is that any way to speak to a lady?" I snarl.

I can't believe I get that out in a mild, sardonic tone.

The sound of his voice alone makes me livid.

Declan goes dead quiet, though in the background I can hear noise—men shouting, things clattering. Sounds almost like a construction site.

"Holt Silverton."

Ah, there's that sneering, slick-talking tone again.

"Who else?" I work my jaw. "Listen, I don't feel like fencing with you, Eckhard. I know you aren't with the bank. I know you aren't what you say you are. I know what you want, and I'll bet you know exactly what *I* want, too."

"Do I now?" he asks slowly, feigning ignorance. "Oh—that's right. You're a bit sweet on the brattier Miss Potter, aren't you?"

"That's one way of putting it."

And that's one way of confirming he's still got Libby.

Shit.

"So you're looking for the Ursa treasure?" I ask. "Because you can dig that whole town up and you won't find squat. Those old bandits were too smart to just leave their whole cache in town. They left clues, though. Clues I've already found. Without me, you'll never figure out where the stash is."

"What is it? Silver? Gold?" Declan sneers. "Why should I believe you?"

"Because I know damn well you've been digging all night, and you've got nothing but broken glass and old pickaxe heads." I pause for effect, then add, "And you don't even know what you're looking for. I just told you. Silver, Declan. Enough unrefined silver ore that you could get yourself out of a hell of a lot of trouble and live pretty high on the hog once you're done."

Silence again.

"Name your terms," he growls back finally.

"Libby," I say. "Safe and unharmed. That's why you took her, isn't it? Information? Tell me where to meet you. I'll show you where to find the cache, and you let us walk. Nobody has to get hurt."

He makes a scoffing sound. "How do I know you won't just double-cross me and try to take the silver for yourself? I know that little bitch needs it bad to pay off the bank."

Because there's no damn silver, I think to myself.

All I say is, "Some shit matters more than money. Libby's life, for one."

"How sentimental."

"Guess I am. It says an awful lot that you haven't once asked why I'm calling you on Sierra's phone, or if she's even safe."

A dark, ugly edge slips into Declan's voice. "I don't have to ask. I know that little whore turned tail and ran to you. She's got no fucking spine at all."

As if he does.

As if any man with a spine would hit a woman, much less resort to his dirty, underhanded tricks.

That's okay.

I'll find a way to make him pay.

For hurting them *both*.

"Sierra's spine is just fine," I say. "Tell me, Declan, do we have a deal or not?"

After a long pause, Declan grinds out, "You come alone."

"One man for backup," I snarl. "You can't expect me to come either alone or unarmed. I'm sure you'll have me plenty outnumbered anyway, but humor me. No guns."

"Whatever. One damn man," he spits. "Midnight tonight. The ghost town. You come by the southern road from the ranch. Whistle three times when you pass the forked tree with the lightning cut split out of it, or you'll get shot. Understood?"

"Understood," I echo back.

Then hang up before he can answer.

I've reached my limit.

One more word and I'd have lost my shit and ruined the whole thing.

As it is, I've only bought less than twelve hours until midnight.

That'll have to be enough time to stall him and turn my bluff into a rescue mission.

I'm already pulling up Blake's number as I race for the door, Sierra's voice trailing after me.

"Where are you going? What's happening?"

"Stay here," I throw back over my shoulder, flinging the door open and launching myself out into the sun. "Stay safe. I'm calling backup. We're gonna bring Libby home."

* * *

I KNOW how to get Declan to believe me.

Just long enough to get him right where I want him.

Sure, there was treasure out in Ursa.

I've got it.

I've also got the proof.

And I stop by the house for a minute, racing inside. It's so empty it reminds me of sleeping alone in Libby's bed last night, never realizing all that time she was in that bastard's hands.

Helpless.

Needing me.

And I wasn't there.

That's gonna change real fast.

I dash through Mark's old journals, his keepsakes, gathering what I need.

The journal with all those numbers written on the inside back cover, for one.

Proof that there's something valuable in Ursa.

Proof it's worth millions, even if I still have trouble believing anyone in their right mind would pay that much for any old rock, even if it's from Mars.

Doesn't matter.

I need enough to distract Declan.

Tucking the journal under my arm, I move—and then, on a whim, I grab that little box with the red rock itself and take it with me, too.

Before I check my Colt, I make sure I've got rounds in the chamber.

Then I head out to saddle up and call in the cavalry.

I'm coming, Libby.

I'm coming for you.

Just hold on a little longer, honey.

XXIII: HOLD YOUR HORSES (LIBBY)

*E*veryone knows I've got a bit of a violent streak.

It's been refined down to an art by the grit it took defending my home from pricks like Declan Eckhard. Anyone who'd dare take the life I've built away.

But that violent streak is nothing compared to the sheer volcanic rage bubbling inside me now.

I swear, if I wasn't tied to a rickety old chair with splinters biting into my ass and a bent, rusty nail head threatening to give me tetanus, I think I'd have launched myself straight at Declan by now and torn his throat out with my *teeth*.

If there was ever any doubt about the kind of man he is, he's more than killed it over the last twelve hours.

Last night, he got me to lower my gun because even if I'm mad as hell at Sierra, she's still my sister. I can't let him hurt her.

So he clubbed me over the head with his pistol.

Knocked me out cold.

He dragged me here to Ursa, where I got woken up by a nice right hook to the cheek, only to find myself tied to this chair with my head throbbing fit to kill.

We've been yelling at each other for hours since then.

He wants me to be afraid of him?

Fuck that.

He wants something.

Even after hours of knocking me around, I haven't given him anything but lip.

Every single verbal middle finger I can manage since he's got my hands bound pretty tight in a mess of ropes.

I guess he finally got sick of my mouth, though.

Since afternoon, he's given up talking, and he's gone digging.

He and his goons brought a bunch of equipment up here. Looks like it might've been stolen from one of Holt's sites. They've been going at it in the graveyard ever since.

I'm left alone inside the church between interrogations.

I can barely see them through the cracked, dusty glass still left in one of the windows. They're working by floodlights now that it's dusk.

The graveyard's a total mess.

Markers tossed over, bits of bone gleaming in the white light.

All they're finding are long-dead bodies.

I wish this town *was* cursed, and all of those people would take revenge for desecrating their graves.

At least I can take comfort that it's not going well for them.

Declan's getting madder by the second, losing his cool, screaming at his people all red-faced with his neck a bulge of tendons.

The guys aren't taking it well.

I get the impression he owes them money. A lot of money, and that's the only reason they're helping him...but he's treating them like lackeys, and they ain't too fond of it.

There've been a few comments I overhear here and there.

Pissy shit, most of it.

But some of it sounds pretty threatening.

I wonder if I could use a little smooth-talking of my own to convince them to turn on Declan?

If only I had something better to offer...

Too bad.

But I overhear a few other things, too.

Yeah.

These boys are the ones who trashed The Nest. They mutter about how it was pocket change, not even half what Declan owed, and it almost got them arrested.

That's the problem with my long-shot plan.

If they're so scummy they'd rob an innocent woman to pay back that bastard's debts...then they're not people I'd trust not to double-cross me even if I got them on my side.

Something's up, though. The last hour or two, Declan's been in more of a hurry.

I wonder why the clock's ticking. It's getting dark and they're not even stopping.

I'm ready to pass out.

It's not safe for me to fall asleep here, but I don't know if I have a choice.

I'm exhausted, whipped, beat to hell and back.

Maybe it's better for me to sleep now while they're distracted. I'll be rested and ready for my moment when they finally call it quits to get some rest themselves.

I don't know how I'll get out of these ropes.

My arms are tied behind my back with the rope woven through the rungs of the chair, while my ankles are hitched to the chair's legs.

But if you think I won't hop down that mountain trail bent over with a chair strapped to my back?

You clearly haven't figured me out yet.

I'm still trying to wiggle my ass so it's not pressing down so hard on that bent nail head and figuring out how I can sleep without hurting myself worse.

That's when I catch a flicker of motion outside on the opposite side of the graveyard.

My chest thumps and I'm wide-awake again.

I go stiff, opening my eyes fully without lifting my head, trying not to give myself away.

If Declan's coming to screw with me again...

No, I recognize a ragged head of blonde hair.

Sierra.

Crap.

She'd skedaddled the hell out of here after Declan back-handed her good when I was brought in last night.

I'd hoped she was gone.

That one of us was safe.

I can't believe she'd come crawling back to that piece of scum after the way he tossed her around.

She still looks like hell, creeping in with a furtive look over her shoulder. She's scraped up and dirty, I guess from running through the mountain pass in the dark last night.

But if she's still Declan's girl, why's she sneaking around, looking at me with her fingers over her lips?

I get my answer when she skitters closer, drops to her knees behind my chair, and starts working at the ropes.

I freeze, staring over my shoulder.

It's hard to believe it at first.

Is Sierra actually turning on her boyfriend and trying to *help* me?

"Sierra?" I whisper.

"Shh!" she says urgently in the quietest hiss, fighting at the ropes, struggling at the knots with little frustrated sounds. "I can't...can't get—"

"Slow down," I whisper. "Look for the loop and try to get your fingers under it. What are you doing?"

She darts me a sharp look from under her brows, a light in her blue eyes that I've never seen before, so fierce it's glowing.

"You're my sister," she says. "Nothing else matters."

I don't know if I want to cry with relief or scream.

I just know we've got to get out of here.

If Declan catches her trying to help me, he'll hurt her even more.

And she's *my* sister, too.

I can't let her get savaged to save me.

So I try to keep my arms as loose as possible so they won't bunch up and make it harder, but she's cursing and pulling and making no progress. I think I feel the ropes loosening just a hair.

Trouble is, this is taking too long.

"You can't get it!" I whisper. "Go back to Heart's Edge. Get Holt."

"I *did!*" she flares, her voice rising for a moment, then dropping again to a terrified hush. "He told Declan some story and agreed to a meeting, said something about getting backup, but I know Declan...I *know* him, Libby. He'll kill Holt and as long as Declan's got you, Holt will let him, that stupid lovesick idiot." Her jaw sets with determination. "I've got to get you out of here before he gets here."

Lovesick? Enough to die for me?

I don't know whether I'm about to break, bawling for that overblown hero of a man or because I'm scared to death she's right about how it ends.

I shake my head sharply.

"Go," I whisper. "We'll work things out. You'll just be in danger. I can't let you—"

"Can't let her *what*, Miss Liberty?" a voice thunders behind Sierra.

A heavy shadow falls over us both.

My heart freezes.

In my peripheral vision, Sierra's eyes widen, the glassy pale blue of defeat.

Right before she suddenly jerks out of my field of view, lifted by a brutal hand.

Thrashing, twisting, I manage to kick the chair around so I can see, but there's nothing I can do to stop Declan from picking Sierra up in one hand like she weighs nothing, grabbing her up by her hair while she kicks and screams and thrashes.

"Let her go!" I snarl, yanking at the ropes, but it's no use.

He ignores me, looking at Sierra with cold contempt.

"So you finally decided to turn on me," he spits. "I always knew you were weaker than—"

He breaks off with the oddest sound, like he's just swallowed his tongue.

Sierra kicks hard, slamming her heel hard into his crotch.

She's wearing some cute little kitten heels, by the way.

Pointy as blades.

Declan doubles over, his face going white, his eyes bulging. His hand goes limp in Sierra's hair before flying over his crotch.

Sierra tumbles to the floor, hitting it hard with a cry.

"Sierra," I gasp out. "Run!"

She struggles up on one arm. "Libby, I—"

"Don't worry about me, just *go!*"

Declan lets out a breathless roar. "I'll fucking—"

He starts to reach for her, still half bent over, wheezing and red-faced and hobbling.

Sierra rolls under his grasping arm, onto her back.

With a vengeful little scream, she drives her foot up again and slams him right in the nuts one more time.

Holy hell!

I don't think I've ever heard a grown man make the sound that comes out of his mouth right now, like someone just punted a seagull in the gut, high and screeching.

I also don't think I've ever been prouder of my sister.

Declan totters backward, his legs buckling, and Sierra scrambles to her feet and darts for the door.

At the doorway, she pauses, looking back with sad, worried eyes. I manage a smile for her.

I nod, just once. No time to waste on words.

It's okay, I tell her. *Go now.*

I'll be all right.

Holt's coming.

And between me and him, we can tackle this idiot clown.

We'll make him pay back every red cent of evil tenfold.

Sierra hesitates a second longer. Her gaze flicks to Declan, and her eyes darken with something I recognize all too well.

Hatred.

Then she's gone, just a faint clatter of her heels on the rickety porch before she disappears into the night.

I'm glad.

Grateful that even if I don't get out of this okay, Sierra surely will.

For now, I just watch as Declan sags on his knees, clutching both hands over his puny dick like a little boy who's really gotta go and tries to hold it in.

His eyes are closed, his expression pained, his jaw a lump of iron.

"That. Fucking. *Bitch*," he wheezes, over and over again, like a mantra he's using to control the pain, rocking back and forth. "That bitch, that bitch, that *bitch!*"

I smirk. "What do you expect? She's my sister, dude."

He opens his eyes to hazy slits, looking at me with abject loathing—then lunges, only to let out a grunt and flop back, wincing and clawing at himself again.

Harsh breaths slip past his lips.

"You might wanna put some ice on that," I point out. "And hold still a bit. No smacking me around or anything. Ruined balls are weird like that. You never really realize how much you pull with your core until you've got a collapsed left testicle."

"My God," he grinds out. "Do you ever *shut up?*"

"Not if I can help it," I fling back cheerfully.

Right now, I just gotta keep him talking. Keep him busy.

I want him distracted when Holt shows up, and not ready and waiting to pull some nasty shit on my man.

"You want me to be quiet now? You were practically begging me to talk before. I don't think flip-flopping's a real attractive trait in a man, you know."

"Enough," he grunts. It's real satisfying that I can tell he's still about to pop from the pain. "Now shut up unless you actually have something useful to tell me about the silver."

Silver?

Oh.

Frick.

That must be what Holt told Declan to get him to meet.

One sly, sexy lie.

Might as well play into it.

If he figures out Holt tricked him, it's over for all of us. So I just shrug as best I can—but that's when I feel it.

The ropes *are* looser.

Sierra made some progress on that knot after all.

Curling my fingers, I try to search for the loose spot in the rope while I keep talking.

"Silver? It's in my kitchen drawer, you idiot," I say. "I dug it all up myself. Melted it down into a pretty silverware set. You were gonna get to eat off it for dinner before you had to be an asshole in my house. You're disinvited to future family gatherings, by the way. Pretty sure a double-stomp to the nuts is an effective Dear John. Pity. You'd have been a good brother-in-law, right?"

"The best," he grits out. "I'm absolutely brokenhearted over your bitch sister. What a missed opportunity, to be part of your family of waspish, irritating little harpies."

"If you'd been nice, we'd even have let you take the Potter name. Better than Eckhard, anyway. The hell kind of name is that? Where are you even from?"

"Better places than this podunk town."

Declan gathers himself with a weird dignity for a smarmy asshole, but I guess he keeps all his smarm in his balls, and Sierra stomped some of it out of him.

He draws himself up, rising to his feet on legs that visibly quake.

Guess he's still too proud to let me see him kneeling for too long.

"Now," he says, looking down at me with this sad attempt at

contempt. "Unless you want me to hunt that sister of yours down like a mad dog and shoot her, I suggest you try being more informative."

I grin.

Sierra's just as much of a country girl as I am.

She knows these mountains, the paths, and our ranch.

She knows how to shoot, too, just as well as I do.

Declan ain't hunting shit.

She's gone, and he's not gonna find her unless she wants to be found.

Which leaves me free to keep shooting my mouth off, while I keep secretly tugging at the ropes.

"What do you want to know? I could tell you how to trim a horse's hooves when they start to overgrow their shoes, or how to prime a pump that's been dry for a while, or—"

I expect the bolt of pain that slams into me like a tornado touching down on my head.

Turns out, expecting it doesn't make the back of his hand hurt any less.

Everything goes whirly as my chair tips over.

Slowly at first, then gravity grabs hold and it's *boom*, down, me flopping on my side like a fish on the floor.

"Ow," I force out. "Was that really necessary?"

"Necessary, but apparently useless. You're still running that mouth," he mutters. "I repeat, unless you have something useful to say...*shut it.*"

The threat's pretty freaking clear.

So is the menace as he strides closer, his dirty boots filling my vision.

I'm already bracing for pain, but I just grin.

"You're so gullible," I say. Nothing like a little truth to make him think I'm lying. "There's nothing here but ghosts. I've never been guarding any treasure. Don't you think if I had silver buried out here, I'd have fixed my money problems?"

"Nice try." He squats down in front of me, bringing his face into my line of sight.

It's hard to see what my sister ever found attractive. "You knew it was here. You just couldn't find it. So you've been keeping people out until you could. I *saw* you, riding out here with your man, looking for the silver to save your ass."

"So you're a stalker on top of hitting ladies? Charming." I let out a harsh laugh. "A big idiot, too. I told you. There's nothing here but ghosts. You should thank me for keeping people safe. The boys who died out here didn't go down happy. And angry dead people tend to stick around."

"Don't insult my intelligence."

"Too late! Already called you an idiot." I'm gonna get myself killed like this, but I need to keep him on the hook. "Believe me or not. But I heard one story about this gang of outlaws. Scum of the earth types. Real violent. And they weren't all that happy about getting outsmarted by the law. And you? You're out there digging up their graves right now. How do you feel about that?"

Me and my big mouth.

Declan drags me up so I'm dangling with the chair tilted against the floor, my whole body dangling from his grip, my scalp on fire.

He brings his face closer so I can smell his wet, meaty breath.

"Stop playing games with me, little girl," he grits out. "You forget. I know all about the dead body. There's no old-time outlaws and no fucking ghosts, *Libby Potter*. That man hasn't been dead that long. How do you feel about jail time as an accessory?"

"A hell of a lot better than I feel about your dental hygiene," I strain out. "Yeah, I know who killed that guy. You wanna hear it?"

His eyes narrow. "Do tell."

I conjure up my nastiest smile. "The same dead bandits who're gonna kill you. That guy tried to steal from this place, so Danny the Rattlesnake and his buddies took him out." I stare right at him like I'm fucking possessed. Might as well play into it. "I can hear them, Declan. I can *feel* them. They're telling me, *you're next.*"

He just stares at me coldly.

I don't know if my acting sucks or he just doesn't care.

But he lets me drop, my vision reeling as I hit the floor hard.

"Sick of your shit!" he snarls.

Then he turns and walks out.

Leaving me alone with the throbbing in my skull and the sound of Declan outside, shouting at his men to keep digging.

* * *

I DON'T KNOW if I fall asleep or pass out.

Everything gets dark, and nothing becomes clear again until Declan's voice wakes me up.

It's like the sound of him talking incites this instant, subconscious fury that slaps me awake as sharp as a punch.

I tense, slitting one eye open, taking in my surroundings.

I'm upright again. No memory of anyone picking up the chair I'm tied to. I must've really been unconscious.

It's darker outside, just a sliver of moonlight through the window.

I can't hear more digging noises or shouting, but I don't get the feeling that people are asleep.

Nah.

It's too tense here.

Declan's shadow hovers, pacing back and forth outside on the porch, his voice drifting inward.

"Don't fucking play me, Silverton."

Holt.

He's talking to Holt.

My heart leaps. I strain to listen.

"We had a deal. Midnight." He pauses.

"Why are you in such a rush?"

401

Another pause.

He passes in front of the door again and leans in to look at me. I slam my eyes shut and let my head hang before he's fully in.

"Of course she's alive! Asleep." He stays silent, then sighs. "Will it get this over with faster? Fine."

His heavy footsteps make the floor creak as he comes inside.

Those thick, horrible fingers dig into my chin, jerking my face up.

"Wake up!" he grunts, but my eyes are already snapping open.

I glare at him mutely, grinding my teeth.

He smirks.

"I'm going to be nice," he says. "Talk to your boyfriend."

He shoves the phone against my ear, still holding my jaw so tight it feels like it's gonna snap right off.

Part of me wants to stay quiet just to spite him. But when I hear Holt on the other end, drawling in that dry way of his, I can't resist.

"Libby," he says—calm as can be, as if he's got everything under control.

I hope like hell he does.

"Hey," I say, trying to keep my voice calm, too.

I don't want him to worry. I want him to know it's okay, and I've got his back.

"Where the hell you been?" I whisper.

"Taking care of business," he answers. "I'm on my way, honey. Coming for you right now."

"You're slow," I retort and swallow back the knot forming in my throat. I won't cry in front of Declan. I *will not*. "Get your butt up here. Turns out Sierra's boyfriend is really crappy company."

Holt chuckles. "Yeah? Doesn't surprise m—"

I don't get to hear any more. Declan rips the phone away with a disgusted sound.

I almost lean after it.

Almost.

But instead I let my pride yank me back and focus on feeling at my ropes, still searching for the right spot.

Declan lifts the phone to his ear.

"One hour," he bites off. "No more delays. Don't make any other 'adjustments,' or I'll know you're bluffing, and I will kill her, Silverton."

I don't hear what Holt says back but it must be enough to satisfy Declan.

He ends the call with a swipe of his thumb, then turns his head slowly, looking down at me with narrowed eyes.

"Well," he says. "Since your darling man's being so accommodating...what do I really need you for?"

It doesn't quite click what he means.

His fist snaps out so fast I don't even see it coming.

He hits like he means it.

There's a crash.

My vision goes white, then black.

Pain storms through me like a red-hot whiplash.

And then I'm gone.

* * *

I'm SURPRISED to wake up again.

I can't breathe.

There's something stuffed in my mouth, something foul and thick that makes my tongue feel like cotton.

I come to slowly, wheezing as I'm tossed around in seasick lurches, my vision fragmenting all over the place.

Oh, God.

I'm gonna barf.

No—no, if I do, I'm just gonna choke myself.

I swallow it back, forcing my eyes to focus, biting off curses around the rag and squirming.

Yep, still tied to the chair.

And as my eyes clear, I realize...I'm staring right at Declan Eckhard's ass.

He's got me tossed over his shoulder, chair and all, and he's carrying me outside.

Ugh.

"Finally awake?" he asks just a little too mildly. He's got a hand clamped down on my thigh, and he digs his fingers in hard enough to make me squirm. "Good. You're lucky I let you live, but you see...I think you're still not telling the whole truth. You *or* Holt. You're going to tell me what we're missing here, and you're going to tell me *before* he gets here."

Everything somersaults in my vision so fast it's a miracle I don't pass out again.

He steps down into the churned-up graveyard and swings me down on the chair so hard my head whacks the tall back of it.

Jesus, if I get brain damage, I'm sending this prick my hospital bill.

He lords over me, his hands on the back of the chair.

"Your army of the dead isn't coming to save you, baby," he says. "Look at them. No ghosts. And you'll be joining them soon, if you don't start talking. What the fuck's here that's so valuable? What did that man in the saloon die for?"

I can't help but stare at what he's done to the graves.

I don't know who these people were.

Sinners or saints, criminals or law-abiding citizens.

It doesn't make what he's done any less of a desecration. Just total disrespectful carnage.

I wish ghosts *were* real. Then they could come kick some asses over what he's done.

"You really are an animal," I whisper. "You just couldn't let these people rest in peace? You're that desperate for money?"

"They're dead. They don't care." He smacks his hand on the back of my chair, a warning. "Now talk. If you're a good girl, I'll even let you see your boy one more time before I dismember you both."

I don't get a chance to retort.

Because suddenly there's a loud whistle—three quick, short bursts.

Plus the sound of hoofbeats, coming in hot.

I know those hooves, they're the sound of my own horses. And I know damn well Declan is in trouble.

It's Holt with somebody else at his side.

"Cut them off!" Declan barks.

His hands are all over me—awful, grabbing, ripping at the ropes, swarming over my hands and legs in a way that makes me feel violated.

That doesn't stop me from trying to kick him off, to pull away. The ropes fall down around my ankles and pool around the chair.

He doesn't give me a chance.

His thick, beefy arm wraps around my neck in a headlock.

There's a metallic click.

And then the mouth of a gun pressed against my temple, cold and steely and round.

"Try anything," he breathes into my ear, his voice almost slimy, "and I'll blow a hole in you right in front of him."

"Fuck you," I hiss, grappling at his arm.

"I'll do that in front of him, too," he leers. "Maybe I'll let him watch me fuck you right before he dies."

The sick horror of those words, that promise, leaves me stiff.

Declan hauls me up, practically carrying me against his chest with my feet dangling.

I don't dare move, kick, or bite.

Nothing while that gun burns against my temple.

He drags me through the town while his men go swarming on ahead.

Eventually we come around the side of the saloon.

Just in time to see Holt and a big, gruff-looking Alaska

emerge from the darkness, Frost and Plath stepping through the trees and underbrush slowly.

Frost looks like a toy pony under Alaska's bulk, but carries him easily while both men ride in with their hands raised, guiding the horses with their knees.

Over half a dozen men train their guns on them.

I could cry at the sight of Holt.

He's never looked more gorgeous. Even now he's easy and relaxed, icy calm in his black leather jacket that makes him belong to the night, jeans laying easy on his thighs.

My heart skips a beat.

He wears confidence itself like designer fashion. Not even flinching when multiple safeties click and seemingly not giving half a damn that he could die with a single pull of a trigger.

The horses stop, surrounded by a circle of men.

Holt cocks his head, a lock of dark hair falling across his brow as his gaze wanders, golden brown eyes glinting in the moonlight.

He smirks.

Of course he freaking does.

"Not even a hello? Hardly a warm welcome," he calls out, pitching his voice to Declan.

"I told you, no more surprises," Declan growls, hefting me up. "You're late. Don't play games with me."

Holt arches a brow, keeping his hands held high.

"I'm not the one playing treasure hunt like a kid pretending to be a pirate," he says. "Now would you mind putting my girl down?"

"Only when I'm good and ready."

Declan sounds calm, if irritated.

I can feel what he's not saying, the violent pounding of his heart against my back.

Something's making him nervous.

He's a small-time criminal, I bet. I don't think he's ever truly killed anyone before.

He's probably always just been fine making big threats, using that intimidating bulk and bearish attitude to make people think he'd just as soon kill them as look at them.

But really?

He's all talk—and he runs once he's been found out.

Maybe he's piss scared.

Afraid he'll have to put his money where his mouth is and actually murder someone when he's so weak he'd be terrified of the consequences.

Or else have the men who are already mad at him realize he's just a big trash-talking bully and turn on *him* with those guns when he doesn't deliver.

I catch Holt's eye.

The look he gives me is long, steady, reassuring, and fierce as hell.

Like he's holding me across the distance, whispering *it'll be okay, honey. I swear.*

Protecting me when he can't even touch me, keeping me safe and warm.

I just need him to understand what I'm getting at without Declan realizing.

So I move my lips carefully, mouthing out soundless words.

Keep.

Him.

Talking.

Buy me time.

Because the second Declan tries to bluff about shooting me and then doesn't follow through, I'll gnaw through his arm if I have to. Seize any chance to get loose.

Once he can't use me as collateral anymore, we'll get out of here just fine.

Holt looks at me oddly for a second, then nods.

A small thing, but it's there.

Slowly, he lowers his arms, and Alaska follows suit.

Every last one of Declan's men bristle, shoulders going up hard as they take aim.

"Calm down," Holt says, casually laying his hands on the saddle horn. I can't see a gun on him anywhere, but if he's smart, he's packing. "My arms are just getting tired."

Declan makes an irritated noise. "Do you not realize how serious the situation is?"

"Sure do," Holt says. "No reason we can't be comfortable, though. We came to talk. Don't need guns to do that. We can all get what we want and walk away from here nice and peaceful."

"And if I tell you I don't need you anymore?" Declan says. "Your girlfriend's been pretty chatty."

"Has she?" Holt asks mildly. "I'm sure anyone would talk if they'd been tossed around as much as Libby. I just might have to change my mind about getting violent."

I feel a vicious grin splitting my lips.

Even with the gun pressed against my temple, I dig my fingers into Declan's arm. "You don't get to kill him. I'm gonna do it first. One bullet for every time he smacked me."

"Fuck, you really don't shut up," Declan mutters, jamming the pistol harder against my skin, grinding the metal into me. "The two of you don't understand when you're at a disadvantage, do you?"

"We're not," Holt answers, shrugging. "It's simple, Eckhard. You hurt Libby, I don't tell you shit. You can't force me to say a thing. I don't respond well to torture and shit-talkin' threats. Just makes me more ornery. And if you put a bullet in my brain, well, won't be talking then, will I?"

Declan looks like he might explode.

Holt tilts his head, his gaze flicking past us toward the grave-yard. "Looks like you think you can make dead folks talk. How's that been working for you?"

"Don't you people ever get sick of the sound of your own voices?" Declan snarls.

"No." Holt grins. "Want to hear a few more ways you're

fucked if you don't stop screwing around and do things my way?"

Declan's chest rises and falls heavily against my back in a deep, long-suffering sigh.

"Do enlighten me," he mutters.

I almost grin.

I kinda know how he feels.

Except this is part of what I love about Holt.

And he's in full snake charmer mode, smooth and casual, his velvety-rich voice hypnotic and rolling.

"The thing is," he continues, "you haven't figured out you're interfering with an active crime scene. Sheriff Langley's been all over this place. Once he realizes you've fucked up his investigation, you're in jail for obstruction and probably a lot more."

He lies so smoothly he almost makes me believe it, if I didn't know it was pure bull.

But the next part isn't as he glances at one of the men holding a gun on him.

A man with a sleeveless shirt on.

He's sporting a bared bicep, grimy with dirt and sweat from digging...all wrapped up in a bloodied bandage.

"Hey, friend," Holt says. "Sorry you took a bullet."

The man flinches, eyes widening, giving himself away.

Oh, hell. It's one of the assholes who attacked me. The man I shot.

"I hate to tell you this, but you left a little DNA evidence back at Libby's place. The cops have it. They'll trace it back to you, and then nail you right to Declan. Is this scumbag worth jail time? Does he owe you that much money?"

"Shut up!" Declan snarls, though whether at Holt or the white-faced, stricken-looking man, I don't know. Not until he adds, "Don't fucking answer him."

"Why not?" Holt asks blandly. "You've put these guys in a bad position, Declan. After swindling them out of their money, too. All this work for nothing. Treating them like your flunkies.

Making them dig all over hell when what you're looking for isn't even buried in the ground."

"The fuck are you talking about?" Declan's arm tightens on my neck, and I let out a little wheeze. "I know about the old silver mines around here. I've seen their equipment. I know they'd hide it in secret caches until they were ready to sell so no one would pocket it. It's in all those old books lying around. You told me you fucking know where the silver is."

He lets out an angry, guttural grunt, grinding that pistol against my temple again.

"I lied," Holt says bluntly.

I swear to God, my life flashes before my eyes when I feel Declan's hand shifting and can tell his finger's tightening on the trigger.

Before he can yell, though, Holt holds a hand up. "Don't get stupid. We can still talk. Just let me get something out of my saddlebag. I ain't going for a weapon, so don't shoot."

"Stop fucking around, Silverton!"

"I'm not," Holt says, twisting to flip the saddlebag open and slip a hand inside.

It's a miracle they don't shoot him.

But he comes back with something.

A leather-bound book.

Dad's old journal?

Sure enough. He flips the book open to the back and I see the inside cover with my dad's handwriting scrawled all over it.

"Take a look at this," he says.

"I'm not coming a step closer," Declan spits, then says, "Will, grab it."

"I'm not your slave," Will—the guy with the bandage—bites off, but edges closer to Holt, eyeing him warily before snatching the book out of his hand.

Holt grins.

Moving backward, keeping his gun on Holt, Will moves to

Declan and shoves the book at him with a resentful glance. He holds it open so Declan doesn't have to let me go.

The scumbag's head brushes mine as he bows to look, muttering to himself, reading numbers over and over again. "Looks like chicken scratch. What the hell does this mean?"

"It means," Holt says, "there was something far more valuable than anyone knew buried in these hills. Something worth a hell of a lot more than silver. It's what the man in the saloon died over. I've got it, but you'll never know what it is or what it's worth if you don't play nice."

"I'm getting damn sick of your mouth," Declan snarls, swinging the gun away from my temple—finally.

Except he points it right at Holt.

Oh, I'm not liking that at all.

"You start talking sense, Silverton," Declan says. "You talk sense right fucking now, or I will blow your head off in front of your girl, then blow hers off so you can die together."

"How sweet," I mutter, tensing up, getting ready to kick free.

Only for Alaska—who'd been so silent it's like everyone forgot he was there—to suddenly sling a sawed-off shotgun from his back, hidden by his broad shoulders.

In half a second, it's pointed at Declan.

Everyone takes aim at him.

Guns swivel around everywhere, a proper Mexican standoff, and the only ones not pointing a weapon at someone are me and Holt.

"Let's be very clear, boys," Alaska says, slowly and calmly. "You might shoot Holt, but not before I get a good shot off and turn a few faces into minced meat. So. Maybe point your shit somewhere else." He glances over the scattered thugs. "Y'all really willing to go to jail for *this* asshole?"

He nods at Declan, a spark of mischief in his eyes.

Uneasy mumbles and two second glances fly around.

"If your choice is jail or death, remember I'll shoot the whole

411

lot of you, too," Declan snarls, frustration boiling over in every word.

Holt actually chuckles.

"Hardly a standoff if you'll kill your own men, is it?" He shakes his head. "You're a terrible damn negotiator, Eckhard. Just plain shit at it. Lucky for you, I'm gonna lay out some fair terms, and you're gonna accept them, and then we're going home."

I guess Declan realizes he's backed into a corner and facing a mutiny.

He lowers the gun with a deep sigh so it's pointing off to the side, instead of point-blank at Holt's face.

"Talk" he says grudgingly.

"You'll let Libby go. As insurance, though, she'll wait in another building." Holt's voice rings with a wild confidence that makes it seem impossible that this could happen any other way. "I just don't want her in the line of fire if this goes south. We'll negotiate, I'll hand over the real treasure, and then Libby and Alaska and I get moving while you hash things out with your men. We never have to see each other again. You're free to fight over money among yourselves."

"Not possible," Declan grunts. "You can't possibly have enough valuables on you here."

"Wrong," Holt says, dipping his hand into the saddlebag again.

He pulls out the little black box from Dad's stuff and flips it open, revealing that dull, rusty blood-colored rock.

"This is what you're looking for, gentlemen," he announces. "All your riches are right here."

There's a moment of silence.

Then men start chuckling in mad derision, while Declan outright scoffs.

"Unless that's one hell of a dirty ruby, you are full of so much shit, Silverton. Did you really come here to gamble with a goddamn desert rock?"

"Yes," Holt says. "Because the desert this rock came from isn't on this planet. You're an idiot, Declan. I'm holding an artifact worth seven figures."

"Bullshit!" Declan's shoulders jerk. "I don't get it."

I sigh, rolling my ears.

"It's from Mars, you jackass," I growl. "It's been buried here. It *made* the crater where this town is. Private collectors and government agencies would chew their arms off for it. You take it, you sell it, you get big money. My dad knew that. So did the dead guy in the saloon."

"No fucking way. That's the most outlandish load of horse shit I've ever heard," Declan says, his eyes flashing venom.

Suddenly that gun's at my temple again.

I freeze.

"Look." Declan raps me with the pistol barrel, enough to make my teeth rattle. "I'm not here for you to tell me some kind of tall tale and pull one over on me. But if that rock's worth what you say it is...nothing's stopping me from taking it by force. Either way, I'm sick of this shit, and we're *done*."

"For once, you're right," Holt says coolly. "We're very fucking done."

A noise in the distance makes me perk my head up.

An engine blaring.

Lights flash bright over the entire town, bathing Ursa in shadows and white glow.

Then there's a scream...a freaking siren?

Something huge comes barreling out the other side of the mountain pass, and it's pure chaos.

Everyone's screaming, running like maniacs, and that big roaring beast of a machine plows on right at Declan.

Right at *me*.

Now!

I kick back *hard*, and as much as I'd like to sock Declan another good one in the nuts, I end up nailing him in the knee instead.

Just for good measure, I bite down hard on his arm, sinking my teeth in deep.

He makes a strangled sound, flailing around.

But he drops me.

I go rolling out of the way, just as what I swear to God looks like a *fire truck* comes whipping through and smashes into the church.

Holy hell.

Didn't I see something like this at the last Winter Carnival when everything went nuts?

There's no time to decide.

Declan's thrown himself to the side.

Dammit! I was hoping they'd gotten him, but he's not getting far.

Not when three big men leap off the back of the truck and bring an instant smile to my face.

Warren, Doc, and Leo, the Heroes of Heart's Edge. They're huge, swift shadows in the night, chasing down the idiots trying to make a break from bedlam.

The fourth musketeer, Blake, climbs out of the driver's seat with a big grin, while Holt thunders in on horseback, into the panicked goons in full retreat.

It's a total flipping riot.

Dust billows up everywhere and the church starts collapsing in on itself, the siren piercing the night with another ear-splitting shriek.

Maybe that's why I'm the only one who sees it.

Declan rises, his face twisted into the nastiest fit of rage I've ever seen. He staggers to his feet and whips around to take aim at Holt.

Like hell!

Before I can even think, I throw myself at him.

I'm small, but I hit like a cannonball, diving at his legs and taking him out at the knees.

We go down hard together.

A loud gunshot cracks off and zings past me. So close I feel the heat kiss my shoulder before it slams into the church and hits something, but I'm focused on Declan.

He's not getting up again if I have anything to say about it.

I lift up.

Raise my elbow.

And then pile-drive it down into his nuts so fast they crunch.

Never let it be said I didn't learn anything from Sierra. She was on a real self-defense kick for a while—I just wish she'd used her skills more on the trash men she keeps dating.

Tonight, I do it for her.

Declan flops forward with a howl, but I guess all that pain gets him blazing mad, because this time he comes up swinging, charging me like a drunken bull.

But I'm already rolling away, just as the thunder of hooves rolls in.

The timing is sweet perfection.

Declan freezes as Holt pulls up behind me, tall and proud on Plath's back.

He shoves that Colt of his right between Declan's eyes.

"You dropped your gun," Holt says—his voice light, but his eyes are pure steel. "And your men are scattering. Choose wisely."

Not that they're gonna get far.

I can hear the boys whooping, taunting Declan's goons as they round them up like cattle, practically having *fun* with it.

"You okay, Libby?" Holt asks, never taking his eyes or his gun off Declan's frozen, furious face.

"Nothing I can't fix by socking this swamp rat in the face a few more times," I snarl, dusting myself off.

Holt thumbs the hammer on his Colt. "What do you say, Declan? Want to let the lady use you for a punching bag, or should I drop you dead right here?"

Declan curls his upper lip. "You don't have the balls."

"Shit. You're spoiling to be wrong *twice* tonight?"

415

I tense. That's just the thing. I could totally see Holt ending him.

Right here, right now.

He's got that strength and killer instinct in him.

The willpower to knowingly take a man's life to save someone else's, even though he'll have to carry that weight for the rest of his days.

If the reasons were right, if there were no other options...he'd kill for me.

Something Declan never could.

But Holt leans down over Plath's neck, bringing himself close to the thug, meeting his eyes with a dark, heavy promise.

"Lucky for you," Holt growls, "I have a fucking conscience."

Right before he draws back, quickly reversing the Colt with a practiced ease.

He swings it across Declan's face, pistol-whipping him so hard I hear the resounding *crack* of bones as his head tears to the side.

Then, with a moan, he falls down in a heap that's almost pathetic for a man who tries to have so much bluster.

Suddenly it's just me and Holt while the ghost town erupts into stray shots and wild hollering around us.

We stare at each other like there's nothing else in the world.

I've never been so happy to see someone in my life.

I knew he'd come for me.

I knew he'd save me.

I knew there was no way in hell I was letting someone like Declan take me out without seeing my man, my knight, my hero again.

But now that he's here, looking at me with those intense bourbon-gold eyes, practically devouring me in this endless breath between us, I feel it.

That hot emotion inside me I've been trying to deny. It comes up like magma ready to burst through to the surface.

I know it. I dread it. I need it.

Love.

It can't be anything but love for this brave, crazy, infuriating beast of a man.

It's on my lips, my mouth opening at the same time as his.

"Holt—"

"Libby—"

We both break off in a laugh, but before we can say anything else, Plath shakes her head with an impatient snort and shoves her nose against my chest, nearly knocking me back.

"Calm down, girl!" I tell her. "I'm okay. I'm getting to it."

The hollering has died down around us. I'm guessing Declan's men have all surrendered. No match at all for the men of Heart's Edge.

I let out a soft *oof*, then chuckle and stroke her mane, her face, her velvety nose.

"She missed you," Holt says, voice thick and alluring as a bonfire. "She's not the only one."

I angle my head, looking up at the gorgeous man sitting so tall and proud on Plath's back. "So you missed me, huh?"

"A hell of a lot, honey. More than that, too. Think we need to do some talkin', but for now..." He offers me his hand. "C'mon. Let's help the boys finish rounding up the trash before Langley gets here."

I grin and slip my hand into his, savoring the sweet thrill of his voice, his touch, his strength as he lifts me up into the saddle effortlessly, settling me in front of him with his thighs flanking mine and his body wrapped hot around me.

One thing's for sure.

Holt sure knows the way to my heart.

Maybe it's a path laid in the blood of my enemies instead of rose petals.

But who wouldn't love a man who gives her first dibs at vengeance?

XXIV: TIME TO PONY UP (HOLT)

*I*t's a few more days before Libby and I get to have that talk.

I haven't even figured out what I want to say to her that won't have me sounding like an addled, lovestruck idiot.

Falling all over myself to tell her how much I love her, need her, want her to stay in my life.

How bad I want to help her turn that ranch into a home full of light, laughter, and family.

We've been a little busy for heart-to-hearts, handling the fallout of that mess in Ursa, and then passing out stone-cold tired next to each other at night.

Libby snores a tiny bit in her sleep when she's that exhausted.

No plans to tell her—I like living.

Frankly, I'm amazed we even survived.

Sure, Declan's men were chickens who turned tail and ran.

Libby almost outdid a whole crew of heroes and put the fear of pint-sized firecrackers into those boys that night.

After that dustup, it's mostly been dealing with the police.

A very put-out Langley, who's sick of this town's bad habit of leaving him out of the loop until it boils over and someone needs to clean it up and put a nice, neat legal stamp on things after asses have been kicked.

It couldn't be helped.

We also couldn't hold back the truth anymore with Declan and his guys tied up, then turned over to the police.

Gerald Bostrom's bones finally came to light.

Nothing we could do except turn everything over to law enforcement and tell Langley the truth about Ursa.

That Libby knew about the dead body, and so did her dad.

We just left out the part about Mark Potter killing the guy.

That's a detail he can figure out on his own. Hell, maybe it's his shot at sussing out loose ends we couldn't.

I can't blame Libby for being nervous as hell—especially when Langley calls and says he wants to talk to us in Ursa.

It could mean nothing.

It could mean everything.

It could rip apart her life and her world.

So I've gotta be the strong one today.

While she's a jittery mess, bouncing off the walls, I try to keep it together quiet and steady.

I hold her hand tight, until I've got to let her go to hand her up into Frost's saddle and mount up on Plath.

The road through the pass has actually been cleared out pretty well in the last few days.

It's the shortest path to the ghost town, and the police have been driving in and out a lot. I don't even know what the boys did to the tires to get that big honking fire truck through the brush.

Still, horseback's the easiest way for us. We make good time trotting down the packed earth under the bright morning sun.

We hear the noise of investigators still working over the town and trying to figure out what happened long before we break around the last bend.

I slow Plath, nudging her over until my knee bumps Libby's thigh and Frost's flank. I reach over to capture her hand.

"You sure you're ready for this talk?" I ask as our horses jounce to a halt. "If it turns out to be...you know."

Her eyes are a little too wide, but there's no doubt or hesitation in them as she squeezes my hand and nods.

"I've put this off too long. Whatever it is, I'll face it. I know I *can* face it with you, Holt."

Hearing her say that fills me with a joy I can't describe.

I hope I'll always be worthy of this wild woman's faith.

I know I'll always aim to keep it.

We hold hands as long as we can manage while mounted, heading forward to take those last few yards into town at a slow, steady walk.

There's crime scene tape everywhere.

Mostly around the half-demolished church, the graveyard, and the saloon.

A couple of cop cars, a forensics van from the FBI, people in uniforms and jackets with alphabet agency patches slowly picking things over with gloved hands, taking photos and tagging evidence.

Sheriff Langley sticks out like a sore thumb in his old-school sheriff's browns.

He's standing around uselessly, just watching people with his gloved thumbs stuck in his belt loops.

When he catches sight of us, though, he waves like we're showing up for a picnic instead of stopping by a crime scene as witnesses.

Libby and I exchange dry looks, then dismount and get the horses hitched up.

At least if Langley's his usual cheeky self, it's probably not bad news.

Probably.

By the time we're on the ground, he's come stomping over to us on his pointy-toed cowboy boots.

"Morning, Libby, Holt," he says. "Good of you to come out."

"No problem, Sheriff," I say.

Libby takes a deep breath, scrubbing her hands on her thighs, trying to force a smile.

"Morning, Sheriff," she says sweetly. "You have something to show us?"

"Right this way." He walks across the dusty road to where his cruiser's parked.

Several evidence boxes are stacked on the trunk, a bunch of old ledgers and books piled inside. While we're walking, Langley talks over his shoulder.

"There was this lectern that got shot open and busted up during your mess with that Eckhard guy. Found a bunch of old church records in it...but found some stuff I think belonged to Mark Potter, too, and might have something to do with the case. Figured you could confirm."

Libby darts me a nervous look. I give back a warm smile.

It'll be okay.

I know it will.

"Okay," she says a bit breathlessly. "Let me take a look."

Langley rummages inside the box, then comes up with a slim journal, leather-bound like the others, and passes it to Libby.

When she edges closer, holding the thing like it's burning her, I don't hesitate to wrap my arm around her shoulders, gathering her up.

Anything to support her.

I watch with my heart beating to kill as she flips the pages open.

It's not as big a scribbled mess as the others.

It's mostly a lot of other pages, all taped in. It takes me a minute to realize what I'm looking at.

More lab test results on the rock, I think, from various places all over the country.

Multiple independent assessments confirming it's exactly what Mark Potter thought.

A visitor from another world. Worth far more than Bostrom would've paid him, if he'd pulled off his double-cross.

There's stuff on Bostrom, too.

Damning stuff, illicit deals on antique goods with falsified receipts worse than the government's infamous golden toilets. Stuff that's clearly a lie to cover for other purchases.

I also see what looks like someone's fudged accounting records, plus several newspaper clippings about valuables going missing from museums all across the Pacific Northwest.

He's even got Polaroids.

Guess Mark did his homework on Bostrom.

If I'm being honest...it doesn't look good.

Almost looks like Mark was fixated on Gerald Bostrom.

And if Bostrom has any surviving kin, I can easily see them using it to spin a story of Mark being paranoid and obsessed, building up a narrative in his head until he shot without cause.

I start to say something to Libby, anything to offer comfort, but her expression looks weird.

She's numb, flipping through more pages, and when I make a single sound, she holds a hand up sharply, shaking her head.

I shut up quick and give her silence.

Finally, she stops, like she knows what she's looking for, and here it is.

It's just a few lines on a page.

One of Mark's silly poems, I guess.

But I feel my world shift when I read the title.

He Shot First.

No fucking way.

It's like the sky opens up with a message from the great beyond. What Mark's been trying to tell us all this time.

Crowding Libby, both of us barely breathing, we read it together.

Mark Potter will never go down as a good poet.

It reads almost like an elegy, a lament for the dead, or even a song.

It's a story about a man finding a cursed blood stone here in this dead little town and shooting a man who tried to double-cross him and kill him.

The hero of the poem realizes all the rock can ever bring is greed and death.

He vows he'll throw it off a cliff...but there's something almost ominous in the way it casts its spell over him, and he keeps it instead.

He cuts away a fragment to try to break the curse, turning it into something good by grinding a piece of it down into polished gemstones, setting them into a necklace for his daughter.

Giving the stone to the stars, and the stars to her eyes, he writes.

Libby catches a breath, one hand drifting up to her little necklace and the polished red bits inside.

"Holy Toledo. So I've been...wearing a piece of the stars around my neck my whole life, and I never realized it?" she whispers, her voice breaking. "A piece of *this?*"

"Seems like it." I squeeze her tighter. "But look what he keeps coming back to, sweetheart. What he says over and over again. Bostrom shot *first.*"

She lifts her head, looking up at me with eyes that glimmer with something that might almost be hope. "If...if Bostrom shot at Dad first..."

"It was self-defense, Libby," I finish, while her eyes widen. "He wasn't a bad man. Mark shot that shady fuck defending himself, and maybe his family too. Who knows what he'd have done if he'd killed your old man out there with no witnesses. Mark had to save his own life, maybe even others."

Libby goes quiet. "Better than nothing, I guess, but it's still just a poem. One-sided, even if I believe it. Not proof."

Langley clears his throat, sounding almost embarrassed.

"Yeah, about that...I need to show y'all something." He ducks his head. "Come out here, please."

He turns to lead us toward the saloon with a murmur to *mind your step* as we move around the evidence markers and crime scene tape.

Inside, the whole saloon's been covered over with tape and forensics markers—including something on the wall I hadn't noticed before, marked by a bit of orange tape and a scrap of paper.

"There," Langley says, nodding toward the wall.

It's a bullet hole.

I don't even need to get closer to tell.

Someone shot there, all right, and it looks like it came from a gun fired not too far from the remains of Gerald Bostrom.

Libby goes pale. "He...he said find the gun."

"And we did, Miss Liberty," Langley drawls. "The boys pulled an old Smith & Wesson out of the debris behind the bar, crushed under the spot where a shelf collapsed. Probably went flying when he got shot. Near as the forensics folks can piece together, someone was standing right where that bullet hole was. Dead guy shot at 'em, missed, and hit the wall right where we pulled out a slug matching that Smith & Wesson. And then the guy standing here shot back, leaving the fella in the suit to rot with a shotgun slug in his chest." He squints at Libby.

My hands go to her shoulders, holding her up, because I can tell she's about to faint.

"Easy, honey," I whisper.

"Mark was real fond of shotguns for defending the homestead, wasn't he?" Langley asks.

"Y-yeah!" Libby says, pressing her fingers over her mouth sharply, breathing in a hard rattle. "He s-sure was."

There's only a half-second warning in her eyes spilling over before she breaks.

The woman just busts out sobbing, turning and flinging herself into me, and no matter how tiny she is, she nearly knocks me clean over.

I catch her with an *oof*, then wrap my arms around her tight, my chest seizing. "Libby, what's wrong—"

"I'm *happy!*" she belts out, even as she shows her joy by beating her fists against my chest, overwhelmed with emotion. Not gonna lie, she's smacking me like a little twister, but I'm not letting her go. "Oh my God. I knew it. Knew he was a good man, I knew it, I knew it...Gerald freaking Bostrom shot first."

That's when Libby starts jumping up and down, using my shoulders for balance.

I can't help but smile, seeing her this happy.

"Yeah, he did," I say and kiss her hair, letting her release all the pent-up emotion. "Now we know it for a fact, and everything's gonna be a-okay."

Even if I don't know how.

There's still her issue with the bank, the taxes, not to mention having to start from square one with Silverton Construction.

Still, I wonder...could that damn Mars rock help?

If it was really worth killing and dying over, maybe it's as cursed as Mark Potter thought.

Maybe we should find our own way.

Then again, maybe that thing could finally do some good.

* * *

IT'S like a whole new world by the time we leave Ursa.

Instead of going back to the ranch house, we go for a ride.

I think we both need it, and so do the horses.

We chatter back and forth about how we can't wait to hear Declan's put away for life. Probably won't take long.

Sheriff Langley told us feelers started coming from other states for Declan Ekhard almost as soon as his ass was booked and we gave our statements. The trail of warrants he's left all over the continent swindling *millions* of dollars out of hardworking folks should do a fine job of keeping him locked up.

And if they don't, the human trafficking cases he's been involved with will. Found out he hauled illicit cargo a few times for Jupiter Oil, a shady and now defunct entity dealing kidnapped girls on the black market. They went down last year in North Dakota and made national news for the hell they raised.

Thankfully, there's only so much Declan talk worth blabbing about when his thieving ass isn't our worry anymore.

We're laughing as we race each other along the plains below the cliffs, then slow as we take the trails that start to wind up to the upper bluffs.

Libby looks brighter than I've ever seen her.

There hasn't been a dull moment since I met her, not since I came back to Heart's Edge, when she hasn't been under pressure.

Even so, she's been full of fire that never went out.

And now she's free to burn all the brighter, her face open and fresh and full of joy, her eyes glittering. She's let her hair down, this tumbling mess around her shoulders the soft summer breeze picks up and threads out behind her like spun gold, tumbling and waving everywhere.

She sits easy in the saddle, the tension gone from her body, leaving her moving fluidly with Frost's gait, her hands light and sure on the reins.

Libby's this woman of wild extremes.

And I don't think anyone could blame me for falling head over heels in love with her stubborn, crazy ass.

We're almost to the cliffs behind the Charming Inn, following well-worn paths where the trail widens in front of us. We can ride side by side without crowding.

She reaches over and catches my hand, squeezing it with a look full of so much warmth it stops my heart, before slowly drawing away to take her reins in both hands again.

"So," she says lightly. "What the hell do I do with that rock?"

"Toss it over a cliff? That's what your old man wanted. Doesn't seem to do much but bring ruin and misery. Then again..."

"Yeah, it kinda saved our asses, too," she chuckles. "God, I almost want to sell it. I mean, Sierra's let up, but there's still the bank, and I don't know how I'm going to fight them off forever, Holt."

"Your choice, woman. Whatever you decide to do with it, I'll be standing by your side."

We're breaking out into the sunlight now, stepping out of the trees and into the field of flowers behind the inn, leading up to the cliffs where every lover in the history of the town wished for their forever.

I hadn't meant to bring her here today.

It's almost fitting that we've found our way.

I dismount from Plath, swinging myself down and holding a hand lightly on the mare's neck to keep her steady, but my eyes are just for Libby as I look at her glowing on Frost's back.

"Look," I say. "You don't need to sell the damn rock tomorrow. Or worry about money at all. Pulling together, we can manage. We can figure out the debt. You've got me now, and I'll put in everything if it'll help you."

Libby gives me a wry, affectionate look. "Um, I hate to break the news but...you're about to be broke after giving up that mega-mall contract."

"Alaska's working on more contracts in Heart's Edge and five towns over. Maybe things will get a bit tight while I build out our work, but I can still help, Libby." I offer her my hand.

I start off into the sunset then, knowing something deep down in all this chaos.

This is the perfect place.

Next time we're out here, I'll have a better reason for her to smile.

* * *

Months Later

427

IT'S AMAZING how fast time blurs by with a weight bigger than King Kong off our backs.

Hectic weeks drift into a lazy late summer, giving way to a fall where the days get shorter and cooler. The hills around Heart's Edge come alive with late wild blooms and the first hints of brilliant autumn.

It's a fine day when we can finally march into Reid Cherish's office with a check to pay off everything in full. That robot of a man snaps off a frigging salute when we're finished, and it's a chore to man up, shake his hand, and walk out without giving him shit.

Even Cherish deserves a reprieve today. We're celebrating.

It took a whole lot of wrangling, but it's done.

Last week, we turned that Mars rock over to a rep from a big museum and space center down in Texas. They gave Libby an eye-popping check. She split part off for Sierra, part for charity, and part she damn-near forced on me. I only agreed to take it as an investment in my company I'd pay back.

Then we waited a couple weeks to see if we'd break out in hives or fall over dead from food poisoning or black cats crossing our paths.

So far, so good.

Seems like that old space rock wasn't as cursed as Mark thought.

Now we're standing on the hills overlooking that special heart-shaped cliff where all the locals here go when it's time to make a big damn promise in the name of love. The same place I picked out on that hazy day after we found out her father's name was clear, the first day we found hope for a normal life.

Libby blinks, gasping and slipping her hand into mine.

Even as she swings her leg over and slides off Frost's back, she looks around as if she's just realized where we are.

"Holt Silverton...what...what are you doing?"

I wait until she drops down lightly to the ground before I sink down on one knee, still clasping her hand tight and grinning. "What does it look like, honey?"

"You can't! You don't—"

"I can, and I do. For once, it's too late to argue."

Well, maybe it's a little early for those words.

It's not too early to pull out the ring I've been carrying in my back pocket since this morning.

I've had it for a couple months. It'd been an impulse buy when I went into town to the jeweler's, after Cindy called me with an appraisal and a sale offer. Only forty-thousand dollars on the old designer ring, but when you're hard-up, you'll take it.

I'll tell her about that in a little bit, though.

Libby stares at me like her eyes might fall out.

I swear to God my bright, brassy girl *trembles* as I open that box.

Inside is a delicate silver ring.

For her it's gotta be silver since she's all radiant gold. Silver makes me think of the stars, and she's my whole damn sky.

The diamond's not huge.

It's not some obscene thing that used to belong to some kind of royal or something.

But I picked it just for her, and that's what matters.

From the way her breath catches and the overwhelmed swallow she makes...

Yeah, I think she likes it.

It's a simple setting—a diamond cut into a four-point star, surrounded by smaller diamonds like a constellation.

And tangled around the ring? That crescent moon bracelet, a memory of the night I realized I was falling head over boots for her.

"Liberty Potter," I say. "When I came back here looking for home, I never thought I'd find it in a hellcat who pushed me down in the muck and called me every filthy name in the book."

429

She lets out a shaky laugh, pressing her hands to her mouth, eyes gleaming.

I grin. "But I did. After dancing with you that night at the Norton place, looking down at how beautiful you were under the moon, that's when I knew. Didn't know how to say it then, but I sure do now."

I pause, watching a crystal tear come sliding down her cheek.

"Holt..." she strangles out.

"I'm past falling, Libby. Way the hell past falling. I'm just *in*. All in with you." I can't even find words for how my heart thumps, putting it out there like this. "I love you, Miss Potter. If you'll do me the honor of having my hand, I'd like to make you Mrs. Silverton."

Libby lets out another overwhelmed laugh, turning her face away, tucking her hair back and scrubbing at her eyes with a little sniffle.

"Aw, hell. Can't you just say 'will you marry me' like a normal dude instead of making a smooth speech?"

"No." My grin widens, because I think I can feel her answer coming and that hope lifts me up until I'm a hot mess. "But I'll say them too. Will you marry me, Liberty?"

"You're the biggest fool in the world if you don't already know my answer," she snaps, beaming like the sun.

Then she reaches out to touch the ring, fingering the fine chain of the bracelet.

Her fingers are so warm as that touch shifts to me, resting on my lips, gentle and sweet, as if she'd caress that proposal from my skin to hers.

Her eyelids slip down.

I still can't believe this stunning firecracker looks at me with that much emotion in her soft blue eyes.

"Yes!" she whispers. "Holt, *yes*. Because dammit if I don't love you too...and it's been building up for so long I think I'm gonna burst if you don't kiss me right now."

I'm springing up off my knees in a heartbeat, clasping that

ring box to keep it safe while I bury my fingers in her hair and drag her in.

Nobody told me how sweet a kiss can taste until I'm sharing the first kiss I've ever had as someone's fiancé.

Nobody warned me I didn't know love or passion until Libby goes loose in my arms in a way that says she trusts me completely—now and forever. Body, mind, and soul.

Nobody said I wouldn't know joy until the person who means more than anything else says I matter just the same to her.

And I don't know how I ever called myself a man until I became the man I needed to be for Libby.

Our kiss comes slow, soft, like we've just transformed from lovers to betrothed, and now we've got to test it out to settle into our new identities.

That subtle hint of something *else* that makes every stroke of our lips somehow richer, fuller, filled with so much emotion it rocks through me.

I devour my fiancée, my future wife, my everything like a starved wolf.

We're both breathless by the time we pull back.

Breathless, but smiling like the lovestruck fools we are. And her smile gets bigger as I steal her hand.

First I loop that bracelet around her wrist, then slide the delicate ring home on her finger. I'd guessed her size.

Guess I was an eagle eye because it goes down snug like it's always belonged there.

Her eyes gleaming, Libby spreads her fingers, looking at the ring in awe.

"I never really thought about what kind of ring I'd like," she murmurs. "Never even thought about getting married. But it's like you picked what I'd choose for myself. It's simple but it's delicate and lovely and just...it's perfect, Holt. How did you find the perfect ring for me?"

"By trying to know you better than I know myself, honey.

Watching what you love, and what you care about. That's what love means." I curl my hand over hers, relishing the feeling of the ring captured between us, warming our fingers as I give her a tug toward the cliff. "Now let's go throw some flowers, lady."

XXV: ONE HORSE TOWN (LIBBY)

*F*irst, a few words of advice.

Never make your sister your maid of honor.

Never let your sister plan your wedding.

Never let your sister sweet talk you into Ladies' Night at Brody's with dick-shaped drinking straws; never let your sister pick out her own bridesmaid's dress, and never, *ever* let your sis know you forgive her for a lifetime of pure bull.

Because by the time it's over?

You might just be down one sister.

I know I'm about to be, if Sierra doesn't stop driving me out of my mind—and if she doesn't stop *fussing with my freaking hair.*

I still don't even have my dress on.

She's standing over me in front of the mirror in the room at the Charming Inn that we reserved for bridal prep. I fidget in my chair while she curls my hair up into this mess on top of my head.

I look like I should be presenting a car or something on The Price Is Right.

Not like I'm about to get married.

"Stop it," I growl, swatting at her. Carefully, seeing how she's holding a hot curling iron. "Jesus, pile this up any higher on my

433

head and they're gonna think I'm a backup singer for Conway Twitty."

"Who?" she asks, blinking at me in the mirror.

She's looking better now.

She's calmed down with the gaudy Vegas showgirl looks, and gone natural with her hair loose and breezy, comfortable in jeans and cute flowy sleeveless blouses.

She doesn't look so starve-yourself-thin-until-you-die anymore, either.

I help, feeding her fresh-baked pies until she's blue in the face every time she comes around the ranch. I'll remake a country girl of Sierra Potter yet.

Her bruises are long healed.

Outside, anyway.

What's hurting her deep down will take more than time to heal, and it'll happen on her schedule.

But it feels like maybe she's ready to try as she smiles at me in the mirror.

"Quit it, Libby," she says, flicking the curling iron off and setting it down. "You're giving me sappy looks again."

"Am not!" I half-heartedly jab my elbow back at her. "Look, just let me have a moment of being glad you're back, okay? It's my wedding day. Can't I do that?"

"You can." She leans down, draping her arms over my neck and resting her chin on one of my shoulders.

When you look at us in the mirror like this, we don't look that different.

"I'm sorry, Libby. Sorry I left you here to handle things alone."

"Enough apologies. You had your reasons." I curl my hand against her forearm and lean into her. "Crappy reasons, but still...reasons."

"*Hey*." She nudges her cheek against mine with a laugh. "Please don't forget I got the crap beaten out of me by a gorilla pretending to be a man, just trying to save your butt."

"And you're gonna remind me of that every time I give you hell?"

"Yep!"

We both laugh—but it's a quieter laughter, a sweeter humor that reminds me of when we used to play together as girls.

"Hey," I murmur, squeezing her arm. "Remember the first time I tried to learn to ride?"

"I remember you eating a faceful of dirt," she teases.

"Yeah." I chuckle. "And you got down and kissed my fore-head, picked me up and made sure I wasn't broken, and then put me right back on that horse. Remember what you said to me?"

"I do," she answers, her voice softening with emotion. "We don't fall. We never fall. We just learn how to stand up again."

I smile. It's surprising how hard that hits me.

"I feel like I've been falling down and learning how to stand up again too much, Sierra. All by myself. And now I've got Holt, and you..."

"Now now, no getting teary-eyed on my account." She squeezes me tight. "But I know the feeling. I just...I ran away, yeah. I kept falling and was so stubborn that I couldn't admit that where I wanted to be was *here*." She bites her lip. "I missed y'all so much, but I felt like you didn't see me at all. You and Dad had each other, after Mama died. So I thought you wouldn't even notice if I was gone."

"I noticed," I say thickly. "We noticed. You messed up, but we all do. You're my sister, and I love you."

"Dammit, Libby, I'm going to ruin your hair." She buries her face in the messy tower of curls on top of my head. "I love you too."

I let out a shaky laugh.

"Gonna ruin my makeup if you make me cry." I scrub at my eyes, making sure not to smudge my liner and eyeshadow, and nudge her. "Screw the hair, let me take this mess down and get in my dress. Can you do me a favor?"

In truth, she's already done me a lot of favors.

Sierra's half the reason we've been able to get the ranch up and running again so fast with my new money. It helps having her to hire folks and show 'em the rounds.

The other half?

Totally Holt, the man who's waiting on his "I do."

God, it feels good to be able to pull together after pulling alone for so long.

I smile as Sierra gives me a puzzled look in the mirror.

"Sure, what can I do?" she asks.

"Go outside," I say, "and get me a handful of flowers."

* * *

I CAN HEAR the crowds outside by the time I shimmy into my wedding dress and take my hair down into a deliberately messy tumble.

Then strew it with flowers, Sierra and I rushing to thread the stems of the delicate pink and blue blooms in so they're scattered evenly throughout.

A lot like stars against the sky.

Just like the stars in the constellation necklace I still wear around my neck. It makes me feel like Dad's here today with us. And I think he'd be glad at the man I picked to marry.

Sierra gives me a tight hug before rushing out to take her place in the bridal procession, thrusting my bouquet of daffodils into my hands before she's gone.

I start to follow...

...and then nearly trip on my heels.

And my dress.

Look, I'm not used to this, okay?

But even if I'm rough and foul-mouthed, I want my wedding to be *that* kinda day.

A little extravagant, a little overblown, where I get to be a little bit of a princess.

So while my dress looks simple, a pretty white silk sheath with stars embroidered along the bodice in little specks of diamond, it's long enough to trail the floor in flows that look graceful.

Just wish I could say the same for the heels. They're taller than what I'm used to with my boots.

I right myself, grabbing at the wall—only for a thin, wizened hand to gently take my arm, helping me up.

"I've got you, dearie."

Ms. Wilma.

Pretty as a picture in a slim white skirt and matching jacket with a daffodil pinned to her lapel.

She hooks her arm in mine, holding me steady in more ways than one when my heart races a mile a minute. We step outside, where my future husband waits.

Maybe we're a cliché in Heart's Edge, having our wedding here on the cliff like so many before us.

I don't care.

I want our forever.

I want the happy ending that legend promises.

I'll be a cliché today and walk down an aisle of silk cloth laid over a meadow of flowers.

We head out into the open autumn sun with half the town watching. All of my friends plus his friends and family, gathered neatly in chairs to either side.

Up by the altar, next to the arch of flowers, it's *him*.

Holt Silverton, looking finer than ever.

Alaska, Blake, Warren, Doc, and Leo stand behind him, his men of honor, while Felicity and Sierra and a few of my other friends are there as bridesmaids.

Honestly, they're just pretty blurs of color eclipsed by the bright light of one man.

Holt looks like a natural lady-killer, clean-cut and perfectly groomed in his tux.

Underneath that fine-tailored wool, that tightly trimmed

beard and combed hair, there's a wild man who's ready to take on anything.

Including me and my ridiculous heart.

He's my Zorro. He's my Rhett Butler. He's my Lone Ranger.

He's my everything, and the moment those whiskey-fire eyes lock with mine, I forget everything else.

There's music somewhere. Ms. Wilma walking me down the aisle when my feet can't remember how.

Everyone turning their heads to watch, soft approving murmurs, warm encouragement as I pass by.

They're all just background noise when all I hear is the beat of my heart growing louder and louder the closer I get to Holt.

There's a heat between us that sizzles the closer we are to each other.

It's nearly burning by the time I stop in front of him, and Ms. Wilma gently hands me off to take her place in the front chairs.

There's a hushed, pure silence.

Reverence for this moment when we stand here looking at each other, mere seconds away from being man and wife in the eyes of all.

Don't cry, don't cry.

I've said it so many times, fighting with everything in me.

Only now I don't bother.

Not when I'm so happy I can't stop the tears as I look up at him and smile.

"Hi, you," I whisper.

Holt's eyes flash, his smile so warm, so tender, it captures my heart more than anything.

"Hey," he answers, reaching up to stroke my cheek with his thumb, wiping away the tracks of my tears. "Ready to get married?"

"Ready as I'll ever be!"

He grins. "Never thought wild horses would drag us here, huh?"

"Kicking and screaming all the way," I tease, laughing.

But there's no kicking. No screaming. No second guesses.

No protest, no hesitation, no doubt.

The priest begins reading off the litany that leads us to our vows.

I know.

I know one thing as sure as I know the stars will come out and the heavens will turn and the constellations will come and go with the seasons.

I flipping love Holt Silverton.

And I want to be with him for the rest of our lives.

I feel like I'm floating on a dream as that ring slips on my finger, then his, and then it's all echoes.

With this ring, I thee wed.

"With this ring, I thee wed."

I do.

"...I do."

Just like that.

A few simple words and it's real, and suddenly everyone is shouting and cheering, and the dazed bubble around me bursts. Reality swoops in on us with my pulse pounding and my entire body buzzing with joy and—

And Holt pulls me close. His hands drift to the small of my back, downright possessive, hotter than that ring of his I can feel through the thin silk, imprinting against my skin.

He's kissing me now.

Oh my God.

My. Husband. Is. *Kissing*. Me!

And I'm kissing him back with a force that moves the world.

Because as long as I have Holt, I have everything.

I have my world, my sky, my stars.

I'll never let anything take him away.

* * *

No matter what the rom-com movies say, nobody has a clue

how exhausting a wedding and reception really are until they've lived through their own.

Or planned someone else's.

I think Sierra might faint soon.

I'm feeling pretty burned out myself by the time we're through speeches, toasts, cake, dancing, tossing the bouquet right into Felicity's clenched hands, and being whirled through everyone who wants to congratulate us, tease us, or give Holt ginormous heaps of crap.

He doesn't know what to do with it when Blake and the guys tease him relentlessly.

Honestly, it's adorable.

But I remember one night months ago when Holt told me about how he always felt shut out from his older brother and his friends. Now they're good friends.

Being part of something big with them and getting accepted into their pack must be kinda jarring in a good way, I guess.

It's almost evening before we steal away.

We're supposed to be escaping to our honeymoon.

Everyone pretends to not notice we're sneaking off behind their backs, piling into Holt's truck—rickety as it is—in our fancy duds, the whole vehicle tricked out in ribbons and flowers that just make it look even shabbier.

Before we hit the road, we've got one more stop.

I get to watch in my wedding dress while Holt and Alaska, both of them in tuxes, break ground with a shovelful of dirt each on the site that will be a new road leading to Ursa.

It's officially a state-endorsed historical protection site.

So now we've got a genuine tourist spot on my property, and guess who'll be making bank on a revenue share agreement by the time it launches next summer?

We'll never be afraid of losing our home ever again.

Once that's done, with handshakes and a few beers from the guys—and you can bet I have one too, skirt gathered up in one hand and can in the other—we're off again.

This time it's just us, the wind in our hair through the open window.

Then miles of road between us and Colorado.

I've always wanted to try whitewater rafting. We're taking a river tour honeymoon, but for now, all I care about is us, alone, not even needing to talk.

I've never felt more peaceful than I do right now, leaning against Holt with one hand twined in his, watching hours of highway fly past.

Everything's gonna be all right.

I watch the sun set, and then the stars come out, and up there in the night sky...

I hope you're watching, Dad.

I hope you know I'm happy.

I hope you know I kept my faith in you till the end.

Maybe I'm imagining it, but the stars seem to twinkle just a little brighter.

I'm half asleep by the time we pull into the tiny one-horse town that's almost nothing but rental cabins and amenities for vacationers and honeymooners, a resort made up to look like a rustic village.

I let Holt handle checking us in at the main building and getting our keys, and apparently let Holt do the walking for me, too. He pulls the truck's passenger door open and scoops me out.

"Up we go, my darling bride," he teases, laughing as I yelp and clutch at his neck.

"Idiot," I murmur.

He grins because he knows the translation from angry Libby-speak. Idiot means *I love you.*

And I love, love, *love* this gorgeous fool of a man who put everything on the line to save me, then helped me save myself.

I can't take my eyes off him as he carries me across the threshold of our cozy little log cabin.

That moment, that little tradition, ignites something in us both, still shaking off the lazy peace of the drive.

There's barely a second to admire our surroundings—single room, shadowed in cool and comforting recesses, the bed large and luxurious—before our eyes lock.

That thread of tension stretched tight between us snaps in a single breath.

Curling my hands against the back of his neck, I drag him down.

We meet in the middle in a kiss that blazes hotter than the brightest stars.

You'd think we'd go soft and gentle on our honeymoon.

Our first time as man and wife should be slow, special, savored.

Nope.

We're like rabid animals. Thank God I'm not attached to this wedding dress because he shears it right off me, seams shredding against my skin and biting into me before giving way.

I'm not wearing much underneath, translucent white lace picked out just for this, a flimsy bra that barely holds up enough to cup my breasts and a pair of panties that doesn't hide a single thing.

Especially not how much I want him.

I'm practically dripping.

"Honey, fuck." Holt stares at me like I'm an offering waved under a tiger's nose, husky growls rising in his throat as he dips me back onto the bed.

I don't even get to catch my breath before I get his teeth, leaving wet marks on the lace and delicious spots on my skin that burn even after his mouth moves on.

He's a tornado. Hands wild and everywhere, stroking, caressing, molding me, while I rip at his shirt, his slacks, dragging them off his body like a woman possessed.

I need him.

Need more than just his body.

Need him inside me like yesterday, his flesh as close to mine as my heart is to his.

I don't know how I peel my husband out of his clothes without committing a felony.

It's all a blur of sensation, of his touch and his kiss and his taut, tawny skin under my fingers, the hot ripples of his muscles and the fire in his breath every time it meets my skin.

Sweet, sweet hell.

In the shadows of the cabin, he's a feral beast, hulking over me, eyes glowing in the dark like how a golden latte steams.

I've always thought he was too beautiful to be real, to be human.

No man should be the freakish kind of hottie Holt Silverton is with that perfectly sculpted, swarthy tanned body and the inky blackness of his hair, his beard; that stone of a face cut in handsome planes of sinful grace.

No, I don't think he's the devil incarnate anymore—except when he gives me his tongue.

But he's real.

He's human.

And now I see deeper.

The powerful heart beating inside that strong, broad chest, just as perfect as the rest of him.

Maybe he's brash, arrogant, and still has the worst sense of humor I've ever known.

But he's kind. He's good. He's faithful. He's brave.

He's utterly mine, and I can't even fathom being anybody else's again.

Best of all, tonight he's totally *with me.*

I slide my thighs against his hips and spread my legs. I open, giving myself to him, surrendering to the wildfire building between us, to this wild animal on top of me, the only man I've ever met who's as relentless at life as I am.

And it's more than perfection as he jerks my hips up, as he grasps on tight with a heady, growly possessiveness.

As he fits himself to me.

As he whispers "Libby" with all the love and passion in the world.

As he drives into me so deep, so hot, that I can't help screaming his name to the rafters, the moon, the stars.

There's no mercy in this man.

Not when his body surges over me, in me, rampaging through my helpless insides with heat and pleasure. His cock's friction moves faster in deep, claiming strokes, a low frenzy on his lips.

God, it's savage—as savage as the story of our love, and it has the perfect ending.

If I could stay like this forever, twined with Holt, locked in this passion, I don't think heaven itself could ever hold a candle to this.

And if I have my way...

I will.

This is us. This is everything I've needed.

Not just insane pleasure, but someone who can go head to head with me without backing down. Someone I can trust to have my back, through thick and thin.

Someone who can weather the storm.

I'm not standing on my own anymore.

I'm not carrying everything by myself.

For the first time in my life, I have a man I can lean on.

A hero who's been there for me, no matter what.

"Holt," I whisper, pressing my lips to his jaw, his throat, then his mouth, breathing in his scent, rising up to meet him, gasping as he lifts me and holds me like I'm something precious, even as he fucks me like a beast. "Holt...Holt, I love you."

He stops—our bodies locked so tight together, those dark bearish eyes nearly scouring.

His mouth traces over mine, taking my lower lip gently, like he can taste those words on my lips.

"Really, Mrs. Silverton?" he breathes, and I shiver to hear it said out loud for the very first time. "Then it's a damn good thing I've loved you since the moment I set eyes on you."

I can't speak.

It's too overwhelming.

Too much.

He's too much and somehow always just enough.

And you'd better believe he's more than I ever wanted when he pins me down, picks up where he left off, and thrusts me right over the cliff into a screaming, shuddering tsunami.

Before my senses give out, before he growls his heart out, I hold fast to Holt, to our love, to this shared explosion as we crash together, driving into the sweetest ecstasy I've ever known. Judging by the roar in his throat, I think it might be his best ever, too.

My world's officially upside down.

Tonight and forever.

Not just my body, as I spasm and pant and surrender to my husband.

Thanks to this unshakable man, the void's been filled forever with light and laughter and so many kisses.

With Holt by my side, my dark knight, there'll always be stars, and this life of ours will never be empty again.

EXTENDED EPILOGUE: PUT OUT TO PASTURE (HOLT)

Years Later

THEY SAY BE careful what you wish for.

Once upon a messed up time, I wished for a home, a family, a life that I could carve out of this world and call my own.

Turns out, I didn't get my way.

I got something better.

Because I didn't make my life all on my lonesome.

I couldn't have.

I made a life together with Libby and this strange, mixed up little town.

Our life—and a life for our kids right here in Heart's Edge.

In hindsight, maybe I should've been careful what my fool head wished for.

Libby never told me she's got a history of *twins* in her family, all on her mother's side.

Maybe she and Sierra weren't, but she's got a whole gaggle of doppelganger aunts.

Presto, and I've got not two, but *four* bright-eyed daughters.

And they're all currently climbing me like a tree while I try to get one of our newest ponies saddled up so I can start to train him on working with kids. If all goes well, he'll be a sweet addition to Libby's classes.

It's my weekend. The construction crew's out of commission for a couple of days, even though we're up to our elbows in new contracts.

I talked the city out of the shopping mall years ago. Hell, I even helped organize the resistance among local business owners when they tried to put that thing elsewhere. We banded together, threatening the entire council in the next election if they didn't listen for once.

And listen, they did.

Libby was right, that place would've destroyed every mom and pop shop in a thirty-mile radius.

Though I've heard hints of the bank trying to push away under the surface, always fighting to transform Heart's Edge into something it shouldn't be with their real estate investment arm.

For now, though, we're working on building up local tourism by building out existing attractions, and creating new ones and, well, all those little contracts add up.

We keep busy.

The days are long, fulfilling, and sometimes hard.

Nothing's easier than coming home to my girls, though, even when they're busy piling all over me.

"Oof, Stella, let up," I say, catching the chubby arms around my neck. Stella and her twin sister Aurora, both a healthy four years old, are dangling down my back. "Daddy can't breathe when you sit on his neck."

"I'm not Stella, I'm Aurora!" Stella chirps, and next to her Aurora giggles.

"Uh-huh. You oughta know better than to try that cow poo with me," I say, laughing. "Daddy knows his girls like the back of his hand."

I tighten Twain's girth strap. The pony snorts, pawing at the ground—but very carefully staying comfortably away from the two three-year-olds hugging my legs.

Good boy. He's been trained to watch out for little human arms and legs.

I sink down in a crouch, where one particular pair of little feet dangling down my back can reach the ground. "Be good now. Get down and shoo your little sisters out of the way."

Reluctantly, Stella and Aurora let me go, and gather up Dawn and Celeste like good big sisters, taking their sticky little hands and guiding them on wobbly toddler steps to the side of the area outside Twain's stall.

They're all as blonde as their mama, but with my hazel-gold eyes, until they're just golden lively things all over. You'd think they were children of the sun, as brown as they get tumbling around to play, instead of being named after the stars.

I watch them with a fond smile I can't help.

My heart swells with pride to see my girls looking after each other with such sweet attentiveness, before I return to saddling up the pony and making sure he's comfortable, paying special attention to his cues that tell me his strap is too tight or his bit is uncomfortable.

You can't ever be too careful with an animal you're training to work with kids.

Give them one reason to buck at all, and you're looking at a world of hurt.

Once I'm sure he's settled, I turn to lead him out into the training paddock.

"Come on, girls," I call, taking it slow so their chubby little legs can keep up. "Who wants to ride first?"

There's a chorus of *Me! Me! Me!* plus a few incoherent gurgles, little hands reaching up—only for one of them to get swooped up by slim, strong hands.

Libby comes stepping around the barn with a loud laugh, lifting Celeste high onto her hip.

"Nobody," she says, looking at me with those blue witchfire eyes that make my heart beat harder every damn time. "You just went and saddled that pony up for nothing, hon. Did you forget?"

I blink. "Guess I did. Uh, what'd I forget again?"

Laughing, Libby nuzzles Celeste's hair, while our little girl burbles happily and her twin sister tugs at Libby's pretty paisley skirt.

She's still just as gorgeous as the day I met her, but she seems *more* now.

Stronger. Content. Relaxed.

Brighter than all the damn stars in the galaxy combined.

Libby Potter was a handful and a half.

But Libby Silverton's been the entire frigging bushel, able to make steam shoot out my ears or make me grin like the world's biggest fool on demand.

She's full of so much life and purpose, every day of hers filled with the business of running both this ranch and the Historical Ursa tour. It's amazing how far folks will come to see a genuine, bonafide old outlaw town.

We trade off parenting duties. We've both always got one finger on the pulse of our businesses, and every other finger on wrangling those little ferrets we call our kids.

We manage pretty well, and I think we're doing a fine job of parenting.

We haven't dropped any of them yet, at least.

They're alive and nothing's broken, they laugh a lot, and we both love them so much we'd give our own lives for any one of those munchkins.

Good start, right?

Libby tilts her face up to me in that gesture that I know now means *hands full of baby, give me a kiss.*

I'm more than happy to oblige, leaning down and brushing my mouth across hers—sweet and chaste, keeping it clean in front of the kids, but you know damn well I'm not averse to making a couple more sooner or later the dirty way.

Whether we wind up with four or eight...we'll manage.

For now, though, I pull back and ask, "You gonna keep a man in suspense forever? What'd I forget?"

"The inaugural ceremony?" she says.

I start to curse—then clap a hand over my mouth, stopping myself before little ears can hear.

"Right. Fu—oh, truck. I'll go get changed, and we'll get in the *truck*."

Her eyes glitter slyly as she watches me with that fondness that says I'm the dumbest man alive, but I'm hers. "You do that. I'll call Sierra to keep an eye on the girls."

"You're the best, honey." I lean down to steal another kiss, then swoop up all three of my remaining daughters in my arms and hug them all at once, squeezing them and gently jostling them around while they laugh and squeal and wriggle like puppies.

Then there's number four, as Celeste whines to be with her sisters and Libby deposits her in my arms. I make sure I get my fair share of Daddy kisses and clumsy hugs before I set the giggling mass of babies down and pry myself free.

One more grin for Libby, and a salute.

Then I turn and race into the house.

It's been a good, long while since I've worn anything that wasn't work duds.

Haven't needed to.

But for this, I dig out a pair of slacks and a nice white button-down, and even some cufflinks—while Libby's sleeker than a panther in a pretty black dress. Might seem a bit dressed-up since we're just going out to Ursa, but it's the principle of the thing.

There's a new road leading through the cut into the town.

Laid it myself, all cobblestone, keeping with the rustic look but still making it easier for the ghost town tours to pass through on horseback. The path's cleared and the stones are sure to protect against muddy seasons.

So we actually get to drive back there, bouncing along in my old truck that's actually been faithful all these years.

Plenty of other people are already gathered here, dressed in their Sunday best.

Warren and Haley Ford, two little kids hanging on their arms. Warren flashes a thumbs up when he sees me, which I return.

Haley holds on to Ms. Wilma's wheelchair. The woman's older than Methuselah and has to be fought into her wheels for the long distances to places like this, but I knew she wouldn't miss this day for the world. She's the oldest person in town with any memory of Ursa's secrets in her granny's stories.

Then Doc and Ember, his green eyes flashing behind his spectacles as he holds his woman's hand real tight. They're gunning to surpass everybody in the baby department.

Leo and Clarissa Regis. Guess Sweeter Things isn't just the name of her popping candy shop when Leo grins at everybody, flashing his wife a knowing look. If anybody knew how freaky this town's history can get, it's them.

Their son, Zach, he insisted on flying in just for this from college. The kid's barely sixteen and he's already away at MIT, working on killer robots or some shit.

Oh, yeah. There's also Blake. Grinning like the big brotherly dummy he is, one arm throwing out a floppy wave for me, and the other wrapped tight around his woman, Peace, who's swapped out those swaths of purple in her red hair for pink lately. Libby must've paid her thousands for massages by now.

Andrea, too, also visiting from college. She's not the foul-mouthed rebel she used to be, looking more like a grown-up now in her artsy dress splashed with stylized birds.

With the road laid through, the town's been fully restored after decades of neglect and that last dustup with Declan and his crew.

Even the little church steeple towers over everything, a fresh white coat of paint on it, the graveyard put back into place and those poor souls laid to rest.

Including Danny the Rattlesnake.

The town called in a special archaeological team specializing in restoration to get things back together. They're the ones who matched up one of the bodies and the dates on the grave marker.

1831-1869.

He's become a new local legend of sorts, a mad man who wanted to play robber god and wound up canonized as a sort of hometown saint for putting Ursa back on the map.

But it's not him we're here for.

Just because this place caused Heart's Edge a whole lot of grief in the early days doesn't mean it has to stay that way.

Mark Potter believed his red rock was cursed, too. Pretty heavy words for a former NASA scientist.

I'm happy we proved him wrong.

Without that rock and the sale it brought in, we never would've built this kind of life. The scientists studying it would've lost an asset, and all these people gathered here, smiling under the warm evening sun?

They would've lost their claim to local history and a togetherness that must make the bandits of old Ursa spin in their graves.

The restoration project cleaned up the town hall, too, and added something new. Its highest little cupola tower is a mini-observatory now, telescopes freshly installed, where people can come and see the stars up close.

Today, the historical society that oversees this place is renaming it.

The Mark Potter Town Hall and Observatory.

A far cry from being scared Libby's old man was ever a

merciless, cold-blooded killer, keeping those secrets about Bostrom for years.

And it's not hard to tell the weight's been lifted off Libby's shoulders forever as we take a place of honor near the front of the crowd for the speech, the champagne, the ribbon cutting.

It feels like a fresh start.

A reset button on all the troubles that ever plagued us and Heart's Edge since the first brick of this little town was laid. The curse of the rock has been lifted, if it ever existed at all.

For Libby and me, that's a big hell no.

She's free, smiling and clapping as the tears stream down her face.

I can't help the smile that eats up my face.

Can't even remember what it's like to be a drifter, lost in the wind.

Not here. Not in this place where I belong.

This town, this woman, this tribe I've always belonged to.

I just had to wander for a little while to figure my shit out.

But now?

Now I'm home.

And I'm never going anywhere away from her again.

* * *

ONE FINE SUNNY DAY, I stepped out of my shiny car, looking to cut a big deal with a hellcat.

That hellcat laughed at my shit, threw me in the mud, knocked some damn sense in me, and my world's never been right-side up ever since.

Thank God.

Without Libby, I'm not the best I can be. Nobody's knight and nobody's friend. Nobody's papa and nobody's builder.

It takes a long time for some dudes to plant their stakes and settle down. No denying I'm one of them.

Then again, there's damn sure no denying I've found my place, my woman, and my family.

It just took a little hell from her lips to show me the way, and now that I've got my path laid down, I make sure I give it back every night.

I'll always show Liberty Silverton the love, the warmth, and the stars that'll be ours in every breath, every word, and every last growl she pulls out of my heart.

ABOUT NICOLE SNOW

Nicole Snow is a *Wall Street Journal* and *USA Today* bestselling author. She found her love of writing by hashing out love scenes on lunch breaks and plotting her great escape from boardrooms. Her work roared onto the indie romance scene in 2014 with her Grizzlies MC series.

Since then Snow aims for the very best in growly, heart-of-gold alpha heroes, unbelievable suspense, and swoon storms aplenty.

Already hooked on her stuff? Visit nicolesnowbooks.com to sign up for her newsletter and connect on social media.

Got a question or comment on her work? Reach her anytime at nicole@nicolesnowbooks.com

Thanks for reading. And please remember to leave an honest review! Nothing helps an author more.

MORE BOOKS BY NICOLE

Heroes of Heart's Edge Books

No Perfect Hero

No Good Doctor

No Broken Beast

No Damaged Goods

No Fair Lady

No White Knight

Marriage Mistake Standalone Books

Accidental Hero

Accidental Protector

Accidental Romeo

Accidental Knight

Accidental Rebel

Accidental Shield

Stand Alone Novels

Cinderella Undone

Man Enough

Surprise Daddy

Prince With Benefits

Marry Me Again

Love Scars

Recklessly His

Stepbrother UnSEALed

Stepbrother Charming

Enguard Protectors Books

Still Not Over You

Still Not Into You

Still Not Yours

Still Not Love

Baby Fever Books

Baby Fever Bride

Baby Fever Promise

Baby Fever Secrets

Only Pretend Books

Fiance on Paper

One Night Bride

Grizzlies MC Books

Outlaw's Kiss

Outlaw's Obsession

Outlaw's Bride

Outlaw's Vow

Deadly Pistols MC Books

Never Love an Outlaw

Never Kiss an Outlaw

Never Have an Outlaw's Baby

Never Wed an Outlaw

Prairie Devils MC Books

Outlaw Kind of Love

Nomad Kind of Love

Savage Kind of Love

Wicked Kind of Love

Bitter Kind of Love

Printed in Great Britain
by Amazon